The BEST INTENTIONS

The
BEST INTENTIONS

A NOVEL BY

INGMAR
BERGMAN

TRANSLATED FROM
THE SWEDISH
BY JOAN TATE

ARCADE PUBLISHING • NEW YORK

First North American Edition

Originally published in Sweden by Norstedts Förlag, Stockholm, under the
title *Den goda viljan*

Library of Congress Cataloging-in-Publication Data

Bergman, Ingmar, 1918–
 [Goda viljan. English]
 The best intentions / Ingmar Bergman.
  p. cm.
 ISBN 1-55970-207-9
 I. Title
 PT9875.B533G6413 1993
 839.73′74—dc20   92-54828

Published in the United States by Arcade Publishing, Inc., New York
Distributed by Little, Brown and Company

10 9 8 7 6 5 4 3 2 1

BP

Printed in the United States of America

PROLOGUE

The Åkerblom family were great ones for taking photographs. After my father's and mother's deaths, I inherited a marvelous collection of albums, the earliest dating from the middle of the nineteenth century, the most recent from the beginning of the 1960s. There is undoubtedly a great deal of magic in those photographs, particularly when looked at with the help of a gigantic magnifying glass: the faces, the faces, hands, postures, clothes, jewelry, the faces, the pets, views, lighting, the faces, curtains, pictures, rugs, summer flowers, birches, rivers, coiffures, angry pimples, budding breasts, handsome mustaches— this could continue ad infinitum, so it is best to stop. But most of all the faces. I go into the photographs and touch the people in them, the ones I remember and those I know nothing about. It is almost more fun than old silent films that have lost their explanatory texts. I invent patterns of my own.

Ever since the autobiographical *The Magic Lantern*, I have had it in mind to make a film about when my parents were young, the beginning of their marriage, their hopes, shortcomings, and good intentions. I look at the photographs and feel a strong attraction to those two people, who in almost every way are so unlike the somewhat introspective, mythical, larger-than-life creatures who dominated my childhood and youth.

Because film and photography are my particular form of expression, I started rather aimlessly to draw up a pattern of action based on statements, documentation, and, as I say, photographs. In my imagination, I roamed the streets of Upsala, when Upsala was a small, inward-looking, and sleepy university town. I visited Dufnäs in Dalarna when Våroms, my maternal grandparents' summer house, was still a special and illusory paradise off the beaten track.

I wrote as I have been used to writing for fifty years, in cinematic, dramatic form. In my imagination the actors spoke their lines on a brilliantly lit stage, surrounded by somewhat softened but wonderfully clear decorations. In the center of this considerable staging moved my mother and my father in Pernilla Östergren's and Samuel Fröler's personifications.

I do not wish to maintain that I have always been so conscientious with the truth in my story. I have drawn on my imagination, added, subtracted, and transposed, but as is often the case with this sort of game, the game has probably become clearer than reality.

Since I knew, with no bitterness, that I would not be directing my saga, I was extra thorough with my explanations, right down to describing fairly insignificant details, even certain things that would never be registered by a camera. Except possibly some suggestions to the actors.

In that way, the story unfolded during six months one summer on Fårö Island. I cautiously touched my parents' faces and destinies and felt I learned quite a bit about myself, things which had been concealed under layers of dusty inhibitions and conciliatory wording with no real content.

This book has not in any way been adapted to the finished film. It has had to remain as it was written: The words stand unchallenged and I hope have a life of their own, like a performance of its own in the mind of the reader.

Fårö, August 25, 1991
Ingmar Bergman

I

I choose an early spring day at the beginning of April, 1909. Henrik Bergman has just turned twenty-three and is studying theology at Upsala University. He is on his way up Östra Slottsgatan toward Drottninggatan and the Grand Hotel, where he is to meet his paternal grandfather. There is still some snow on Slottsbacken, but it is thawing fast, the water rushing along the gutters and the clouds marching along.

The hotel is a long, two-story building squeezed below the cathedral, the jackdaws screaming around the tower and a small blue tram cautiously making its way up the slope. There is no one in sight. It is Saturday morning; the students are all asleep, and the professors are preparing their lectures.

A distinguished elderly man is sitting at the porter's counter reading *Upsala Nya Tidning*. He keeps Henrik waiting for an appropriate spell of time, then lowers the paper and says with nasal courtesy, "Yes, your grandfather is expecting you in room seventeen, up the stairs there, on the left." After which he straightens his pince-nez and returns to his reading. Clattering sounds and women's voices can be heard coming from the kitchen, and the smell of stale cigar smoke and fried herring combines with the fumes from a huge coal stove rumbling away in one corner.

Henrik's impulse is to flee, but his legs take him up the creaking carpeted stairs, along the mud-yellow corridor to door seventeen. His grandfather's polished boots are standing by the doorpost. Henrik takes a deep breath, then exhales and knocks. A rather light, sonorous voice says, "Come on in, the door's open."

The room is large, with three windows facing onto the cobbled

3

yard, the stables, and the still bare elms. Two beds with mahogany ends are against one wall; a commode is enthroned against the opposite wall, with jug and basin, and towels embroidered in red. The rest of the furnishings include sofa and chairs and a round table with a breakfast tray on it. A worn rug of doubtful oriental origin lies on the knotted floorboards, and engravings of hunting scenes hang on the dimly patterned brown wallpaper.

Fredrik Bergman rises from his armchair with some difficulty and goes to meet his grandson. He is an impressive man, taller than the boy, broad and gnarled, with a large nose, iron-gray hair cut short, and sideburns, but neither beard nor mustache. Behind the gold-rimmed glasses are dark blue, slightly red-rimmed eyes. He holds out a powerful hand with ragged but clean nails. The two men greet each other without smiling. The old man gestures to his grandson to take a chair with a worn cover and carved legs.

Fredrik Bergman remains standing, gazing at Henrik with curiosity but noncommittally. Henrik looks out the window. A carriage drawn by two horses rumbles across the cobbles in the yard. When the noise has subsided, the grandfather takes the floor. He speaks ceremoniously and clearly, a man used to being understood and obeyed.

Fredrik Bergman: As you may have heard, your grandmother is ill. Professor Oldenburg operated on her at the Academic Hospital a few days ago. He says there is no hope.

Fredrik Bergman falls silent and sits down. He traces the pattern on the rug with his stick, an activity that seems to interest him. Henrik hardens his heart and remains indifferent. His handsome face is calm, his eyes large and mildly blue, the mouth below the neat mustache clamped shut: I'll say nothing. I'll listen. The man over there has nothing of importance to say to me.

His grandfather clears his throat, his voice steady, his speech slow and clear, with a slight touch of dialect.

Fredrik Bergman: Your grandmother and I have been talking about you over the last few days.

Someone out in the corridor laughs, then walks quickly away. A clock strikes three quarters past the hour.

Fredrik Bergman: Your grandmother says, and has said for a great many years, that we wronged you and your mother. I maintain each and every man is responsible for his own life and his own actions. Your father broke away from us and moved elsewhere with his family. That

4

was his decision and his responsibility. Your grandmother says, and has always said, that we ought to have taken care of you and your mother when your father died. I thought he had made his choice, both for himself and his family. In that respect, death changes nothing. Your grandmother has always said that we have been without mercy, that we have not behaved like Christians. That's an argument I do not understand.

Henrik (*suddenly*): Grandfather, if you have summoned me here to clarify your attitude toward my mother and myself, then I have known that as long as I can remember. Everyone is responsible for himself. *And* his deeds. In that we are agreed. Please, may I go now? I'm actually studying for my exams. I'm sorry Grandmother is ill. Perhaps you would be kind enough to give her my regards.

Henrik gets to his feet and looks at his grandfather with calm and genuine contempt. Fredrik Bergman makes a gesture of impatience, which transmits itself through his whole great body.

Fredrik Bergman: Sit down and let me finish. I shall not be long-winded. *Sit down*, I say! You have no cause to love me, but that's no excuse for being discourteous.

Henrik (*sitting down*): And . . . ?

Fredrik Bergman: Your grandmother has told me to seek you out. She says it is her last wish. She says you are to go and see her in the hospital. She says she wishes to beg your forgiveness for all the hardships both she and I, as well as our family, have inflicted on you and your mother.

Henrik: When I was born and my mother was a widow, we traveled the long way down from Kalmar to your farm to ask for help. We were directed to two small rooms in Söderhamn and an allowance of thirty kronor a month.

Fredrik Bergman: My brother Hindrich took care of all the details. I had nothing to do with the financial arrangements. Your grandmother and I were living in Stockholm when I was a member of Parliament.

Henrik: Nothing could be more pointless than this conversation. It is also embarrassing to have to witness an old gentleman I have always respected for his inhumanity suddenly changing and becoming sentimental.

Fredrik Bergman gets up and places himself in front of his grandson, then whips off his gold-framed glasses, a gesture of violent rage.

5

Fredrik Bergman: I can't go to your grandmother and tell her you have rejected me. I can't go to her and tell her you don't want to go and see her.

Henrik: I don't think that'll be necessary.

Fredrik Bergman: I have a suggestion to make. I know your aunts in Elfvik have guaranteed a loan so that you can study here in Upsala. I also know your mother earns her living as a piano teacher. I am offering to pay off that loan. I am offering you and your mother an appropriate allowance.

Henrik does not answer. He looks at the old man's forehead, his cheeks, his chin, where there is a small cut from his morning shave. He looks at the great ear, at the neck and the pulse beating above the stiff collar.

Henrik: What do you want me to say, Grandfather?

Fredrik Bergman: You're very like your father. Did you know that, Henrik?

Henrik: So they say, yes. Mother says so.

Fredrik Bergman: I never did understand why he hated me so terribly.

Henrik: I understand that you have never understood, Grandfather.

Fredrik Bergman: I became a farmer, and my brother became a priest. No one asked us what we wanted or didn't want. Is that of any great significance?

Henrik: Significance?

Fredrik Bergman: I never felt either hatred or bitterness for my parents. Or else I've forgotten.

Henrik: How practical of you.

Fredrik Bergman: What? Oh, practical! Well, yes, you could say that. Your father had such vivid ideas about freedom. He was always talking about having to "have his freedom." So he became a bankrupt pharmacist in Öland. That was his freedom.

Henrik: You're mocking him, Grandfather. (*Silence.*)

Fredrik Bergman: What do you say to my offer? I'll be responsible for your studies. I'll pay a monthly allowance for the rest of your mother's life and pay off your loan. All you have to do is to go to ward twelve at the Academic Hospital and make things up with your grandmother.

Henrik: How do I know you won't cheat me, Grandfather?

Fredrik Bergman laughs briefly, not a friendly laugh, but it contains appreciation.

Fredrik Bergman: My word of honor, Henrik. (*Pause.*) You'll have it in writing. (*Cheerfully.*) Let's draw up an agreement. You decide on the sums of money, and I'll sign it. What do you say, Henrik? (*Suddenly.*) Grandmother and I have lived together for almost forty years. It hurts now, Henrik. It hurts most horribly. Her physical torment is terrible, but they can relieve that sort of thing at the hospital, at least for the time being. What's difficult is that she is suffering spiritually. I beg of you for one moment of mercy. Not toward me; I don't ask that. But toward her. You're going to be a minister, Henrik, aren't you? You must know something about love. I mean Christian love. To me, that's all talk and evasions, but to you, talk about love must be something real. Have mercy on a sick and desperate person. I'll give you whatever you want. You decide on the sum. I won't haggle. But you must help your grandmother in her distress. (*Pause.*) Are you listening to what I'm saying?

Henrik: Go to the woman who's called my grandmother and tell her from me that she lived a whole life at her husband's side without helping Mother or me. Without standing up to you, my grandfather. She was aware of our misery and sent small presents at Christmas and birthdays. Tell that woman she chose her life and her death. She will never have my forgiveness. Tell her that I despise her on behalf of my mother, just as I loathe you and people like you. I will never become like you.

Fredrik Bergman takes the boy's arm in a hard grip and slowly shakes him. Henrik looks at him.

Henrik: Are you going to hit me, Grandfather?

He frees himself and slowly walks across the room, closing the door carefully behind him and going down the dark corridor, some gas lamps flickering in the faint daylight from three dirty windows high up in the roof.

Henrik has an oral exam in church history with the dreaded Professor Sundelius in the first week in May.

7

This is Monday, half past five in the morning. The sun is bright behind the tattered blind in the young man's modest lodgings, containing a sagging bed, a rickety table heaped with books and files, a chair, a heavily loaded bookcase that has seen better days but never better books, a washstand with a cracked basin, a jug, a pail, and a chamber pot. A three-legged armchair propped up on four volumes of Malmström's unreadable exegetics. Two paraffin lamps (a surprising luxury!), one hanging from the low ceiling, where damp patches form continents, the other on the table, watching over two photographs: his mother when she was still young and pretty, and as a fiancée, white and good-looking with bright eyes and wide smiling mouth. On the sloping floor, a few rag rugs of the indestructible kind. On the bulging wallpaper, reproductions with motifs from the Old Testament. In the corner by the door, a tall narrow tiled stove with a floral pattern on the tiles. The room breathes poverty, ingrained Lutheran cleanliness scrubbed with soft soap, and stale pipe smoke. The view out to the courtyard is of a blank wall and seven outhouses anxiously propped up against each other and the wall. Small birds are chattering away in the lilac bushes, now almost in bloom. The old wood cutter in the basement has already started sawing. Somewhere, a baby is crying for its mother's breast. As mentioned before, it is half past five, and Henrik wakes with a stab in his stomach — the church history exam. The dreaded Professor Sundelius.

Justus Bark comes in without knocking. He is Henrik's contemporary, but small and stocky, with dark eyes, a large nose, and black hair. He speaks with a Hälsinge accent and has bad teeth. He is clad in a dark suit, white shirt, loose collar, loose cuffs, black necktie, and frenziedly polished but worn shoes.

Justus: *Ecclesia invisibilis, ecclesia militans, ecclesia pressa, ecclesia regnans, and,* last but not least, *ecclesia triumphanus.* You know what's the worst thing about old man Sundelius? Gyllen told me last night. He flunked ecumenics because he didn't know the Roman Catholic Church had held twenty assemblies, but that the Greek Orthodox Church only approved the first seven. Which assemblies did the Greeks approve?

Henrik: Nicaea in 325 A.D., Constantinople in 381 A.D., Ephesus in 431, Chalcedon in 451. Constantinople again in 553 *and* in 680, and Nicaea in 787.

Justus: Bravo, bravo. Gyllen failed, and the dreaded Sundelius threw him out. First question, wrong answer, out. We're scared now, scared

8

stiff. I have consumed far too much coffee or something called coffee. Can you lend me some tea? My stomach's burning like Gehenna.

Henrik: The cupboard, Justus. See you in ten minutes. At the bottom of the stairs. Fully conscious.

Justus: Gyllen is wealthy. He'll be chucked out by Sundelius in three minutes, will shrug his shoulders, and will take a summer holiday after the Spring Ball. Then he'll scrape through church history at Christmas. Would you like to be . . . ?

Henrik: No thanks. *Amicus.*

Justus: What are those blue marks on your chest?

Henrik: That's Frida. She bites.

Justus: See you in ten minutes.

Henrik: *Pax tecum.*

After Justus has left, Henrik stands naked for a moment in the bright sunlight, trying to breathe calmly, then says quietly: "Lord, are you going to help me? If it goes badly today, it'll be a catastrophe. Old man Sundelius could be a little unwell, couldn't he, and will send his kindly senior lecturer instead. It's happened before."

But on this particular morning, the dreaded Professor Sundelius is not the slightest bit ill. At ten to eight, the three candidates are sitting and waiting in the spacious hall. The professor has married into money and lives in a handsome twelve-room apartment in Vaksala Square. The door to the dining room is open, and two servant girls in blue and white are clearing away breakfast. For a few moments, they glimpse the professor's wife, handsome but lame. She briefly raises her lorgnette to the three young candidates and their pale faces. They rise to their feet and bow respectfully with ingratiating smiles — as if that would help. The salon clock dully strikes eight. "Hear it not, Duncan; for it is a knell that summons thee to heaven or to hell," thinks Henrik, quoting *Macbeth*, act 2, scene 1. The secretary to the professor (he actually has a secretary, so he is very wealthy; it's rumored he will be a minister in the next cabinet shuffle) is a fairly dusty creature with psoriasis and watery eyes, secretly enjoying the terror he is spreading as in humble tones he summons the three young men into the professor's study.

Professor Sundelius is an impressive man in his fifties, with an open face, ruddy complexion, thick hair, and beard streaked with gray. He is wearing a well-fitting frock coat, which enhances his well-

9

proportioned figure. He walks swiftly across the oriental rug, smilingly holding out a muscular hand and heartily shaking the hands of the delinquents.

His study is spacious though rather dark, for heavily draped curtains keep out the brilliant spring day. The fragrance of books and silence prevail. A desk, huge as a fortress. Leather upholstery. Three dark-stained chairs set out, with cane seats and straight backs; glittering armatures; dark pictures in gilt frames and faintly shimmering bodies of women.

The professor sits down at his desk and invites the three of them to be seated on the proffered chairs. He chooses a cigar (first cigar after breakfast) from a silver cigar box, tops it carefully, and lights it.

Professor Sundelius: Nothing as good as a breakfast cigar. With confidence, I can tell you that this is a genuine Cuban cigar. Look how nobly it glows. Look how the fine veins of the tobacco leaf absorb the fire and how gently they are turned to ash.

For a few seconds, the professor and his candidates contemplate the beauty of cigar smoking, then, in silence, Sundelius leans forward and reaches out a large hand. The students at once realize they are to hand over their examination books. The professor places them in a row on his blotter.

Professor Sundelius: Which of you gentlemen would like to start? Who'll take the first shot? As you gentlemen are sure to know, I am considered exacting. Not from pettiness, but from a reasoned attitude, which has brought on me a great many less flattering epithets over the years. Well, never mind about that for the moment. We have far too many lazy, stupid, and ignorant theologians. By making reasonable demands, I am able to help you improve your reputation and raise your status. It is often said that a priest is a spiritual guide, whatever benefit his congregation gains from the good pastor's knowledge of Boniface VII and his works. That's a seductive but faulty argument. A thorough knowledge of church history requires industry, interest, a broad view, a good memory, and self-discipline. Qualities that are good for a priest. I hold up a net and ensure that the idiots, the slackers, and the drivelers are caught in it. That's always a sight to behold, don't you agree, gentlemen?

Three bleak smiles and some silent agreement. Then silence. Baltsar, the third man in the trio, clears his throat. There's not much to say about him. He is one of the diners at "Cold Märta's" restaurant, is thin, and has a sickly yellowish complexion, protruding eyes, and bad

10

breath. Baltsar is not destined to last long on this earth. In a few years, he will put a cartridge of dynamite into his mouth and explode among the town's famous fritillaries, right after they've burst into bloom. Nothing much is left to bury.

Professor Sundelius (*soberly*): Good, good, Mr. Bejer. Let us talk about Scholasticism, a broad and sustaining subject, and let us begin with what is called Early Scholasticism, the foremost representatives of which were . . . ?

Baltsar: Johannes Scotus Erigena, and Anselm of Canterbury. Early Middle Ages. Tenth century.

Professor Sundelius: Well, yes, roughly. And what was characteristic of those two gentlemen?

Baltsar: Johannes Erigena maintained that true religion and true philosophy are identical. Anselm of Canterbury said that general concepts, that is, ideas, are realities and not just words. *Credo ut intelligam.*

Professor Sundelius: . . . *nihil credendum nisi intellectum.*

Baltsar: Anselm did not say that, but his opponent, Abelard, did to some extent. To him, reason played a decisive role. He wanted to limit authoritarian belief, which he thought risky. That meant he acquired powerful enemies.

Professor Sundelius: Let's go back to High Scholasticism and Thomas Aquinas for a while. Mr. Bergman, your subject will be the "Apostleship." Would you name a few of the Apostolic Fathers? Which authors are considered to have been immediate apprentices of the Apostles?

Henrik: Barnabas.

Professor Sundelius: That's right. But there are other *very* important figures, are there not?

Henrik: Clemens of Rome. (*Pause.*) Polycarpus.

Professor Sundelius: Three more, Mr. Bergman.

Henrik: No.

Professor Sundelius: What is meant by the Apostolic Assembly?

11

Henrik: They are the assemblies the Apostles themselves instituted in Rome, Ephesus, and Corinth.

Professor Sundelius: More?

Henrik: Ephesus.

Professor Sundelius: You've already mentioned Ephesus.

Henrik: Alexandria.

Professor Sundelius: No, but Antioch. Jerusalem.

Henrik: Yes, of course.

Professor Sundelius: What is meant by *Symbolum Apostolorum*?

Henrik: Something to do with profession of faith. I don't know any more.

Henrik studies his nails. The catastrophe is a fact. Baltsar and Justus have stopped breathing. Professor Sundelius says nothing. A drowsy spring fly buzzes in the narrow ray of sunlight coming through the gap in the heavy window draperies.

Almost thirty seconds vanish into infinity. The professor looks attentively at Candidate Bergman, then turns back to his desk, leafs through the examination book, and finally hands it to Henrik.

Professor Sundelius: I suggest, Mr. Bergman, that you take a walk in the botanical gardens. There is a great deal there to marvel at at this time in the spring. Either one believes in Almighty God, or one doesn't. Good-bye, Mr. Bergman, and welcome back at the end of November. Perhaps I should add that my introductory statement does not apply to you. I think you will be a good priest, regardless of the Symbolum or the Apostolic Fathers.

The professor nods, indicating thereby that Henrik should retire. No one can maintain that the Dreaded Sundelius smiles, but he looks at Henrik Bergman with something resembling curiosity. Then it's all over. Out through the door. Out into the dining room where the parquet floor is being polished on all fours. Out into the hall to take down his student cap. Down the marble staircase, which echoes. The great door bangs. A band is blaring away in the middle of the street, the sun blazing down, people stopping to stare or marching along in time. A gangling youth, bareheaded, with thin dark hair, dark eyes, and a trim mustache, stops in front of Henrik and touches his arm with an elegant walking stick.

Ernst: Hello, Bergman. You won't forget choir practice tonight, will you? Hugo Alvén is coming. At the Zwyck afterward.

He nods and is gone.

Now we'll talk about Frida Strandberg, Henrik's fiancée for the last two years. Of course, it's a very secret engagement, known only to their closest friends. Neither Henrik's mother nor the Elfvik aunts know about it. The girl's family in Ångermanland know nothing either. But it is an engagement all the same, with an exchange of rings, sacred promises, lighted candles, and tender kisses.

Frida is three years older than her fiancé, and she works as a waitress at the Gillet, the town's most genteel hotel. She and several of the other staff live in wretched, drafty hovels right at the top in the attics of that massive building. The moral consequences of this mixed residence do not bother the management, but going in and out of bedrooms at night is prohibited. The only staff entrance is guarded by a Cerberus and his wife, who seem to lack the normal need for sleep.

Frida is beautiful, a fine figure of a woman, big-boned, with high breasts and round hips under her long tight skirt. She wears her ash-blonde hair in bangs over her forehead and gathered into a knot on the top of her head. Her eyes are large, almost round, and observant, appraising and curious. She laughs often, surprisingly loud laughter, her lips shapely and chin round and definite. She looks determined with a chin like that. Her nose is long and nobly shaped. She speaks rapidly, with a broad accent, moves quickly, and carries herself well, whether bearing heavy trays in the hotel dining room or taking a Sunday walk in Fyris Park with her fiancé.

They had met by chance. One of Henrik's friends who often joined him for a meal at Cold Märta's had inherited some money from an aunt and wanted to celebrate. They went to the Flustret down by Svandammen. Frida had a temporary summer job there, working upstairs in the private rooms. It was a warm evening, with heavy balmy scents coming through the open windows and military music from the pavilion.

They were very drunk, Henrik most of all. When the party broke up to make their way to the brothel in Svartbäcken, the theologian proved impossible to resuscitate, so was left to his fate or Frida, who eventually (after finishing work at two o'clock in the morning) got hold of a cab. She managed to coax his address out of him and, with the help of the cabdriver, carried and dragged the still blind-drunk student up the stairs to his room. Nothing happened that night, except that Henrik vomited on Frida's skirt, hit his head on the edge of the table, and bled fairly profusely.

Two days later, Henry set off for the Flustret with a bunch of what to him were expensive flowers. He found her at the sordid back quarters, where she happened to be taking a break with a cup of coffee and a cigarillo. Both of them were profoundly confused. Henrik apologized for his appalling behavior and offered to pay for the cleaning of Frida's skirt. She did not know what to say, since the skirt was ruined and couldn't be washed, and she realized it was unlikely that Henrik could afford to buy her a new one.

She finished her coffee, carefully stubbed out the cigarillo, and put the rest of it into a little tin. Then she got to her feet and said that her break was now over — but if he cared to come and meet her, she finished work at two o'clock. He sat down at a round marble table out in one of the large lilac arbors, ordered a mineral water, and sat watching the people and listening to the regimental music, the ducks quacking, and the water rushing under the bridge.

When the time came, he went with Frida to the Gillet, where he kissed her hand, something he had learned from his mother, and he also explained that he was alone in Upsala, in Sweden, in the World, and in the Universe. Frida laughed, surprised and slightly uneasy, and suggested an outing to Graneberg. She had the next Sunday off.

Thus began their time together, which rapidly developed into living together. Henrik was tormented by a sense of sin, lechery, and an ungovernable jealousy. Frida used cunning, wisdom, white lies, and strategy to calm this disturbed and confused child. She also taught him how to avoid consequences, which in turn brought on attacks of retrospective jealousy. Frida coaxed, and Henrik made a fuss. They were soon inseparable.

After a while, they became engaged . . . secretly. Henrik didn't dare tell his mother about Frida, but Frida had no objections. She was biding her time. To be the wife of a minister might be a future. She often hoped and dreamed about such a life but kept her dreams to herself. Frida was well aware of the realities and was wise enough to draw her own conclusions and make plans. Henrik, on the other hand, was aware of nothing, because a mountain of demands blocked his view. He lived in a mire of his own constraints and other people's expectations. With Frida, he would suddenly feel a stab of happiness, or whatever he was to call this unfamiliar feeling, which surprised him and caused hot tears to rise in his eyes.

When Frida came back home to Henrik on the evening of the oral

14

exam, it was already rather late. With the gracious permission of the head waiter, she had managed to change her hours. As the cathedral clock struck ten, she arrived to find the door open and the room almost in darkness. Henrik was lying on the bed with his arm across his face. As she cautiously approached, he sat up.

Frida: Justus came by and told me. Have you had anything to eat? You haven't eaten all day? I thought as much, so I brought some beer and cold cuts with me from the kitchen. Miss Hilda sends her regards — you know, we met her at the concert in Holy Trinity Church. She said she thought you were good looking but far too thin. Can I light the lamp and then set the table — I could move the books a little, couldn't I?

She busies herself in silence, stubbornly. Henrik looks at her, feeling both burdened and relieved, but he is also bursting to relieve himself.

Henrik: I must go and have a pee. I haven't had a pee all day.

Frida: Surely no one can be that miserable!

Henrik smiles faintly and disappears out into the corridor, and she hears him clattering down the stairs. Frida pours beer into a glass, sits down at the table, lights a cigarillo, and looks at the photograph of Henrik's mother. Then she turns her eyes to the window and looks down at the wall and the courtyard. Henrik is standing there, faintly illuminated by the light in the doorway. He is buttoning his trousers and probably senses she is looking at him, so turns to look up at the light from the window and sees her there framed in the yellow square. She smiles, but he does not smile in reply. She waves to him to come on up, raising her glass and taking a sip. Then she opens her blouse, pulls down her bodice, and exposes her right breast.
Frida gets up at dawn to make her way home.

Frida: No, you stay there. It'll be light soon, and I like walking along the river when the town's empty and quiet.

Henrik: I have to go home next week. Can you imagine what it'll be like? Mother waiting there on the platform, fat and expectant. I'll go up to her and tell her I've messed it up, failed the exam. And then she'll start crying.

Frida: Poor Henrik! I could come with you.

They laugh somewhat joylessly at such an inconceivable idea, and Henrik jumps out of bed and dresses. Then they're on their way through the chilly, still morning. When they get to Ny Bridge, they stop and look down into the dark, swiftly running water.

Henrik: When I was a child, Mother got a carpenter to make a little altar. She made a lace altar cloth herself and then bought a plaster model of Thorwaldsen's Christ, took two pewter candlesticks from the dining room, and put them on the altar cloth. We held communion on Sundays. I was the minister in cassock and dog collar. Mother and some old girl from the old people's home were the congregation. Mother played the organ, and we sang hymns. We even took communion — just imagine! Later on, I had to ask Mother to stop all that embarrassing playacting. I began to think we were committing some awful sin — it was all so silly and humiliating — I thought God would punish us. Mother was somehow so reckless. She was miserable, of course. She had gone and done all that for my sake, and I — anyhow over the last few years — had done it for her sake. It was a miserable business. And now, on a day like today, I wonder whether I am going to be ordained for Mother's sake and because my father didn't want to be a priest, although the whole family thought he ought to be. And I wonder what he thought when he gave up his studies, after being so promising. I wonder what he thought. And a pharmacist — he became a pharmacist! Can you imagine what Grandfather and the rest of the family thought? The shame of it! Yes.

Frida: Why shouldn't you become a priest, Henrik? It's a good profession. Honorable, solid, and good. You'll be able to support yourself and family, and not least your mother.

Clearly, Frida is teasing. Or perhaps her dialect makes the problem seem meaningless. Or perhaps Frida simply thinks her theologian is being awkward. It's not easy to know.

Johan Åkerblom, the superintendent of traffic, is resting, that is, he is shortening the boredom of the afternoon by taking a nap. He is also quite right to rest. He is over seventy and has retired from railway bridges, shunting yards, and signal systems, constructed and developed during the period of the greatest expansion of rail traffic. As a young man and a newly qualified engineer, he had applied to the State Railways and was noticed almost immediately for his quick and practical ideas. He advanced swiftly and easily in his career.

When he was twenty-four, he married the daughter of a wealthy wholesaler, purchased the newly constructed building at 12

16

Trädgårdsgatan, and moved into a ten-room apartment on the first floor. Three sons were born in rapid succession: Oscar, Gustav, and Carl. After twenty years of outward success and marital difficulties, his sickly wife died. Johan Åkerblom was left alone and nonplussed. His three sons were not yet adult and had been brought up much too strictly. The home, run by a housekeeper, was falling apart at an accelerated rate.

The superintendent of traffic played the cello in his spare time and consorted with the Calwagen family, whose head of household had written a German grammar book destined to plague generations of Swedish children: *Die Heeringe der Ostsee sind magerer als die der Nordsee* (The herrings of the Baltic are smaller than those of the North Sea). And so on.

Together they formed a string quartet, which could be expanded into a quintet when necessary, for the elder daughter, Karin, was an ambitious amateur pianist, who made up for her lack of musicality with enthusiasm and determination. Karin felt great sympathy for this widower, more than thirty years older than herself. She could clearly see his household disintegrating after his wife's death, and one spring day, without beating around the bush, she suggested that she and Johan should marry. Overwhelmed by so much generosity and energy, moved and stammering, Johan could hardly do anything else but gratefully accept. They married six months later, and after what was for those days an extremely short honeymoon at a new railway junction in the town of Halle, Karin, twenty-two years old, and overflowing with goodwill, moved into the ten-room apartment on Trädgårdsgatan.

The three sons, all more or less contemporaries of hers, reacted with dismissive suspicion and the sophisticated bad behavior of those who've been brought up too strictly. Among themselves they were enemies, but now they suddenly found reason to unite against someone who was clearly threatening their freedom. Within a few months, however, the three young men knew they had met their match. After a period of severe defeats, they decided to lay down their arms and surrender unconditionally. Karin was an instinctive strategist even in her early years and clearly realized that she must not use her advantage to humiliate her opponents. On the contrary. She heaped blessings on them, not only from wisdom but also from affection. She liked her awkward, kind, and confused stepsons, and met their growing affection with gruff and cheerful tenderness.

Karin is now forty-four and has two children of her own, Ernst and Anna, both in their twenties. The household has four servants and a large circle of friends. The two older brothers have also married and have families of their own, and they often come on more or less improvised visits.

When Karin married, she discontinued her training to be a teacher, a decision she never had occasion to regret. Daily life provided her with a continuous occupation. She was good with people, clear-sighted, humorous, friendly, and cheerfully energetic. She was also quick-tempered, dictatorial, ruthless, and sharp-tongued. No one could say she was beautiful, but her whole little person radiated charm and physical vitality. It is scarcely credible that the superintendent and his thirty-years-younger wife loved each other in the romantic sense, but they acted their roles without protest and gradually became good friends.

So Johan Åkerblom is resting. His Protestant heritage forbids him to get undressed and rest his back and aching hip in his comfortable bed. So he sits in his big reading armchair in an elegant short smoking jacket and with a scholarly treatise within reach. He has only pushed his glasses up onto his forehead. His afternoon pipe, the tobacco jar, and the little glass of absinthe are on the table by his chair. His light room faces the courtyard, hence the quietness. A tall tree keeps the sun off the window and casts flickering green shadows on bookshelves and pictures with Italian motifs on the walls. A solemn grandfather clock measures the time with courteous ticks. A light-colored patterned oriental carpet covers the floorboards.

Anyhow, the door now opens, very gently, and the main character of this story comes in quietly. Anna is just twenty, small and neat but well developed, with long brown hair with a reddish tinge at the ends, warm brown eyes, finely shaped nose, a sensually friendly mouth, and childishly rounded cheeks. She is wearing an expensive lace blouse, a broad belt around her narrow waist, and a long tailored skirt in light woolen material. She is wearing no jewelry except a pair of light diamond earrings. Her boots are fashionably high heeled.

That's what she looks like — Anna, my mother, whose name was really Karin. I neither want to nor am able to explain why I have this need to mix up and change names: my father's name was Erik, and my maternal grandmother's was Anna. Oh, well, perhaps it's all part of the game — and a game it is.

Anna: Are you asleep, Papa?

Johan Åkerblom: Of course. I'm asleep and dreaming I'm asleep. And

I'm dreaming I'm sitting in my study, asleep. Then the door opens and in comes the most beautiful — the most loving — the most affectionate of them all. And she comes over to me and blows on me with her gentle breath and says, Are you asleep, Papa? Then I dream I'm thinking: this must be what it's like to wake up in paradise.

Anna: You should take your glasses off when you're resting, Papa. Otherwise they might fall on the floor and break.

Johan Åkerblom: You're just as would-be-wise as your mother. You should know by now that with me everything is intentional and well thought out. If I push my glasses up onto my forehead when I take my little midday rest, that gives the impression of a creative state with my eyes closed. No one — except you — may surprise Johan Åkerblom with dropped jaw and open mouth.

Anna: Oh, no. You were sleeping correctly and upright and under control. As always.

Johan Åkerblom: Well, what do you want, dear heart?

Anna: Dinner will be ready in a few minutes. May I have a sip of your absinthe, by the way? They say it's so depraved. Just think how Christian Krohg and all those brilliant Norwegians went mad about absinthe. (Takes a sip.) If you're going to drink absinthe, then I suppose you have to be just a little depraved to be capable of drinking absinthe. Sit still now, Papa, and I'll fix your hair so you look nice.

Anna disappears into an inner room and comes back at once with a hairbrush and comb.

Johan Åkerblom: Weren't we going to have a guest to dinner? Wasn't Ernst . . . ?

Anna: It's a friend of Ernst's. They sing in the Academic Choir together. Ernst says he's studying theology.

Johan Åkerblom: What? Is he going to be a minister? Does our Ernst mix with an apprentice priest — the end of the world must be nigh!

Anna: Don't be silly, Papa. Ernst says this boy — I've forgotten his name — is awfully nice, rather shy but awfully nice. He's also said to be terribly poor. But handsome.

Johan Åkerblom: Oh, yes, yes, now I understand this unexpected interest in your brother's latest friend.

Anna: Papa, you're being silly again. I'm going to marry my brother Ernst. He is the Only One for me.

Johan Åkerblom: But what about me?

Anna: Oh, you, too, Papa of course! Hasn't Mama told you to trim those tufts of hair in your ears? How can anyone hear with so much hair in his ears?

Johan Åkerblom: They're particularly fine, so-called hearing hairs, and no one may touch them! With my hearing hairs, I have a very special kind of hearing, which tells me what people are thinking. Most people say one thing and think another. I hear that immediately with my hearing hairs.

Anna: Can you say what I'm thinking at this moment?

Johan Åkerblom: You're too close. Too much strain on my hearing hairs. Stand over there in that ray of sunlight; then I'll tell you at once what you're thinking.

Anna (*laughing*): Well, Papa!

Johan Åkerblom: You're very pleased with yourself. And you're also very pleased your father loves you.

As the clock on the cathedral, the clock in the dining room, the clock in the drawing room, and the introspective clock in the study all strike five, the door opens and the superintendent of traffic enters the salon with Anna at his side. He has put his right arm around her shoulders and leans heavily on his cane with his left.

Everyone rises and greets the Head of the Household. Perhaps this is the right moment to describe those present. Karin has already been mentioned, as has her son, Ernst, who is the same age as Henrik. The three brothers, Oscar, Gustav, and Carl, are standing slightly to one side, sorting out some of Carl's constant money troubles, all of them talking at once. When their father comes into the room with Anna, they at once fall silent and turn to smile politely at the two of them.

Oscar is like his father, a well-off wholesaler, self-confident and taciturn. He is married to Svea, a tall thin woman of sickly appearance, her glasses concealing her pain-filled gaze. She is always considered to be on the brink of death. Every autumn, she goes on cures and takes the waters in southern Germany or Switzerland, and each spring she returns bowed, swaying slightly, a tortured apologetic smile on her face: I didn't die this time either. You must be patient.

Gustav is a professor of Roman law and a bore, something those around him are given to pointing out. He has become quite stout to protect himself. He laughs good-naturedly and shakes his head at his own sorrows. His wife, Martha, is of Russian origin, speaks Swedish with a broad accent, and is good-humored. She and her husband are united by an intimate love of the delights of the table. They have two lovely and somewhat unruly daughters in their early teens.

Carl is an engineer and inventor, largely unsuccessful. Most people consider him the black sheep of the family. He combines intelligence with misanthropy, is a bachelor and not particularly clean either spiritually or physically, the latter to his stepmother's constant annoyance. Yes, there is something fishy about brother Carl, and I will return to him in a moment.

Also present is Torsten Bohlin, a young genius with bold features and flowing hair, who is carelessly elegant and loved by the family. At twenty-four, he is writing his doctoral thesis (on the Gregorian chant in pre-Protestant choirs as reflected in the collection of melodies found in Skattungbyn Church during the 1898 restoration). Last but not least, young Bohlin is regarded as Anna's intended. It's said that the two young people have been observed expressing their warm feelings for each other.

Upright Miss Siri appears in the doorway to the dining room, apparently slightly put out. Karin Åkerblom says from across the room, "Our extra dinner guest has not arrived. We'll wait a few minutes and see if he appears."

Karin (*to Ernst*): Are you sure you told your friend that we have dinner at five o'clock?

Ernst: I emphasized that we are insanely punctual in this family. He pointed out that he himself was a desperate enthusiast for punctuality.

Johan Åkerblom: What kind of creature is he?

Ernst: Papa dear, he's not a creature at all. He is studying theology and is going to be a priest, God willing.

Carl: A priest, a priest! Why not a priest in the family? A professional addition to this gang of hypocrites.

Martha: Has this fabulous creature a name?

Ernst: Henrik Bergman. From the Gästrike-Hälsinge student hostel. We both sing in the Academic Choir. He's an excellent baritone, and he's also got three unmarried aunts on his father's side.

Oscar: The ladies of Elfvik.

Ernst: The ladies of Elfvik.

Johan Åkerblom: Then Fredrik, the member of Parliament, must be his grandfather.

Karin: Do we know him?

Johan Åkerblom: A really cunning old fox. He's keen on a special alliance — an Agrarian party. That would be a fine old mess. Conflicts and splinterings. For that matter, we're supposed to be related somewhere along the line. Second cousins or something of the kind.

This gives rise to some hilarity, which is silenced when the doorbell rings. "I'll go," says Anna firmly, stopping Miss Siri, who is on her way with the special look of disapproval on her face that would frighten anyone. Anna opens the door, and there is Henrik Bergman. He is petrified.

Henrik: I was delayed. I'm late.

Anna: You can have some dinner all the same. Though I expect you'll have to sit in the kitchen.

Henrik: I'm terribly . . . I'm usually . . .

Anna: . . . a stickler for punctuality. We know that already. Come on in. Otherwise dinner will be later than ever.

Henrik: I don't think I dare. No.

Henrik turns abruptly and takes a few quick strides toward the steps. Anna goes after him and grasps his arm, suppressing her desire to laugh.

Anna: We are apt to be rather dangerous when we're all together as a family, especially when we don't get our food at the prescribed time. But I think you should really pluck up your courage. The food'll be terribly good, and I have made the dessert all by myself. Come on, now. For *my* sake.

She takes off his student cap and smooths down his hair with her hand. "There we are now. You look fine," and she shoves him ahead of her into the salon.

Anna: Mr. Bergman says he is very sorry. He has been at a friend's sickbed and had to go to the pharmacy. There was a line there. So he was delayed.

22

Karin: How do you do, Mr. Bergman. Welcome to our home. I hope your friend isn't seriously . . .

Henrik: No, no. He has only . . .

Anna: . . . broken his leg. This is my father.

Johan Åkerblom: Welcome to my home. I do believe you're quite like your grandfather.

Henrik: So they say, yes.

Anna: My brothers Gustav and Oscar and Carl, and Martha who is married to Gustav, and Svea to Oscar, and the girls are Gustav and Martha's daughters, and this is Torsten Bohlin, who is considered to be my intended. Now you know the whole family.

Karin: Then I suggest we at last go in to dinner.

Ernst: Hello there, Henrik.

Henrik: Hello.

Ernst: Who's broken his leg?

Henrik: No one. It was your sister who . . .

Ernst: Ah yes, you must watch out for her.

Henrik: I've no longer . . .

Karin (*interrupting*): Perhaps, Mr. Bergman, you would please sit down over there beside Mrs. Martha. And Torsten, you sit beside Anna. Then we can say grace.

All: For what we are about to receive may the Lord make us truly thankful.

They all hurriedly bow and curtsy, then sit down among much cheerful chatter. Miss Siri and Miss Lisen in black and white, and starched caps, appear with fresh asparagus and mineral water.

Henrik Bergman is now afflicted with further trials. He has never seen asparagus before. He has never before had a four-course dinner. He has never drunk anything but water, beer, or schnapps with his food, and he has never in his life seen a finger bowl with a small red flower swimming around in the water. He has never seen so many knives and forks, and he has never before conversed with a sarcastically good-humored lady with a strong Russian accent. Walls loom high and chasms open.

Martha: I'm from St. Petersburg. Our family still live in a large house near Alexander Gardens. St. Petersburg is very beautiful, especially in the autumn. Have you ever been to St. Petersburg, Mr. Bergman? I go home every year in September. That's the most beautiful time of year, when everyone has come back from their summer holidays and the season starts, the parties, the theaters, and the concerts. So you're going to be a priest? Your looks are most appropriate. You have lovely sorrowful eyes, Mr. Bergman, and the women are sure to fall for such looks. But you must keep your hair off your forehead when you've got such a lovely poet's forehead. Let me help you! My husband, Gustav, that nice old fat gentleman sitting over there, yes, him! I'm talking about you, my darling. He's a professor of Roman law. You wouldn't think so to look at him, would you (*laughs gaily*)? I've been in Sweden for almost twenty years. I love your country, but I'm Russian. No, Gustav looks like a baker. But he's got a warm heart. He was on a visit to St. Petersburg, and we met at a charity banquet. He proposed later that evening, and I said to myself, Martha, stupid girl, no doubt you could find a more handsome man, but *that* man has a heart of purest gold, and so we married a year later and I have indeed wondered occasionally about this country and its peculiar people, but I have never really regretted it. Regrets aren't compatible with nature, anyhow. Are you a man for regrets, Mr. Bergman? (*Laughs, grows serious.*) The churches are so poverty-stricken in this country, the hymns so poverty-stricken, no great moments. My dear Mr. Bergman, sometimes I think I worship two quite different gods. (*Laughs quietly.*) Now I'll . . . no, wait a moment. I'll show you how to eat asparagus. It's the tip that's the good part. We have to take the stalk in our fingers. It tastes better that way — and is more enjoyable; then you put it to your mouth and bite, but *carefully.* And then this is what you do with the finger bowl. Look at me now, Mr. Bergman.

In addition to asparagus, the menu includes salmon mousse with green sauce, spring chicken (hard to handle), and Anna's masterpiece, a trembling crème caramel.

After coffee in the salon, they make music. Dusk is falling, and they light candles around the musicians, who are playing the slow movement of Beethoven's last string quartet. Johan Åkerblom plays the cello; Carl is a good amateur violinist, member of the Academic Orchestra. Ernst plays the second violin, with great feeling but less success. A retired member of the Royal Opera House orchestra comes down for coffee from his apartment above, with his viola, a courteous shadow, benevolent and somewhat haughty. He can hardly bear to

24

make music in this company, but the superintendent of traffic has underwritten loans for him and his suffering is prescribed.

Music and dusk. Henrik sinks . . . all this is dreamlike, outside and beyond his own colorless days. Anna is sitting by the window, looking steadily at the musicians and listening with attention, her profile outlined against the dying light outside. Now she senses she is being watched and controls her first impulse, but then gives in and turns to look at Henrik. He is looking gravely at her, and she smiles slightly formally, slightly ironically, but then becomes grave in response to Henrik's solemnity. I see you, all right. I see.

Now it is time to leave, and farewells are being exchanged. Henrik bows and says thank you in all directions and for a brief moment finds Anna in front of him. She stands on tiptoe and whispers quickly into his ear, her hair fragrant, a light touch.

Anna: My name's Anna and yours is Henrik, isn't it?

She at once goes and stands beside her father, taking his arm and leaning her head on his shoulder, all of it a trifle theatrical, but affectionate, not without talent.

Henrik is quite dumbfounded (that's what it's called, banal but at the moment there is no better word, dumbfounded). So he's standing in bewilderment on the corner of Trädgårdsgatan and Little Ågatan. He ought to go home and write that painful letter to his mother, but it's early and he's lonely. Ernst was off on some escapade and had been in a hurry, rushing down Drottninggatan with his coattails flying.

The chestnuts are out, and band music can be heard from the city park. The cathedral clock strikes nine, and the Gunilla bell replies with delicate clangs from the hill above the Sture Vaults.

Someone pokes Henrik on the shoulder. It's Carl. He is benevolent now, exuding brandy.

Carl: Shall we walk together, Mr. Bergman? Shall we, for instance, take this street straight down to Svandammen and look at the three cygnets, *Cyg-Nus Ocor,* or the black swan, *Chenopsis Atrata,* which has just been imported from Australia? Or shall we extend our promenade by exactly a hundred meters, take a glass of liqueur together — and last but not least, look at the three brand new whores they've acquired from Copenhagen? We'll go to the Flustret, Mr. Bergman. Let's go to the Flustret!

Carl smiles winningly and pats Henrik on the cheek with a soft little hand.

They sit out on the Flustret's glassed-in veranda. The evening is still; people have settled out-of-doors in the mild early summer twilight. Only a few seedy lecturers huddle indoors in bitter solitude, guarding their night drinks. A slim, strikingly lovely waitress comes up to the table to take their order. She gives a little bob and greets them.

Frida: Good evening, sir. Good evening, Mr. Bergman. What would you like this evening?

Carl: Half a bottle of punsch liqueur, Miss Frida, if we may? The usual — and some cigars, please.

Frida: I'll tell the girl.

She nods and turns on her heel. Carl watches her go, a blue gaze behind the pince-nez.

Carl: You seem to know Miss Frida, Mr. Bergman.

Henrik: No, not really. We sometimes come here to eat when we have any money. No, I don't know her.

Carl (*sharp-eyed*): Color has come into the pastor's cheeks, Mr. Bergman. Is this a denial? Are we going to hear the cock crow?

Henrik: I know only that her name's Frida and she's from Ångermanland. (*Pulls himself together.*) Nice-looking girl.

Carl: Very nice looking, very. Doubtful reputation. Or? What do you think, Mr. Bergman? Theological training is said to provide insight into human weaknesses. Or should I say a nose for them?

The cigarette girl comes with her tray and supplies the gentlemen with Havana cigars. Carl pays and tips her generously. The girl clips and lights their cigars. They puff away and lean back.

Carl: Well, Mr. Bergman, what did you think of the evening?

Henrik: In what way, Mr. Åkerblom?

Carl: What did you think of us, to put it bluntly?

Henrik: I've never had a four-course dinner with three different wines before. It was like being at the theater. I was sitting there in the middle of your play, expected to perform with you, but didn't know my lines.

Carl: Very well put!

Henrik: It was all very attractive but also repelling. Or rather, inaccessible. I don't mean to be critical.

Carl: Inaccessible?

Henrik: Even if I wanted to get into your world and had ambitions to act in your play, it would be impossible.

Frida brings the liqueur in a cooler and two small glasses with no stems, slightly misted over. Carl looks at Henrik with mild attention. Henrik doesn't dare meet Frida's eyes. Supposing she kisses me on the mouth, or puts her hand on the back of my neck? What would that matter? Actually, things are inaccessible in her direction, too. Perhaps in all directions? Outside? thinks Henrik with bitter voluptuousness. Outside?

Carl: My stepmother, Karin, plays the main part in our insignificant family drama. Mammchen is a remarkable character, considerably larger than life. Some people say that's our little bit of luck; others maintain she's an out-and-out bitch. If anyone happened to ask *me*, I would say she wants what is good and does what is evil, to para- phrase — yes, it's Romans, isn't it? Her ambition is to keep the family together, whatever point there is in that. If something doesn't fit in with the pattern, she cuts it out, amputates it, deforms it. She does that well, the charming little lady.

Carl raises his glass to Henrik, who answers his toast, and they look at each other with sympathy.

Carl: May I be so bold as to suggest a fraternal toast? My name's Carl Ebehard, '89. Thank you.

Henrik: Erik Henrik Fredrik, '06. Thank you.

The ritual is carried out, and the newly created brothers carefully observe the quiet that usually follows such a significant event.

Carl: I'm an inventor, really, and have had a few minor inventions accepted by the Royal Patent Office. I'm a failure in the eyes of the family, the black sheep. I've been in the lunatic asylum a couple of times. I'm no madder than anyone else but am considered somewhat incoherent. Our family has produced so damned much normality that there's some surplus craziness, and I see to that. *In addition*, I happened to clash with the law a few years ago. I imitate other people's handwriting far too well. To be a priest, one should believe in some kind of god, shouldn't one? Isn't that one of the principal conditions?

Henrik: Yes, that's probably a principal condition.

Carl: How the hell can any young person today believe in God? Excuse the intentionally tactless way I put it.

Henrik: . . . difficult to explain. Just like that.

Carl: . . . an inner voice? A feeling of being in someone's hands? Of not being left out, excluded? Like a warm breath on your cheek? Like being a small pulse beating in an immense circulation system? A not insignificant pulse, despite the vastness of the network of arteries and veins. Purpose, pattern, moments of grace? No, I'm not being ironic. It's just my throat never ceases throwing up sarcastic belches. I'm being terribly serious, young man.

Henrik: Why do you ask, if you know?

Carl: I think a man born blind can perfectly well imagine things in red, blue, and yellow.

Henrik: I'm an irresolute person. I like to think the cassock may perhaps be a good corset. I'll probably be a good priest for my own sake. Not for humanity's.

Frida returns, puts the bill down on the table beside Carl, then glances at Henrik.

Frida: I'm sorry to bring you the bill, but as you gentlemen perhaps saw on the notice down in the hall, we're closing early tonight. We have a breakfast for the whole Senate tomorrow morning, and we have to set all the tables tonight.

Carl: So Miss Frida is . . .

Frida: . . . busy this evening? (*Laughs.*) You could say that.

While Carl is paying and putting back his wallet with some ceremony, Frida leans over behind Henrik and pinches his ear. This occurs swiftly and unnoticeably. She smells good, slightly pungently of sweat and rosewater.

Carl Åkerblom and Henrik Bergman are standing by the railing around Svandammen looking at the black swan floating as if dreaming through the dark mirrorlike water. Fine rain has begun to fall.

Henrik (*after a long silence*): And your half sister? Anna?

Carl: Anna? She's just twenty. You saw for yourself.

Henrik: Yes. Yes, of course.

Carl: She's training at Sophiahemmet's school of nursing. Mammchen maintains that young women must have an education. That they must stand on their own two feet, and so on. Mammchen believes that she believes that. She herself gave up her teacher training in order to marry.

Henrik: Your little sister is very . . .

Carl: . . . attractive. Exactly. We've had a great many suitors coming to the house, but Our Lord Father has frightened them all away with his appalling but extremely sophisticated jealousy and Our Lady Mother has frightened them even more with the scarcely cheerful prospect of having Karin Åkerblom as mother-in-law. At the moment, that young genius Torsten Bohlin is frequenting the family. Nothing at all deters him, and he appears to be amazingly tolerated. But then he's a man of the future, too, and he'll obviously be a cabinet minister or an archbishop. Anna seems unusually amused by his attentions. Though my theory is that Anna's destiny is written in another book.

Henrik: Look, here comes the other black swan out of their house. This rain's very pleasant.

Carl: After the drought. Yes. Anna's destiny will probably be to love a madman or a sex murderer or perhaps a nonentity.

Henrik: Why are you so sure of that?

Carl: Our little princess is so well adjusted and clever and purehearted and tenderhearted and loving; there's no limit to it.

Henrik: But that sounds good. All of it? Or?

Carl: You see, my boy, she possesses a splinter of glass, a sharp splinter that cuts. (*Laughs.*) Now I've terrified you all right!

Henrik: I don't understand what you mean.

Carl: Nor is it something you can understand just like that. But I know her. I *recognize* her.

Henrik: That sounds like a more sophisticated kind of literature.

Carl: Of course, of course.

Henrik: Let's go, shall we? It's raining quite hard now.

Carl: You can share my umbrella. Since I have a markedly tragic view of the ways of the world, I always carry an umbrella. Whether I use it later on or not is my own free choice. It's my shrewd way of combating determinism and deceiving chance.

Henrik (*smiles*): For obvious reasons, I can't share your . . .

Carl: . . . view. I have no opinions, but I chatter. Do you know what, Henrik? I think Miss Frida would be an *extraordinarily* splendid minister's wife.

Henrik does not reply to that. He is, quite simply, rendered speechless.

The term has ended and Henrik goes home.

It's a hot day in mid-June, and the train chugs through the summer countryside, making a lengthy stop at each station. Silence, the buzz of flies. Chestnuts in flower reach out toward the closed windows of the compartment. No one is in sight, either at the stations or on board the train. Then on it chugs, first through the pine forest and then along the coast. It takes all day to travel by passenger train from Upsala to Söderhamn.

Henrik arrives at the west station at twenty-seven minutes past eight in the evening. Mama Alma is waiting at the entrance. He sees her at once — her heavy figure seems to be surrounded by an invisible aura of tearful desolation. Henrik smiles, puts down his suitcase, and embraces his mother.

She is very fat. Her face is round, her eyes wide open and anxious; she has a small snub nose, large sensitive mouth, and short neck. She is wearing a tight summer coat that is rather shabby and has a button missing. Her black hat with a feather in it has been knocked awry by their embrace. She laughs and cries in utter despair. Henrik makes an effort to return his mother's show of affection. She smells of dried sweat and is wheezing asthmatically. "Let me look at you, my son. How pale you are, and how thin you are. I suppose you've not been bothering about food, of course! How nice of you to come back to your old mother for a few days. Are you really going to have a mustache? I don't think your mama is all that keen on that mustache. You'll probably have to shave it off now that you're to be my darling boy again."

Alma Bergman lives in three small rooms at the top of the inner courtyard block on the corner of Norralagatan and Köpmangatan. One of the rooms is Henrik's and is rented out during the winter months.

Alma's bedroom is a very small room, and then there's the dining

30

room, connected to a spacious kitchen by a curious serving passage. The apartment is very cluttered, as if its occupants had suddenly had to move from something much bigger and had not had the courage to part with bulky furniture, pictures, and other objects.

Over everything lies a sticky layer of proud poverty. Perplexed abandonment. Hopelessness and tears.

While Alma produces something to eat, Henrik goes into his boyhood room: The narrow sagging bed. The broken wicker chair with cushions, the rickety desk with its old wounds from the ravages of his penknife, the unmatched chairs. The wardrobe with its cracked mirror, the bookcase of tattered books, the washstand with its ill-matched jug and basin, the worn towels. The dirty window, its pelmet slipped from the curtain pole. The pictures of biblical scenes from his childhood (Jesus with the children, the return of the prodigal son). Above the bed is the photograph of his father. A young, handsome face; thin, wispy hair, brushed back off a high forehead; large blue eyes; a small self-conscious smile — pride, vulnerability, integrity, and suffering; the features of an actor.

In one corner by the window, somewhat cramped, is the altar with its altar runner and silver candlesticks, Thorvaldsen's Jesus, and an open prayer book. In front of the altar, a prie-dieu embroidered in green and gold. The altar frontal is purple with a cross in dull red. A dazzling bunch of freshly picked cowslips stands at Jesus' feet.

Henrik sinks down on one of the odd chairs, hides his face in his hands, and breathes deeply, as if suffering from an attack of asphyxiation.

He finds it hard to swallow, although he ought to be hungry, for he has eaten nothing but a few sandwiches he had taken with him for the long journey. His mother sits opposite him at the table, the paraffin lamp lit, dusk fallen outside the square windows.

Alma: Everything's got so terribly expensive recently. Of course, *you* don't have to think about things like that, but I hardly know how I'm going to manage. Just think, paraffin's gone up by three öre, and five pounds of potatoes cost thirty-two öre. I can hardly afford beef nowadays but have to get ordinary pork, or perhaps another kind of meat for soup. And coal — you've no idea what a winter we've had — coal and wood have doubled in price. It meant wrapping up indoors, though I have to put the heat on for my piano pupils, and that costs an awful lot. What's the matter, Henrik? You look so miserable. Has something awful happened? You know you can tell your old mother anything.

31

Henrik: I failed my church history exam.

He makes a helpless gesture and stares at his mother's ear. She carefully puts down her teacup and places her fat little hand on the table, the heavy wedding ring glistening dully.

Alma: When did this happen?

Henrik: A few weeks ago.

Alma: And what will the consequences be?

Henrik: I'll retake it at the end of November. Professor Sundelius won't let me try any earlier.

Alma: So your finals will be delayed.

Henrik: By six months.

Alma: How are we going to manage, Henrik? The loan is almost all gone, and everything's grown so expensive. Your fees and books and your keep. I can't think what we can do. I've never been able to handle money.

Henrik: Neither have I.

Alma: And we promised to pay back the loan as soon as you were ordained.

Henrik: I know, Mama.

Alma: I try to get more pupils, but piano lessons are the first thing people give up when things get so expensive. One can understand that.

Henrik: Yes, one can understand that.

Alma: I could start cleaning again, but my asthma's got so bad, and my heart's acting up, too.

Henrik: Mama, dear, you're not to start cleaning.

Alma gets up with a sigh, filled with tenderness. She embraces her son and showers him with kisses, prattling away at the same time: "My little boy, my darling, my heart! You're all I have. I live for you and you alone. We'll help each other. We'll never abandon each other, isn't that right, my darling boy, isn't that right?"

Gently but firmly, Henrik frees himself and puts his mother onto a chair. Holding her arms, he looks into her bright, tear-filled eyes.

Henrik: I can give up my studies, Mama. I'll give them up and look for work and move back here again. Then first of all we'll pay back the loan to the aunts in Elfvik. Then perhaps I could start studying again, when I've saved enough to manage on my own and not be a burden to anyone.

Alma laughs, a large hearty laugh of white teeth, and strokes her son's face with her soft, fat hand.

Alma: My poor dear boy, you really are even sillier than me. Surely you don't think we should stop *now*, just when we're nearly there? Surely you don't think I'm going to let you be some telegraph office clerk or a tutor? You . . . who's going to be a priest. *My* priest!

His mother laughs again and gets up, filled with sudden energy. She goes across to the monstrous sideboard taking up all the space between the windows, gets out a bottle of port wine and two glasses, and pours it out. Henrik also starts laughing — this is all so familiar and charged with a remarkable sense of security — both of them in distress, then suddenly a laugh, irresistible, Mama laughing — so it's not that bad. They toast each other and drink. She leans forward and sighs.

Alma: I've heard that really talented frauds never bother with small change. They go straight for the big money. In that way they're regarded as more trustworthy and can finagle even more money for themselves.

Henrik: I don't really understand.

Alma: Don't you understand? We've been far too meek! The aunts will have to hand over a decent sum of money now. We'll pay them a visit. At once. Tomorrow.

The mythical aunts live in a handsome wooden villa overlooking the Ljusnan River, twenty kilometers south of Bollnäs. They are Henrik's grandfather's sisters and are very old. Grandfather is their baby brother, the tail end of the family. The names of the aunts, from eldest to youngest, are Ebba, Beda, and Blenda.

Briefly, this is their situation: Grandfather's father was a man who owned forests and land and possessed a good business sense. When the exploitation of Norrland began in all seriousness, the enterprising Leonhard created a fortune for himself, and when he died, he left a considerable inheritance. Grandfather Bergman thought that none of it should be touched, and that it ought to become part of and increase the working capital of the family farm. No one had dared oppose him except Blenda, who claimed a share of the inheritance for herself and her sisters. Their brother objected, but Blenda took the dispute to the county court in Gävle. Before this scandal had become public, Fredrik Bergman gave in, and with his heart trembling with hatred, he realized he would have to pay out the shares of the inheritance to his unmarried sisters. From then on, he refused to speak to them again, and the hatred on both sides became a well-established fact. Neither births, nor marriages, nor deaths could bridge their mutual bitterness.

Blenda, the youngest sister, who had shown so much enterprise, took over the management of the fortune. Through good sense and business acumen, she increased its value even more. She had a handsome wooden villa built, with a view over the most beautiful part of Lake Ljusnan. The house was filled with the most comfortable furniture of the day and decorated with the most tasteless wallpapers, tapestries, and pictures of the century.

The villa has a garden, almost a park, which runs down in terraces toward the river. The sisters work in it every spring, summer, and autumn, in white linen dresses, overalls, wide-brimmed hats, gloves, and clogs. All the love, tenderness, and inventiveness they possess are scarcely wasted on one another, but instead bestowed on the garden. The garden returns their devoted attentions with lush greenery, laden fruit trees, and dazzling flower beds.

Ebba is the eldest and a trifle out of it, which she has always been. She is also deaf and doesn't say much. She has a faithful friend, a very old labrador with rheumatism. Ebba's face is like a withered rose petal. She was probably a beautiful girl.

Despite her age, Beda's hair is still dark, her eyes also dark, and tragic. She reads novels, plays Chopin with more passion than instinct, is quarrelsome, and complains loudly about almost everything. Now and again, she departs, but she always comes back. Her departures are sensational and her returns ordinary. In contrast to her sisters, it is said that she has experienced passion.

Finally, Blenda is small, quick, and controlled. She has a renowned capacity for getting her own way. Her hair is iron gray, her forehead low and broad, her nose large with a reddish tinge, her mouth sarcastically curved, appropriate for lightning attacks and ironic invective.

Once a year they go to the capital, mixing in circles, going to concerts and theaters, ordering expensive and stylish items from the leading fashion houses in town. Occasionally, they go for a cure at a resort in southern Germany or Austria.

That's the situation with the aunts of Elfvik.

The sisters' bedrooms, though horribly cluttered, are furnished according to each woman's personal taste. Ebba inhabits bright florals, Beda purple and art nouveau, while Blenda lives in blue, pale blue, dark blue, dull blue. At this particular moment, agitation reigns. They are dressing for dinner, advising, helping one another, squabbling. Their rooms are interconnected with doors that are often locked, but at the moment they are all wide open.

Blenda: Can you see them?

Beda: What are they doing?

Ebba: Bless my soul! They're down at the bathing hut.

Blenda: What! Are they going swimming in that cold water?

Ebba: Bless my soul! They are indeed!

Blenda: How foolish. Alma, that fat cow. How foolish.

Beda: Move over, so I can see.

Blenda: They're going into the bathing hut.

Ebba: They're going to go into the water.

Beda: At this time of year! The water can't be more than ten degrees.

Blenda: Can I wear my pale blue?

Beda: Isn't that too elegant? Alma might feel socially degraded. She's probably only got something black.

Blenda: Then I'll take the pale gray.

Beda: My dear, that's even more elegant.

Ebba (*trumpets*): Bless my soul! The Ljusan's rising.

Blenda: What did you say?

Ebba: Alma, that mountain of flesh, has gone into the water.

Beda: Don't stand there staring. Put your corsets on, and I'll help you lace them.

Ebba: What did you say? Dear Henrik's naked now!

Beda: No! I must see that.

Blenda: Don't push. God, he's good-looking, that boy!

Ebba: Goodness, how thin he is.

Beda: But lovely shoulders. And handsomely built.

Blenda: I wonder why they've come, I really do.

Beda: That's not difficult to guess.

Ebba: He's swimming very strongly.

Blenda: Shall I really take the pale gray?

Beda: Yes, I think it's all right. It'll look really good with your red nose.

Ebba: Now they're going back to the bathing hut. Heavens above, what would we have done if they'd drowned?

Blenda: Paid for the funeral, I suppose.

Beda: Ebba, come on now, so that I can get you dressed.

Ebba: No, no. I must see them as they come out.

Beda: Are they coming out now?

Ebba: What? They're coming in, and they're holding hands!

Blenda: I've a good idea why they've come.

Beda: So what, you old miser.

Blenda: They'll not get a cent out of us, I'm telling you. Not a cent. They've had their loan, and they don't have to pay it back until Henrik's ordained.

Ebba: How good-looking he is, dear Henrik! But going naked like that, both of them. How extraordinary.

Beda (*to Ebba*): I've got your pink out. (*Shudders.*) The pink!

Ebba: No, I don't want that. I want the floral one. The one with roses and lace.

Beda: Oh, goodness. That makes you look even more hideous.

Ebba: Now that was really nasty of you. I heard.

Blenda: She's dolling herself up as if she were going to perform at the Royal Theater.

Beda: What's wrong with that, may I ask?

Blenda: There's nothing really wrong with the dress.

Beda: I want to look really nice for the boy. He may need to see a little style and beauty, perhaps.

Blenda (*laughing maliciously*): Ha ha!

Ebba: Who's taken my perfume? (*Squeals.*) My perfume!

Beda: An old biddy like you shouldn't use perfume. It's obscene!

Ebba: Now you're being nasty again. Where's my ear trumpet?

Beda: Supposing this is about money again. Do we have to be so impossible?

Blenda: Certainly, Beda dearest. Times are hard, and people have to learn to live according to their means.

Beda: They don't appear to be living off the fat of the land.

Blenda: Alma's never been able to manage money. Do you remember when we sent her fifty kronor when Henrik's father passed away? Do you know what Alma bought? A pair of very elegant shoes to go with her mourning clothes. She told me herself! Is that a way to be economical? I'm only asking.

Ebba: They're on their way back from the bathing hut now. Heavens, what a lovely way he looks at his mother. What a nice boy he is.

The living room and dining room meet at an angle to the big window facing the sunset. Everything here is light: airy summer curtains, white handmade furniture à la Carl Larsson, yellow wallpaper, large basket chairs, a piano, a lime-green sideboard, brightly colored rag rugs on the wide, well-scrubbed floorboards. Modern art of a kind on the walls — women as flowers and flowers as women, comely young girls in white, vaguely gazing into a delightful future.

The sisters march in in single file: Ebba, Beda, and Blenda. Alma and Henrik are already in place, the mother in a much too tight purple silk dress, tortured by her tightly laced corset, Henrik in a neat but shiny suit and stiff collar and necktie. Blenda at once says dinner is served, and when they have taken their places, she presses a concealed electric bell. Immediately, two young serving girls appear with a steaming tureen and warm plates. Nettle soup with egg-halves.

After dinner, they have coffee on the veranda. Alma and Henrik are put on the rattan sofa; Blenda takes the rocking chair, strategically placed outside the horizontal sunlight. Beda has sat down on the steps to the terrace. She is smoking a cigarette in an elegant holder. Ebba is sitting with her back to the view with her ear trumpet at the ready.

So the time has come. Alma is wheezing slightly, whether from the tension or the good food and excellent wine is hard to say. Henrik is pale and keeps tying his fingers into knots.

Blenda: We assume that Alma and Henrik have not come this long way out of family affection. I seem to remember it is three years since we last saw you. The reason for your journey at the time was the loan that would cover the costs of Henrik's studies.

Blenda rocks cautiously in her chair and gazes at Alma with cool benevolence. Beda closes her eyes and allows herself to be exposed to the last rays of the sun. Ebba has her ear trumpet at the ready and is sucking at her false teeth.

Alma: The money's come to an end. It's as simple as that.

Blenda: Oh, so the money's gone. It was supposed to last for four years, and not even three have gone by.

Alma: Everything's got more expensive.

Blenda: You decided on the size of the loan yourself, Alma. I don't remember haggling.

Alma: No, no, Blenda, you were very generous.

Blenda: And now the money's all gone?

Alma: I reckoned on Henrik's grandfather helping us, because after all, Henrik was to keep up the family tradition and become a priest.

Blenda: But Henrik's grandfather didn't help?

Alma: No. We begged for a whole day. We got nothing but twelve kronor for our railway tickets. So that we could get back to Söderhamn. Plus a pittance of a monthly allowance.

Blenda: That was generous.

Alma: Times are hard, Blenda. I have piano pupils, but that doesn't bring in much, and some of them have stopped taking lessons.

Blenda: And now you want another loan, Alma?

Alma: Henrik and I have *thoroughly* discussed whether he should interrupt his studies and apply for a job with the Telegraph Office in Söderhamn. That was our only way out. But then something happened.

Ebba: What?

Alma: Then something happened.

Beda: That sounds plausible!

Alma: Something pleasant.

Ebba: What is she saying?

Blenda: Something pleasant happened.

Alma: I think Henrik should tell you himself.

Henrik: You see, I had an oral exam in church history with the dreaded Professor Sundelius. Three of us took it, and I was the only one to pass. After the exam, the professor asked to speak to me alone. He offered me a cigar and was extremely friendly. Quite unlike his usual sarcastic self.

Alma (*excited*): He offered Henrik a cigar!

Henrik: I've said that, Mama.

Alma: Sorry, sorry.

Henrik: Well, we chatted for a while about this and that. Among other things, he said that anyone good at church history shows industry, good memory, and self-discipline. He thought I had shown unusual talent when I'd elucidated the Apostolic symbolism. That's quite complicated and requires some scholastic classification.

Ebba: What's he saying, Blenda?

Blenda: Not now, Ebba. (*Hoots.*) Later, later.

Henrik: He suggested I should go over to the academic side. That I ought to write a thesis for a doctorate. The professor offered to be my adviser. Then later on I would be sure to get a fellowship. He said most theologians were idiots and they had to nurture the few talents they have.

Alma: Flattering for Henrik, you see, Blenda. Professor Sundelius will become archbishop or a cabinet minister any moment now.

Henrik: Then I told him the truth, that I had no means. I hadn't even enough capital to complete my theology exams. Then the professor said that if I could arrange for the first years on my own, later on I would be awarded something called a postgraduate scholarship. That's quite a lot of money, you see, Aunt Blenda. Nearly all those who get them are married with children and servants.

Blenda: Well I never!

Alma (*diving in*): Now we've come to you to ask for an interest-free loan of six thousand kronor. Professor Sundelius reckoned that was just about what was needed.

Blenda: Well I never!

Alma: We wanted to turn to you *first*. I mean, before we went to the Upplands Bank. The professor promised to write a recommendation. He would guarantee the loan, he said.

Blenda: What do you think, Beda?

Beda (*laughs*): I'm speechless.

Ebba: What are you talking about? Is it about money?

Blenda: Henrik's going to be a professor! And needs six thousand kronor, apart from the two thousand he's already borrowed. Do you understand?

Ebba: Have we got that much money?

Blenda: *That* is the big question.

Blenda laughs with a crackling sound. Beda smiles and peers at Henrik from under her long dark eyelashes. Henrik's pallor has turned to scarlet. Alma is breathing heavily. Suddenly, Blenda gets up and claps her hands together.

Blenda: If we're going to get something done, then we'd better do it at once. Would you mind coming with me into my study, Alma and Henrik?

Blenda's study has a special entrance from the hall and is rather cramped. The shelves are crammed with office books. In the middle of the floor there's a sloping office desk and over by the window an ordinary desk and some chairs of stained wood. In a corner a leather sofa and armchair, a round table with a brass top and everything for the smoker. Blenda turns on the electric light, frees a little key from a gold chain around her neck, opens the middle drawer of the desk, takes out some shiny metal keys, and opens the safe skulking behind a screen by the door.

Neither Alma nor Henrik can see what she is doing behind the screen. When she appears again, she has a bundle of banknotes in her right hand. She puts the money down on the desk, locks up the keys to the safe, and fastens the drawer key back onto the gold chain. Then she starts counting. Six thousand riksdaler in notes. When at last she stops counting, she hands the money to Alma, who is standing there as if she had been struck by lightning.

Alma: Maybe I should sign a receipt.

Blenda: Henrik, please go out to your aunts for a moment. I would like to talk to your mother alone.

Henrik bows and goes to the door. He has a nasty feeling something may have gone wrong. After he has left the room, Alma is asked to sit down. Blenda starts leafing through the telephone directory.

Blenda: Funnily enough, we have the Upsala telephone directory here in the office. I was going to telephone Professor Sundelius and thank him on behalf of the family for his worthy contribution to the family's promising youth. Yes, here's the number, one-five-four-three.

She lifts the receiver and, smiling, looks at Alma, whose face has turned ashen, tears dimming the wide-eyed gaze. Blenda slowly hangs up the receiver.

Blenda: Maybe I'll phone another day. It's not very polite to disturb such a prominent man after eight in the evening.

Blenda sits down opposite Alma and looks at her with something that might be described as tender irony.

Blenda: Alma, you know perfectly well my sisters and I are proud to be able to help Henrik toward a brilliant future.

She pats Alma's plump knee and her plump cheek, where a tear is on its way down to the corner of her mouth. Alma mumbles something about how grateful she is.

Blenda: You don't have to be grateful, Alma. I'm doing this because your boy is so splendidly gifted. Or perhaps for no particular reason. For your love for the boy, Alma. I don't know. Shall we go back to the

41

others? I think we should celebrate this evening with a bottle of champagne. Come now, Alma, *don't cry like that*. I haven't had such fun since our brother lost the inheritance case.

At the height of his career, the superintendent of traffic had had a summer residence built close to the river, the lakes, the forests, and the low, bluish mountains. Every year in mid-June, the move to the summer place was made, a massive undertaking, involving a whole host of special procedures. Curtains were taken down, rugs rolled up with moth-proofing and newspapers, furniture covered in ghostly yellowing sheets, chandeliers covered in tarlatan, a wagon loaded with necessities such as Johan Åkerblom's special bed, special cushions for the little girls' dollhouse, Miss Siri's incomparable cake tins, Mrs. Martha's paintbrushes, and Anna's novels.

It is now early July, and a quiet sleepiness combined with shimmering heat has descended on people and the reflections in the water. The croquet balls roll listlessly. Someone is playing the piano, a sentimental romance by Gade. Miss Lisen is dozing on the viewing bench without noticing that her ball of wool has fallen to the ground. Mrs. Karin, the ruler of the household, is sitting on the upper veranda, white-clad and mild, in a broad-brimmed hat to shade her eyes. She is busy with a letter that doesn't get written, her gray-blue gaze lost in the light above the hills. The superintendent of traffic himself is asleep in a hammock, his glasses on his forehead and a book on his stomach. Nevertheless, in the kitchen a certain limited industry reigns.

Miss Siri and Anna are preparing the strawberries. It's a burden, of course, but they are making good headway. The atmosphere is confidentially talkative: some chat and some silence. Flies buzz on the sticky yellow strip of the flypaper, and the fat cat is purring half-asleep on the windowsill.

Miss Siri: . . . well, I came to the house when you were born, Anna. I was to help Stava, but she was already ill, so I had to take over from the very start. She spent most of the time in bed in the maid's room, issuing orders. No one knew how ill she was, so it was rather annoying, I'll have you know, Anna. Then suddenly one morning she was dead. I was quite good at things, even then, though I was no more than twenty. But there was an awful lot to do. Mrs. Åkerblom wasn't much older, either, and her stepsons were really unruly, yes, indeed. And the master didn't do much to help with their upbringing, either. He was much too busy with his railway bridges. Then Rike and

Runa — they were nice, willing girls but as thick as two sticks. So Mrs. Åkerblom and me had to take the responsibility and clear up the mess. We did that, too, although when the missis got with child again she was really ill, I'll have you know — so I said to her . . . don't wear yourself out, Mrs. Åkerblom, but get as much rest as you can, and I'll take care of everything as long as you tell me how you want things. Well, that's what I did. And then the missis got better again, and it's been like that ever since, I mean, how things are to be done. The missis and I don't always agree, but we both wage war on carelessness, dirt, and disorder. We don't tolerate disorder in any way, if you know what I mean, Anna. (*Pause.*) Well, that's how it's been and that's how it is.

Anna: Have you never been in love, Miss Siri?

Miss Siri: Oh, yes, there was someone at first who tried to pull my skirts over my head. But we had so little time, I never found out whether he had intentions or not.

Then Ernst saunters through the kitchen, pulls his sister's pigtail, kisses the nape of Miss Siri's neck, and asks if there's any orange juice, then sits down at the table and greedily starts eating the finished strawberries. Miss Siri waits on the boy. She even hacks a piece of ice off the perpetually dripping block in the icebox, and then the glass of juice is on the table together with currant cakes. Ernst yawns and says he is going for a bicycle ride to the Gimmen. "Coming, too, Anna?" "In this heat!" cries Anna as Ernst takes the opportunity to tickle her. "We're going swimming, too. Come on, lazybones! We must just tell Mama that we're off."
  They go to the stairs leading up to the first floor. "Mama!" cries Ernst. Karin Åkerblom wakes from her dreams over the half-written letter, goes out to the stairs, and says sternly, "Ernst, what a noise. You'll wake Papa." "We're going to the Gimmen for a swim. Are you coming, too, Mama?" "Anna, have you asked Miss Siri if there's anything to do in the kitchen?" "Nothing for the moment," says Anna. "Anyhow, the girls might help a bit more. They've gone and hidden themselves in the playhouse and are reading *Countess Paulette's Secret Lovers*. Lovers in the plural, please note." "Oh, yes," says Mrs. Karin, resignedly. "That's not my responsibility. Martha will have to deal with that." "We're off, anyhow," says Ernst, rushing up the stairs and embracing his mother. "Thank you, that was nice of you," says Karin Åkerblom, giving her son's hair a tug. "You must get your hair cut. You're inappropriately shaggy."
  So off they go on their shiny bicycles, first a few kilometers along

the main road, then at right angles in among the trees. It's a winding, sandy forest trail running along the shallow and stony Gima River, even now in the hottest summer months racing and tumbling wildly along.

The Gimmen is a long glacial lake, right in the middle of an endless forest landscape. The water is clear and icy cold, the shores stony, at first sloping gently, then suddenly plunging steeply into the depths.

The two have left their bicycles at the derelict mill and are making their way along a cattle track beneath alders and the darkening trunks of birch trees along the shore. They find their bathing place, a narrow, sandy strip of shore shaded by thick foliage.

After going for a swim, they share a melting bar of chocolate, a few sleepy flies keeping them company, but otherwise it is still, cloudless yet stifling, like thunder on the horizon, looked forward to but threatening. Ernst does a handstand. He's quite a skilled gymnast. Anna has put on a vest and petticoat and is lying on her back staring up at the leaves. She stretches up one arm and follows the contours of the branches against the white vault of the sky.

Anna: Do you have any ideals?

Ernst: What?

Anna: Ideals!

Ernst: What a question.

Anna: Maybe so. But I'm asking you all the same, and I actually want an answer.

Ernst: Ideals. Of course I have. To earn money. Not to have to work. Erotic mistresses. Lovely weather. Good health. Immortality. I want to be immortal. I don't ever want to die. Immortality in the sense of being famous doesn't interest me. I want the people I like to have as good a life as I have. I don't want to hate anyone. I'll never marry anyone. But I'd like to have children. Yes, I certainly *do* have ideals.

Anna: Don't you ever take anything seriously?

Ernst: No, Anna my pet, I don't take anything seriously. How could I, when I see the way the world behaves. I have a great need to maintain my sanity. So I don't bother to think. If I started thinking, then "I'd go cuckoo," as Fröding says.

Anna: At nursing school, we get quite a lot of theoretical teaching.

44

Most of it awfully miserable, but sometimes it's so disturbing and captivating that . . .

Ernst: . . . you've a talent for compassion, and I haven't. In that respect, I'm like Mother.

Anna: You know, one day a woman doctor came, a professor of pediatrics. She started by just telling us about her practice and giving us examples from it. Mostly about children with cancer. She talked about such hideous suffering that we found it hard to control ourselves. We just wanted to cry so as to escape from all those horrors. Children in terrible pain. Little children, Ernst, who don't understand and see clumsy grown-ups all round them. They're tormented, crying, brave, silent, stoic. And then they die. There's no cure. Sometimes unrecognizably cut to pieces. That woman professor talked about it quite calmly. Her compassion was total, all the time. Do you understand, Ernst?

Ernst (*slightly sarcastically*): No, Anna, my dear cranberry heart. What is it you want me to understand?

Anna: I want to be like that professor. I want to be right in the middle of unfathomable cruelty, Ernst. I want to help, to soothe and console. I want to acquire all conceivable knowledge.

Ernst: Then the nursing school must be good?

Anna: Oh, yes, I suppose so. Half the girls in the program get married as soon as they qualify. To me, it's something greater and more difficult. You know, Ernst, sometimes I think I'm incredibly strong. I imagine God has created me for something important — something important to other people.

Ernst: So you believe in God?

Anna: No, unfortunately I don't believe in any god.

Ernst: You think too much. That's why you get stomachaches.

Anna: I'll speak to Mother and Father about this business of training to be a doctor.

Ernst: That won't be easy, Anna, my pet. Think of Upsala! Think of those medics you know. Think of the professors!

Anna: What *she* managed, I can manage, can't I?

Ernst: But what about us two if you become a professor?

Anna: We can get married, and you can look after the household.

Ernst: But I want children.

Anna: You've got your mistresses, for goodness sake!

Ernst: You'll just be jealous and make a fuss.

Anna: That's true. No one may touch my darlings.

Ernst: What darlings have you got?

Anna: Wouldn't you like to know! Papa, of course. And you, of course. (*Falls silent.*)

Ernst: And Torsten Bohlin?

Anna: No, no. Heavens, how stupid you are. Torsten's no darling.

Ernst: But *someone* is.

Anna: Maybe so. But I don't know.

Ernst (*abruptly*): By the way, would you like to come with me to Upsala for a few days?

Anna: I don't know if Mama would let me.

Ernst: Don't worry about that. I'll fix it.

Anna: What are you going to do in Upsala in the middle of July?

Ernst: They've just set up a meteorological institution. Professor Beck has suggested I apply.

Anna: And you'd like that?

Ernst: Watching the skies and clouds and horizons and perhaps going up in a balloon. Eh?

Anna: You'll have to speak to Mama. I don't think she'd let me go.

Ernst: Who's going to cook my meals! Who'll darn my socks? Who's going to see to it that Mother's little darling goes to bed on time? You know, we could have a good time.

Anna: It's tempting.

Ernst: I'll go by bike, and you can go by train. Then we'll meet at Trädgårdsgatan. This summer idyll is beginning to get on my nerves.

Anna (*kisses him*): You're a cunning beast, Ernst.

Ernst: You're also a cunning beast, Annie-Pannie Cranberry Coot. Though of another kind.

Summertime tutoring. Reluctant and depressed pupil with scabs on his knees, half-asleep. Reluctant and depressed tutor with suppressed rage and lewd thoughts. The window is open to the July summer. Far away, but visible, four young women are bathing, shrieking, and laughing. The garden's balmy scents. Åkerlunda Manor, Åkerlunda estate, twenty or so kilometers northwest of Upsala. The Åkerlunda River, the estate road, the waterfall, the beehives, some leisurely stray cows in the rye field.

The young count is called Robert and is glaring sulkily at an open German grammar. He is expected shortly to recite the present tense, the imperfect, and the pluperfect, and if possible the future of the auxiliary verb *Sein*. Henrik, in a tie and shirtsleeves, is sitting on the other side of the table reading church history, occasionally underlining something with a blunt pencil stub. Robert and Henrik, two slaves chained together at the very bottom of the galley of learning. The bathing girls shriek. Robert raises his eyes and stares out the window, the white curtain lazily billowing. Henrik takes his feet off the table and slams his book shut.

Henrik: Well?

Robert: What?

Henrik: Have you learned it?

Robert: Can't we go for a swim?

Henrik: What do you think your father would say to that?

The young count lifts one buttock, farts, and shoots a look of hatred at his tormentor, then unbuttons his trousers. Robert is really a handsome youth and his mother's darling, but now he is caught between the hammer and the anvil — the count's arrogance and ambition.

Robert: Oh, bloody fucking hell.

Henrik: Do you think I like this any more than you do? Let's make the best of the situation.

Robert: At least you get paid! (*Scratches his crotch.*)

Henrik: Button up your trousers, and chuck the grammar over here.

47

Robert throws the book at Henrik and reluctantly tucks in his bluish, slightly floppy dick. He puts his arms on the table, his head on his arms, and takes up a sleeping position.

Henrik: Well, start now . . . present tense first.

Robert (*rapidly*): *Ich bin, du bist, er ist, wir sind, Ihr seid. Sie, sie sind.*

Henrik: Bravo. Dare I ask for the imperfect?

Robert (*equally rapidly*): *Ich war, du warst, er war, wir waren, Ihr wart, Sie, sie waren.*

Henrik (*surprised*): Listen to that. And now . . . well, what?

Robert: Perfect, for Christ's bloody sake.

Henrik: The perfect?

Robert: *Ich habe gewesen.* (*Silence.*)

(*Henrik stares at him.*)

Robert: *Du hast gewesen, er hat gewesen.* (*Silence.*)

Victim and tormentor look at each other with irreconcilable repugnance, though at this particular moment it is hard to say who is playing which role.

Henrik: Oh, yes . . .

Robert: *Wir haben gewesen.*

At that charged moment, the old count comes in without knocking. Maybe he has been listening outside. Svante Svantesson de Fèste fills the room with his bulk, his voice, his sideburns, and his nose. His eyes are childishly blue, his face red merging into purple. Henrik has got to his feet and is straightening out his clothing. Robert hunches up, well aware of what is coming.

Count Svante: Ah, yes. German grammar. Well now, what was it I was going to say? Yes. A young gentleman called Ernst Åkerblom has arrived on his bicycle and wishes to speak to you. I informed him that you were occupied with my son until one o'clock, and urged him to visit our girls down at the bathing place, advice he clearly accepted with pleasure. Yes, well, that was that. How are things going for Robert? Is he ineducable, or have you managed to knock into him some of the education expected of a nobleman? — now that the old parliamentary system has been abolished. How's it going?

48

Henrik: I think Robert's very able and is making good progress. If there are gaps . . .

Count: Do you *mean* gaps, not chasms?

Henrik: . . . there are gaps, as I said, but with mutual efforts, we shall no doubt achieve something before the beginning of the autumn term.

Count: Really? You don't say! Well, that sounds hopeful. What do you say, Robert? Eh?

The count slaps the back of Robert's neck so that the boy's teeth rattle. The gesture is intended to be encouraging, but Robert lowers his head, starts sniffing, and a tear trickles its way down his dirty cheek.

Robert: Yes.

Count: What? Are you blubbering?

Robert: No.

Count: I was mistaken. I thought you were. Blow your nose, boy! Don't you have a handkerchief? What sort of sloppiness is this? Here. Take mine. Stop sniveling. I want to talk to Mr. Bergman alone. Take your grammar with you, and go and read in the arbor.

Robert slouches off, a walking misery. After he has closed the door, the count lowers his bulky frame onto an unsteady chair with a broken back and sits there hunched up, growling to himself.

Henrik: You wish to speak to me, sir?

Count: His mother says I'm unfair. That I drive him too hard. I don't know. She says I don't love him. I don't know. Perhaps I'd better stop this cruelty to animals. What do you think, Mr. Bergman?

Henrik: One should never give up hope.

Count: Nonsense, Mr. Bergman! My son Robert is an ineducable sluggard, a damned idiot. A tearful slouch. He'll grow up to be a spendthrift, a ne'er-do-well. He reminds me of his uncle, my wife's brother. In him, you can see the final result.

Henrik: I feel sorry for him.

Count: What? Sorry for someone who's had everything? Who's never had to make the slightest effort? Who's his mother's spoiled brat? If you're sorry for that creature, then you're sorry for mankind.

Henrik: Perhaps I am sorry for mankind.

Count: What sort of damned nonsense is that, Mr. Bergman? That sort of morbid fantasy — no thanks! *Ich habe gewesen!* What? Mankind is a muck-heap, Mr. Bergman. An excrescence on the face of the earth. Thank Christ for horses, Mr. Bergman. If I didn't have my horses, I'd put a bullet through my head. *Horses* — you can be sorry for them. Their great mistake was at the beginning of time when they made a pact with man. They've had to pay dearly for that agreement. (*Abruptly.*) So we're agreed to stop this nonsensical coaching of Robert?

Henrik: That's for you to decide, sir.

Count: Exactly, Mr. Bergman, the count decides. We'll send the cry-baby to his grandmother in Hägersta, where there are plenty of old biddies to spoil him. And he'll have to repeat a grade next year. What's the date today? Saturday, July 9? You're finishing at your own request as of today and will be paid up to Friday the fifteenth. You can stay or leave, Mr. Bergman, whichever you like. Does that suit you?

Henrik: May I remind you, sir, that I was appointed until the first of September. I lack resources and have counted on this appointment.

Count: Well, I'll be damned. Are you saying you should be paid for doing nothing?

Henrik: It would be quite impossible for me to find another post this late in the summer. I have to live, sir.

Count: You certainly have pretensions, Mr. Bergman. And you're insolent, to boot. I hadn't expected that of an apprentice priest.

Henrik: I'm sorry, but I stand by my rights. If you refuse, sir, I shall be forced to turn to the countess, for the written agreement was in fact signed between her and me.

Count: Don't you *dare* speak to the countess.

Henrik: I'll have to.

Count: You're a damned scoundrel, Bergman. Clearly you weren't thrashed enough in your childhood.

Henrik: And you, sir, if I may say so, are a bounder who was presumably thrashed far too much in your childhood.

Count: What if I make up for some of your father's sins of neglect by giving you a good thrashing here and now?

Henrik: If you do, sir, you can count on me hitting back. Go ahead. You may strike first since you, sir, are undoubtedly the elder. The nobler.

Count: I have high blood pressure and am not supposed to get annoyed like this.

Henrik: May one hope for a slight stroke. In that case, God is merciful, freeing the earth of such a scoundrel.

Svante Svantesson de Fèste now starts laughing and punches Henrik in the chest with his fist. Henrik smiles in confusion.

Count: Damn it, you're quite something of an apprentice priest. Well, not bad at all, young man. If you're to get anywhere in this rotten world, you have to stand up for yourself. Did you say the first of September? Then I owe you for July and August. That'll be two hundred and fifty riksdaler. Let's settle up on the spot, and not a word to the ladies, eh?

Henrik: Our agreement actually included food and lodging until the first of September. But I'll forego that.

Count: Stay on, won't you? It's pleasant here. And pretty girls! And good food! You must admit we eat well.

Henrik: No, thank you.

Count: Christ, you really are stuck-up. Don't you forgive easily, either?

Henrik: Not in this case.

Count: Come on then, we'll go and have coffee with the countess and the girls. And your companion. What was his name again?

Henrik: Ernst.

The count, in a good mood, slaps Henrik on the back.

The day is growing hot, the dust swirling around in the dry puffs of wind. Henrik and Ernst are on their way to Upsala. They are cycling side by side along the bumpy road. Sandals, trousers rolled up a little, shirts open at the neck. Rucksacks filled with diverse necessities. Jackets, underclothes, socks rolled up in raincoats on the carriers. Student caps. Leisurely pace. They set off at five o'clock and after a great many rests and swims have got as far as Jumkils Church.

There are people about, standing in groups and walking along the side of the road, men in their best suits and round hats, collars and

51

ties. Suddenly Ernst gets a lump of earth between his shoulder blades. He stops and turns around. Henrik stops a little ahead of him. A group of men pass, talking to each other, but not looking at Ernst. A tall, thin man suddenly rushes up and snatches off Henrik's student cap, spits on it, hurls it to the ground, and stamps on it. Henrik is dumbfounded. Ernst pedals past and signals for him to get a move on.

They pass Bälinge station. A special train with a large number of cars has stopped on a siding, and there's a great deal of activity near the train, a brass band unpacking its instruments, flags being unfurled. A hundred or so men are moving about on the dusty sunny-white open space outside the station.

Ernst: We'll see if there's going to be any autumn term at all.

Henrik: Why shouldn't there be an autumn term?

Ernst: Don't you ever read the newspapers?

Henrik: How can I afford to?

Ernst: They say there'll be a general strike and a big lockout. In August at the latest.

Henrik says nothing. He is confused and embarrassed because, as usual, he is ignorant of such matters.

They arrive at about one o'clock at an Upsala empty of people. The sun is straight above Trädgårdsgatan, and the shadows have retreated far in under the chestnuts. They put their bicycles in the cobbled court-yard and unstrap their packs. Anna has already seen them and comes running out. Her cheeks are red, and she is sunburned, her hair in one thick braid. She wears a big kitchen apron with pleated shoulder straps as wide as angel wings on top of her linen dress. She embraces Ernst and kisses him on the mouth, then turns to Henrik and, smiling, holds out her hand.

Anna: How nice you could both come. Good day, Henrik. Welcome to Trädgårdsgatan.

Henrik: It's very nice to see you again, Anna.

They are formal and a trifle embarrassed. All of this is in fact unlawful, taking place without parental knowledge and permission.

Ernst: Cold sponge-down, cold beer, two hours' sleep, and a good dinner, and *after that*, festivities and improvisations. Does that sound good?

52

The huge tin bath is dragged out onto the kitchen floor, and buckets full of water are poured into it. Henrik and Ernst wash themselves and each other with soap and sponge. Anna has put out two bottles of beer, chilled in the icebox. After they have toweled themselves dry — Anna sitting on the wood box in the hall — and poured the water down the drain by the courtyard pump, they repair to their rooms: Ernst in his usual room and Henrik in the maid's room behind the kitchen. The latter room faces north, is cool and a little dark. The wallpaper is verdigris green and smells of arsenic, the ceiling is high and has damp patches all over it. Henrik stretches out on the narrow, protesting bed. On the wall is a picture of a stagecoach stopping at a country inn, people moving busily around carriages and houses, dogs barking, a horse rearing. A four-legged gilt clock stands on a tall brown-painted chest of drawers with brass fittings, busily and kindly ticking away. The sheets and pillow smell of lavender. The heavy foliage just outside the window is quite still. Then a little breeze comes; the leaves turn slowly and rustle for a moment. Then all is quiet again.

Henrik can hear the brother and sister laughing and talking somewhere deep inside the apartment. He suddenly feels a profound peace. He hardly knows what it is that makes tears come to his eyes. What's really the matter with me? he says to himself. Then he falls asleep.

Ernst rudely shakes him awake: "God, you're a demon for sleep. You've slept for three hours. Come on now, wake up, and I'll show you something amusing. But quiet, go quietly, so that she doesn't notice anything." Ernst takes Henrik by the hand and leads him out into the kitchen where some preparations for dinner are evident. The door into the hall is half-open. They can hear Anna's voice from the hall. She's talking on the telephone.

Anna: How nice of you to phone, Mama! Yes, Ernst has arrived all in one piece. What? He was fine. I told you. At the moment he's snoring his head off. I can't hear you very well. I said I couldn't *hear you* very well. Has Papa got a stomachache? He's always having them, poor Papa. What are we going to do this evening? We'll probably go to Odinslund and take in a concert there. Are we alone? What do you mean, Mama? There's only Ernst and me. Goodness, this'll be an expensive call, Mammchen. Give my love to everyone! Big kiss, Mammchen, and don't forget to give Papa a hug from me. What did you say, Mama? My voice sounds peculiar? You imagined it. The line's so bad. Good-bye, Mama. We'll ring off at the same time.

Anna puts down the receiver and winds the handle, then rushes out into the kitchen, pulls her brother's hair, and flings her arms round his waist. "Watch out for my sister," says Ernst with tenderness. "Do watch out for her! She's the most honest hypocrite and the cleverest liar in Christendom."

Dinner is perhaps not particularly well cooked but is festive nonetheless. Ernst has coaxed open the lock to the traffic superintendent's wine cellar and chilled a few bottles of white Burgundy, and there's port wine in the medicine cupboard. The windows are open onto the dusk and the silent street. A thunderstorm is on its way somewhere, and the sun has disappeared, sunk below a purple cloud beyond the copper roof of the library. Anna has got dressed up and is wearing a thin sepia-colored silk blouse with a square neck, long sleeves, and lace cuffs. Her skirt is elegantly tailored, her belt wide with a silver buckle. She has put up her hair into a low knot. Her earrings are small and glitter discreetly, but expensively.

What are they talking about? Well, the strange experience at Bälinge station, of course, and then about Torsten Bohlin, who has gone to Weimar and is to continue on to Heidelberg. He has written several letters to Anna, which she now finds here at Trädgårdsgatan. No one put in a request for the mail to be forwarded. "I've only myself to blame," says Anna. "Papa never likes my admirers." "Only Ernst," says Ernst, and all three of them laugh. Anna takes her brother's hand. "Go and see if there are any cigars in Papa's box," she says.

And there are — rather dry of course, but passable. Ernst persuades Henrik to tell her about the row at Åkerlunda. Then Henrik suddenly turns to Anna, looks hard at her, and says, "You're going to be a nurse, aren't you?" That prompts Anna to go and fetch a small album. "This is Sophiahemmet, you see, and here at the back, with the windows facing the park and Lill-Skogen, that's where our lecture room is. And those are our bedrooms. It's quite grand, only two to each room. The food's good, and the teachers are excellent. Though strict. And the days long, never less than twelve hours. From half past six in the morning until long past six in the evening. You're pretty well beat by then, I'll have you know, Henrik." Anna is kneeling on a dining room chair, close to Henrik. She smells fresh and sweetish, not exactly of perfume, but perhaps good soap. Or perhaps she just smells like that. Just of herself. Ernst is sitting at the end of the table, rocking his chair, his cigar between thumb and forefinger. He is looking at his sister and his friend with a smile on his face, and may well be a little drunk. Henrik can feel her upper arm against his own, and her hair tickles him when she bends her head, looking for herself in one of the photographs. *There I am,* she says. "You may not believe it. The uniform is not exactly becoming, though the cap's pretty, but we don't

54

get that until we've qualified." "My sister's going to be a sister, my sister Sister Anna," says Ernst, and they laugh. "You two look sweet together," he adds.

Anna at once closes the album and leaves a space between herself and Henrik. "Do you think my sister's attractive?" "She's more than that," says Henrik gravely. "What do you mean by that?" Ernst persists. "Don't spoil everything just when we're having such a nice time," says Anna, slightly annoyed and pouring out some port wine for herself. "I've splashed some on my skirt," she says. "Henrik, dear, give me the water carafe, would you. Ordinary water's best to get it out. Damn! My lovely skirt!" Ernst and Henrik watch while Anna rubs at the spot with her table napkin. The skirt tightens over the curves of her hips and thighs.

They drink up and do the dishes together. Ernst washes up, Henrik dries, Anna sorts and puts things away in cupboards and drawers. What are they talking about now? The siblings are probably talking about Mammchen. Mama does the deciding, Mama controls, Mama decides. Mama goes to Papa, just as he has sat down in his favorite chair with the morning paper and his morning cigar, and says: "Johan, listen to me now," or, if it's something serious, "Listen to me now, Åkerblom, we really *must* decide whether we're going to help Carl with his debts this time, too, or whether we let him go to the dogs. It'll be the moneylenders as usual, you know that." "You must decide," says Papa Johan. "No, Johan," Mammchen protests, sitting down. "You know I *always* defer to you in money matters. You mustn't wear that jacket any longer. It's beginning to shine at the elbows!"

The siblings are clever at acting comedy. They laugh and act the fool, and Henrik is drawn into it. He has never seen such beautiful people before. He feels a violent yearning but doesn't really know what he's yearning for.

"Or like *this*," says Anna eagerly, imitating Mama Karin. "Now listen to me, Ernst. Who was that lady you were with in Ekeberg's coffeehouse on Thursday? I saw you through the window, all right. What were you talking about that was so secret you forgot both your hot chocolate and the Napoleon cakes? Yes, yes, of course she was quite pretty, very pretty, I'll admit, but was she a really *nice* girl? What's happened to Laura? We really liked her, both Papa and I. Such a pity you don't settle down, *dear* Ernst. You're *much too spoiled* with girls. All you have to do is to crook a little finger, and they come galloping up in droves. Your young friend, whatever his name is, Henrik Bergman, that's it, isn't it? He's another of those gadabouts who's sure to be up to all sorts of things with girls. He's far too good-looking for a young girl to dare trust him."

It starts raining in the evening. They have sat down in the green drawing room among the shrouded armchairs and draped pictures. In the fading light, the carpetless wooden floor looks whiter than ever, the contours of the curtainless windows even sharper. Ernst is singing a Schubert song. He has a light baritone voice, and Anna is accompanying him on the piano. It is *Die schöne Müllerin*, the eighteenth song: *Ihr Blumlein alle, die sie mir gab, euch soll man legen mit mir ins Grab.* The notes float gently through the dusky room. Two candles illuminate Ernst and Anna as they lean over the notes. *Ach Tränen machen nicht maiengrün, machen tote Liebe nicht wider blühn* . . .

Henrik sees Anna's face, the soft line of her mouth, the gentle shine of her eyes, the shimmering wave of hair. Close to her with his face turned to Henrik, Ernst with his soft, thin hair brushed back from his forehead, the pale mouth, the determined, strongly marked features.

Henrik stares steadily at the two siblings, calling a halt to time. It's not to slip away in the old way this time. Nothing has ever been like this before. He didn't know such colors existed. A closed room opens. The light gets stronger, and his head whirls: Naturally it *can* be like this. So it can be like this for himself as well.

Ernst: Schubert knew something about space, time, and light. He put together unimaginable elements and breathed on them. In that way they became comprehensible to us. The minutes tormented him, and he freed them for us. Space was cramped and dirty. He freed space for us. And the light. He lived in the cold, raw shadows and turned the gentle light toward us. He was like the saints. (*Falls silent. Silence.*)

Anna: I suggest we take a walk to Fyris bridge before we go to bed.

Ernst: It's raining.

Anna: Only drizzling. Henrik can take Papa's old raincoat.

Henrik: I'd like that.

Ernst: I certainly would not.

Anna: Come on now, Ernst, don't be silly.

Ernst: You and Henrik can go. I'll stay at home and finish off what's left in the bottle.

Anna: I *want* you to come too. Not only do I want you to, but I *insist* that you come. Just so you know.

56

Ernst: Anna is her mother's daughter. In every way.

Anna: My brother lacks the most elementary sensitivity. It's a pity.

Ernst: I really don't understand what you're talking about now.

Anna: Exactly. Exactly that.

So they walk through the drizzling rain of the summer night, Anna in the middle, quite small and plump, with the tall young men on either side of her. They link arms and slowly stroll along. No streetlights on to disturb the night light. They stop and listen.

The rain rustles in the trees.

Anna: Ssh! Can you hear? A nightingale.

Ernst: I don't hear any nightingale. For one thing, they don't come this far north, and for another, they don't sing after midsummer.

Anna: Quiet now. Don't talk all the time.

Henrik: Yes, it *is* a nightingale.

Anna: Ernst, open your ears!

Ernst: Anna and Henrik hearing nightingales in July. You're lost. (*Listens.*) Well I'll be damned, if it isn't a nightingale after all!

At about two o'clock that morning, flashes of lightning can be seen against the blind in the maid's room. Sometimes there's a faint rumble of thunder. The rain rustles, sometimes a little louder, sometimes dripping and faint. Suddenly it can be so quiet, Henrik can hear his heart pounding and his pulse beating in his eardrums. He can't sleep, anyhow. He's lying on his back with his hands behind his head, his eyes wide open. That's it. So that's how it can be. For *me*, too, Henrik! The opening into the room that used to be tightly closed gets wider and wider. It is like vertigo.

Someone is moving about in the kitchen, and the door opens, creaking noticeably. This is no dream. Anna is standing in the rectangle of light. He can't see her face, and she is still dressed.

Anna: Are you asleep? No, I knew you weren't asleep. I thought I'd go in to Henrik and tell him what's happened.

She stays in the doorway without moving. Henrik doesn't dare breathe. This is serious.

Anna: I don't know what to do about you, Henrik. It's not just that you are here with me. But it's much much worse when you're away from me. I've always . . .

She falls silent and ponders. Now it's presumably vital to be truthful. Henrik is about to say something about his confusion and the closed and open room, but it's too complicated.

Anna: Mama says that the most important thing is to keep one's emotions under control. I've always been sensible about that. So I think I've become a little self-confident, actually.

She turns her head away and takes a step back. The dawn light from the kitchen window falls on her face, and Henrik can see she has been crying. Or perhaps she is still crying. But her voice is calm.

Anna: One can't — Mama and other people, my half brothers, for instance, say I have inherited too much cleverness from both Mama and Papa. I've always been rather proud when I've been praised for my cleverness. I've thought that was the way life should be, and that was how I wanted it. I certainly don't need to be afraid. (*Long silence.*) But now I'm afraid, or to be quite honest, if what I feel is fear, then I'm frightened.

Henrik: I'm afraid, me, too.

He has to clear his throat. His voice has dried up somewhere along the way. Now, right now, his heart stops, quite briefly, but stops all the same.

Henrik: Besides, my heart stopped. Just now.

Anna: I know what it's like, Henrik. We're in the middle of a crucial moment. Can you imagine anything so amazing and puzzling? Time stops, or we think time stops, or "your heart," as you say.

Henrik: What shall we do?

Anna: There are really only two possibilities. (*Soberly.*) I say to you: Go away, Henrik. Or: Come into my arms, Henrik.

Henrik: You think both alternatives are bad?

Anna: Yes.

Henrik: Bad?

Anna: Of decisive importance.

Henrik: Can't we play a little?

Anna: Besides, I don't even know what sort of person you are.

Henrik: I'm not in the slightest peculiar.

There is a note of terror, comical terror. Henrik has not much self-insight, never has had, and never will have. Anna shakes her head with a smile: "Now you can see for yourself how risky this can be!" She steps over the threshold and into the room, sits down on the end of the bed, and smooths out her skirt. Henrik struggles up into a sitting position.

Anna: I don't think you know anything about anything. I think you're obscured. I can't find any other word for it at the moment.

Henrik: Obscured?

Anna: You just keep repeating what I say all the time. Tell me the way you want things to be.

Henrik: I'll tell you exactly. I have never, and I say *never*, and I swear it's true, I have never in my life had a day and an evening and a night like this day, evening, and night. I swear. I know nothing else. I am confused and grateful and frightened. I think all this will be taken away from me. It's always like that. It has always been like that. I am empty-handed. That sounds dramatic, but it's true. I think, quite simply, why should any of what I've had today fall to my lot? Do you understand, Anna? You and Ernst live in your world, not just materially, but on all levels. Inaccessible to me. Do you understand, Anna?

Anna slowly shakes her head and looks at Henrik with sorrowful eyes. Then she smiles and gets up, goes over to the doorway, and turns around.

Anna: Oh, well. I suppose we can postpone the decision for a few hours, or even days or weeks.

When she has said that, she smiles indulgently and says good night. Then she closes the door, which creaks loudly.

I can see them sitting in the dining room at the large cleared table with its lion feet. They have the superintendent of traffic's chessboard between them. The protective sheets have been removed from two of the windows. It is raining quietly and persistently. I see Ernst, too, standing in the doorway in a raincoat, his student cap in his hand, saying he

59

must be off to the meteorological institution for a while, because the professor wishes to speak to him. "Dinner at five o'clock," mumbles Anna, moving a bishop. "'Bye, then, and good luck," says Henrik, rescuing his queen. The hall door slams, and quiet descends. Somewhere in the building, a piano is being played, slowly and hesitantly.

Anna suddenly knocks the chessmen over and hides her face in her hands, then peeps through her fingers at Henrik and giggles. Henrik leans over the board and tries to reinstate the chessmen. After one lame attempt, he sits still and watchful.

Anna: We needn't tell everyone that we . . . well, that we're thinking of . . .

Henrik: No, of course not.

Anna: I'm suddenly terrified when I think about that we don't know the slightest thing about each other. We ought to sit at this table for a hundred days and just talk and ask questions.

Henrik: It wouldn't be enough.

Anna: We decide to live together for the rest of our lives and know nothing about each other. That's a little unusual, isn't it?

Henrik: And we haven't even kissed.

Anna: Shall we kiss now? No, that can wait.

Henrik: First we must state our failings.

Anna (*laughs*): No, I don't dare. You'd run away!

Henrik: Or you.

Anna: Mama says I'm obstinate. That I'm selfish. Pleasure-loving. Impatient. My brothers say I've a damned bad temper and get angry about nothing. Well, what else can I think of? Ernst says I'm coquettish, that I love looking at myself in the mirror. Papa says I'm lazy about things I *must* do, cleaning, cooking, doing boring homework. Mama says I'm much too interested in boys. Well, as you hear, there's no limit to my failings.

Henrik: My greatest failing is that I'm confused.

Anna: Surely that's not a *failing*.

Henrik: Yes, that's just what it is.

Anna: What do you mean?

60

Henrik: I'm confused. Understand nothing. I just do what other people tell me. I don't think I'm particularly bright. If I read a complicated text, I find it difficult to understand what it means. I have so many feelings. That also confuses me. I've nearly always got a guilty conscience, but mostly don't know why.

Anna: That sounds difficult.

Sorrow and uneasiness. What kind of strange game is this? Why are we going on like this? Why don't we kiss each other? Today's a celebration, isn't it? They sit in silence and avoid each other's eyes.

Henrik: Now we're both miserable.

Anna: Yes.

Henrik: It's loneliness that frightens us. If we're together, we find the courage to understand and forgive our own and each other's failings. One should be careful not to start at the wrong end.

Anna: Shall we kiss each other now, so that we're happy again?

Henrik: Wait a while. I've something important I must tell you. No, don't laugh, Anna. It's necessary that I tell you that . . .

Anna: Oh, I'm sick of all these stupidities!

She places herself opposite him, takes his head in her hands, turns his face upward, leans over him, and kisses him ardently. Henrik lets out a moan; her fragrance, her skin, the small, strong hands holding him fast, the hair welling over her shoulder.
He grasps her around the waist and presses her to him, his forehead against her breast. She doesn't let go of his head, and they stagger, joined together. They stay like that a long time, not daring or able to free themselves from the embrace. What will really happen after this? What will happen to us?

Anna: . . . I suppose we're engaged now.

She frees herself and pulls her chair up next to his. They are sitting opposite each other, but now the table is no longer between them and they are holding each other's hands. They are disturbed and try to subdue their breathing and their hearts. Henrik is also in great distress. He ought to say what he must say, but he can't. She senses something is wrong and searches his face.

Anna (*smiles*): . . . now we're engaged, Henrik.

Henrik: No.

Anna (*laughs*): Oh, *aren't* we engaged?

Henrik: I knew from the very beginning it would be wrong. I must go away. We'll never see each other again.

Anna: You have someone else.

(*Henrik nods.*)

Anna's face turns ashen, and she puts her forefinger to her lips, imposing silence on them. Then she quickly runs her left hand over Henrik's forehead and lets it rest on his shoulder for a brief moment. Then she goes around the table and sits at the short end behind Henrik's back. She stays there, biting a nail, not knowing what to say.

Henrik: We've been living together for almost two years. She was as lonely as I was. She likes me. She's helped me many times. We've got on well together. We're engaged.

Anna: You've nothing to reproach yourself for. Not *really*. You might possibly have said something last night, but everything was so unreal then. I understand that you said nothing. What about our beautiful future now? What do you really want?

Henrik: I want to live with you. But I didn't know that yesterday. Everything has changed — like this!

He gestures with his hand, which then falls heavily and disconsolately onto the table. Then he turns to her and shakes his head.

Anna: So you mean you're thinking of abandoning — whatever her name is — whoever she is?

Henrik (*pauses*): If you want to know, her name is Frida. She's a few years older than me. She's also from the north. She works at the Gillet Hotel.

Anna: What does she do?

Henrik (*angry*): She's a waitress.

Anna (*chilly*): Oh — a waitress.

Henrik: Is there anything wrong with being a waitress?

Anna: No, of course not.

Henrik: You must have forgotten to name one of your more serious failings. You are clearly conceited. *You* thought up this business of our future together. Not me. I have always been prepared to live in reality. And my reality is gray. And dull. Ugly. (*Gets up.*) Do you know what I'm going to do now? Well, I'm going home to Frida. I'll go home to her and ask her forgiveness for my stupid and foolish betrayal. I'll tell her what I said and what you said and what we did and then I'll ask her forgiveness.

Anna: I'm cold.

Henrik is not listening. He goes out.

In the hall he bumps into Ernst, who has just come through the door and is taking off his raincoat. Henrik mumbles something and tries to get past, but is grabbed.

Ernst: Hey, hey, hey, what's all this?

Henrik: Let me go. I really want to leave and never come back again.

Ernst (*imitates*): ". . . want to leave and never come back again." What are you talking about? Is this a Schubert romance?

Henrik: It was stupid from the start. Please let go of me.

Ernst: And what have you done with Anna?

Henrik: I suppose she's still in there.

Ernst: Quarreling already. You don't waste much time. But Anna's an impatient girl. She likes to get on with things.

He presses Henrik down onto the white-painted wood box in the hall and stands over by the glass doors so Henrik can't possibly escape. At that moment, Anna emerges. When she sees her brother, she stops abruptly and slaps her thigh with her hand. Then she turns roughly to the window.

Ernst: What the hell's going on?

Henrik: I really do beg of you to let me go. The next step will be to punch you in the jaw.

Anna (*calls*): Just let him go.

Ernst: Don't disappear, Henrik. We can have dinner at Cold Märta's at five, can't we? What about it?

Henrik: I don't know. There's no point.

He has his pack in his arms and takes his student cap down from the hat shelf. Ernst opens the hall door, and Henrik disappears down the stairs, taking great strides. Ernst closes the door and slowly goes in to his sister. She is still standing by the window, showing all the signs of anger and pain.

Ernst: Anna, my cranberry heart, how have you brought all this about?

Anna turns to Ernst and puts her arms around his neck, then cries very dramatically and possibly enjoyably for a few seconds. Then she falls silent and blows her nose on the proffered handkerchief.

Anna: I'm sure I love him.

Ernst: And he?

Anna: I'm sure he loves me.

Ernst: Why are you blubbering then? Listen, Anna.

Anna: It *hurts* so.

Ernst sits down on a chair and takes his sister on his lap, and there they sit in tender intimacy without saying another word. The rain stops, and the sun draws hard white squares and rectangles on the protective curtain over the windows. The whole room appears to be floating.

Henrik does as he said, and makes his way to the Gillet Hotel, trudging up the six flights and banging on Frida's door. After a while she opens up, drowsy with sleep and wearing a capacious flannel nightgown with a stocking wrapped around her neck. Her nose is red and her eyes are glazed. She stares at Henrik as if he were not real. Despite this, she steps aside and lets him in.

Frida: Are *you* in town?

Henrik: Are you ill?

Frida: I've got a terrible cold and a sore throat and temperature. So I had to go home at half past nine last night. I almost fainted. Would you like some coffee? I was just thinking of making something hot.

Henrik: No, thank you.

Frida: How nice of you to come and surprise me. I would never have expected that. Thanks for your nice letter, by the way. I was just going to answer it, but there's so little time and I'm not much good at writing.

Behind a screen is the room's only luxury article, a small gas stove with a weak, sooty flame. Frida makes coffee and spreads sandwiches. Despite his feeble protests, Henrik allows himself to be waited on. Frida patters about, barefoot and fussing, then finally sits down on the bed, pulls the quilt around her, and blows on the hot coffee, which she sucks through a sugar lump. She suddenly looks carefully at Henrik, who is sitting on the only chair in the room and has put his cup of coffee on the bedside table.

Frida: Are you ill, too? You don't look well yourself.

Henrik: It's nothing.

Frida: How can you say anything so silly? As if I couldn't see that something's up.

Henrik: I suppose I'm miserable.

Frida: Oh, *that*, of course. Is there something you want to tell me? I can feel there is.

Henrik: No.

Frida: I can *see* there is.

Henrik: . . . no.

Frida: Come here and I'll give you a hug.

She puts her cup and sandwich down and pulls him to her. He is not unwilling.

Frida: Are you afraid of catching my cold?

Henrik: . . . no.

Frida: Get undressed and come to bed.

She gets briskly off the bed and pulls down the ragged blind. Then she unwinds the stocking around her neck and swiftly does her hair in front of the blotchy mirror above the commode. Before she creeps back into bed, she pulls off her nightgown. Underneath she is wearing a short tricot vest and a pair of fairly long-legged underpants. She slithers out of the pants but keeps on the vest.

II

The atmosphere in the Åkerbloms' summer residence, with its magnificent view over the river and the bluish mountains, is oppressive, not to say brooding. No happy cries from the bathing place, no croquet balls rolling across the terrace lawn, no piano music, no glasses of fruit juice, or novels in hammocks. Everyone is keeping quiet, listening for the voices from the traffic superintendent's study. Nothing can be heard properly, except an occasional word here and there, or perhaps a loud, emphatic sentence. Otherwise mumbling and silence.

Papa Johan is sitting at his desk, smoking an almost extinguished pipe, which he now and again tries to light. Mrs. Karin is seated on the green sofa beneath Ottilia Adelborg's painting entitled *Departure to the Outfield*. She is pale with fury. Her daughter, no less furious, is standing in the middle of the floor, her face a bright red. Ernst has taken up a strategic position by the door.

Karin: Charlotte telephoned yesterday evening and assured me you and Ernst had a male guest. She was very upset and said she had heard talking from the maid's room all night. Is that true?

Anna: Yes. (*Angry.*)

Johan: Watch your tongue when you're speaking to your mother.

Anna: Mama should watch her tongue when she speaks to me. I am in fact grown up now.

Karin (*coldly*): As long as you eat our bread and live with us, you are our daughter and must abide by the family rules.

Anna: I won't abide Mama and Papa treating me like a child.

69

Johan: If you behave like a child, you'll be treated like a child. (*Clears his throat.*)

Karin: Don't you understand what a scandal you are bringing down on our heads?

Anna: Aunt Charlotte is a telltale old bitch, and I'm glad she's got something to dish up at her next coffee party.

Johan: Ernst, you're not saying anything?

Ernst: What can I say? Anna and Mama keep quacking away at each other like a couple of angry ducks. You can't get a word in . . .

Johan: Was it you who invited this youth back home?

Anna (*angry*): No, just imagine, *I* was the one who had the audacity to be so bold.

Johan: I was asking Ernst.

Ernst: *I* invited him.

Karin: But Ernst, how *could* you be so stupid!

Ernst: He's a good friend of both of ours. You know him, anyhow. He came to dinner with us one Sunday.

Karin: What's his name? A young man who accepts an invitation to stay overnight in a home where the parents are absent must be either arrogant or badly brought up.

Anna: Mama, you really are being utterly absurd.

Karin: But I know *nothing*. Perhaps you two have a bag of secrets and carry on all the time behind my back.

Anna: Considering the fuss you're making, it wouldn't be surprising if we did keep our secrets to ourselves.

Karin: Johan! You must tell your daughter to behave properly. I have been very patient with you and your spoiled ways. Now I see the results.

Anna: It's not my fault I've been spoiled.

Johan: No, you're right there, my girl. It's been mostly my fault, and your mother has warned me about it on several occasions. Now I see that we must deal with you more harshly. (*Clears his throat, twice.*)

Anna (*laughs*): Spank me and send me to bed without dinner?

70

Johan (*trying hard to remain serious*): Don't be silly, Anna. This is no joking matter. What's the boy's name?

Anna: His name is Henrik Bergman. He's studying theology and is going to be a priest. And I love him and actually intend to marry him.

Now it is truly silent in the traffic superintendent's study; in fact throughout this lovely summer residence, and far beyond it as well.

Karin: Oh, yes. Really. Yes. Well now. Really.

Johan: Well, that's quite clear then.

Anna: You won't be able to stop me.

Johan: My dear daughter, I fear that to some extent you have misjudged your situation. You don't in fact come of age for another whole year, and until *then*, legally and morally, you are under your parents' jurisdiction.

Karin (*angrily*): Is that boy going to be a priest! Who hasn't the wits to respect a young woman's honor. You went into his room at night. Wasn't it his voice and yours that wretched Charlotte heard through the wall? It was you and him?

Anna: Yes, so what? We were talking about our engagement.

Karin: Maybe you slept with him in the bed?

Anna: No, I didn't. But if he'd asked me to, I would have.

Johan (*darkly*): That's quite enough!

Anna: Mama asked me, and I answered her.

Johan: Where was Ernst?

Ernst: I was asleep. I knew nothing about all this.

Karin: And if you get pregnant?

Anna (*with a smile*): Difficult at that distance.

Karin: Johan! Did you *hear*!

Johan (*sorrowfully*): Yes, yes, I heard. I heard all right. I heard. (*Clears his throat again.*)

Karin: I really don't know what we shall do.

Ernst: May I suggest something?

Johan (*frowning*): Go ahead.

Ernst: I suggest that my honored parents don't do anything at all. What's happened is just thoughtlessness on Anna's and my part. We've made fools of ourselves, quite simply. We're certainly prepared to apologize to you both for the unpleasantness and anxiety our thoughtlessness has caused you. Aren't we, Anna?

Anna: What?

Ernst: Apologize to Mama and Papa.

Anna: I'll really have to think about that.

Ernst: While you're thinking about it, I suggest that Anna writes a nice formal letter to the boy. Mama then adds a few benevolent lines inviting him here for a week.

Karin: Never! That scoundrel and seducer.

Anna (*flaring up again*): If anyone's a seducer in this place, it's me! Don't forget that, honored parents! And if you start being difficult, then I really will seduce him and get pregnant. Then whatever happens, you'll have to marry me off to the child's father.

Karin: I think you underestimate your parents' determination, my dear Anna.

Anna: *Your* determination, you mean. Papa and I have always agreed. Isn't that true, Papa?

Johan (*slightly embarrassed*): Yes, yes, of course, my child. Of course. Hm!

Karin: On second thought, I think Ernst's suggestion is a sensible one. We'll invite the oaf here and take a closer look at him.

Anna: Poor Henrik. That would be *frightful*.

Ernst: *I* will look after him.

Karin: What do *you* say, Johan?

Johan: Me? Nothing. What have you done with Torsten Bohlin, by the way? Is he out now?

Anna: Oh, him! He was only a sort of playmate.

Johan: Oh, I see, yes. And to think I was jealous of that stroppy little professor-to-be.

Karin: Don't talk nonsense, Johan.

Johan: No, no, all right, I'll keep quiet. I'm asked a question and answer it, then get scolded. (*Laughs quietly.*)

Karin: Please, Johan, do try to be serious for a little while longer. If I . . . I mean *we* . . . invite this young man here, Ernst, would you mind making it quite plain to him that he is not to come with any ideas of an engagement in mind?

Ernst: That I can guarantee.

Anna: *I* don't guarantee anything.

Karin: Nobody asked you! Shall we join the others now? They must be wondering. It's ten past five, and dinner is waiting.

Märta's dining rooms are inside the courtyard and two floors up in a shabby block on the corner of Dragarbrunnsgatan and Bävern Alley, and consist of three greasy, dirty-brown rooms, quite spacious, with connecting hallways. The cramped, dark kitchen is on the other side of the hall, which is a long, dark passage with no daylight, at the end of which is a badly ventilated toilet. The sun never penetrates these premises, not even in high summer. When the tiled stoves and the coal stove are out, a tomblike chill smelling of mold reigns in Märta's dining rooms, from which comes the name Cold Märta. Miss Märta herself and her two helpers reside in a narrow passage and two cubbyholes beyond the kitchen.

There are some good things to say about this eating place for students, alcoholic telegraph clerks, and incurable bachelors. Märta's food, though not all that great, is certainly plentiful. If required, it is possible to have, in secret, a schnapps before and a brandy after the meal. As medicine. Credit is also generous, not to say intrepid. The establishment is run good-heartedly on infinitesimal margins. There are better (much better) but also worse places in this city of learning. The Friday meatloaf is the tour de force of the house, though when it reappears in disguise on Tuesdays, it is as dicey as Russian roulette.

It is now the middle of August, about half past five in the afternoon. The dining rooms are almost empty. Beef stew and thickened fruit syrup are on the menu, served together with home-brewed, very weak beer. Outside it is still high summer and a general strike is underway. Inside it's dusk, ingrained cooking smells, indeterminate scents from the toilet, and pent-up dissolution.

The three theology students from Professor Sundelius's examination are sitting at a corner table in the farthest room. Henrik, confused and lethargic, is staying in town instead of going back home to his mother and Söderhamn. He is camping out on a wretched sofa at Justus Bark's lodgings, the latter keeping the wolf from the door by tending flower beds in the botanical gardens. His inadequate allowance is not due until the beginning of September. The future suicide, Baltsar, is always flush with money and is self-taught. He devotes his time between terms to the Chinese language as written in the seventh century, when the Empress Wu tse-t'ien persecuted and annihilated many of the most powerful T'ang dynasty.

The three men are downing quantities of thickened fruit syrup with skimmed milk. Miss Märta passes and asks kindly whether the stew was good. Polite mumbles. She stops as if wanting to say something, but changes her mind. Then she says it all the same.

Miss Märta: I'm sorry to have to tell you, but I must raise my prices. It's the general strike. Everything has become so insanely expensive, you see, gentlemen, so my monthly rates must go up from the first of September. Twenty öre a meal, that is, thirty-five kronor a month, or thereabouts. I have no wish to reduce the quality. And then we must have it nice and warm in the winter. Perhaps I may offer you a brandy with your coffee.

Appeased mumbling. Miss Märta fetches four glasses, unlocks the sideboard, takes out a bottle, locks the cupboard up again, and sits down. The theologians have fetched their coffee. They toast one another, after which, silence.

Perhaps it should be mentioned that Miss Märta Lagerstam does not look as one might expect. She is a small, white-haired lady with dark eyes and a pale, fine-featured face. She has narrow shoulders, a thin body, and moves easily. No one dares play hell with Miss Märta.

She lights a cigarette in a long holder and leans back, looking at her guests through the veil of smoke, her eyes half-closed. Miss Märta's helpers have begun clearing the tables — the big table in the middle room, and the small tables the few guests have now left. Miss Gustava is a fat, silent girl with a sorrowful gaze; Miss Petra, scarcely beautiful but friendly, is forty years old and a widow.

"Let's put the gramophone on," says Miss Märta, ordering Gustava to fetch the machine and the records. Justus offers to help her. When they go into Miss Märta's cluttered room beyond the kitchen, the theologian at once begins to lick and pinch the melancholy, passive girl, pressing her against the wall, and is just about to pull down her drawers when, without warning, Miss Petra comes in. She doesn't take much notice of the commotion by the stove but just says, "I'll take the records. You have to mind that they don't fall on the floor and get broken." Justus loses interest, and Gustava tucks her big breast back inside her blouse.

Miss Märta has now stood them another brandy, the girls have sat down on the two chairs drawn up for them, and the theologians are smoking proffered cigars. Out of the red gullet of the gramophone comes Enrico Caruso's beseeching voice: *Principessa di morte! princi-pessa di gelo! Dal tuo tragico cielo, scendi giu sulla terra!* The lamp has been pushed forward and glows sleepily through the tobacco smoke and brandy fumes.

Miss Märta looks at her guests with a maternal smile. "Now, isn't this nice? Aren't we having a nice time? This is how it should be. Such nice boys! Henrik shouldn't bite his nails, and that Baltsar, what can we do about him? He starts crying as soon as you look at him, though young Bark looks as if he'll be all right, now that he's down inside Gustava's bodice, though someone should see to it that he gets some new top teeth, poor boy.

"Come over here and sit by me, Mr. Bergman! Why do you bite your nails? You shouldn't do that when you've got such nice hands. Well, what have you got to say for yourself? How do you get on with the ladies? Spoiled, of course, and courted. Picking and choosing. Now listen to me, young man. Don't look so terrified. I won't eat you. That's right!"

Justus Bark and Miss Gustava have lost their balance and fallen to the floor with a lot of long-winded and soundless giggling. They help each other to their feet, the girl's knot of hair now undone. Miss Märta leans across the table and changes the record. Now it is from *Die Fledermaus*, the party at the palace of the bored, lecherous old Prince Orlofsky. The choir sings caressingly beneath the scratching of the needle: *Brüderlein, Brüdelein und Schwesterlein Du, Du, Du, immerzu. Erst ein Kuss, dann ein Du . . .*

Baltsar postpones his suicide for a few more hours and rests his narrow white forehead on Miss Petra's curvaceous shoulder and ex-pertly caressing hand. Miss Märta turns her lips, her well-formed sensual lips with their two small transverse wrinkles, toward Henrik's lips and kisses him fleetingly at least three times. "Christ Almighty," says Justus Bark suddenly. "I've got a letter for Henrik! It came this afternoon when I was at home freshening up. Sorry about the delay, but we were so occupied."

Justus pulls a crumpled envelope out of his top pocket and hands it over to Henrik, who focuses on it: the handwriting is unquestionably Anna's. It is undoubtedly a letter from Anna! Anna has written a letter to him! Anna has written!

He takes the letter very carefully, excusing himself with more confusion than courtesy, and tumbles out onto Dragarbrunnsgatan, now deserted in the rosy light of the setting sun. From the nearby shunting yards he can hear a puffing shunting engine and the clanging of train cars striking the buffers. He trots up Bävern Alley toward the river, then sinks down on a bench and reads the short and affectionately formal letter, in which, in a few lines at the end, Anna's mother has invited him to visit the family.

Ernst has been given a camera with a delayed action release as a birthday present, and a family photograph is to be arranged. (The photograph actually exists, though it is from a somewhat later period, probably the summer of 1912, but it fits better into this context, and anyhow this isn't a documentary.) After breakfast, the clan reassembles in the little meadow at the edge of the forest. It is a warm, sunny day, and everyone is in light clothes. Well, then . . . two chairs have been taken out. On one sits the traffic superintendent with his cane and breakfast cigar. If you look carefully with a magnifying glass, you can see that his calm, handsome face is distorted with pain and sleeplessness. Next to her husband sits Karin Åkerblom. There is no doubt whatsoever which of the two is the head of the household. The plump little person radiates authority and possibly smiling sarcasm. She has a stately summer hat on her well-tended hair, a kind of seal on her authority, clear eyes looking straight at the camera, and a small double chin. She has got herself into position to be photographed, but a few seconds later, she gets up full of vitality to issue orders. The older sons with their wives are grouped around the parents. Carl is standing alone, in profile, looking to the right, pretending he isn't there. Gustav and Martha's girls are laughing, and so are blurred. They have hunched up their shoulders and are holding each other around the waist, wearing blouses with sailor collars and calf-length skirts. Nearer the camera, on the left in the photograph, Anna is sitting on the grass. For some reason, not hard to guess, she is looking very grave, her gaze open and ingenuous, her lips slightly parted — so many stolen, passionate kisses. Behind Karin, kneeling, are Ernst and Henrik, both in student caps, neat jackets, collars, and ties. It is quite clear that Henrik has been invited to the traffic superintendent's summer residence as a friend of their son's and not as a possible fiancé for their daughter. Slightly in the background, but quite visible, are Miss Lisen and Miss Siri, a dignified pair in dazzling white aprons and serious expressions.

Fourteen people, summer, August 1909. No more than a second. Go into the photograph and recreate the following seconds and minutes! Go into the photograph as you want to so badly! Why you want to so badly is hard to make out. Perhaps it's to provide some somewhat tardy redress to that gangling young man at Ernst's side. The one with the handsome, naked, uncertain face.

When the family portrait has been taken, the traffic superintendent, with the aid of a cane and gently supporting hands, is guided to the open loggia facing the sun and the view. The old gentleman is put into a special chair with an adjustable back and armrest and a green check rug. He is given a cushion behind his back, a stool under his feet; a wicker table is brought forward for the day's mail, yesterday's newspaper, a glass of mineral water with a few drops of brandy in it, and a pair of field binoculars. With her own fair hands, Mrs. Karin spreads a rug over his knees, kisses him on the forehead just as she does every other morning, before she herself sets about her day's multifarious exercising of power.

"You wanted to speak to young Bergman? He's waiting in the dining room. Shall I ask him to come here, or do you want to read your mail and your newspaper first?" says Mrs. Karin urgently. "No, no, let him come," mumbles Johan Åkerblom. "It was actually you who wanted to speak to the boy. I don't know what to say." "Of *course* you do," retorts Mrs. Karin, without smiling, and goes to fetch Henrik.

He is invited to sit in a basket chair of indefinite form, neither stool, nor chair, nor armchair. The traffic superintendent smiles slightly apologetically as if to say: Don't look so terrified, my young friend, things aren't that bad. Instead he asks if Henrik would like to smoke, a cigar, a cigarillo, or perhaps a cigar-cigarette? Oh, he wouldn't? Of course. Of course you can smoke your pipe. Is that English tobacco? Yes, of course. English pipe tobacco is the best. The French is so harsh. Johan Åkerblom takes a sip of his brandy-colored mineral water and puffs at his cigar.

Johan Åkerblom: If you use the binoculars, you can see the station building down there just beyond the curve of the tracks. If you look carefully, you can see the siding. I usually amuse myself by checking arrivals and departures, you see, Mr. Bergman. I have a timetable here for express trains, passenger trains, and freight trains. I can watch and compare. It's an old man's little amusement for someone who's spent his whole professional life with railway lines and locomotives. I remember when I was a little boy, I kept insisting until I was allowed to go and watch the trains at the railway station — we lived in Hedemora at the time. There's nothing more beautiful than those new engines the Germans have started making: "F 17," or whatever they're called. Well (*clears his throat*), perhaps you're not particularly interested in locomotives, Mr. Bergman?

Henrik (*disoriented*): I've never thought about railroad engines in that way.

Johan Åkerblom: No, no, of course not. How are your studies going, by the way?

Henrik: I can manage what I'm interested in. What I don't understand is less easy.

Johan Åkerblom: Yes, yes. Fancy there being so much to learn to become a priest. One wouldn't have thought so.

Henrik: What do you mean, sir?

Johan Åkerblom: Well, what do I mean? One thinks perhaps, seen from a noninvolved, lay point of view, that being a priest is more of a matter of talent. One has to be — what is it called now? — a fisher of men, a fisher of souls.

Henrik: One has to have convictions first and foremost.

Johan Åkerblom: What kind of convictions?

Henrik: One has to be convinced that God exists and that Jesus Christ is His son.

Johan Åkerblom: And *that* is your conviction, Mr. Bergman?

Henrik: If I were equipped with a sharper mind, then perhaps I would call my convictions into question. The really brilliant religious talents always have their periods of terrible doubt. I sometimes wish I could be a doubter, but that's not so. I'm fairly childish. I have a childish view of faith.

Johan Åkerblom: Then you're not afraid of death, Mr. Bergman? For instance?

Henrik: No, I'm not afraid, but I prefer to shy away from it.

Johan Åkerblom: Then do you believe man is resurrected into eternal life?

Henrik: Yes, I'm quite convinced of that.

Johan Åkerblom: Well I'll be damned! And the forgiveness of sins? And the Sacrament? The blood of Jesus to thee given? And punishments? Hell? You believe in some kind of hell, whatever it'll look like?

Henrik: One can't say I believe in this and this, but I don't believe in that.

Johan Åkerblom: No, no, naturally not.

Henrik: Archimedes said, give me a fixed point and I shall move the earth. For me the Sacrament is the fixed point. That's how, through Christ, God came to an agreement with Man. That was how the world was changed. From its very foundations and through and through.

Johan Åkerblom: Oh, yes. Did you think that out yourself, or did you read it somewhere?

Henrik: I don't know. Is it that important?

Johan Åkerblom: Well, what about all the devilment that surrounds us? How does that match up with God's agreement?

Henrik: I don't know. Someone has said that we are satisfied with perspectives that are far too limited.

Johan Åkerblom: I would say you have your answers down fairly pat. And when will you be qualified?

Henrik: If all goes well, I shall be ordained in two years. Then I'll be given a chaplaincy almost immediately.

Johan Åkerblom: Not much to start with, I suppose?

Henrik: Not that much.

Johan Åkerblom: Not enough to start a family, eh?

Henrik: The church likes her young priests to marry. The pastor's wife plays an important role in the parish.

Johan Åkerblom: And what is she paid?

Henrik: Nothing, as far as I know. The pastor's stipend is also his wife's stipend.

Johan Åkerblom turns toward the dazzling summer light, his face gray and sunken, the gentle gaze behind the pince-nez darkened by physical pain.

Johan Åkerblom: I suddenly feel rather tired. I think I'll go and lie down for a while.

Henrik: I hope I haven't caused you any inconvenience.

Johan Åkerblom: No, not in any way, my young friend. A sick man who seldom thinks of ultimates understandably may be somewhat shaken by talk of Death and ultimates.

Johan Åkerblom looks at Henrik benignly and signals to him that he would like to be helped out of his chair. As if by magic, Mrs. Karin and Anna appear and take over.

So that Johan Åkerblom does not have to bother with the stairs, the nursery, the sunniest room in the house, has been made into a bedroom for the invalid. He sinks down on the bed with a pillow under his right knee. The shade has been pulled down, coloring the air a gentle pink. The window is open; outside, the birch trees rustle, and the express train to Stockholm, which doesn't stop at the little station, signals before the railway bridge. Johan Åkerblom winds up his gold watch and checks the time. Karin is standing at the end of the bed, unlacing his boots. "No," says Johan Åkerblom, sighing. "I wasn't able to talk to our guest. I simply couldn't bring myself to talk to him about what you wanted me to say to him." "So I suppose I'll have to deal with it," says Karin Åkerblom.

That evening there is reading aloud around the dining room table. The paraffin lamp shines gently on the entire assembled family. Outside the windows, the August dusk thickens into night.

They all have their prescribed places at the evening ritual, in this case Mrs. Karin enthroned at the head of the table, reading from Selma Lagerlöf's *Jerusalem*. Next to her are the girls with their handwork, the wives together down one long side, Martha painting on parchment with a fine brush, Svea with her eyes and face enclosing her grinding illness. At the other end, Anna and Ernst are leaning over a large jigsaw puzzle tipped onto a wooden tray. The traffic superintendent is in his rocking chair by the window (no one else in the family would dream of sitting in that chair). He is outside the circle of light and turns his head toward the darkening landscape and the cold moonlight making the flowers of the pelargoniums take on a pale violet color. Carl has brought in a special table and put out a lamp for himself. He is leaning and quietly wheezing over a construction of balsa wood and thin steel wires. He maintains he is constructing a machine for measuring the humidity in the air. Oscar and Gustav are benevolently dozing in each corner of the long sofa below the wall clock, their evening drinks, bottles of mineral water and brandy, on the low table in front of them.

Henrik has finally placed himself on the very edge of the company, or perhaps outside the company, it's hard to know which. He has sat down on a narrow basket chair by the door into the kitchen and is sucking on his empty pipe, observing the family, looking from one to another, looking at Anna. Anna, apparently so absorbed by the puzzle, Anna leaning toward her brother, Anna, who has gathered her hair into a knot today. Anna's smile, Anna's intimacy, Anna safely enclosed in her family. Look at me, just for a moment. No, she is absorbed, inaccessible inside the magic circle of the ceiling lamp. She is whispering to Ernst. That swift, conspiratorial smile. See me, just for a moment! No. Henrik cultivates a mild grief, an elegiac sense of being outside. At that moment, he is wallowing in something he likes to call hopeless love. At the same time he realizes with a shudder of satisfaction that he is worthless. He is wandering in the shadows, far beyond Grace. He is seen by no one, and that is true.

Mrs. Karin's reading is well articulated, subdued yet dramatic. When she comes to dialogue, she gives her performance a little character, coloring it according to her own judgment, and is fascinating in a simple way, allowing herself also to be captivated by what she is reading:

Karin: "When the Dean's wife came into the doorway, she stopped and looked around the room. A few of them tried to speak to her, but she could hear nothing at all that day. She raised her hand and said in that dry hard voice of the kind often used by deaf people: 'You no longer come to me, so I have come to you to tell you you must not go to Jerusalem. It's an evil city. That was where they crucified Our Saviour!' Karin tried to answer her, but she heard nothing and simply went on: 'It's an evil city and wicked people live there. That was where they crucified Christ. I've come here,' she went on, 'because this has been a good house. Ingmarsdotter is a good name. It has always been a good name. You must stay in our parish!' Then she turned and went out. Now she had done what she had to do, and she could die in peace. This was the last act life was demanding of her. Karin Ingmarsdotter wept when the old lady had gone. 'Maybe it's not right for us to go,' she said. But at the same time, she was glad the old lady had said: 'Ingmarsdotter is a good name. It has always been a good name.' That was the first and only time anyone had ever seen Karin Ingmarsdotter hesitant when confronted with the great undertaking."

Karin Åkerblom closes the book with a little bang; the clock above the sofa strikes ten, and it's time to disperse. "Think of all those good intentions," says Svea, opening her eyes and peering up at the ceiling lamp. "All that goodwill that caused so much misery. For it all came to nothing but misery."

Karin (*benevolently*): Have you read the Jerusalem books, Svea? I didn't know that.

Svea: My dear Karin, I read them seven years ago. You read a lot when you can't sleep.

Karin makes a dismissive gesture and pats Svea on the arm. Like all very healthy people, she doesn't like hearing about illness.

Karin: You'll see, Svea, that new bromide pill will do the trick. Tidy up behind you, won't you, girls. Off you go! Come on now, Johan Åkerblom, I'll help you with your shoes. Oscar, you'll have your breakfast at seven tomorrow morning, so that you can catch the Stockholm train without having to hurry. I've told Lisen you're to have breakfast at seven. Come on now, Johan, where's your cane? Anna, would you take the tray of drinks and put the brandy away in the cupboard? Anna, Ernst, and Mr. Bergman, you three wait here. I'll soon be back. We have a few things to talk about. Would you please open the door, Martha? That's right. Mind the sill, Johan! It really is unnecessarily high, in fact isn't really necessary at all.

"Good night"s and "sleep well"s crisscross the room. Martha slips out onto the veranda for a last cigarette. Mother-in-law doesn't approve of women smoking. Henrik, Anna, and Ernst put away the puzzle, which turned out to be of a castle in Normandy with a bridge and an ox-cart. Oscar hurries out to the outhouse, the lantern fading away into the night. Carl carefully carries both table and lamp up to his attic room — his boyhood room. Gustav gets something to read out of the glass-fronted bookcase. Good night, good night, and another day leaves our time and never comes back. Good night, good night.

Anna, Henrik, and Ernst remain seated at the table. Mrs. Karin comes in from the hall. She has put on a soft violet-colored peignoir (very correct, with her guest in mind). She sits down at the head of the table and runs her hand over the checkered oilcloth that is always put on after dinner. She makes the same gesture once again, her broad engagement and wedding rings glimmering on the strong hand.

Karin: Ernst has suggested that you three young people go off on a cycling trip to the farmland at Bäsna. The idea was, as far as I have

82

understood it, that you should stop overnight. By chance, I heard that Elias has brought his people and cattle back unusually early this year. So the buildings are empty. Ernst tells me he has Elias's and his father's permission to use the buildings for a few nights. (*Pause.*) Naturally, I am totally against your plans.

Ernst: But, Mama dear!

Karin (*raises her hand*): Let me finish. I am utterly against your plans, but I am not going to forbid them. (*Smiles sarcastically at Henrik.*) My children maintain quite forcefully that they are grown up and must take responsibility for themselves. Their parents will have to be satisfied with awaiting the consequences. The alternatives are not that wonderful. The threads between young and old are fragile. We old feel strongly about the link and guard it with constant compromises. The young, on the other hand, find it easy to cut through anything that doesn't suit them. I am not blaming you, for that is what it's like. You profit from your boldness and youthful ruthlessness. Our task is to look on. To make a long story short, I intend to be passive up to a certain point. One more thing: I shall always tell you where I stand. But you must always be quite clear about what I think. Any questions?

Anna: How do you know that you're always right, Mama? We might just as well be right. Isn't that so?

Karin: To some extent you've misunderstood my argument. I have experience; you haven't. I have learned to see our actions in a wider perspective. You go by your own desires. That's what you do when you're young. I did, too, when I was your age.

Anna: Of course, you spoil some of the enjoyment, Mama, by talking in this obscure and threatening way. Actually, it's rather sophisticated.

Karin: If you could read my thoughts, if you could see into my heart, as they say, then you would see neither threats nor whatever you called it — sophistication. You would probably find a mindless love for you and your brother. That's what you would see.

Anna at once goes over to her mother and embraces her. Karin Åkerblom allows herself to be embraced and pats her daughter lightly on the backside. The young men have been sitting speechless during this conversation, which indeed has been in their mother tongue, but which nevertheless has been incomprehensible to them.

Ernst: Mama, you really are a game old thing. Don't you think so, too, Henrik?

Henrik: To be honest, I don't really know what's going on. You'll have to explain to me.

Karin (*energetically*): Exactly. Now let's all go to bed. I mean, *I'm* going to bed. I suppose you want to stay up for a little while longer? There's an opened bottle of red wine in the sideboard. Good night, Ernst, give your mother a kiss. Good night, Anna, make sure you don't talk too loudly and remember Papa is right next door. He'll be reading for an hour or two more. Then it must be quiet. Good night, Henrik Bergman. My husband tells me that your conversation this morning made quite an impression.

Henrik (*bows*): Good night, Mrs. Åkerblom.

Karin: Anna, don't forget to put out the lamp and make sure the veranda doors are locked.

They set off at about five in the morning. A few hours later, the day has become stifling and windless, a gray mist hiding the sun and the light strong but with no shadows. There is a lot of uphill work, and back-pedal braking puts a fierce strain on backs and necks. Things get better after the old ferry crossing. The wind gets up over the heath, and they swim in the cold waters of the deep, swiftly running Boda River. They eat sandwiches and drink fruit juice, feeling better. Ernst starts laughing and complaining bitterly that no one can understand how grown people with their senses intact can, every summer, every year, be so self-destructive as to pack themselves together into the traffic superintendent's summer residence and, in addition, declare that everything is delightful. "Between ourselves, I have to tell you, my dear Henrik, that the situation has grown worse as my father's fatigue has increased. Mama feels she has to take on the whole responsibility, and she's developing a dreadful talent for manipulation and oppression. Now, however, we are about eighteen kilometers away from that dreadful accumulation of misunderstandings, confusions, and surrenders. Here's to freedom, my children! And then we toast in red currant juice."

"It's easy to be ungrateful," says Anna. "Mama makes efforts far beyond her strength. Then she doesn't sleep and is restless. And the more tired she becomes, the more she feels she has to handle the most minute details in the household. Then she complains, and we get angry and unfair." "Yes, yes," says Ernst, complementing his sister. "Anna and I keep up a perpetual conversation about Mama. We are most unjust toward her. But we have to take care of our safety valves. Think about Papa in his heyday, and Mama and her consuming efficiency. No wonder the brothers have become what they are. Anna and I have got off lightly." "I shall certainly keep Henrik away from our family," says Anna suddenly, then turns scarlet.

By midday, they have reached their destination and quickly make themselves at home. There is a huddle of smallish buildings on the edge of the forest below the mountain. The grassy slope runs down to a circular pool called Duvtjärn, where there are water lilies along the opposite bank, their stalks disappearing into the brownish black water.

The cottage consists of a single room that serves as both kitchen and sleeping quarters. The people who usually live there have just gone back to the village for the harvest and threshing, so it's clean and scrubbed, but full of dead flies. It smells of sour milk and smoky stove. A tangle of wild raspberries leans on the corner of the cottage. The old well with its lever is built over a spring. The water is cold and tastes of iron. Two felled and withered young birches are wilting by the porch.

After they have moved in, Ernst says he is going into the forest to fish for trout and politely asks whether anyone wants to go with him. Neither Anna nor Henrik seem inclined to. Ernst says he understands perfectly well, but adds that he will be back for dinner, and they are to have fresh fish. Then he says good-bye, puts his long fishing rod over his shoulder, and disappears on the path to the mountain.

Anna and Henrik are left to themselves and each other. The tension in the silence crashes all around them, deafening and confusing and, despite everything, unplanned. They start kissing on their way to the pool, where they are going to look at the water lilies. They turn back to the cottage and lock themselves in and go on kissing. "No," says Anna. "We can't be together. It's impossible, Henrik. I'm bleeding."

So they go on kissing and take off some of their clothes. They land on a bed with a bedspread as coarse as a bed of nails, but that is no real obstacle. Then suddenly there is quite a lot of blood, pretty much everywhere. Anna says it hurts, be careful, it hurts. Then she forgets it hurts, and it doesn't hurt any longer. She no longer cares that blood is all over the place and that the pulse in Henrik's neck is beating against her lips. She sobs and laughs and holds him tightly. For a few moments this is a pastime — but a decisive one.

So much becomes decisive when one tries to examine an event

85

after the fact and knows what happens later. An event that also consists of a few loose odds and ends. It means filling in the account with understanding and possible inspiration. Occasionally I can hear their voices, but very faintly. They encourage me, or say dismissively: It wasn't like that *at all*. It *really* didn't happen like that.

As far as this episode is concerned, I have heard no comments, either one way or the other. I remember Mother once saying: "Oh, yes, we often went on cycling trips to the farmlands at Bäsna. When we got there, Ernst went off to catch trout. When he came back, he produced a fat eel. I refused to kill it, so we released it into the Duvtjärn and then we fried pork and potatoes for dinner. I remember that."

They are now sitting on the jetty, much damaged by the ice, with a scrubbing brush and green soft soap, scrubbing away at the old bedspread, which only reluctantly relinquishes the blood.

Anna: This spring, we were doing our practical at Sabbatsberg Hospital. My roommate and I ended up in a ward for old men in the last stages of consumption. It was terrible, terrible. So much horror and misery. At first I had to go out and vomit several times a day, and Paula fainted when the doctor showed some poor wretch who had suppurating sores all over his body. It was a strange time, you see, almost like a dream. We had to wash the patients when they messed themselves, and we learned to put in catheters both here and there. They were dying like flies all the time. A screen was just pulled round, and sometimes at night you had to sit and hold someone's hand and just watch while his life simply ran out. I thought I'd never again be the same Anna as I had been, and I was pleased about that. Then I thought about you, Henrik. Do you think the stains have all gone now? No, there's another one. I thought about you, Henrik. And I thought about us, when we get married. Do you understand what an *unbeatable combination* you and I will be? You a priest and me a nurse! It's as if you could see *a plan* for our life. We've come together to accomplish something for other people. You bandage the soul and I the body. Isn't that magnificent! If it weren't so impossible, I could believe that God had thought it up. What do you think?

Henrik covers his face with his hands and sits like that for a few moments, far too dazzled by the enthusiastic and loving look in Anna's eyes.

Anna: What's the matter, Henrik?

Henrik: I don't think it's allowed.

86

Anna: I don't understand at all what you mean.

Henrik: This much joy just cannot be allowed. Some punishment must be on its way.

Anna: The sun shines after rain. (*She stretches out a hand, throws back her head, and is silent for a moment.*) A mild wind is blowing. We love each other, and we're going to live together. We'll . . . (*She takes down the hand and puts it against Henrik's cheek.*) We shall live *for each other and be useful to other people.* And our children shall be as clear-minded as we are.

Henrik: You must stop now. I think there's a secret cosmic envy that punishes people who talk like that.

Anna: Then I challenge that cosmic envy to a duel, and I promise you I know who'll win! Now let's hang up this bedspread and let it dry in the sun. Then our sin will be obliterated.

It has been said and decided from the start that Henrik's visit would end on Thursday the twenty-second of August. On Wednesday afternoon, Henrik is sitting in Ernst's room at the brown escritoire, trying to go through his examination sermon. The house is silent and empty, the family gone to the hill with the grand view with some guests who had arrived from the capital in their own automobile. The superintendent of traffic is slumbering in his chair on the veranda. Siri and Lisen are sitting on the bench overlooking the sunset, preparing chanterelles from a basket between them.

As if by chance, Karin Åkerblom has stayed behind and not gone on the outing, pleading a slight cold. As if by chance, she knocks on her youngest son's door and, without waiting for an answer, looks in. Henrik at once rises to his feet. Mrs. Karin apologizes and says she has no wish to disturb him, but just wants to know whether Ernst has left his cardigan at home, so that she can mend it, for there is a large hole in the elbow. As if by chance, she comes into the room and looks around with two swift glances. She has her ingeniously fitted-out mending bag over her arm. She smiles benevolently at Henrik and asks if she is by any chance disturbing him. Henrik bows and tells her that she is not disturbing him in the slightest.

"Then may I ask your assistance, Mr. Bergman?" she says, swiftly digging out a skein of thick wool and threading it over Henrik's outstretched hands. She suggests that they sit down opposite each other by the open window. The creeper climbing all the way up to the eaves has begun to turn red, and a faintly acrid scent of autumn is coming from the marigolds in the beds below. But it is still summer weather, and a summer wind is blowing across the river, which is glittering in the bright afternoon light.

If Henrik had known anything about Mrs. Karin Åkerblom, that knowledge would have warned him. He now tumbles headlong into all the pitfalls and walks innocently into all the traps. Her ability to get people to confess has been testified to. She is now sitting there with a quiet smile and has tied Henrik's hands together with blue wool. The ball is being nimbly wound up.

Karin: Are you going back home to Söderhamn and your mother tomorrow, Mr. Bergman?

Henrik: I'll probably be going straight to Upsala.

Karin: But the term doesn't start for a while, does it?

Henrik: I have to find a room and get myself settled. I'm also retaking church history.

Karin: Oh, so you've had your exam in church history, have you? That's Professor Sundelius, isn't it?

Henrik: Yes. It didn't go too well.

Karin: Professor Sundelius is a real tormentor of students. I remember him as a young man. He used to come to our home. He was a handsome youth, but terribly self-important. Then he married into money and a big stone house and made a career in liberal politics. People say he'll be a cabinet minister, from what I can make out.

Karin Åkerblom looks out the window and seems to be thinking. Then there's a tangle in the wool, and she leans forward to separate the threads.

Karin: Have you enjoyed your stay here with us, Mr. Bergman?

Henrik: Very much, thank you. Ernst is a very good friend.

Karin: Ernst is a fine boy. Johan and I are immensely proud of him. We try to keep our enthusiasm in check. The danger is that we might otherwise inhibit him with our expectations.

Henrik: I don't think Ernst seems oppressed. He's an unusually free person. In fact, he's the only truly free person I know.

Karin: I'm glad to hear you say so, Mr. Bergman.

Henrik: I'm very fond of him. He's like a brother to me.

Karin: I think Ernst is also happy that you're friends. He's said that many a time.

Henrik: You were kind enough to ask me, Mrs. Åkerblom, whether I had enjoyed my stay. Naturally I replied that I had, very much so. But that's not entirely true. I have been frightened and tense.

Karin: Frightened? But my dear boy, why frightened?

Henrik: The Åkerblom family is an alien world to me. Although my mother took great trouble with my upbringing.

Karin: But my dear boy! Has it been so difficult?

Henrik: Most of it would have been bearable, if only I hadn't been so aware of the criticism.

Karin: Criticism?

Henrik: The family is critical. I am weighed on the scales and found wanting.

Karin (*laughs*): Now, listen, Mr. Bergman! All families are like that. We're certainly no worse than any other. And you know, Mr. Bergman, you have two very competent and devoted defenders.

If this were a conventional novel, now would be the time to describe what Mrs. Karin is thinking and perhaps most of all Henrik's fluttering emotions when faced with Mrs. Karin's clear looks. Far too late, Henrik has realized that the trap door has slammed behind him. His chances of making a case for himself are extremely limited.

Henrik: Perhaps it is worse than that, Mrs. Åkerblom. I have felt unwelcome.

Mrs. Karin smiles a little and goes on winding. She waits a while before saying anything, and that makes him uncertain. He thinks perhaps he has gone too far, that he has overstepped the boundaries of courtesy.

Karin: And you think that?

Henrik: I do apologize. I didn't mean to be discourteous. Nevertheless, I can't shake off the feeling that I am not tolerated. Particularly by the mother of Ernst and Anna.

Another silence. Mrs. Karin nods as if in confirmation. I have received your message, Mr. Bergman, and I am mulling it over.

Karin: I'll try to be honest with you, Mr. Bergman, although I may well have to hurt your feelings. In that case, it will be unintentional. My antipathy, or whatever I should call it, is nothing personal. I even think I would be able to entertain friendly and motherly feelings toward Ernst's young friend. I see that you are a sensitive and vulnerable person, who has in many ways already been afflicted by harsh reality. My antipathy, if that is what we are to call my combined attitude, is entirely to do with Anna. I like to think I know my daughter fairly well, and I believe a liaison with you, Mr. Bergman, would lead to a catastrophe. That is a strong word and I know it may seem exaggerated, but nonetheless, I must use the word. *A major catastrophe.* I cannot think of a more impossible and fateful combination than between our Anna and Henrik Bergman. Anna is a spoiled girl, willful, strong-willed, emotional, tenderhearted, extremely intelligent, impatient, melancholy and cheerful at the same time. What she needs is a *mature man* who can nurture her with love, firmness, and unselfish patience. You are a very young man, Mr. Bergman, with little insight into life, with, I fear, early and deep wounds beyond remedy or consolation. Anna will despair in her helpless attempts to heal and cure. So I am asking you . . .

Mrs. Karin looks at the blue ball of wool that is growing in her hands. She bites her lip, and red patches appear on her cheeks.

Henrik: May I say something?

Karin: Yes. (*Absently.*) Of course.

Henrik: I refuse to accept this conversation. As Anna's mother, Mrs. Åkerblom, you may well have good reason to poison me with accounts of my appalling spiritual life. I can assure you that most of your arrows have struck home. The poison will no doubt have the intended effect. And yet your attack is unforgivable, Mrs. Åkerblom. An outsider, even if she happens to be the Holy Mother, can never interpret what happens in two people's minds. The family reads Selma Lagerlöf in the evenings. Has it never occurred to you from what you read that the author speaks of Love as the only earthly miracle? A miracle that transforms. The only real salvation. Does the family perhaps believe the author has invented that to make her dark sagas slightly more attractive?

Karin: I have lived quite a long time, but I have never even caught a glimpse of any miracles, either earthly or heavenly.

Henrik: Exactly, Mrs. Åkerblom. Australia does not exist because you have never seen Australia.

Mrs. Karin gives Henrik Bergman a sharp but appreciative look, then smiles quickly.

Karin: I fear our conversation is beginning to be far too theoretical. The facts are that with all my power and *all my means*, I will put a stop to any further dealings in love on the part of my daughter.

Henrik: I think that is an unrealistic decision.

Karin: What is unrealistic about it?

Henrik: You can't possibly stop Anna. I think any such attempt would simply result in hatred and conflicts.

Karin: Only time will tell.

Henrik: Exactly, Mrs. Åkerblom! Time will reveal the consequences of a devastating mistake.

Karin: Whose mistake?

Henrik: I shall now go to Anna and tell her of our conversation. Then we'll have to see what we'll do.

Karin: Apropos that, what has happened with your engagement, Mr. Bergman? I mean, of course, your engagement to Frida Strandberg? As far as I can tell, it is still on. Anyhow, Miss Strandberg denied that it had been broken off.

Henrik lowers his arms and the remains of the blue wool. A nail has been driven through his heart. His eyes are glazed.

Henrik: How do you . . . ?

Karin: How do we know? My stepson, Carl, has been making inquiries. We already knew the truth a week before you came here.

Henrik: And you're going to tell Anna the truth, Mrs. Åkerblom?

Karin: I have no intention of saying anything to my daughter. Presuming you and I come to an agreement.

Henrik: An agreement? Or an ultimatum?

Karin: All right then, an ultimatum, if you wish to call it that.

Henrik: Then I'll leave.

Mrs. Karin nods urgently. She is calm and dignified, with no trace of anger in the plump face or the sharp, blue-gray eyes.

Henrik: May I write a letter?

Karin: Naturally.

Henrik: Does Ernst know?

Karin: He knows nothing. The only person who knows anything is me. And Carl, of course.

Henrik: And what reason shall I give?

Karin: You're good at lying, Mr. Bergman. In this case, a quality of that kind can come in handy. I'm sorry, that was very nasty of me.

Henrik: I must say it as it is.

Karin: Do as you think best, Mr. Bergman. Whatever happens, there will be a great many tears.

Henrik: May I ask one last question?

Karin: You may.

Henrik: Why did you let me come here, Mrs. Åkerblom? Despite what you knew. That's quite incomprehensible.

Karin: Do you think so, Mr. Bergman? I wanted to see my daughter's love at close quarters. And the misfortune had already occurred.

Henrik: What do you mean by "misfortune"?

Karin: I mean just what you do.

Henrik: In that case, I can say that you made a serious misjudgment.

Karin: Did I indeed? And now?

Henrik: That actually concerns no one but Anna and me.

Karin: Go and write that letter, Mr. Bergman! And take the three o'clock train. Anna won't be back until later and then . . .

Henrik: . . . then I'll have gone.

The skein of wool runs out, and the ball is complete. Karin Åkerblom and Henrik Bergman rise to their feet without looking at each other. During the last few minutes, they have established a life-long and irreconcilable hostility.

After this conversation, Mrs. Karin is exhausted and restless. She sits with a book but cannot read, pushes her gold-framed spectacles up onto her forehead. Stands in the middle of the room with the fore-finger of her left hand against her lips and her right hand on her hip, then catches sight of herself in the mirror and turns away. Walks away and touches the edge of the rag rug, bends down and straightens out the fringe.

The kitchen door can be heard opening and shutting. She peers cautiously from behind the curtain. Yes, it's Henrik standing on the steps, Lisen coming out with a packet of sandwiches. He thanks her dumbly, shakes her hand, picks up his shabby suitcase, and strides briskly toward the gate and the forest road. Karin is tempted to open the window and call him back, but at the same time realizes that there is no way back from what has occurred.

She is prepared to take the responsibility. She always takes the responsibility, and that stranger must be got rid of. For Anna's sake alone. Or? Henrik goes out through the gate but doesn't shut it. Other reasons? He's a liar and deceiver, and Anna must be protected. He is now disappearing down the steep slope of the forest road, the tree trunks obscuring him. That open, vulnerable face. A child's face. It was for Anna's sake. Now he's gone. I can't stand that sort of dangerous, appealing pliancy.

Mrs. Karin puts her hands down flat on the spotless green desk top, fatigue coming in waves, then bends over and bows her head. Now there will be conflicts, strife.

In the kitchen, Lisen is preparing baked pike and gooseberry fool for dinner. Siri is setting the table. As if by chance, Karin goes through the kitchen and says that at the end of the outing, they are to stop off at Berglund's to taste Aunt Greta's fresh cheeses. "So they won't have much appetite for dinner," says Lisen curtly. "I just hope they come on time. The pike's good. And what about Mr. Bergman, who's just left?" Lisen goes on expressionlessly. "Something to do with his mother," mutters Karin absently, her hand on the door handle. "But she lives in Söderhamn, doesn't she?" says Lisen, still in passing. "So why was he in such a hurry to catch the Stockholm train?" "I expect he'll change trains in Borlänge," says Karin, moving out into the hall, where Johan Åkerblom is just on his way to his room, walking slowly, leaning on his cane. "We ought to get an indoor toilet," he says and stops. "I've been going on about that for several years," his wife replies. "The slope'll be troublesome in the winter," says Johan. "You'll have to use the pail," says Karin benignly. "Like hell I'll sit on a pail!" Then, as if in an aside: "I think Henrik Bergman has left, hasn't he?" "Yes, he has," says Karin on her way up the stairs. "Something to do with his mother." "I suppose you drove him away," says the traffic superintendent, halfway into his room. "Just as well, I suppose. I didn't think him suitable." "You were so taken with him," says his wife sarcastically. "Well, you know," replies Johan. "A young man with opinions. But Anna was much too interested, though she's at that age, of course."

The door closes, and Karin stands on the stairs, not knowing whether to go up or down. She is tired again. Must be the menopause, she thinks suddenly, and feels some relief. When she gets to her room, she hears the Stockholm train signaling as it comes into the station.

Down in the yard, Ernst gets off his bicycle and flings his knapsack and pack to the ground. His mother opens the window.

Karin: Oh, so you're the first one home?

Ernst: I thought I'd have a quick dip before dinner. Is Henrik in?

Karin: Henrik has just left.

Ernst: What? Has he gone?

Karin: He took the Stockholm train.

Ernst: Why?

Karin: I don't really know. Something to do with his mother.

Ernst: Does Anna know he's gone?

Karin: How could she? Mr. Bergman said he was going to write a letter.

Karin closes the window. "What's really happened?" says Ernst, but his mother pretends not to hear the question and shrugs her shoulders. Then she lies down on the bed and pulls a rug over her feet.

After a short — all too short — spell of stillness, she hears the horses and carriage, the bustle and noise of unloading, happy cries from the girls and the tinkle of a bicycle bell (Carl insists on cycling). The noise spreads through the house, laughter and talk and heated arguments about a swim before dinner. Martha's voice, annoyed. Oscar and Gustav on the terrace with a whiskey. Suddenly Anna's quick footsteps. She has seen the letter; she is opening it; she is reading it. Then rapid footsteps, the door, short hard knock. Mrs. Karin hasn't time to answer; the door is jerked open, and Anna is standing on the threshold, dry-eyed and raging. She has the letter in her hand and holds it out accusingly toward her mother, who has sat up on her bed, pulling vainly at the rug.

Anna: I won't submit to this! *Mama!* I *won't* submit to it.

94

Karin: Don't stand there making so much noise the whole house can hear. Come in and shut the door. Sit down.

Anna slams the door shut but remains standing. After a few moments, she has her voice under control.

Anna: He says that we'll never see each other again.

Karin: He may have his reasons.

Anna: There isn't a single sensible reason in this letter. Who made him write it? Did you, Mama?

Karin: No, I didn't make him. But when I found out about the circumstances, I advised him to leave and never show himself again.

Anna: What circumstances?

Karin: I would prefer not to say what I know.

Anna: If I am not told the truth, I'll immediately go and find him. No one can stop me.

Karin: You're forcing me to.

Anna: What is it you know that I don't? Is it his fiancée, that Frida woman? He has told me about that. I know everything. He's been completely honest.

Karin: I don't think he's been entirely honest.

Anna: You're deliberately hurting me, Mama.

Karin: Now listen to me, my dear. Your brother Carl has absolutely reliable information that Henrik Bergman is still living with that woman. If you like, I can . . .

Anna (*gestures*): No.

Karin: If you like, I can ask your brother Carl to come here and confirm his information.

Anna: . . . no.

Karin: I refuse to go into detail. You'll have to draw your own conclusions.

Anna (*gestures*): . . . no.

Karin (*calmly*): . . . from the very first moment, I felt there was something unpleasant about that man. Naturally, he is to be pitied, I

95

mean, fatherless, poor, a difficult upbringing. It is all very touching, and I don't deny I felt a certain pity that made me hesitate. (*Pause.*) You're saying nothing.

Anna: So Carl has been spying?

Karin: That was hardly necessary. Let us say he was informed and thought I ought to be told.

Anna: . . . I won't submit to this.

Karin: . . . what will you do?

Anna: . . . I won't tell you.

Karin: . . . in any case, it's time for dinner. Perhaps you would like something in your room? I'll tell Lisen to bring you up some milk and sandwiches.

Mrs. Karin's fatigue has gone, and she gets up from her bed with lively movements, folds up the rug, smooths down the bedspread, and checks her hair in the mirror. Then she goes over to her daughter, who is still standing by the door.

Anna: . . . this I'll never forgive.

Karin (*mildly*): . . . who won't you ever forgive? Is it me you won't forgive? Or your friend? Or Life, perhaps? Or God?

Anna (*darkly*): Don't say another word.

Karin: When you've had time to think it over, you'll be sure to understand a little better.

Anna: . . . can't I be left alone?

Karin: My poor little girl.

Anna: . . . don't! Don't give me that pity!

Mrs. Karin is about to add something, but changes her mind and leaves Anna standing there speechless.

An icy wind is blowing across the plain and sweeping over the town, which crouches down submissively. Is the misery of winter to start as early as the end of October? It's bound to be both long and wearisome. The cathedral bell is tolling loudly. It's three o'clock on an

96

iron-gray Thursday afternoon, the jackdaws screaming around towers and projections and the brown Fyris River flowing sluggishly under the bridges. In university lecture rooms, glowing eyes of iron stoves glare at sleepy students and mumbling professors ensnared in their bitter intrigues. The fading light struggles listlessly with the dirty yellow gaslights in stairwells and corridors: to think freely is great, to think correctly is greater. Not to think at all is safest. This is the day when you die because you've stopped breathing. Immanuel Kant totters along with his head thrust forward, pursed mouth, and bad breath through this stronghold of knowledge: "To be moral one must bow to the laws of morality out of sheer respect for this moral law as it appears in the categorical imperative: act so that the maxim of your will can always be a principle for public legislation!"

At four o'clock, it is almost dark. Snow has now begun to fall, sometimes swirling, sometimes gentle, covering streets and roofs. But things are at least better now: the lecture came to an end, and the students are throwing snowballs at each other and at the statue of Erik Gustav Geijer.

Henrik has left his friends, who have hurried off to Cold Märta's steaming pea soup and warm wood stoves. He goes to stand opposite 12 Trädgårdsgatan and remains there for an hour, then another, snow-covered and stiff with cold in body and soul. No one is in sight; no one comes or goes; the street is deserted. There's a light on in a first-floor window, and occasionally a shadow flits across the white curtain. Behind him, inside the grammar school's dark, deserted yard, a door slams in the wind. Squeaks and creaks in between. Sometimes it is completely quiet, and Henrik can hear his own heart beating. The lamplighter comes, crosses the street, reaches up with his long pole, and pulls the lamp's steel loop. The snow whirls and dashes against the sources of light. The clock strikes quarter to seven, three ringing notes far away in the darkness. A small tram works its way up the curve from Drottninggatan toward the cathedral, screeching violently, the snow swirling, figures just visible behind its misted-up windows. Then all is still again. Henrik stamps his feet, his toes frozen in his thin boots, but otherwise he has made himself numb. I'll stand here until she comes. She must come. She's sure to come.

And then she does come, not alone, but with her sister-in-law, fat Martha. They emerge from the porch entrance, well wrapped and chatting amiably. Anna at once sees Henrik, says something to her companion, and crosses the street. Her face is suddenly illuminated by the streetlamp.

Anna: Don't stand watching for me. No, you may not touch me.

Henrik: Surely we can talk to each other! Just for a few minutes?

Anna: You've misunderstood everything, Henrik. *I* don't want to talk to *you*. We have nothing more to say to each other. Can't you leave me in peace?

Anna starts crying openly and vehemently, like a child. Martha comes waddling over in her gleaming matt fur coat and Russian fur hat. She is annoyed and tugs at Henrik's arm.

Martha: You must leave the girl alone. Don't you see you're frightening her?

Henrik: Please don't interfere. This is none of your business.

Martha: You're behaving like a fool. For that matter, we haven't time to stand here. We're going to a concert in the university hall, and it's nearly seven o'clock.

Anna: Can't you leave me in peace? Please, Henrik, I'm asking you as kindly as I can. Leave me alone!

Henrik: How are you? You look ill.

Anna: Yes. No, I don't know. I'm probably just miserable.

Henrik: I can't go on living.

Anna: Oh, don't be so dramatic! Of course you can go on living, and so can I.

Henrik: Anna, *speak to me!*

Anna: Don't touch me, I say. Don't *touch* me! You mustn't touch me. You're disgusting.

Henrik is paralyzed by her tone of voice. He has never heard such a tone of voice before. He sees the contempt in her eyes and has never seen anything like it before. (Henrik is a sheltered person, as if invisible. He has lived with his invisibility without it worrying him. He has always been rather indifferent to Frida's comments. Anna is looking at him with obvious contempt, no doubt about it, and he cannot misunderstand the look in her eyes — it is for him in particular, or rather someone a long way inside the role-playing, someone who for one painful moment realizes the extent of his destitution. That's what it was like, and that's how it would be, a lifetime. *He has at last been seen.*)

He drops Anna's arm and lets her go. She is no longer crying. The two women soon vanish into the darkness and the swirling snow.

After Christmas, Anna was to return to the nursing school. Nothing had been as usual. The traffic superintendent had had a slight stroke and was paralyzed on one side, a paralysis which seems to be easing. Carl had been threatened with personal bankruptcy a week before Christmas. His parents and Oscar had rescued him, but had put him in the hands of a financial guardian, his stepmother declaring herself willing to oversee his finances in the future. The girls had measles. Svea had proclaimed that this was probably her last Christmas on earth, and Anna was suffering from grief and love sickness, combined with a persistent cough that would not go away. The day after the new year (1910) began, she received a letter in an unfamiliar handwriting, very neat and well written. She read it with rising astonishment.

> Highly Esteemed Miss Åkerblom. I apologize for troubling You, but I find myself compelled to write to You, on an urgent matter of extreme importance to both You, Esteemed Miss Åkerblom, and to the Undersigned. May I be so bold as to request a Conversation? In that case, I suggest that we meet at Lagerberg's coffeehouse on Thursday at two o'clock. The Undersigned will be easy to recognize. I have a dark red winter coat and ditto hat. If the Esteemed Miss Åkerblom considers it worth the trouble to meet me, I would be singularly grateful. If not, I request You to disregard this letter. With great respect, Yours Faithfully, Frida Strandberg.

A few minutes after two o'clock, Anna goes into Lagerberg's coffeehouse on the corner of Drottninggatan and Västra Ågatan. It is almost empty. Two older ladies with well-groomed coiffures and large aprons are talking quietly to a professor of civil law in a top hat. Outside, it is snowing gently. Inside, the tiled stoves spread a fragrant warmth, releasing a multishimmering, roseate harmony over the seduction of the coffeehouse's delicious and much-renowned confectionary, while the pervasive aroma of freshly made coffee serves as a provocative counterpoint.

One of the well-groomed ladies asks Anna if there is anything she would like, and Anna says "hot chocolate with whipped cream and a small coffee cake," and "please, can I have it served in the inner room?" "Yes, of course, please go on in, Miss Åkerblom."

Frida Strandberg is already there and gets up when Anna approaches. She holds out her hand, and they greet each other with reserve and no attempt at false cheer. Frida's wine-red woolen coat is

99

simple and becoming, her hat of the same material trimmed with fur. Anna is wearing the fur coat she had received as a Christmas present, tailor-made and elegant, and a small sable beret is perched on her back-combed hair.

Frida: Have you ordered, Miss Åkerblom?

Anna: Yes, thank you. I have.

Frida: It was kind of you to come.

Anna: I suppose I was curious. (*Coughs.*)

Frida: Aren't you well?

Anna: A cold that won't go away.

Frida: Have a little mineral water. I haven't used the glass.

Anna: Thank you. That's kind of you.

Frida: There's been an unusual amount of illness going around this year.

Anna: Oh, has there?

Frida: People get sick when they're unhappy. I think there's been an unusual number of unhappy people this autumn.

Anna: Why just this autumn?

Frida: The general strike, of course, and all that that's brought with it.

Anna: Of course, the general strike.

Frida: You're going to be a nurse, is that right, Miss Åkerblom?

Anna: I'm just going back to the school of nursing.

Frida: I would love to have been a nurse. But I had to earn my own living rather young, so . . .

Anna's order arrives, a large cup of hot chocolate beneath a mountain of whipped cream, the coffee cake in its crinkly paper, and a glass of water. The well-groomed lady smiles maternally and makes herself scarce. Frida watches her go.

Frida: Do you know her?

Anna: When we were children, Papa used to bring us here almost every Saturday.

A silence arises that foreshadows a turn in the conversation in the direction of its real purpose. Anna suppresses a cough and takes a sip of water, her cake still untouched. Frida looks at her own hand and the engagement ring. The letter, written on a kind of impulse, had not been difficult to compose. Now the undertaking has become almost unbearable.

I asked my mother how much she remembered of the situation. She hesitated, then answered that she had immediately liked Frida Strandberg, that she seemed older and more mature than her age, and that "she was good-looking." She also remembered that both of them had noticed the engagement ring at about the same time and Frida had been slightly embarrassed.

Frida: I must go to work in half an hour. So I want to say what I've got to say without dillydallying. It's not that simple. When I wrote that letter, I thought everything seemed so clear, but now it's difficult.

She smiles apologetically and shakes her head. Anna feels a wave of fever in her forehead and mouth. She starts to take her handkerchief out of her bag, but then stops.

Frida: It's about Henrik. Miss Åkerblom, I'm asking you to take him back. He's . . . I don't know how to put it . . . he's . . . falling apart. It sounds peculiar when I say it like that, but I can't find a better expression. He doesn't sleep; he studies late into the night; and he looks so bad, one could just cry. I'm not saying this to arouse your pity. If there's no pity, I mean no feelings, then it'd be both stupid and tactless. I don't know much about the situation. He hasn't said anything. I've just guessed most of it.

A gesture of impatience and a quick smile. I suppose she wants me to say something, thinks Anna. But what is there to say?

Frida: I try not to be angry and hurt. But no one can help their feelings. I can't help getting furious, for instance. Or that I like him, although he behaves so feebly. Do you know what I think, Miss Åkerblom? I think he's the most agonized person on two feet. He doesn't want to be with me any longer now, but do you think he dares say to me, now, Frida, let's leave it at that, it's over between us, I'm in love with someone else? He can't bring himself to say he doesn't want to be with me any longer, because he knows I'll be cross and miserable. And then he hurts me even more by saying nothing. I don't know that much about what's gone on before, or what you think, Miss Åkerblom, about all this. But I think we are three poor wretches all suffering and crying in secret. So I feel that I must be the one to strike the first blow, so to speak. I must tell Henrik I won't go on with it any longer. For my own sake. I'm not going to let myself be hurt and — humiliated, yes, humiliated. He lies in my bed crying for someone else. It's humiliating for both him and me. It's humiliating. I'll tell you something, Miss Åkerblom, something I think about all the time. In a sense, he hasn't got a real life, poor thing. So nothing's worthwhile. The reason he's so miserable isn't hard to figure out. He's got a mother who — well, it sounds awful to say so — he's got a mother who's killing him. I don't know how she does it, because I know she loves him so much, he goes crazy with fear. In my profession, you learn quite a lot about people, you know, Miss Åkerblom. And I've only once ever seen him together with his mother. He hasn't even dared tell her we're engaged, rings and all. No, I was given the honor of waiting on them while they were having coffee at the Flustret. I arranged that. I wanted to see that woman. I can't call her anything better. No, I must go now if I'm to be there on time.

Anna: . . . what shall I do?

Frida: . . . take him, Miss Åkerblom, just decide. Henrik's the finest and best person I know. The kindest, and so good. I know no one better. I just want him to have a good life at last. He's never been happy in his whole life. He needs someone to love; then he won't have to hate himself so much. Now I really must go, or I shall get into trouble. Though that doesn't matter all that much, because I'm leaving and going to Hudiksvall for the summer. (*She smiles slightly.*) Maybe it's interesting to know that I'm getting out of town. I have a good friend — no, not in *that sense* — a good friend who lives in Hudiksvall, and he's got a fine boardinghouse he's going to sell, and he's building a hotel. He wants me to go there and run the restaurant, together with a girl who's been to catering school in Stockholm and in Switzerland. Lots of people think Norrland is going to be the place of the future, and it could be fun to be in on that future right from the beginning. So I'm leaving, though it'll be sad for me and I know I'll cry. But it's best that way. May I please pay for us both? I'll pay on my way out, if you wouldn't mind staying for a moment. Perhaps it wouldn't be exactly right if we paraded along the river together. Good-bye, then, Miss Åkerblom, and be careful with that cough. (*She goes, turns.*) Yes, one more thing. Don't ever tell Henrik . . . I mean, about my letter and our talk. That wouldn't be a good thing. He would just complicate matters. He'll always complicate everything, poor boy!

Suddenly, Frida Strandberg looks miserable, her eyes glistening, her lips trembling. She gestures dismissively. "I haven't cried all this time. Why now? How silly."

Then she is gone, the red curtain swaying.

The cold descends after Epiphany, smoke rising straight up out of the chimneys, the sunlight glowing for an hour or two above the great brick structure of the castle and dusk soon falling. Children and sparrows are making a lot of noise around Carolina Hill; crystals of ice bloom on the windowpanes; and the sleigh bells jangle shrilly.

Anna has put on her uniform and is packing, back to nursing school now that the Christmas holidays are over. She has a temperature and feels wretched, coughing as she moves slowly between the cupboard, the chest of drawers, the wardrobe, sitting down on her bed, standing by the window, going to the door, going to her desk, starting a letter, tearing it up, throwing it into the wastepaper basket. "Dear Henrik, I want us to . . ." — and then she doesn't know what to say. Fever throbs in her body, and sometimes she finds it hard to breathe, especially after an attack of coughing.

Ernst opens the door. "Are you really going to go? You're not well. For God's sake, there must be limits to your sense of duty. I've been skiing in Old Upsala. It's twenty-five below zero. I'm going to have a brandy. Then I'm off to work. I'm working in the afternoons, so I won't see you for a while. I'll be coming to Stockholm sometime next week. We'll go to Dramaten and see Strindberg's latest play. Look after yourself, beloved little sister. Give me a kiss. Shall I take a message to Henrik? We'll both be singing tomorrow evening. Shall I give him your regards? All right, I *won't* give him your regards. Farewell, then, my little cranberry heart!"

So Ernst leaves and Anna weeps, is weeping again. She doesn't want to cry and doesn't really know why she is. Mama Karin looks in: "Wouldn't you like a little Ems water, dear? Let me feel your forehead. You really are ill. I'll telephone the matron and tell her you're ill. I'm not going to let you go in that state!" Anna sulkily shakes her head: "Leave me in peace, leave me alone. I forbid you to telephone Matron. She hates us making a fuss. A little Ems water would probably be nice."

Mrs. Karin goes down to boil some Ems water. Anna sits at the desk. "Dearest, dearest Henrik, we must . . ." But she doesn't know what they must and tears up the sheet of paper. There's a discreet knock on the door, and her father pokes his head into the room. When he sees Anna, he smiles and comes right in, making his way with the aid of two canes and ending up on the nearest chair.

The temptation is irresistible. Anna flops down to her knees and embraces her father: "Papa, dearest Papa, can't you look after me? I can't cope with anything anymore! I don't know what I'm going to do. I know I have to be responsible, but Papa, I just *can't cope!*"

At long last Anna is really weeping, coughing, sniffing, and crying, just like when she was a little girl — utterly inconsolable. Mrs. Karin comes in with a glass of steaming-hot Ems water. She is almost horrified, puts the glass down on the bedside table, and pulls up a chair to be close to her daughter, patting her now and again on the shoulder and back.

Karin: I'm going to tuck my little girl into bed and phone for Dr. Fürstenberg, and to Matron. I'll come and sit with you after dinner, and then we can have a little talk. Then you'll be given something to make you sleep and you'll feel much better tomorrow, so we can decide what to do. Wouldn't that be nice, my dear?

Anna nods in silence. Yes, that might be nice.

The next scene takes place a few days later. The setting is Henrik's room. An unexpected guest is sitting at the desk. It is Oscar Åkerblom, the wholesaler, in a fur coat, galoshes on his feet, his Astrakan cap set aside on top of the Holy Scriptures. Henrik makes his entrance and expresses astonishment. Oscar at once starts to speak.

Oscar Åkerblom: Good day to you, Mr. Bergman. Please excuse my unannounced intrusion, but your good friend Justus Bark thought he could let me in without running too great a risk. It really is hellishly cold in here, Mr. Bergman. Please excuse an old man for keeping his coat on. No, no, please don't light the stove for my sake. Wild young minds perhaps need a little cool around their foreheads. How would I know? Please be so kind as to sit down. I won't take up much of your precious time, Mr. Bergman. Please sit down, I said.

Henrik: What's this about?

Oscar Åkerblom: It won't take long, I promise you it won't, young man. Don't look so indignant. I'm not your enemy. I'm just a conveyer of information. The family considered that you should be told and that I was the most appropriate messenger.

Henrik: Tell me what you have to say and then go.

Oscar Åkerblom: Oh, so that's how it's going to be, is it, young man! Well, that makes things very much easier.

Henrik: Good.

Oscar Åkerblom: I've been sent here to tell you the following. Please listen carefully now, Mr. Bergman. My young sister Anna is ill. She has tuberculosis. One lung is affected, and the other is at risk. She is being cared for at home at the moment. As soon as her health permits, her mother will take her to a sanatorium in Switzerland, where she will be well looked after. Please be silent, Mr. Bergman. May I finish speaking without interruptions. My sister Anna sends her regards and says she no longer wishes to have anything more to do with you, Mr. Bergman. She *expressly* asks you not to write or telephone or wait for her outside the gate or in any other way force yourself on her. She wishes *unconditionally* to forget your very existence, Mr. Bergman! Our doctor says that this will be of great importance to her recovery. My last message is an undeserved benevolence on the part of my family. In this envelope there is a thousand kronor. Here you are, Mr. Bergman. I'll leave the envelope on your blotter. Our conference is over now, and I shall leave. Allow me just to add a personal reflection on what has just been said. I'm sorry for you, and I regret your unhappiness. I'm sure you're a very pleasant young man. My brother Ernst maintains quite definitely that you're eminently suited to the serious vocation of the priesthood. In time, you will no doubt benefit from what has oc-curred. (*He leans forward.*) Invisible barriers run through our lives. It is pointless to try to force these barriers, in either direction. Think about that, Mr. Bergman. And now a speedy farewell. There's no need to see me out.

Let's speed up the telling of this story. Thus, two years are annihilated, plunging into the river of time and vanishing, leaving almost no trace behind them. But this is no chronicle, requiring a strict accounting for reality. It's not even a document. I'm reminded of my childhood, when I used to work on a kind of picture in magazines that consisted of nothing but dots and numbers; the objective was to draw lines be-tween the numbers and gradually an elephant or a witch or a castle appeared. I possess fragmentary notes, brief tales, isolated episodes. Those are the numbered dots. I draw my lines in what may well be a vain hope of a face appearing. Perhaps a glimpse of the truth of my own life. Why should I otherwise take so much trouble?

Father's old watch ticks indefatigably on its stand on my desk. I took it from his bedside table one afternoon at the end of April 1970. The watch ticks. It's almost a hundred years old. But one day it inexplicably stopped. That made me downhearted; I thought that my father disapproved of my writing, and that he was gratefully declining this belated attention I was paying him. However much I wound, shook, poked, and blew on it, the second hand refused to move. I put the watch into a compartment in my desk — a little separation. I would miss the ticking heartbeat and the discreet reminder that time is measured. The watch lay in its compartment and pondered. The next morning I opened the drawer and looked, but with no expectations. The watch was ticking away to its heart's content. Perhaps that was a good omen. I relate this as an episode to smile at. However, I am serious.

Two years go by. Gustav Fröding dies and is acclaimed a prince of poetry. A new hymn book comes out. In an automobile race on the stretch of road between Gothenburg and Stockholm, the winner sets a record time of twenty-two hours and two minutes. Prime Minister Staaff's second cabinet takes over. There are a thousand cars in the capital. In the summer a mixed bathing place was opened in Mölle, the international press and photographers all present. An adventurer flies across Öresund, and Archbishop Ekman opposes Bengt Lidfors's nomination as professor of botany on the grounds of the latter's irregular life-style. Cellar-master Johan Alfred Ander commits his bestial murder and is executed with the humane and newly imported guillotine. Halley's Comet is thought to predict a worldwide catastrophe, perhaps the end of the world.

Actually, it's less than two years later: April 1911. Henrik Bergman has just been ordained. Anna is still in a sanatorium called Monte Veritá by Lake Lugano and is considered practically cured. Svea Åkerblom has undergone a major operation for the removal of both breasts, her womb, spleen, and ovaries. She has grown whiskers and shaves every day. Carl has a new invention with which he is assaulting the Patent Office: with short but harmless electrical impulses, bed-wetting and ejaculation can be prevented in youths. Gustav Åkerblom's wife, the jolly, plump Martha, has acquired a lover. Every Thursday she goes to Stockholm, where she is taking instruction in the painting of miniatures. Her husband has similarly increased in girth and does not begrudge his wife her distraction. Their daughters have started senior high school and intend to take university entrance exams, something fairly unusual in those days. Oscar Åkerblom the wholesaler has

106

expanded his empire and opened branches in Vänersborg and Sundsvall. He is not just well-off these days, but regarded as wealthy. Ernst
has applied for a post as a meteorologist in Norway, a country far
ahead of his own in this new science. Johan Åkerblom, the traffic
superintendent, is rather fragile, the aftereffects of his stroke overcome
but the pains in his leg and hip troublesome. Mrs. Karin, busy govern-
ing her extensive empire, has put on some weight, which does not
worry her much. On the other hand, she has hemorrhoids and is also
troubled with permanent constipation despite figs, prunes, and a
special herbal tea of elderberry and dandelion.

After these interruptions, which would presumably make any experienced dramatist's hair stand on end, we shall return to the story or the
action or the saga or whatever.

The scene is the marital bedroom one spring evening at the end of
April. It is past ten o'clock and quiet in Trädgårdsgatan. Noise and
music can be heard coming from the Gästrike-Hälsinge student residence, which is closer to the cathedral, where preparations for Wal-
purgis Night are underway.

Mrs. Karin is putting her long hair into a thick braid for the night.
As usual, she is standing in front of the mirror in the spacious bathroom beyond the bedroom. This contains a newly installed bath and
running water, tiled walls, and a bulky radiator below the window
with its colored panes. It cannot really be said that Karin is beautiful,
but her lips are victorious, her complexion fair and unlined, her forehead broad, nose determined, her mouth even more determined. "Not
lips for kissing but for issuing orders," as Schiller says. The gray blue
eyes can be cold and observant, but can also turn black with rage.
Mrs. Karin has never uttered the words "I love" or "I hate." That would
be inconceivable, almost obscene. Nevertheless, this does not mean
that Karin Åkerblom, who is just forty-five, is a stranger to passionate
emotional outbursts.

Johan Åkerblom is sitting on the edge of his bed in his red-
bordered nightshirt, his pince-nez on his nose. He is reading an
English magazine called *The Railroad*, which describes in voluptuous
terms a new steam locomotive of astonishing performance. The bedside light illuminates his thin, newly washed hair, the rather hunched
figure, and the long nose. The ceiling light is already out, the room
dusky, white-painted beds, side by side. Light curtains, artistically
draped, a huge wardrobe with double doors and mirrors, comfortable
pale-green upholstered armchairs, a wide rug in soft colors, sturdy,

ingeniously fitted-out bedside tables for carafes of water, medicine bottles, appropriate bedside books, and chamber-pot cupboards.

Inherited oil paintings hang on the walls: Karin when young in a white summer dress; a leafy tree against a brilliant summer sky; an Italian basilica in a square, three women in colorful costumes having stopped on the sun-drenched piazza.

Mrs. Karin closes the door into the bathroom. She has her glasses on her nose and pair of curved nail-scissors in her hand. She sits down on a low stool by the bed and starts cutting her husband's toenails.

Johan: Ow, now you've cut my little toe off.

Karin: It's so hard to see. Can't you turn a little?

Johan: Then I can't see to read.

Karin: I can't think *what* you do to your toenails.

Johan: I bite them.

Karin: You ought to go to a chiropodist, a foot person.

Johan: Never! I'm no sodomite, am I?

Karin: Here's a callus. You must let me scrape that away.

Johan (*reading the magazine*): If you take it away, I'll lose my balance. I find it difficult enough to walk as it is.

Karin: My patience is incredible. Incredible. Really.

Johan: Don't be so namby-pamby, my darling. You love poking in ears, putting on bandages, squeezing pimples, lancing boils, pulling hairs out of anyone's nostrils. *And* not least — cutting toenails. You find it voluptuous.

Karin: You could at least lift your foot up a bit.

Johan: I don't like seeing you at my feet.

Karin: I sit at your feet so that you don't get totally filthy.

Johan: As long as you have a pure mind, you don't need to wash your feet.

Karin: And you have?

Johan: What do I have?

Karin: You don't even listen to what you're saying yourself.

108

Johan: Because you disturb me all the time. On these new great engine cylinders, they use what they call *airway ventilators*, which automatically open a link between the two ends of the cylinders, so no air compression shut inside the cylinder and consequent counterpressure can arise when the engine runs with the steam shut off. Listen to that now. Thank you, thank you, that's enough toenail cutting for now.

The traffic superintendent puts the magazine aside, swings his legs up with some difficulty, and creeps down under the covers. Mrs. Karin presses the button of an electric bell and patters around her bed. She is wearing a full-length peignoir. Standing by her bed, she takes three pills in rapid succession, tossing her head back and taking a gulp of water after each pill.

Johan: When you take those pills, you look like a hen with a bad throat. And you blink.

There is a knock on the door, and Miss Siri comes in with a little silver tray holding a cup of steaming bouillon and a plate with two oatcakes spread with slivers of mild cheese. She puts the tray down on the traffic superintendent's bedside table, wishes them good night, and departs as soundlessly as she had come.

Johan munches on an oatcake and blows on the hot soup. Mrs. Karin is sitting on her bed writing in her diary with a thin pencil.

Johan: Well?

Karin: I don't know. I'm writing down what happened yesterday, but the strange thing is I can't remember anything. What happened yesterday? Can you tell me?

Johan: No. Yes, we had a letter from Martha. And I went to the dentist and had a wisdom tooth pulled. You bought an Arvid Ödmann gramophone record.

Karin: Sometimes I feel so mournful, Johan. (*She sighs.*)

Johan: What's worrying you?

Karin: I don't know. Yes, as a matter of fact I do.

Johan: If you know, you should say what you know.

Karin: Don't you think Ernst comes to see us less and less often?

Johan: I haven't thought about it.

Karin: Yes. Less and less often.

Johan: *You* were the one who wanted him to move away from home and set up his own household.

Karin: Has it never occurred to you that I was so enthusiastic because I wanted him to contradict me: "No, no, Mammschen dear, I like it much better here at home with you and Papa."

Johan (*astonished*): Don't tell me you hoped that would happen?

Karin: The opposite happened. He was still enthusiastic.

Johan: And then our little girl is away. In a hospital. Far away. Thank goodness almost better, at last! But the house has been damned empty.

Karin: Yes, of course. But she likes it there at the sanatorium and has learned German properly. She doesn't seem to have missed us.

Johan: And now you're going over there to bring her back.

Karin: Would it upset you if Anna and I made a detour through Italy? I think it'd be fun to go to Florence just once more in my life.

Johan: Then you'd be away quite a long time?

Karin: Four weeks at the most. You could come with us, Johan!

Johan: You know I couldn't.

Karin: We could take it carefully. You'd enjoy a little trip, Johan. Imagine . . . Tuscany in the spring!

Johan: *You* must go. Not me.

Karin: Anna would be so pleased.

Johan: I'll stay at home and count the days.

Karin: It's good that Anna's not coming home just yet. May can be so cold and wet. In June, we'll go straight to the country.

Johan: Do you think she'll want to wait that long?

Karin: What do you mean? Tell me what you mean.

Johan: I just meant that perhaps there's someone she wants to come back to. Now that she's well again.

Karin: I don't really understand. Do you mean . . . ?

The traffic superintendent looks at his wife with a thoughtful expression on his face: It is a moral and strategic dilemma for him. He

110

doesn't like keeping secrets from Karin. He ought to keep quiet. But he doesn't. Quick decisions and extensive consequences.

Karin: What is it, Johan? I can see you want to tell me something that's worrying you.

He doesn't answer, but opens the bedside table drawer and takes out a letter. It's a letter from Anna. To Ernst. Not sealed. Quite thick.

Johan: When the afternoon mail came, you weren't at home. So I took it. Here's a letter from Anna to Ernst. It was posted in Ascona four days ago.

Karin: Ernst's coming back from Christiania next week. There's no point in forwarding it.

Johan: Anna seems to have forgotten to seal the envelope. Or she did it so carelessly, it's come open by itself.

Karin: Why do you say it like that? That's nothing remarkable. It often happens . . .

Johan: There's another letter inside the letter.

Karin: . . . another letter? To Henrik Bergman.

Johan: It says on the envelope "to be forwarded because I don't know his address."

Karin: But that letter's sealed.

Johan: That letter was sealed, but I've opened it.

Karin: What do you think Anna'll say . . . ?

Johan: It was simple. A little steam from the kettle.

Karin: Have you read the letter?

Johan: No, I haven't read it.

Karin: Why haven't you read it?

Johan: I don't know. Ashamed to, perhaps.

Karin: If we read that letter, it'd be for Anna's good.

Johan: Or from jealousy. Or because we're furious that the girl is going behind our backs. Or because we don't accept young Bergman.

Karin: Naturally, Johan. It's easy to complicate one's deepest motives. You can read about that kind of fun in novels.

111

Johan: Read it! I find it difficult to make out Anna's handwriting.

Karin takes the letter to Henrik Bergman, opens it, puts on the glasses she has just taken off, unfolds the many pages, and reads in silence. She shakes her head.

Karin: Oh, just listen to this!

But Johan is not allowed to listen to anything. Mrs. Karin turns the pages, frowning and scratching her cheek.

Johan: I was given nothing to listen to.

Karin (*reads*): ". . . all long ago. When I think back, I realize how childish, immature, and spoiled I was. The long time I've spent here at the sanatorium and the proximity of contemporaries who are much sicker than I am have made me think again. And then I've said to myself . . ."

Johan (*quietly*): . . . you mustn't read any more.

Karin: . . . if *you* don't want to hear it, then I'll read it to myself.

Johan: It's not right.

Karin (*reads*): ". . . and then I've said to myself, I feel a responsibility for you, Henrik, a responsibility I thought I hadn't the energy to bear and so I tried to unburden myself of you. I was ill, too. I couldn't think clearly. It was nice just to sink into a fever and be looked after. I felt humiliated and deceived. I thought you'd lied. I was convinced I'd never be able to trust you again. Now, afterward, this all seems unreal and distant. And also, my guilt is at least as great as yours, if it can be called guilt when you're blinded and confused."

Mrs. Karin stops and puts down the crisply folded sheets of paper with the golden emblem of the sanatorium on the left-hand edge. She finds it hard to control an emotion leaping up her throat and forcing her to swallow.

Johan: . . . strange to think . . .

Karin (*reads on*): ". . . I know nothing. But if it is true that after almost two years you still look on me as you did when we were sitting on the jetty at Duvtjärn washing the blood out of that bedspread . . ."

Johan: . . . one must blame oneself . . .

Karin: ". . . it's so easy to say you love someone. I love you, dear Papa. I love you, brother dear. But you are really using a word you don't know the meaning of. So I dare not write that I love you, Henrik. I don't dare do that. But if you will take my hand and help me out of my great grief, then perhaps we can teach each other what that word entails . . ." (*Pause.*)

Johan: Now we know more than we wanted to know.

Karin: Yes, it's going to be difficult now.

Johan: We can't suppress the letter.

Karin: He shouldn't have it.

Johan: I beg of you, Karin.

Karin: For Anna's sake.

Johan: And if she finds out that we . . .

Karin: Letters get lost. It happens every day.

Johan: It mustn't happen.

Karin: That's silly, Johan.

Johan: Do as you please. But I don't want to know.

Karin: Just as I thought.

Johan: Do you really imagine we can stop . . . ?

Karin: Maybe not. (*Pause.*) But now I'm going to tell you something important. Sometimes I am *quite sure* when something is right or wrong. I am so sure, it's as if it were written down. And I am sure that it is wrong with Anna and Henrik Bergman. So I'll burn the letter to Ernst and the letter to Henrik. And I'll go to Italy with Anna and stay away the whole summer if that proves necessary. Are you listening to what I'm saying, Johan?

Johan: In this case, you're going too far.

Karin: I don't think so.

Johan: Evil breeds worse evil.

Karin: That remains to be seen.

Johan: I don't understand how you dare!

Then silence falls in the bedroom: despondency, anxiety, revulsion, anger, jealousy, grief: Anna's leaving me. She has already left me. Anna is going away and taking the light with her.

113

Mrs. Karin leafs through the many closely written pages, reading here and there, her forehead scarlet: I know that Anna is uncertain deep down. She only opposes us when she's angry or upset. I must be careful. She really wants to please her mother. Her looks can be pleading . . . tell me what to do. I know so little.

Karin (*suddenly*): Yes, well, it says here that Henrik Bergman has been ordained. (*Reads*) "I grieve that I couldn't be at your ordination, and I think about how your mother must have . . ." Oh, yes. Then he promptly disappears from town, what a . . .

She falls silent. It's painful that Johan doesn't understand. Even distances himself. It's been like that so often in their life together. She has had to carry out all the unpleasant decisions on her own.

Karin: Johan.

Johan: Yes.

Karin: Are you miserable?

Johan: I'm at a loss and miserable.

Karin: Can't we try to be nice to each other although we disagree on this matter?

Johan: But this is *vital*, Karin.

Karin: Just because of that. I don't want you to retreat. I don't mind taking the responsibility, but you mustn't retreat.

Johan: But it's *vital*.

Karin: I heard you say so.

Johan: For you and me.

Karin: For us?

Johan: If you carry out what you plan to do, then you'll harm Anna. If you harm Anna, you harm me. If you harm me, you harm yourself.

Karin: How can you be so sure that I'll harm Anna? It's horrible of you to say that.

Johan: You'll stop her from living her own life. You can only make her anxious and uncertain, but you can't change anything. You can damage but not change.

Karin: And you're sure of that?

Johan: Yes.

Karin: You know?

Johan: Sometimes, though not often, I think about the future. Both you and I know that I'll soon be leaving you. We know that, though we never talk about anything so embarrassing and unfortunate. You'll be left alone and will go on ruling your kingdom. I think you'll find yourself rather isolated. Don't make yourself lonelier than you need to.

Karin is sitting upright in her bed, not leaning back against the pillows. With a hasty movement, she takes off her glasses and puts them, not on the bedside table, but in front of her, right across the scattered sheets of paper. Her face is in the shadow, her hands on the covers. For a brief moment she is open, vulnerable. Johan tries to take her hand, but she withdraws it, though not roughly.

Karin: I don't think I can be lonelier than I already am.

Johan: I don't understand.

Karin: Ernst is moving to Christiania. For good.

Johan: Does that seem so bad?

Karin: Yes, it does.

Johan: Ernst is really the only person . . .

Karin: I don't know, I can't classify. But Ernst . . .

She gets no further, and slaps the covers with her hand, once, twice.

Johan: Is it so *bad?*

Karin: I'm not going to complain.

Johan: Our children are leaving us. That's a fact.

Karin: I'm not complaining.

Johan: But I presume it's a terrible desolation.

Karin: You use such dramatic words.

Johan: I presume it's like this — this moment had to come. We're not prepared for it. And now we're nonplussed and close to tears.

Karin: That's not true. I have given the children a free hand. I have tried to protect them, but I've never shut them in. Neither Ernst nor Anna. You can't say I've ever forced them.

Johan: Yes, yes, yes. I've sat there in my study and sometimes listened to voices and footsteps. Then I hear the hall door and I know Anna's back from school. And my heart starts beating. Will she come running through the salon, fling open the door without knocking? Will she come to me in the study? And give me a hug? And then start telling me something important at top speed?

Karin: But that's so long ago.

Johan: Yes I suppose it is. Is it?

Karin (*decisive*): There's no point in us sitting here grieving over something irretrievable. The main thing is that we're all healthy and more or less content with life. You and I are largely worn out and must have the sense to retire from the scene. (*Smiles.*) Isn't that so, my dear?

Johan: But you're about to start steering Anna's life. How does that fit in?

Karin: I can't stand aside while a misfortune is happening before my very eyes.

Johan: So you've decided.

Karin: Decided? That would mean I had once hesitated.

Johan: Good night then, Karin.

Karin: Good night.

She leans forward and kisses him on the cheek, pats his hand, then gathers up the sheets of paper and puts them back in the envelope, which is then slipped into the bigger envelope, places the latter in the drawer of the bedside table, and turns the key. After that Mrs. Karin puts out the bedside lamp and lies comfortably on her back with her hands on her chest. A few minutes later her deep breathing confirms that she has left all her troubles for the next seven hours.

Johan Åkerblom lies awake for a long time, partly because he has to empty his bladder every three hours, partly because he has a grinding pain in his left side, and partly because his knee and hip are aching quietly but persistently, presumably indicating a change in the weather. The light by his bed is out, but the streetlamp sends a pale light through the blind and throws shadows on the ceiling. I'm not crying, but I'm certainly *desolated*.

Henrik Bergman is ending Sunday evensong in the medieval church in Mittsunda. It's a quiet evening in the middle of June, the sun shining below the clouds and coloring the squat tower and the tops of the limes. A slight coolness is rising off the brilliant smooth surface of the little lake. The church porch has recently been tarred and gives off an astringent smell. The paths are raked, graves tended, silence. The cuckoo calls from various directions.

Henrik takes off his cassock, hangs it up in the yellow varnished cupboard in the sacristy, and sits down at the table where the church-warden has just counted the evening collection. That is soon done and soon recorded. "I'll stay for a while," says Henrik. "Don't forget to lock up," says the churchwarden. "I'll leave the key in the usual place. Good night, Pastor." And so Henrik is alone.

Later on, he is standing down by the water's edge, staring out over the pale stillness. Dusk is light and transparent. No one speaks, no one replies, no one prays, and no one is listening. Henrik is alone.

Later still, he is sitting in the guest room at the parish priest's in Mittsunda. The pastor's wife has put out milk and hard crispbread sandwiches for him. Henrik drinks and munches. Then he gets up and lights the paraffin lamp, stands there, and listens to his loneliness, a wound.

He can hear subdued talk and laughter from the dining room. The parish priest has some guests to supper.

Sleeplessness. Getting up at dawn, shaving, washing, dressing, and going out. Drizzle and a mild wind. Strong scents from the garden. The elms rustle. Henrik stands still. It hurts. He walks a few steps. That hurts almost as much. It's not possible to hurt so much. It's nothing physical. Wordless. Shut in. Shut out.

Suddenly he hears footsteps on the gravel path. Henrik turns around. A man is coming toward him, broad forehead, brushed-back hair, high cheekbones, snub nose, wide mouth, strong chin, broad shoulders, lively, energetic movements, walking lightly, holding his hand out to Henrik, looking at him with glowing eyes. Henrik knows him at once. It is Nathan Söderblom, professor and author of a theo-logical encyclopedia, but more than that: admired, almost worshiped by his students, in all likelihood an archbishop within the near future, international capacity, a deadly threat to the mechanisms of academic intrigues. Musician. He is wearing baggy trousers, his waistcoat un-buttoned, no collar to his shirt, a worn cardigan.

Nathan Söderblom: Sleepless?

Henrik: Good morning, Professor. Yes, I'm sleepless.

Nathan Söderblom: The light nights. Or your soul?

Henrik: My soul, more likely.

Nathan Söderblom: I listened to your discourse yesterday evening.

Henrik: Were you in church? I didn't see . . .

Nathan Söderblom: No, you didn't see me, but I saw you. I was sitting with the organist, you see. We'd been playing Bach preludes for a few hours, working the bellows and playing in turns. Old man Morén is one of our great musicians. Did you know that? Well, then I thought I might as well stay and listen to you.

Henrik: Just as well I didn't know.

Nathan Söderblom: Maybe so, yes.

The professor stops and neatly fills his pipe. Despite the drizzle, it seems easy to light. His hands are broad, with protruding veins. His pipe belches smoke and squeaks.

Henrik: I've had the good fortune to have been given a temporary position over the summer. Naturally I'm not at all mature enough for the task, but the parish priest is friendly and doesn't complain. I don't think my discourse yesterday evening was anything special. I keep rewriting and *re*writing, I'm so desperately dissatisfied with my achievements. Baptisms and funerals I find easier. Then I don't have to prepare. Then I see the people right up close to me. Then the words come by themselves. I'm sorry I'm talking so much.

Nathan Söderblom: Just keep on talking.

But no more comes. Henrik realizes he has said too much and is embarrassed. The two men walk slowly up to the gate and the narrow road to the church and churchyard. The professor is smoking his pipe. The mosquitoes dance.

Nathan Söderblom: I'm staying temporarily in the annex over there. The parish priest is an old student friend of mine and offered me a refuge. I must finish my book. There's always so much hullabaloo going on in Upsala.

Henrik: What are you writing?

Nathan Söderblom: Well, that's not easy to say. I'm writing about Mozart evincing God. That artists demonstrate God's presence. Roughly that.

Henrik: Is that true?

Nathan Söderblom: You certainly may not ask me that.

Henrik: For me it's absence, silence. I speak, and God says nothing.

Nathan Söderblom: That's unimportant.

Henrik: Is it unimportant?

Nathan Söderblom: You're here on earth to serve people, not God. If you decide to forget all that about God's presence and God's absence and direct all your strength toward people, then your deeds will be God's deeds. Don't demean yourself by constantly flirting with your faith and your doubts. You can't *demand* clarity, security, insight. Try to understand that God is part of his creation, just as Bach lives in his B-minor mass. You're interpreting a composition. Sometimes it's puzzling, but that's unavoidable. When you let the music sound — then you evince Bach. Read the notes! And play them as best you can. But don't doubt the existence of Bach and the Creator.

The pipe has gone out, and the professor stops. He stands still to relight it once, several times, and at last succeeds. Henrik is trembling, but not from the morning chill or the gentle rain.

Nathan Söderblom: On the other hand, you cannot demand perfection. There's no point in raging over the cruelty of Creation. It's pointless to demand responsibility. Your task is to be concrete. Don't put God on trial. A great many of the best minds in the world have failed on that score. I think it's really beginning to rain now.

They turn off toward the church and go in through the porch. Henrik leans against the rough wall.

Henrik: I'm imprisoned. And I'm frightened it's a life sentence, although no one has said anything.

Nathan Söderblom: That's also unimportant.

Henrik: Unimportant?

Nathan Söderblom: Yes, my son. It's unimportant. I think you're capable of great devotion. I can see that you bear within you a profound desire to sacrifice yourself, but you don't know how. Your sense of being worthless stands in the way. You are your own worst enemy and jailer. Get up out of your prison. To your surprise, you will find that no one will stop you. Don't be afraid. The reality outside your cell is never as terrible as your terror inside your imprisoning darkroom.

Henrik (*hardly audible*): How can I do that?

119

Nathan Söderblom: Next week I have to go to London to a conference. When I get back at the end of June, you must get in touch with me. Maybe I am mistaken, but if things are as I think, there's a faint sign of a quick solution to your difficulty.

Henrik: Bless me!

Nathan Söderblom: No. Not like that. Get up!

Henrik (*grasping his hand and kissing it*): Bless me!

Nathan Söderblom: Get up. You've taken the first step toward freedom. Stay here for a while after I've gone. Weep if you feel like it. I'm leaving you now.

Henrik: Professor, you don't even know what my name is or who I am.

Nathan Söderblom (*at a distance, turning around*): I know your name. God be with you.

Karin Åkerblom makes up her mind, carries out her plans, and takes responsibility for her actions. Despite a grinding sense of approaching doom, at the end of May she sets off for Switzerland and fetches her daughter for a trip to Florence, Venice, and Rome. In Amalfi, they are to rest for a few weeks with their friends the Egermans. Then it's time to return to the family and the summer residence.

Mrs. Karin finds Anna well, and round cheeked, but quiet, assuring her with a polite smile that she is pleased to see her mother, that she has recovered, and that summer will soon be here. She also energetically maintains that she is pleased about the trip to Italy. She asks with interest after the family, and says she is looking forward to seeing her brother Ernst again. Yet despite this amiable young woman's amiable efforts to please her mother, one can sense an underlying stillness and an inaccessible melancholy.

One Thursday in the first week of June, mother and daughter are standing in the ancient enclosed courtyard of the Museo Nazionale. Mrs. Karin has her glasses on her nose and is lecturing from a thick little book. Anna is propped up against the well, listening politely. They are sensibly and elegantly dressed in lightweight, tailored summer suits, Karin in a hat, Anna with light headgear of thin lace.

Karin (*reads aloud*): "The trend of realism in the fifteenth century brought with it a newly awakened study of nature. Interest in man and tangible reality predominated in sculpture. The true creator of Renaissance sculpture was Donatello, the greatest artist of the century, whose profound study of Antiquity inspired his inherent talent for original creation."

The white light draws sharp contours across the stone flags of the courtyard. Tourists move around in leisurely groups, and a fat cat with a malicious expression watches little birds bathing in a small puddle left from the night's rain.

Karin: Are you tired?

Anna: No, no. A little perhaps.

Karin: We didn't get much sleep. Thunder and rain almost all night.

Anna: It was the subject of conversation at breakfast.

Karin: You should ask to have your breakfast taken up to your room, as I do. It's much nicer.

Anna: I like the chatter in the breakfast room. Mr. Sellmér is particularly attentive.

Karin: Shall we go back for lunch, or shall we eat out? I know an excellent place quite near here.

Anna: You decide, Mama.

Karin: Then I suggest we eat at the hotel, so we can have a long siesta afterward.

The hotel's justifiably famous view is over Ponte Vecchio and the river. Inside, it is all English courtesy, shadowy public rooms with dusky red walls, expensive, somewhat faded tapestries and upholstery, huge paintings in shimmering gold frames, wide marble staircases, thick carpets muffling footsteps, and dazzlingly polished brass. The building surrounds an inner courtyard with lush greenery, two fountains, and afternoon music.

Karin Åkerblom and her daughter have rooms on the third floor with a connecting door between them, the windows facing the river. The ceilings are high, the lintels over the doors ornamental, and the beds spacious. Their common bathroom has recently been installed. All the pipes are outside the walls and play their own tunes. There is good reason to listen to the conversation at lunch, which runs like this:

Karin: By the way, did you know that Count Snoilsky used to stay at this hotel? My mother knew him and met him several times. I mean, she was really better acquainted with Countess Piper, Ebba Piper. It was a notorious scandal. Almost thirty years ago. And now Count Snoilsky is almost forgotten — a fine man, but sad.

(*Anna smiles politely, but doesn't answer.*)

Karin: I had a letter from your brother Oscar. Did I tell you that this morning? Goodness. Well, so like him, but so thoughtful, the nicest of you all. Well, he says everything's fine at Trädgårdsgatan and he and Papa even went for a little walk! It's nice of Oscar to take care of Papa when we're away. Otherwise he'd probably be so lonely. Though Papa does say that he likes being on his own, and Einar Hedin goes to play chess with him on Friday evenings, but now that Ernst is in Christiania — I don't know. Papa writes to say he is looking forward to us coming home, and of course he's particularly looking forward to seeing you, but he never complains.

(*Anna doesn't answer, empties her glass of wine.*)

Karin: . . . I mean, Papa also thought this trip of ours was a good thing. We ought to try telephoning home someday. Just think how surprised they would be, though you never know, they might be terrified something had happened to us.

(*Anna doesn't reply, is served.*)

Karin: The main thing is that you're better. I say that to myself every day.

Anna: I wonder why we've heard nothing from Ernst.

Karin: Ernst! You know where he is, don't you?

Anna: I wrote to him seven weeks ago.

Karin: He knows you'll soon be home.

Anna: Yes.

Karin: You mustn't worry.

Anna (*impatiently*): I'm not worrying.

Karin: He knows Papa and I write to each other nearly every day.

Anna (*impatiently*): That has nothing to do with it, has it?

Karin: What do you mean? No, of course not.

Anna: I want to go home.

Karin: Of course, my heart. We're on our way.

Anna: Can't we go home tomorrow? Straight home?

Karin: But our plans are all set!

Anna: Can't one ever change things?

Karin: What do you think the Egermans would say?

Anna: I don't care what the Egermans say. They're friends of yours, not mine.

Karin: Elna's actually a childhood friend of yours, Anna.

Anna: Elna doesn't interest me. Damn Elna!

Karin: Sometimes you behave like an unruly child.

Anna: I *am* an unruly child.

Karin: Anyhow, we can't forsake the Egermans in Amalfi. They'd be sad and offended.

Anna: You go to Amalfi, Mama, and I'll go home.

Karin: This is silly, Anna. We'll do what we agreed to do. And that's that.

Anna: What *you've* agreed. Not me.

Karin: It's cold and wet at home. The doctor also thought we ought to stay where it's warm for a little transitional period. We'll be home by midsummer.

Mrs. Karin has an inimitable way of ending a conversation. She smiles encouragingly and lightly strikes her little beringed hand on the tablecloth, as if she were wielding a chairman's hammer, rising to her feet at the same time. Two servants are there at once, pulling back their chairs. Anna has no real chance of remonstrating, of staying there, raising her voice, or buying her own train ticket.

Siesta: drawn venetian blinds, semidarkness in both rooms, the door barely ajar. From the town they can hear bells ringing, newspaper vendors in the street below, trams clanging. The two women are resting on their beds in dressing gowns and bedsocks, their hair down. The pleasant sleep that would surely come after the night's disturbing thunder simply does not materialize. Silence. Distance. Perhaps sorrow. Almost certainly sorrow.

Then, surprisingly, there is a knock on the door of Mrs. Karin's room. Then another. Then a third, this time resolute. Karin asks her daughter to find out what it's about, and Anna wraps her dressing

123

gown tightly around her, tucks her hair behind her ears, and patters out to the little hallway. Astonishingly, one of the hotel's managers is standing outside the door in his impeccable tails and waxed mustache. He hands over a telegram in a blue envelope. When Anna indicates with a helpless gesture that she has no change for a tip handy, the man raises his hand in a dismissive gesture, bows gravely, and hurries away toward the corridor. Anna closes the door and stands there with the envelope in her hand, hesitant and ill at ease. Karin asks what it is, and Anna says it's a telegram. "Bring it here, then," says Karin impatiently.

Anna closes the door to the hall and goes in to Karin, who has now sat up in bed, switched on the bedside light, and stretched out for her glasses. Anna hands her the sealed envelope. She slits it open and unfolds the handwritten message. She reads it and draws a deep breath, then hands the paper to Anna. There are only a few words on it.

PAPA DIED LAST NIGHT.
OSCAR.

It is night in this strange hotel and in this strange city. Mrs. Karin and Anna have been very busy all afternoon, packing, canceling bookings, talking to Mrs. Egerman in Amalfi. An almost inaudible conversation with Gustav and Oscar in Upsala, new reservations on the Northern Express from Milan. (In those days, the journey took almost two days.) No time for thoughts, afterthoughts, pain, tears.

When evening comes with its harsh, bright yellow light between the slats of the blinds, the clang of bells from the nearby Maria Church, and distant music — when evening comes, Mrs. Karin suddenly turns very pale. She is standing by the dinner table that has been ordered in their rooms. They haven't eaten much. She pours herself a glass of wine, her hand trembling. She is pale, with dark shadows under her eyes. Anna is leaning over her suitcase.

Anna: We must make sure we've not forgotten anything. Everything's packed except our toiletries and traveling clothes. We've canceled our rooms in Venice and Rome, and settled things with Mrs. Egerman, thank goodness. The porter assures me we have first-class seats on the Northern Express tomorrow afternoon from Milan — then we'll be home by the evening the day after tomorrow. We've also spoken to Oscar and Gustav. Mama, I don't think we've forgotten anything, do you?

Mrs. Karin has raised the glass of wine to her lips, but doesn't drink it. The pain is so unexpected and so violent that she has to stay still, quite still, to survive the next second and the next and the next.

Anna (*gently*): What is it, Mama?

Her mother turns her head toward her daughter and looks questioningly at her, like a child.

Karin: I don't understand. (*Shakes her head.*) Don't understand.

Anna: Mama dear, come over here, and we'll sit down. I'll draw the curtains, shall I? Does the sunlight bother you? It'll soon be gone, anyway. Would you like some more wine? It'll do you good, Mama. Let's sit quite still here, you and I together.

Anna takes her mother's hand and holds it tightly. The sharp pattern of sunlight on the wall's gold-framed pictures and the red wallpaper slowly fades. The clang of bells ceases; the day becomes quiet. All they can hear now is the waltz from the *Merry Widow* played by the hotel orchestra far down inside the great house. *Lippen schweigen, 's flüstern Geigen, hab mich lieb! All die Schritte sagen, Bitte, hab mich lieb!* Mrs. Karin takes a drink of her wine, leans back against the sofa cushions, and closes her eyes.

Karin: The worst of it is that I left him alone. He was alone, Anna. And it was at night.

Anna (*pleading*): Mama!

Karin: He was alone, and I wasn't there. He was in pain and got out of bed. Then he sat down at his desk and switched on the desk lamp. He'd taken out paper and pen; then he fell to one side and down to the floor.

Anna: Mama, don't think about it.

Karin: I'll tell you something strange, Anna. When I decided I was going, when everything had been arranged, when I had said goodbye to Papa and was going out through the front door, I suddenly thought, quite inexplicably: *Don't do it!*

Anna: Don't do what?

Karin: Don't do it. Don't go. Stay at home. Cancel it all. For a brief moment, I was overcome with anguish. How strange, Anna.

Anna: Yes, that was strange.

Karin: I had to sit down. I broke out in a cold sweat. Then I got cross with myself. I've never given in to whims and fancies of that kind. Why should I give in this time? There was no reason to at all.

Anna: Poor Mama.

Karin: Exactly. Poor Mama. I make decisions and carry them out. It's been like that all my life. I never change my mind.

Anna: I know.

Karin: Most people don't like making decisions. So I have to.

Anna: You shouldn't blame yourself, Mama.

Karin: No, that's pointless. (*Pause.*) I've made a lot of wrong and stupid decisions, but I wouldn't say I've ever had any regrets. But this time . . . (*Draws breath.*) Oh, God!

For a short while she holds her hand over her eyes, but then at once takes it down, as if she thought the gesture was exaggerated or perhaps melodramatic, and takes another sip of wine.

Anna (*holds Karin's hand*): Mama.

Karin: When your father asked me if I wanted to marry him, although he was more than twice my age and had three sons, I decided without even thinking about it. Mother warned me, and Father was very upset. I didn't love him. I wasn't even in love with him, I knew that. But I liked him. I was sorry for him. He was so terribly lonely with his wretched, lazy housekeeper who cheated him out of money and didn't look after the home properly, and then those three badly-brought-up, lost boys. I was also a little lonely, and so I thought we'd be sure to alleviate each other's loneliness.

Anna: Surely, that wasn't a wrong thought.

Karin: Yes, Anna. It was wrong. *One* loneliness is all right. Two are unendurable. But in the end you must never probe it too deeply. Then you and Ernst came along. That saved me — was my salvation.

Mrs. Karin smiles apologetically. She hears herself using words she has never used before. She sees herself making gestures she has never made before. She struggles with a weighty, swelling grief, a grief she has never before experienced. She empties her glass.

Karin: Would you give me a little more wine, please? Aren't you going to have any yourself?

Anna: I have some, thank you.

Karin: That's how we came out of our loneliness, Johan and I. I don't know, for that matter. Perhaps those are just things you say. But you and Ernst became a great joy, something we had in common. We had to busy ourselves with the two of you, and every little thing became important.

Anna: And so Ernst became mother's boy, and Anna became daddy's girl.

Karin: I don't know. Is that what happened?

Anna: But Mama!

Karin: Yes, yes, perhaps you're right.

She is sitting turned away, the wound bleeding quietly, scarcely hurting anymore. It grows darker. The streetlamps are turned on. Through the stillness and the faint rumble from the city they can hear the murmur of the river.

Anna (*gently*): Shall we go to bed now, Mama? We've got to get up early.

Karin (*absently*): Yes, perhaps we should.

She leans her forehead against Anna's shoulder, then bends right down and rests her head on Anna's lap, a puzzling movement, almost prohibited. Anna draws her mother's hands to her and holds them against her breast. She doesn't know what to do next. Then she is seized with a sudden impulse and takes her mother in her arms and holds her tight. A few long, ragged sobs come from Karin, very unfamiliar and frightening.

Suddenly she frees herself from Anna's embrace, almost brutally. She sits straight up, runs both hands over her face, and touches her hair, twice, running the palm of her hand over her forehead, then leaning to one side and switching on the electric lamp by the sofa. She looks at her daughter, coolly, searchingly.

Anna (*terrified*): What is it, Mama?

Karin: There's something you should know.

Anna: To do with me?

Karin: Most certainly to do with you.

Anna: It can wait, can't it?

Karin: I don't think so.

Anna: Then you'd better tell me what it is that's so important.

Karin: It's about Henrik Bergman.

Anna (*suddenly on her guard*): Yes. And?

Karin: You write to him?

Anna: That's true. I have written to him. I sent the letter to Ernst because I didn't know Henrik's address. I've never had an answer, for that matter. The letter probably went astray.

Karin: It didn't go astray.

Anna: I don't understand.

Karin: I must tell you this. I took the letter, read it, and later burned it.

Anna: No.

Karin: I must tell you, because your father warned me. He said it was not right. He said we had no right to interfere. That it would do harm. He warned me.

Anna: Mama!

Karin: I've no excuse. I thought I was doing this for your own good. Johan warned me.

Anna: I don't want to hear any more.

Karin (*not hearing*): Now that Johan's gone, I realize I must tell you what happened. I can't even ask your forgiveness, because I know you'll never forgive me.

Anna: I don't think I will.

Karin: Well, now you know, anyhow.

Anna: As soon as we get home, I'll go and find Henrik and tell him everything.

Karin: There's only one thing I beg of you. Don't tell him I burned the letter.

Anna: Why not?

Karin: If you marry Henrik. Don't you understand? If you tell him, his hatred will be unbearable. We have to live with each other.

Anna: Why?

Anna looks thoughtfully at her mother. An anger she has never felt before is rising inside her, producing a pleasant sensation.

Karin: Now you know.

Anna: Yes. Now I know. (*Pause, change of tone.*) Shall we go to bed? We may need some sleep, and it'll be a long day tomorrow.

She quickly gets up from the sofa and goes toward the door, turns, and politely says good night.

At this time of year (in this case, a July day in 1912), the university town of Upsala can appear so still that it seems to be unreal or perhaps a dream. If it weren't for the chatter of small birds in the dark, leafy trees, the silence would certainly be frightening. The reminder from the cathedral clock of time racing toward annihilation makes the stillness even more immense. The Flustret is closed, and the orchestras have removed themselves and their medleys from the Pearl Fishers and La Belle Hélène to some health resort or spa. In the homes of the wealthy, sheets hang over the windows as if there were corpses indoors, and the smell of mothballs trickles sorrowfully along the hot pavements. The ghost of Gustavianum's anatomical theater has withdrawn into the wall behind the picture by Olof Rudbeckius. The brothel by the Svartbäcken has closed, its industrious occupants gone off to Gothenburg, where the fleet of the British Royal Navy is in port. In the town's ancient theater, dust swirls in the patches of sun that have penetrated the badly fitting stage window-hatches and drawn magical patterns on the sloping floor of the unscrubbed boards of the stage.

Yes, empty, silent, unreal, dreamlike, slightly scary if you happen to be so inclined. The sun is high in a colorless sky; there is no wind, but only a whiff of dried tears, soured grief, suppressed pain, a faint though perfectly perceptible smell, harsh and musty.

There are people who say the world will come to an end with a bang, a crash, a crack. Personally I am convinced that the world will stop, fall silent, be still, fade, languish away in an endless cosmic mist. This July day in this little university town may well be the beginning of such an extremely undramatic end.

The scene is Henrik Bergman's room, at first empty of people and movement. Then the door jerks open, and Henrik comes in backward maneuvering his metal-edged trunk through the narrow door. Everything has already been taken out and flung around on tables, chairs, and floor. He starts packing unsystematically and listlessly and finally sits down on the floor, lights his pipe, and props his elbows on his knees. He sits there, and in that position, for quite a long time.

Suddenly Anna is there in the doorway, behind her the dirty, narrow, sunlit window facing the street. She is in mourning, her hair up under the sable beret, the mourning veil making her face pale and obscuring her eyes.

Henrik (*not moving*): I was almost frightened.

Anna (*not moving*): Were you frightened?

Henrik: I was sitting here thinking about you.

Anna: And then I was suddenly there.

Henrik: It's like in my dream.

Anna: I've something for you.

Now she is in the room. She falls to her knees by his side, searching in her little silky black bag.

Henrik: You're different.

Anna (*looks at him*): So are you.

Henrik: You're more beautiful.

Anna: You look sad.

Henrik: Probably because I am.

Anna: Sad just now, or all the time?

Henrik: I've missed you.

He falls silent and swallows, takes off his glasses and flings them on a pile of books, then looks over at the window.

Anna: But I'm here now, Henrik.

Henrik: Is it true?

Anna: Yes, it's true. I'm here.

Henrik: This is like in my dream. First you come and say something I don't understand. Then you've suddenly disappeared.

Anna: I'm not going to disappear.

She smiles and rummages in her bag, finds a small object wrapped in tissue paper, puts it into his hand, lifts the veil off her

130

face, and pulls off her hat. It lands on the floor. A strand of hair falls over her forehead.

Henrik: Anna?

Anna: Look and see what it is. I bought it the day we left Florence. It's nothing special, and certainly not genuine.

He unwraps the paper. It's a small statuette in darkened wood of the Annunciation of the Virgin Mary. Henrik lets it lie in his open hand.

Henrik: It's Mary without the child. It's the Annunciation.

Anna (*looks at him*): Yes.

Henrik: It's warm. It's warming my hand. How strange. Feel.

Anna takes off her glove, and Henrik puts the figure into her open hand. She shakes her head and smiles.

Anna: No, I can't feel it warming.

She puts the figure on the pile of books beside Henrik's glasses, then picks up her glove.

Henrik: Your father died?

Anna: Yes. The funeral's the day after tomorrow.

Henrik: Is it hard?

Anna: I lived in his love, if you see what I mean. I never thought about it, except when it sometimes bothered me. Now I'm miserable because I was so childish and ungrateful.

Henrik: What have you done with Ernst?

Anna: He's waiting down in the courtyard.

Henrik: Aren't you going to ask him up?

Anna: No, no. Later. I didn't dare come here alone. It was sheer speculation. I knew you'd moved out of town. And yet I couldn't help it. So I said to Ernst: Come on, let's leave this house of mourning and go for a walk; we could go down Ågatan; maybe we'll bump into Henrik. It was like a joke. We laughed. When we came past your house, Ernst said: Go in and see if he's at home; bet you five kronor he is. You nearly always win our bets, I said. So I went in. There you were, and Ernst has won five kronor. Incidentally, I know you never got my letter.

She gets up quickly and goes over to the open window, pushes aside the curtain, and calls out to Ernst in a low voice. He is sitting on a pile of planks, smoking a cigar, bareheaded and in somber clothes, with a white necktie and a mourning armband. He at once turns to look up at his sister and smiles.

Ernst: I'm fine where I am. Just tell me when you feel like company.

Anna: I owe you five kronor.

Ernst doesn't reply but makes a little gesture with his cigar. Anna feels she is bursting with joy all over, in her breast, head, legs, and loins. She turns back to Henrik, who is still sitting on the floor. Maybe he thinks the dream will dissolve if he makes the slightest move. Anna sits down on a rickety wooden chair with a broken back. They are silent and slightly at a loss.

Henrik: You wrote me?

Anna: Yes, it was a rather urgent letter. But it went astray.

Henrik: How do you know it went astray?

Anna: I just know it did.

Henrik: And what did you say in it?

Anna: That's unimportant. It's unimportant *now*.

Henrik: I've got a temporary position in a small parish not all that far from here. They've just extended it by six months. That's why I'm packing. Professor Söderblom, you know who I mean?

Anna: Yes, of course I do.

Henrik: Professor Söderblom has told me to apply for an appointment in Forsboda parish, up in Gästrikland. I've been told it's a difficult parish. Mama was upset, of course. No doubt she'd hoped for something more genteel.

Anna: And now you're not lonely anymore?

Henrik: No, no. I can change, can't I?

Anna (*practical tone of voice*): Of course, we'll go there and see for ourselves.

Henrik: Of course if I'd known . . .

Anna (*soberly*): Henrik, don't be stupid. If you've promised, then you've promised. You can't change things like that.

Henrik: The parish priest is said to be old and ailing.

Anna: We'll take a look at him, too.

Henrik: You realize the stipend is poor.

Anna: We won't bother about that. (*Leans forward.*) And, Henrik! You'll make a *brilliant match* if you marry me. I'll inherit lots of money. (*Whispers.*) A fearful amount of money. What do you say to that?

Henrik: I have no intention of letting you support me.

Anna: Just listen to me, Henrik! (*Practical and decisive.*) First of all, we must get engaged, as soon as the funeral is over. We'll order the rings this afternoon so that we have them on Saturday at the latest. Then we'll get engaged and invite Ernst to an engagement party here in your room, but we won't tell anyone. Next week we'll go and see your mother. I want to get to know her as soon as possible. You write to the parish priest and tell him you and your wife-to-be will be coming to Forsboda at the end of the week to inspect the parsonage, church, and the parish priest himself. Then we'll get married in September, or at the very latest at the beginning of October — and it's to be a *grand wedding*, Henrik. What are you looking at?

Henrik: I'm looking at you.

Anna: We've waited long enough. Mama always says, "You have to make decisions and take the responsibility."

She falls to her knees, takes Henrik's head between her hands, and kisses him on the mouth. He at once loses his balance and falls over on the floor, pulling her with him in the fall.

Henrik: One mustn't forget the kisses.

Anna: No, kisses are important.

And so, ardently and thirstily, they kiss each other. Anna sits up, her black mourning clothes now rather dusty.

Henrik: Your clothes are dusty.

Anna: Yes, goodness, what on earth do I look like! (*Laughs.*) Now let's just tidy up and then we'll go down to Ernst and invite him to our engagement on Saturday.

Henrik: What do you think your mother will say?

Anna: After Florence, what my mother says or thinks is of no importance whatsoever.

Henrik: Has something happened?

Anna: You could say that.

Henrik: And I'm not allowed to know?

Anna: Perhaps. Perhaps one night when we're lying close together in our bed in Forsboda parsonage and the winter storms are raging outside. Then perhaps I'll tell you what happened. But only perhaps.

Henrik: Is it anything to do with the letter?

Anna: Henrik! I think lovers always assure each other they will be honest through and through, and they will never have any secrets between them. That's stupid. I'll never ask you to tell me your secrets.

Henrik: But the truth?

Anna: The truth is different.

Henrik: We'll be truthful. Faithful to the truth.

Anna (*with sudden gravity*): We'll *try* to be truthful.

Henrik: We'll have to practice.

Anna (*smiles*): We'll have to practice. What did you think of my meatballs? Weren't they . . . ?

Henrik: Disgusting!

Anna: You see! (*Smiles.*) And so on. Will you help dust me off?

So they help each other, but also have to hug and kiss, hot cheeks and hands. In the end, they manage to get out into the corridor and down the narrow wooden stairs. Ernst gets up from the heap of planks and gestures with astonishment when he catches sight of the intertwined couple. The friends approach slowly, stop a short distance away, and look at each other with joyful tenderness.

Ernst (*to Henrik*): You look completely improbable.

Henrik: I *am* improbable.

Ernst: And you, little sis. Your lips are so red.

Anna: Yes, they are.

Ernst: A moment ago you were pale. As a whitefish.

Anna: I have proposed, and Henrik says he will have me. Can you imagine how simple things can sometimes be?

Ernst goes up to Henrik and embraces him, takes a step back, looks at him, and embraces him again, striking him hard on the back. Then he kisses Anna on the cheeks, eyelids, and finally on her mouth.

Ernst: You are and always will be the darlings of my heart.

Then off they go to the goldsmith's in St. Larsgatan.

This account turns arbitrary, main issues into subsidiary issues and vice versa. Sometimes it indulges in huge digressions in the tradition of oral storytelling. Sometimes it attaches great importance to a few lines in a letter. Suddenly it wishes to fantasize over fragments that appear out of the dim waters of time. Unreliability on facts, dates, names, and situations is total. That is intentional and logical. The search takes obscure routes. This is neither an open nor a concealed trial of people reduced to silence. Their life in this particular story is illusory, perhaps a semblance of life, but nevertheless more distinct than their actual lives. On the other hand, this story can never describe their innermost truths. It has only its own momentary truth. The desire to continue writing it, the friendly day-to-day insistent desire, is the only tenable motivation of the enterprise. The game itself is the driving force of the game. It is like in childhood — opening the white-painted doors of the toy cupboard and giving free rein to the inherent secrets of the contents. It could hardly be simpler.

Hence, the story takes a long stride across the moment when Anna holds up her hand with its shining engagement ring to Mrs. Karin's tired eyes. She almost certainly says very little: "I know, I know. I hope you can see clearly. There must be peace now. Henrik must know he is welcome in the family."

Nor does the story mention how the bomb exploded the evening after the funeral, when the entire family was gathered in Mammchen's salon to discuss immediate practical problems.

Nor is it related here how Oscar, later that same evening, went to bed with his cancer-ridden, fading Svea. Holes appeared in her brimming reservoir of malice, and she trickled malignancies onto priests in general and Henrik Bergman in particular. In the end, Oscar spoke and said fairly authoritatively: "Svea, shut up. For God's sake, the risk is he may become a relative of ours!"

Mrs. Karin has summoned her family to a meeting in the dining room at Trädgårdsgatan. It is a few days after the funeral, and the July sun is blazing down on the drawn blinds. The huge table with its lion feet has been robbed of its oilcloth and glows black, all in black, black on black against light wallpapers and colorful, shimmering paintings. Mrs. Karin has placed herself at the head of the table by the window, Oscar and Svea on her left, Gustav and Martha on her right. Carl is sweating with abstinence and boredom on Svea's right. The girls are curled up on the straight-backed sofa by the wall, and, finally, Ernst, Anna, and Henrik are sitting opposite Mrs. Karin.

Karin: So I have asked you all to come here to discuss some issues. Before that, I wish to bid Henrik a warm welcome into our family. I now wish all conflicts and bitterness to be forgotten. We must draw a line through the past. If we make an honest effort, both reconciliation and friendship ought to be possible.

Mrs. Karin smiles at Henrik and Anna. The rest of the family do the same, a rather varied collection of smiles. A fly buzzes against the windowpane. Mrs. Karin twists the diamond ring, which is, as always, in its place between the heavy gold engagement and wedding rings.

Karin: We have been to see Advocate Elgérus and gone through your father's last will and testament. If I have construed things correctly, every one of you without exception (*glance at Carl*) has accepted the stated dispositions and found them dictated with care and consideration. I am grateful for our unity. During Johan's lifetime, he and I occasionally discussed what should happen to this building should Johan go before I did. He said that his definite wish was that *I alone* should be the owner and the other members of the family should be compensated with shares and capital. I dismissed the thought, did not wish to talk about it, but when the subject came up after his death, I felt I did not wish to keep it. Under no circumstances. So I asked Advocate Elgérus to investigate its sale. He told me yesterday afternoon that he had received an extremely generous offer from the School of Domestic Science on the other side of the street. The college has been overcrowded for a long time and is prepared to negotiate immediately. I said that I am in agreement with this proposal, but naturally I first have to discuss the matter with my sons, who live in three of the apartments. The college has offered to find equivalent apartments. As for me, I said that I'd be remaining here. But I intend to halve this apartment. I will have a wall built down the middle of the dining room and keep four rooms and the kitchen. I told Siri I will not be needing her after the first of October. Naturally, she was upset, since she has been with us for nearly twenty years, but she will be given a good parting gratuity and will move to her sister's in Småland. Does anyone have any questions?

Henrik looks at his new relatives, closed faces, uncertain glances, compressed lips. No, not Anna and Ernst; they look as if all this has nothing to do with them. Nor has it. The tension soon becomes thick and viscous. Carl has closed his eyes, probably pretending to be somewhere else. Oscar is smiling politely and inscrutably. Gustav is playing with the watch chain across his well-rounded waistcoat, gazing out the window and pursing his lips. Martha clinks her bracelets and puts her hand to her hair. Svea's head has begun to shake on its sinewy neck. Her forehead is red, and small beads of perspiration have broken out on her hairy upper lip.

Svea: As usual, no one dares say anything when Karin presents something to us as a fait accompli.

Oscar: Svea, my dear!

Svea: So I suppose I shall have to say what everyone else is thinking.

Gustav: I really must protest. Svea does not represent the family's views. As far as I know, she represents no one but herself.

Svea: How strange. Gustav, didn't you say only yesterday that Mammchen was highly dangerous? Do you deny it, Gustav?

Gustav: That's a lie, Svea, and you know it. Your hatred of our mother really has no bounds.

Svea: Since I am shortly to die, I am clearly the only member of the family who dares tell the truth.

Oscar (*patiently*): Svea, dear.

Svea: Svea dear, Svea dear. Is that all you have to say?

Carl (*suddenly*): Shut up, Svea. Before you wither with malice. No one believes you have cancer anymore. Naturally it couldn't survive in a body so poisoned by malice. Otherwise, let me say that Mammchen's decision has been a bit of a surprise. When does the boss reckon we'll be thrown out?

Gustav: I think Mama Karin, with her somewhat precipitate chess moves, wishes to indicate to us children that she has tolerated us for almost twenty years and is now heartily weary of both us and our families. We can't blame her for that.

Martha: And we who like our apartment so much, where are we supposed to go?

Gustav: Don't be silly, Martha! We're not exactly going to be out on the street.

Oscar: I personally have no objections. The whole building belongs to Mama Karin. That's stated, clearly and simply, without a shadow of doubt. We're going to be generously compensated. As far as I can see, Mama can do whatever she likes with the place. Besides, have *we* ever taken *her* into consideration?

Svea: But crawled and smiled and agreed with everything . . . that's what you have done! And scorned and mocked her behind her back! Gustav Åkerblom, Carl Åkerblom, Oscar Åkerblom. The Three Musketeers.

Ernst: If this shit is going to continue, I'm leaving. Perhaps we should give a thought to the fact that Henrik Bergman is with us for the first time. For his and for Anna's sake, let's try to curb our tongues. (*To Henrik, smiling.*) Don't worry, it can be worse. Sometimes we're actually really quite human.

Carl: You could say that Papa's death has pulled the cork out of the bottle.

Gustav: A metaphor worthy of my brother Carl.

Carl: You ought to know, Henrik, that my brother Gustav is the spiritual head of the family. If you ask for a piece of advice from him, he will give you three. If you don't follow his advice, you'll get hell for that later on in a sophisticated academic way. The professor is on the Professorship Commission, so he knows the way things work. I warn you in all friendliness, Henrik. Watch out for Mrs. Martha, too. She's far too friendly to handsome youths.

Martha (*lashing out at him*): Carl, you're impossible!

Carl (*sweats*): And Martha will get a big wet kiss from me when this wake is over.

Oscar: I consider Mama's decision judicious. We have lived together in a combination of deceptive security, obligation, and habit. It's been like stagnant water. Our relationships have moldered without us doing anything about them. It'll be good for us to split up the family.

Svea: And what about the summer place?

Oscar: The summer place has always belonged to Mammchen.

Svea: Then we'll be homeless in the summer as well?

Oscar: Calm down, Svea. You've always disliked staying at our summer place, and gone on about spas and trips to Paris. (*Laughs harshly.*) Come to think of it, I don't really know how we've managed to endure one another.

Anna: Why don't you say anything, Mama?

They all look at Mrs. Karin. She has been sitting with her head slightly bowed and playing with a small green ruler. She raises her eyes now and looks at her family with an absent, almost sleepy smile.

Karin: What do you want me to say? You've always squabbled among yourselves. Now that your father is dead, you start on me. That's natural. I have to understand that.

Gustav: Excuse me, Mama, but actually it's only Svea who has to . . .

Karin (*raises her hand*): Let me finish. Sometimes I can't help thinking about what family life would have been like if I hadn't married into it, and been an accessory. (*Smiles.*) Yes, an amusing thought! I was so eager and so well-meaning; order, cleanliness, fellowship — education. Good intentions. Don't think I'm bitter. I'm just thinking.

Carl: And what would have happened to you, Mammchen, if you hadn't had to look after us?

Karin: Well now, Carl! You do ask clever questions although you're so . . . irregular. What would have happened to me? I would probably have gone on to become a teacher. And continued to bring to other people's children a few manners and some education. I have probably never really doubted the rightness of my actions. I may have acted wrongly in minor matters, but in the main ones I have nothing to reproach myself.

Uncertainty. Afterthoughts. Emptiness. Disinclination. Bitterness. Weariness. "What about having coffee in the salon?" says Anna. "I've made a cake." "Of course," says Karin briskly, getting up from the table.

"We're not as bad as we sound," says Gustav, propping his coffee cup on his stomach, cake crumbs scattering onto his waistcoat. "Sometimes, I'll have you know, Henrik, we can even be quite pleasant." "You and Anna must come to dinner with us to celebrate your engagement," says Martha sourly, embracing Anna from behind. "What a sweet boy," she whispers into Anna's ear. "Let bygones be

139

bygones," says Oscar Åkerblom, putting a hand on Henrik's arm. "Call me Oscar. I thought our last meeting extremely unpleasant, but I considered myself obliged to exaggerate it all. I am, if I may say so myself, a good-natured fellow. You and Anna must definitely come to dinner with us before we go to the country!"

Svea caresses Anna's cheek with an emaciated spotted hand. "I'm so terribly ashamed of my outburst. The doctor says it's the drugs that make me so unbalanced. Henrik, you really mustn't believe that your Aunt Svea — Henrik is to say Aunt Svea — that your Aunt Svea is usually so unpleasant." Then Carl sails up and breathes on the confused betrothed: "I warned you and now you're caught! Oh, well, you have only yourself to blame, you poor wretch. Anna is frightfully pretty, but don't let yourself be deceived by her lovely face. She has too much Åkerblom in her. I'm just warning your husband-to-be," grins Carl, breathing all over Anna. "Like hell, I'm warning him, but it's a damned waste of time." "What have you been drinking, Carl?" says Anna with mock indignation. "Well, it wasn't roses," says Carl, sighing.

"Let's go," says Ernst, tugging at Henrik's coat. "I've told Mama that we must give you an airing. Come on, Anna. That was a damned lousy cake you made." "Good-bye, Mrs. Karin, and thank you," mumbles Henrik, bowing behind Mrs. Karin's back. She turns around. She has just told Lisen to put dinner off for an hour. "Good-bye, Mrs. Karin," says Henrik and bows again. "You'll be back for dinner, won't you!" says Mrs. Karin softly, her face pale and eyes tired. "You'll be back for dinner?" "No, thank you, Mama. We won't be back for dinner," says Ernst firmly. "We're going out on the town, Anna and Henrik and I. We're going to get as drunk as lords." Mrs. Karin smiles and shakes her head. "Enjoy yourselves," she says quickly. "You've got some money, I suppose?" "Thank you, Mama dear, we'll manage," says Ernst and kisses his mother on the mouth.

III

After the funeral, 12 Trädgårdsgatan was closed, then invaded at the beginning of August by building workers, craftsmen, and movers. The family dispersed, some to Austria, others to Ramlösa Spa, the children to friends of friends in the archipelago, Henrik to his position in Mittsunda, and Anna to her friend Fredrika Kempe, a fellow student at the Sophiahemmet nursing school. Fredrika had married into a wealthy family right after taking her finals and was already expecting her first child. Mrs. Karin went to their summer residence in Dalarna together with Miss Lisen, who was to stay on with her mistress for the rest of her life, or what turned out to be twenty-four more years.

Mrs. Karin was now alone in both the external and the inner sense. At the end of her year of mourning, she ordered seven identical skirts, blouses, and dresses from Leja's fashion house, all of the same cut, color, and shape. From the spring of 1912 on, she always wore dark clothes: ankle-length skirts, gray shantung blouses with a silver brooch at the throat, black dresses with no waistline, high black boots, and white hemstitched collars and cuffs. Within eight short months, her hair had turned white, still thick and gleaming, but white, not gray.

Anyone who is amused by explanations and interpretations may wonder about the reasons for Mrs. Karin's partial abdication. After all, she was no more than forty-six. She sold the property with no unnecessary comment, divided her apartment down the middle, and shared a considerable portion of the resulting fortune among the agreeably surprised though somewhat confused members of the family. So Anna possessed a capital sum not to be sneered at, and she

143

knew how to manage it, a fact that was for a long time to be a source of annoyance to Pastor Bergman (but of considerable help in the daily life of the family).

Autumn came early that year, brilliantly glowing across the river and the dark edge of the forest, thin ice appearing on the grass and on the tub below the green pump by the well. The nights were crystal clear, windless and starry. Birch-wood fires crackled in the tiled stoves, and the hills beyond Djurås and the Gimmen were sharply outlined. The threshing machines rumbled away in the barns, and the tawny owl was already emerging from the forest at dusk and perching on the outhouse roof.

Mrs. Karin and Lisen spent the summer and autumn in silent but not in the slightest bit hostile symbiosis. When the first snow began falling at the end of October, the news came that the apartment at 12 Trädgårdsgatan was ready. The two women packed what had to be packed, closed what had to be closed; shutters were put up and white sheets draped over the furniture and the piano. Bottles of fruit juice and jars of preserves were packed into wooden crates to be sent to the new addresses of the members of the family. The old ginger cat was boarded out, the door locked, and the two women, both the same age, wordlessly left for Upsala on the morning train. It was a touching day, as departures are nearly always apt to be, a light mist swirling up from the river, white snowflakes falling gently, the light bright and without shadows. The summer house shone like a red patch in all that gray and white, just like the rowanberries.

The brief and insignificant scene that follows occurs ten days before the aforementioned departure. The setting is the spacious light kitchen with its window facing the forest and the hills. Mrs. Karin and Miss Lisen are sitting at the gate-legged table in peaceful accord, cleaning black currants, the fire roaring in the stove, a tall preserving pan exuding steam and fragrance. The top square windows have steamed up. Fresh coffee in their cups, some sleepy summer flies staggering around on the warm stove wall.

Karin: I had a letter from Anna this morning.

Lisen: Everything all right?

Karin: She writes to say she has decided.

Lisen: Is she really going to take that cooking course? Oh, that's good. Then we'll have her home this winter.

Karin: She's not coming home; nor is she taking any course.

Lisen: Anna ought to learn a little ordinary cooking. Though she can do desserts. And cakes. (*Pause.*) Almost as well as I can.

Karin (*smiles*): Well, she isn't coming, anyhow.

Lisen: What's going to happen then?

Karin: They're getting married in November. That's when Henrik starts his pastorate up there in Forsboda.

Lisen: Oh, yes.

Karin: Anna wants to be with him from the start. She says in her letter that that's more important than everything else.

Lisen: Then we're going to have a wedding in November.

Karin: Whether we want to or not.

Lisen: What kind is being considered?

Karin: A grand one, Miss Lisen. (*Smiles.*) A grand party. Sometimes there is good reason to celebrate one's adversities.

Lisen: I think I know what you mean, Mrs. Åkerblom. All one can say is that they'll make a lovely bridal pair. Like in a fairy tale.

Karin: Precisely. Like in a fairy tale.

Their hands move quickly, the cleaned black currants gleaming in the yellow earthenware bowl. Lisen gets up and puts more wood in the stove, then sits down again, sighing with aches in her joints.

Lisen: Have they been to see his mother?

Karin: Anna says in her letter that they're going to Söderhamn today. Then they're going on to Forsboda to look at the parsonage. They've been promised it'll be repaired, Anna says. They're going to stay with the Nordensons. Nordenson is the squire there. He runs the whole estate.

Lisen: Is he related to the Nordensons of Sjösätra?

Karin: Yes, indeed, they're half brothers.

Lisen: There was money there, wasn't there?

Karin: They say so.

Lisen: My sister worked for a cousin of the Nordensons of Sjösätra. His name was . . . if I remember . . . yes, what was his name now? Helmerson. His wife was a real, well . . . Helmerson was, too, for that matter. So it didn't last long.

Karin: Perhaps Nordenson will be all right.

Lisen (*skeptical*): Of course.

Karin: Oscar says the Iron Works are in severe financial difficulties. He usually knows.

Lisen: But the estate doesn't pay for the priest, does it?

Karin: No, he'll get his stipend all right.

Lisen: Our little Anna — just think.

Karin: Yes, it's strange, isn't it, Miss Lisen?

The stove crackles, the lid of the pan rattles faintly and puffs out steam. A fly hits the window and falls on its back. Mrs. Karin stops cleaning black currants, props her elbow on the table, and sits there without moving. Miss Lisen goes on working, but as if at a different pace. She is looking at what her hands are doing.

Lisen (*after long silence*): Yes, yes. Yes, indeed.

Karin: I no longer know anything.

Lisen: It's lonely for Mrs. Åkerblom.

Karin: I don't mind that.

Lisen: Oh, really?

Karin: No, solitude doesn't worry me.

Lisen: But then what on earth . . . ?

Karin: Sometimes I wonder whether I have ever grasped *the innermost reason* why I do this or that. Do you understand, Miss Lisen?

Lisen: I don't understand what you mean by the innermost reason.

Karin: No. No, of course not.

Lisen: If you start thinking that way, then you start getting muddled. For behind what you call "the innermost reason" there might be hidden other reasons that are even farther in. And so on.

Karin: That's true.

Lisen: May I give you some more hot coffee? (*Mrs. Karin holds out her cup.*)

Henrik's mother sends a brief message to say that unfortunately she can't meet the newly engaged couple at the station because her asthma has got worse during the summer. So she has taken up her post at the open front door in her best purple silk dress, a lace cap on the thin, carefully arranged hair, and a large welcoming smile, which nevertheless does not go as far as the sorrowful eyes. Anna allows herself to be embraced and sinks into a shapeless darkness smelling faintly of perspiration. Then Alma holds her fat little hands up toward her son, takes hold of his face, and kisses him on his forehead, cheeks, and chin, her light-colored eyes at once filling with tears and her breathing heavy.

Alma: . . . and you've gone and shaved off your terrible little mustache. (*Teasing.*) We'll see what Anna and I can achieve with our combined forces. We'll probably sort him out, don't you think, Anna! But come on in, dear child, we mustn't go on standing here on the stairs. Let me look at you! Your fiancée is even more beautiful than the photograph you sent me. Dear, dear child, may you be happy with my boy! Let's see now! Are you happy now, Henrik? No, no, how silly I am. You must be quite embarrassed by my obtrusiveness. Now, let's see. This is what I think. Anna can have Henrik's old room. The trouble is, I usually have a paying guest. He's been kind enough to move out for a few days, but he smokes cigars. I've aired and aired the room, but I think it still smells of cigars.

Anna assures her she can't smell cigars but says nothing about the smell of mold oozing out of the dark green, partially faded wallpaper.

Alma: But maybe it will be fun for you to sleep in your fiancé's boyhood room, Anna. Yes, that photograph above the bed is of Henrik's father, taken when we were engaged. I don't think it does him justice at all . . . he was so cheerful and handsome.

Anna: I think he's very handsome, and very like Henrik. He looks like an actor.

Alma: An actor? Well, perhaps, I don't know. He loved singing. He was so musical. And then he went and married a clumsy little fatty like me. Well, I wasn't so fat then as . . . but actually, there were several courting me, so there was competition, you see, Anna.

147

Henrik: Then I'll sleep on the couch in the dining room. That's fine by me.

Alma: No, no. I'll sleep on the couch in the dining room. Then you can be nice and comfy in my room, Henrik. (*Jokingly.*) I'll lie like the drawn sword between the two lovers. (*Laughs.*)

Henrik (*decisively*): Now you're being silly, Mama. I'll sleep on the couch, and that's it!

Alma: Just listen to this dictator! Is he like this with you, or is it just his old mother he orders about? And now here we are, standing around arguing! I've put out some tea and sandwiches in the dining room. Henrik said in his letter that you were going to have dinner at the station restaurant in Gävle. Otherwise, of course I'd have had something extra special for you.

Henrik: That'll be lovely. I promise you, Mama's sandwiches are delicious, artistic masterpieces.

Alma: Now you're making fun of your old mother, Henrik. My asthma means I always have to watch my weight. The doctor's told me so, and food doesn't interest me any longer, not the way it used to.

Alma holds out her hand in silent appeal, and Anna hastily kisses it.

Alma: My child, my dear little child.

For a brief moment, the two women stand close together. Henrik, on his way toward the open dining room door, turns around and sees the quick, indecisive gesture. Alma has put her heavy arm around the young woman's shoulders, her face stiffening in sudden pain. Henrik thinks of a word that opens up like a little shutter somewhere in his mind: inevitable, *inevitable*. Then at the same moment, everything is ordinary again, and he hears Anna's voice: "What is it, Henrik?"

Henrik: I think Mama likes her daughter-in-law. We were a little jumpy, you and I.

Showing the albums, the eternal last resort for the first visit of a fiancée when conversation has run out and the minutes have become long. Showing the albums, on the sofa, lit by the paraffin lamp, Alma and Anna close together, the magnifying glass. Henrik sits on the other side of the round table. He has been given permission to smoke his pipe. Now he is hiding in the half-light and behind the cloud of pipe smoke, so he can watch his mother and his fiancée undisturbed.

Alma (*points with a plump little finger*): There you are, Henrik! One summer in Öregrund. Henrik must be . . . how old were you that summer when we went to all that expense of a summer holiday in Öregrund? You were eleven years old. Eleven.

Henrik: And I got scarlet fever in the autumn.

Alma: No, no, that was the following autumn. I remember that very well. You were so well after that summer by the sea, you didn't get sick once all through the winter. How small he was. And that sailboat, he made it all by himself from drawings in a magazine. He was such a lonely child, poor Henrik. The best thing he knew was collecting plants and examining them and classifying them from the flora. Do you remember your fine collection of plants, Henrik? I've kept it somewhere in the attic. Poor Henrik, I have to laugh, though I ought to cry when I see that photo from Öregrund. Anna, will you have a little more port?

Anna: Yes, please, only not too much.

Henrik: I'll stick to brandy.

Alma: Yes, heavens above.

And Alma laughs and looks at the photograph from Öregrund. Alma's loud laugh is remarkably unlike all her other airs, a friendly laugh of good teeth, amiable and attractive.

Alma: Poor little Henrik! Look Anna, how appalling! (*Points.*) That's me and I'd already become "fat little Mama," but I had a gigantic feather in my hat. And that's one of the sisters from Elfvik; that must be Beda. Yes, it's Beda. She had a wasp-waist and always needed help lacing up her corsets. And my goodness, that summer we had a maid, that was old Rike, just think what we could afford in those days. I've never been any good with money. Nor has Henrik. You'll soon find that out, Anna. I had sold the family jewels — doesn't matter, anyway. And that's my best friend. She was also widowed young. Do you remember Aunt Hedvig, who had eczema? She was so nice and kind, do you remember her, Henrik? She died a year or so later. (*Laughs.*) She wasn't exactly a sylph, either. We were all fat, and then skinny little Henrik whom we all pampered and fussed over! Heavens, how we loved you and spoiled you. Do you remember playing church, and you were the priest and we were the congregation? In that cramped little cottage? How did all us fatties fit into it? (*Laughs.*) You were so good and sweet. We just felt like eating you up, and you were always happy

149

and good-tempered and polite and friendly. Ah me, sad to say, you never mixed with other children, either, although I invited your school friends home, but Henrik used to go and hide, or lock himself in the toilet. (*Laughs, then becomes serious.*) Dearest Anna, you must look after him now. It'll be lonely and sad for me (*she cries*), but life is like that, isn't it? And life has never been particularly kind to Alma Bergman. But I've always been resigned to my fate and thought things would get better. And now Henrik's the priest I dreamed he would be. That's so important. No, I'm not complaining. (*She weeps.*)

Henrik: Now don't cry, Mama dear. We must be happy this evening.

Anna (*cautiously*): You can come and stay with us for long periods, Mama. We'll have plenty of room in the parsonage.

Henrik: Mama, dear, we're not going to abandon you. The hard times are over now. Everything will get better.

Alma (*suddenly*): ". . . the hard times are over" . . . as if you knew! What do you know about my life? I have no intention of sponging on your kindness. I know I'm not very clever, but I'm not that stupid. You two must live your own life, and I shall bring mine to a close. That's it, and that's how it should be.

Alma's eyes are now wide open and calm, almost brilliant. That hermetic combination of slow, destructive, lamentable female misery, and then that dark blue gaze, the laugh, the words full of insight, the sudden sharpness — it is all beyond comprehension.

The photograph from Öregrund actually exists in the real world and is exactly as Alma describes it: a rickety little shack with a veranda and clumsy, fancy decorative fretwork. A small figure sitting hunched up on a garden chair, with stubbly fair hair and a sailor suit, bare legged, holding a sailboat on his lap and a shiny metal vasculum over his left shoulder. On his right are two tall, buxom women in white summer dresses and wide-brimmed hats. On the veranda, behind a bearing beam, you can just see a fat servant girl with a probably toothless but knowing smile. The viewer's spontaneous reaction must be . . . what is it like at night, and where does that spindly creature find space to live and breathe enveloped in all that billowing compact female flesh? How does he defend himself?

When the albums have run out, there is still music to be made. Mama Alma and Anna play duets. There's a great deal to choose from in arrangements for four hands, from the latest waltzes (Alma plays at

150

parties) to Haydn symphonies and choral pieces. However, their playing does not last long, which is a relief, for it turns out that Alma, quite naturally, is a much better player than Anna, something which Alma does not hesitate to demonstrate. Their playing is interrupted by the doorbell ringing.

Alma lifts her hands from the piano and explains with some embarrassment that it's sure to be Freddy — an old friend. She had met him quite by chance down at the market a few days before, and had happened to mention that she was expecting a visit from Henrik and his fiancée. "You remember Uncle Fred," says Alma appealingly, slightly breathlessly. "He's rather eccentric and very obstinate, and insisted on coming to meet Henrik and his wife-to-be. He was an archivist at the Foreign Office and was a member of Parliament for a spell, and now he's retired and has moved to Söderhamn to be near where he was born. Your father and he were friends in their youth. Now, there's the bell again. I must go and open the door. You must forgive me, my dear children." The heavy woman moves lightly and is cheerfully embarrassed. She tugs at her skirt and waistband, smooths down her hair, and disappears into the dark hall, opens the door, greets her guest, and ushers him inside.

The first thing anyone notices about Uncle Freddy is his left eye, which is wide open and darkly penetrating, as if furious. His right eye is obscured by a frosted, opaque monocle. His face is broad and mouth narrow, his forehead high and head almost bald, his beard ice gray and well trimmed. This heavy, Caesarlike head rests directly on broad shoulders and a squat, somewhat stooping body. Large hard hands, silver-topped cane, heavy steps.

Freddy: I see that I am unforgivably breaking into the innermost circle of the family. But your mother, my dear Henrik, insisted, and I have never been able to resist her requests. How are you, Henrik? It's been a long time. I don't think we've met for ten years or so. How do you do, Miss Åkerblom, this is indeed a pleasure. What a lovely young woman. Henrik has inherited his father's eye for female beauty. May I sit down for a few moments? I won't stay long, but I wouldn't say no to a glass of Alma's homemade liqueur. Thank you. Thank you. I'll sit here, no, I'm fine here. Don't let me disturb you. I heard music. Was it Haydn?

Alma: The young people are leaving tomorrow. They're going to Forsboda to inspect the parsonage and the church. Henrik has been appointed to quite a long-term position with the possibility of a permanent post.

Freddy: Forsboda? Beautiful countryside, wild and untouched nature, and then the estate and the manor house in the middle of the forest above the rapids. Do you like fishing, Henrik? If you do . . . (*Falls silent.*)

Freddy Paulin turns his dark, luminous eye on Henrik, who smiles politely, his smile nevertheless remaining unanswered and at once becoming fixed.

Freddy: So you're a priest now, my dear Henrik. Yes, well, I knew your father, the one who broke away, the pharmacist. He was one of my closest friends, you know. Although he was much younger than me. In fact, I was more a contemporary of your grandfather's.

Henrik: I never really knew my grandfather.

Freddy: No, I know. I know. We used to sit on the same bench in Parliament. I can't really say I ever knew him. He wasn't that kind of person.

Henrik: No.

Freddy: But I did get to know your grandmother. She was, as they say, a charming person. We once spent a whole evening talking together, at a party.

Uncle Freddy fixes Henrik with his hideous eye, now impossible to avoid. Now the atrocity is evinced, and the word "inevitable" shines like a beacon in Henrik's egoistical darkness.

Freddy: Your grandmother talked about you.

Henrik: Oh, yes. (*Pause.*) Did she?

Freddy: She thought your grandfather and the rest of the family had committed a great injustice toward your mother and you. She said she had hardly been able to live with the thought of the grandchild who had been taken away from her. She didn't know how to make up for it. She said that thinking about your mother's and your defenselessness and misery made her ill. She also tried to explain her powerlessness. For anyone who knows the Bergman family, that powerlessness was not difficult to understand.

Henrik: No.

Freddy: Then she died, did she, poor thing?

Henrik: Yes, then she died.

Freddy: Did you manage to go and see her before she passed away? She had a great need of . . .

Henrik: She was in the Academic Hospital in Upsala. I was taking exams and put off going to see her. When I finally got around to it, she had died a few hours beforehand.

Freddy: Did you see your grandfather?

Henrik: We met in a hospital corridor but had nothing to say to each other.

Freddy: I was at the funeral, but I didn't see you there.

Henrik: I wasn't at my grandmother's funeral.

Freddy: No, I understand.

Now there's nothing more to say. The rest of the conversation vanishes into thin air. When Freddy Paulin has finished his liqueur, he gets up briskly, as if relieved, and bids them farewell.

Alma bends over the girl, who has already crept down into bed. "Good night, my dear," she whispers. "Good night, and don't forget to count the windowpanes. You should always do that in a new place; then your dreams come true." "Good night, Mrs. Alma," whispers Anna, "and thank you for letting us come. It's been a lovely evening." She declines to throw her arms around Alma. Something stops her, but Alma strokes her cheek. "Will you put the lamp out, or do you want it left on?" "Thank you, I'll put it out in a minute." "Just don't fall asleep over it," warns Alma. "No, no," smiles Anna, and Alma patters out of the room in her gray dressing gown, the thin, severe pigtail down her back. When she has taken off her corsets, her body collapses, her head protrudes, and her back bows as if she were bearing an intolerable burden.

Henrik is sitting on the made-up couch jammed up against the sideboard. He has got his nightshirt on and is winding up his pocket watch with a tiny key, a lighted candle on a chair in front of him. His mother comes toward him out of the semidarkness, moving without a sound, her face glowing chalk-white, but her eyes have vanished. She is like a huge blind fish at a great depth. Now she is there, puts the candle up on the sideboard, and sits down on the chair, her eyes visible again. She is breathing heavily: "Anna's a sweet girl," she whispers abruptly, her breath smelling of sour milk. "Anna's a very nice girl and so lovely, a real princess. You must take good care of her." Henrik shakes his head. "It's still like a dream," he whispers, trying to avoid his mother's breath. "I don't think it has anything to do with me." His mother leans over and kisses him on the mouth. "Good night, my darling boy. Sleep well. You mustn't feel guilty about your grandmother. No one is more guiltless than you are." Alma looks at her son with glazed eyes, her lips moist. Henrik shakes his head, thinks of saying something but changes his mind. "Good night, then," says Alma, kissing Henrik's hand. "Good night, and don't forget to blow the candle out." She nods twice and disappears, wheezing faintly in the darkness, and closing her door soundlessly behind her. Henrik remains sitting there, frightened and at a loss: What's happening? he says to himself.

Alma has taken off her dressing gown and is puttering around her room, silently moving hither and thither. The dining room clock strikes eleven, and the church clock replies; the wind whistles down the street making a signboard screech, then silence returns. Alma has pulled the covers up over her stomach and is sitting upright, looking at the little ivory cross hanging on the wall of the alcove, her hands clasped. "Dear Lord," she says. "Forgive me my sins today, and on all days. Dear Lord, keep and bless my little boy! Dear Lord, forgive me that I cannot love that girl. Dear Lord, take her out of Henrik's life. If I am wrong, if my thoughts are simply dark with malice, punish *me*, Lord! Punish *me*! Not him, or her!"

She turns out the paraffin lamp but lies awake for a long time, staring out into the darkness, listening intently. Something's moving there in the dining room. Sure to be Henrik on his way to that unknown woman. Alma has to sit up, her heart running riot and she almost suffocating. Of course Henrik is on his way to that unknown woman!

Anna is exhilarated when the pale figure appears in the gray rectangle of the door. She flings the covers aside and moves over to the wall. He is at once in her arms. They whisper and laugh. This is a very dignified mutual rebellion against parents.

Anna: Your feet are cold.

Henrik: But they'll warm up now.

Anna: My feet are always warm. I have to stick them outside the covers. Then it's wonderful pulling them back in.

Henrik: You and all your pleasures.

Anna: Yes, I'm pleasure-loving, boundlessly. I'll soon teach you, you'll see.

Henrik: What will you teach me?

Anna: Lie down, so I can kiss you. (*Kisses his mouth.*) Well?

Henrik: Yes, please.

Anna: Supposing your mother hears us?

Henrik: . . . is that also?

Anna: Of course.

Henrik: You're quite ruthless. (*Delighted.*) Are you?

Anna: You're *mine*. I'm quite ruthless.

Henrik: Poor Mama.

Anna: "When my father and my mother forsake me, then the Lord will take me up. Teach me thy way, O Lord, and lead me into a land the Lord shall give me." Isn't that what it says?

Henrik: Not quite, but it sounded good.

Anna: Poor Henrik!

Henrik: Just imagine, here I am, in my old childhood bed, snuggled up with you. I can't believe it.

Anna: But you have to go back to your own bed. We mustn't fall asleep together.

Henrik: I'm not sure Mama would serve us coffee in bed!

Anna: Good night.

Henrik: Good night. Please don't forget me.

Anna: I shall at once begin to think about you.

Henrik closes the door and pads back to his bed in the dining room. He doesn't hear his mother weeping into her pillow.

The remarks made at early breakfast the next day are almost impossible to register. Alma appears in her dressing gown, her hair untidy and face swollen with tears, her mouth trembling and pitiful. Anna and Henrik are cheerful but diffident, politely curbing their delight at departing, their delight in their love, their joy in touching, their joy in belonging.

Alma: Would you like some more coffee, Anna?

Anna: No, thank you. Please, do sit down. I'll get it myself. More coffee, Henrik?

Henrik: Yes, please. Are we in a hurry?

Alma: The train to Sundsvall leaves at quarter past seven.

Henrik: Then I've time for another sandwich.

Alma: Cheese or salami, Henrik?

Henrik: Both, please.

Anna: We have to change trains twice. We won't arrive until this afternoon.

Alma: I've put together a little basket of food for you. It's in the hall.

Anna: How thoughtful of you, Mrs. Alma!

Alma: Oh, my dear child!

Henrik: It's begun to rain.

Anna: Real autumn rain.

Alma: I've got a big umbrella you can borrow. Put it in the baggage room when you get to the station; then I'll pick it up later on.

Henrik: Thank you, Mama dear.

Alma: Oh, that's all right.

Anna: It's fun going by train when it's raining. You can curl up together and eat chocolate and sandwiches — and oranges, of course.

Alma: I have something for Anna.

Alma hurries into her room and stays there. They can hear her blowing her nose and opening a drawer.

Anna (*whispers*): Your mother's been crying.

Henrik: Has she?

Anna: Didn't you see her eyes were red-rimmed and her face swollen? She's been crying.

Henrik (*lightly*): Mama's face is always swollen. And she is also always crying. I think she likes crying.

156

Anna: She knows.

Henrik: Knows what?

Anna: Don't act stupid.

Henrik: Do you mean she heard . . . ?

Anna (*nods*): Yes, I do. And now she thinks a fallen woman is taking away her little boy.

Henrik: Ah, you're imagining things.

Anna: Ssh! Here she comes.

Alma opens the door. She has put on her little lace cap and done her hair. She has also exchanged her down-at-the-heel slippers for shoes. In her hand she has a slim wrought gold chain with a little medallion with *A* engraved on it, surrounded by some very small rubies. Alma holds it out and Anna gets up, almost frightened. There is no friendliness in Alma's gesture.

Alma (*matter-of-factly*): I was given this medallion on the day I got engaged. Henrik's father gave it to me. Of course, it cost far too much, but he wasn't bothered about money. As you see, Anna, there's a big *A* engraved on it. So I think you should have it now as a gift from Henrik's father, as if he were here. There. May I put it around your neck?

Anna: It's much too grand. You really shouldn't . . .

Alma: Hush now, silly girl. It's a simple present. I'm sure you're used to better things.

Anna (*tonelessly*): Thank you.

Alma: You'd better be off now. I won't come with you. I hope you don't mind. I find walking difficult. My asthma. (*Kisses her son.*) Good-bye, Anna. I hope I shall be well enough to come to the wedding. Hurry now! Here's the umbrella. (*Kisses Anna on the cheeks.*) Thank you for taking the trouble to come here.

Anna (*panic-stricken*): We'll be back soon.

Alma: I hope so.

Henrik: Good-bye, Mama.

They race down the stairs and out into the rain. They carry the large suitcase between them, Henrik holding the umbrella over Anna as they dash along the empty wet pavement. They run as if escaping from some danger. Suddenly Henrik laughs.

Henrik: That woman! That woman!

Anna: What is it, Henrik?

Henrik: That woman is my mother!

Anna: Come on, now.

Henrik: Yes, we must hurry.

Is Alma standing behind the curtain? In my grandmother's diary, which is somewhat sporadic, there is a note on the fourteenth of September 1912: Henrik came with his fiancée. She is surprisingly beautiful and he seems happy. Fredrik Paulin called in the evening. He talked about tedious things from the past. That was inappropriate and made Henrik sad.

The guard dashes by in the aisle and says *"Forsboda next!"* Anna and Henrik are sitting side by side, holding hands, tense but solemn. The rain has followed them inland, but sunlight suddenly pours into the dusty compartment and draws sharp contours and rushing shadows over faces and paneling. It is afternoon and the sun is already low. Henrik leans his face against Anna's cheek and says, "Anna, whatever happens, whatever surprises we come across, whatever peculiar people we have to look after, we'll be together." "Yes, now we'll always be together," whispers Anna through the clatter and squealing brakes, the wheels thundering over a small bridge, the engine making one last effort with an extra chug and billowing smoke. Then the train is standing at the shining wet stone platform of Forsboda station. The guard's door slams, the gate's bell rings, the signal is dropped, the stationmaster makes a sign with his arm, and the engine pulls out with its cylinders chugging. This is only a small local train and at once disappears around the curve by the lake. Anna and Henrik are left looking around on the platform, two suitcases between them, one large, the other smaller.

A horse and buggy are waiting beside the wall of the station building, the hood down. Alongside the trap is a man in a long coat with gold braid on his collar and a peaked cap pulled down over his forehead. "Is it the pastor?" says peaked cap, without moving. "That's right," says Henrik. "Then you're to come with me. The squire says I'm to drive the pastor to the parsonage. But he didn't say anything about anyone being with him." "This is my fiancée," says Henrik. "Oh, yes, then your fiancée'll have to come, too, though the squire didn't say anything about any fiancée," says peaked cap, still without moving. Anna and Henrik pick up their suitcases and carry them to the buggy. Peaked cap heaves them in under the seat, and the couple climb up. The driver sits on a board behind the passengers. "Lucky I didn't take the small buggy because it's got only two seats," says peaked cap, smacking his lips at the horse, which sets off at a spanking pace. "You'd have had to stay behind at the station, Miss," peaked cap adds, smiling toothlessly, but not in an unfriendly way.

Henrik realizes this is a joke inviting him to converse, so he asks whether it has been raining all day. "It's been raining all day and there'll be more this evening, so it's just as well I didn't take the small carriage, because it's got no hood. I let the hood down just before the train came in."

Then nothing is said for a long while. "There's the church," says peaked cap, pointing at a huge, unwieldy nineteenth-century cathedral flung down on a slope and surrounded by sparse autumn-red trees. "The pastor won't be preaching much in the big church, I suppose, but more in the estate chapel." His tone of voice is not free of classification. "The pastor's probably mostly for the estate chapel. Gabriel de Geer, the one who started up the Iron Works, and arranged for the Sawmill and built the Manor, that was a hundred years ago, or thereabouts, and he promptly wanted a greenhouse or more like a palm house. He wanted palm trees he could put out in the summer and they had to be indoors in the winter, so he built a special house for his palm trees. But Nordenson's father, who took over after de Geer, naturally thought it was crazy to raise those palm trees and to use all that wood to keep the palms warm. He burned up all the palm trees and presented the palm house to the cathedral chapter, so the people living near the Works and the Sawmill should have a House of God and not have to travel the ten kilometers to the big church. And that was a good thought. Nordenson's father was a good man. But then the Pentecostalists came along. So people preferred to go to the prayer house. Though Nordenson's father was a good man."

After this long speech, peaked cap has drained his resources and is silent for the rest of the journey. They are taken at a brisk pace along a sandy road that runs uphill and downhill between groups of well-built farms and wide strips of darkening forest. There's an icy wind blowing, which may bring snow. The sun is resting on a spiky ridge, the light is raw, yellowish. "You cold, Pastor?" asks the driver. "You needn't worry about us," says Anna, turning around. The driver nods silently.

159

The parsonage is a low building with two wings and a garden with a summer house and tall elms in their autumn splendor. Lights are already on in several windows, and dinner is being prepared in the kitchen.

Henrik knocks on the door, but no one seems to hear or see or be expecting visitors, so he and Anna go through the porch into the front hall. They can hear voices from various directions, and someone is walking quickly across the floor upstairs. A grandfather clock, decorated and painted, strikes five loudly, but reads four o'clock.

A strikingly good-looking woman with graying hair and large dark eyes comes to the stairs, and when she sees her guests she smiles kindly and calls out, "*At last!* We've been waiting all day. The minister lost your letter with your arrival time in it, and Frid has been to meet every conceivable train. We couldn't telephone you because the phone in the parish office has been out of order for three weeks. Anyhow, we didn't know how to get hold of you. No one answered at Trädgårdsgatan in Upsala. Welcome, both of you! My name's Magda Säll and I'm the housekeeper here, and the reverend's niece. Do come in! May I take your coats? Did you have a good journey? It's a shame we live so far from the station. Did you get cold, Miss Bergman? The wind's flared up terribly, so I suppose we'll get snow after all this rain. I'll tell the reverend you're here. Please, do go into the drawing room for the time being. I'll bring coffee in a jiffy."

The lovely and talkative Mrs. Säll disappears into the interior of the house. Anna and Henrik sit down on separate chairs in the spacious drawing room with its pair of crystal chandeliers, Karl-Johan furniture upholstered in silk, and light wooden floor covered with endless patterned rag rugs. Mildly blinking churchmen and bracket lamps are on the walls, and the doors are open into a library of huge bookcases. A dying fire spreading little warmth is burning in the tiled stove, and a heavy imitation baroque wall clock says it is twenty to seven. A pendulum clock under a glass case strikes eight.

The Reverend Gransjö comes in from the library, moving slowly and supported by Mrs. Säll. His face is pale and shapely beneath a large beard, his eyes dark gray behind thick glasses, his hair brushed straight back and in disorder. He is wearing a cassock and slippers. His smile is welcoming but is disfigured by ill-fitting dentures. Anna and Henrik at once get up and go to meet him. Without saying anything or exclaiming, the old gentleman holds out a strong hand and silently greets them, the gray eyes observant. Then he nods as if pleased with what he has seen and signals to the young people to sit down. Mrs. Säll says she will go and get the coffee, and leaves. The

Reverend Gransjö sits down on a straight-backed chair by the drawing room table, a hand cupped around his ear to indicate he is hard of hearing. At the same time, he fishes his gold watch out of the waistcoat behind the buttoned-up cassock, looks at the watch, at the wall clock, and at the pendulum clock.

Reverend Gransjö: A truthful clock should say five past four. All the clocks in this house are wrong. They say it's something to do with an underground magnetic field. My watch, on the other hand, is always right because it seems to be immune to the forces of the underworld.

Henrik fumbles for his own watch. It says ten past four.

Henrik: Mine says ten past four.

The old man is gazing at a spot to the right of Henrik's feet, apparently absentmindedly. The silence is lengthy but not unpleasant.

Reverend Gransjö (*suddenly*): My great friend Professor Söderblom came to see me. He had words of praise for you, Henrik Bergman. I set great store by his judgment. We are old friends. Of course, he's much younger than I am. Nevertheless we are old friends.

The reverend laughs silently and attractively, sucking cautiously on his dentures and turning his gray eyes to Anna.

Reverend Gransjö: He also spoke of you, Miss Åkerblom. I don't know how he knew you, my dear, but he knows everyone. He assured me that Anna Åkerblom would make a good wife to a pastor. I hope you're not offended that I repeat what Söderblom said to me, Henrik?

Henrik (*smiles*): On the contrary.

Reverend Gransjö: Yes, yes. Exactly. Wasn't Magda going to bring some coffee? I won't have any coffee. So I'll leave you two young people, if you'll excuse me. We are to go to Nordenson's for dinner this evening, so I must go and change. And I would like to take a nap.

The Reverend Gransjö gets up rather laboriously, one arm flailing about for a moment, but then he catches hold of the back of a chair and at once regains his balance. Henrik and Anna have also risen.

Reverend Gransjö: Please, do be seated. I can manage perfectly well. It's Magda who insists on propping me up all the time. So I'll leave you now.

The old gentleman waves his big hand and smiles at Anna, who curtsies. Then he disappears through the library, and a door is opened

161

and closed. A large black dog is standing in the doorway to the hall, his tail drooping. When Anna holds out her hand, he approaches suspiciously and sniffs with some reserve, after which he wags his tail three times and goes out again. Magda Säll comes in briskly with the coffeepot, followed by a tall pallid female carrying the tray.

Magda: Sorry I've been so long. Oh, so Uncle Samuel's gone, has he? Well, it's time for his nap, and that's sacred, you see. Thank you, Ottilia, that will do very nicely. Remind Frid that the carriage must be here at quarter past five at the latest and that he is to put in the heating pan, preferably without setting fire to the carriage like last time. Two lumps, Miss Åkerblom? I'm ashamed of calling you Miss Bergman a moment ago. I really do apologize. Cream, Pastor? And one lump? May I offer you a cake? We're going out to dinner with the Nordensons this evening. It won't be exactly fun, I mean, after what's happened, but Mr. Nordenson insists. We would much rather have had a simple meal here at home. Uncle Samuel said the same. But Nordenson was quite insistent, and I think it may have been Mrs. Nordenson putting pressure on him. She's very . . . how can I put it? . . . she's very much occupied with fundamental matters in life and so dreadfully unhappy after everything that's happened this last year. Perhaps you're *schon im Bilde*, Pastor, as the Germans say.

Henrik: I know nothing.

Magda: Is that so? Then I mustn't pass on gossip. But I'm sure you'll find out all about it sooner or later, Pastor.

Henrik: What has happened?

Magda: No one knows for sure. But one thing is quite clear — the Iron Works are in a bad way. And that Nordenson has been involved in some *business* affairs. There has even been talk of prison. All this last year has been a tangle of rumors and stories. But I shouldn't be sitting here chattering. I'll show you your sleeping quarters now. You, Miss Åkerblom, will be in the bishop's room, my goodness. His Grace has that room when he comes on a visitation, and you, Pastor Bergman, are to be in the wing, where we've arranged a very nice room on the top floor. We often have guests. Uncle Samuel is a member of a committee preparing the international ecumenical encyclopedia. He finds traveling difficult these days, so the learned gentlemen come here to us instead.

Henrik finds himself in a square room with a sloping ceiling and floral wallpaper, a starched curtain over a narrow window facing the rustling autumn darkness of the garden. A white bed with high ends, a paraffin lamp, the smell of newly scrubbed floor, and damp chill despite the wood fire in the tiled stove. He considers all this and at once sits down at the desk, where there is pen and ink. In a drawer, swollen with damp — so opening only reluctantly — he finds lined paper, and at once starts writing in his neat, flowing handwriting.

The minister's residence in Forsboda, twelfth of September, 1912. Dearest beloved Anna, you who are my wife before God. As soon as we are separated from each other, however short a time, however insignificant the geographical distance, I am seized with a grinding anxiety that I will never see you again. Everything becomes a dream dissolving into nothing, and I wake up to a loneliness that is extremely painful, for our communion in the dream was so clear. Your hands, your smile, your good voice, the whole of your little person. I try to recall in my inner vision everything that you are, but my fear is too great — you're suddenly gone.

I would prefer to turn myself into your unborn child. I was carried in an anguished womb. Sometimes I seem to remember a terrible cold, that I was frozen already before my birth. Under your heart, I'm sure it is warm. I am envious of our children who will sleep inside you. Forgive me, dearest Anna, if I sound melodramatic, but at this moment I am so afraid and uncertain about all these new and great things that lie ahead! I know that I shall calm down again as soon as I see you. How shall I ever be able to give you the security you need so much? You, who will be leaving a good and sheltered world, together with me, for a reality that neither of us can scarcely imagine! Sometimes I see quite clearly my weakness and my lack of character, all that is floating and indefinite. Sometimes I want to say: Watch out for me! At the same time I cry out: Don't leave me, no, don't ever leave me; only through you can I grow and mature.

After Henrik has signed and read through his letter, he adds a postscript.

As you know, I can be quite pleasant ordinarily. And also, you sometimes say I am handsome. And also, we actually laugh at the same things. The next time you get married, you can surely marry your old beau Torsten Bohlin. I have just read in the papers that he's become professor of exegetics. That's impressive. He's definitely guaranteed more money than I am. Though I sing better!

Forsboda Manor is a high, three-story building with a mansard roof, columns at the entrance, and a broad balustrade up to the level of the first-floor reception and drawing room. The park slopes down to the Storsjön, and in the west corner is the office for the Iron Works, a long, low, eighteenth-century building.

All this seems rather grand but is marred by treacherous decay and lack of maintenance. However, on an evening like this as the September moon rolls up over the wide surface of the water and illuminates the palacelike structure, the cracks in the walls don't show, nor do the flaking paint on the window frames and the wooden shutters on the top windows, the neglected garden, or the dried-up well. The flares flicker along the drive, a servant in livery and white gloves opens the door, and a housemaid takes coats and overcoats.

In the big drawing room, which is well heated, lighted candles mercifully hide the flaws in the wallpaper, the scratches on the parquet floor, the holes in the rugs, and the wear and tear of the upholstery. The guests from the parsonage are warmly, not to say overwhelmingly, welcomed by Nordenson, engineer and managing director of the Works, and his wife, Elin. The other guests are as would be expected. The provincial medical officer, Dr. Algotson, and his wife, Petra, and the manager of the Works, Hermann Nagel.

Nordenson himself reminds one of a shaggy bird of prey. He is tall and gangly, with a large nose and rather thin hair. He regards the world around him with quick looks beneath his bushy eyebrows. His ears are hairy, his forehead far too pale, his mouth wide, with narrow lips. His hands are long and thin, with dark brown liver spots on them. The gangling figure stoops, the head thrust forward, the voice deep and resonant.

Mrs. Elin, like her husband, is impeccably elegant without ostentation (one must after all consider the lower social status of their guests). Elin Nordenson is not what one calls beautiful, but she has a winning smile, warm dark eyes, and softly poised movements. She radiates sensuality and a mild melancholy.

The aging, sluggish doctor and his chattering, florid wife are two of life's first-class supernumeraries, who, without altogether too genuine emotion or altogether too violent participation, testify to our long-drawn-out tragedies and uneasy comedies. I shall waste no words on the Works manager. He dies of a coronary the following week, after helping Nordenson, with uncorruptible loyalty and incompetence, to run the finances of the Works into the ground.

Because Mrs. Magda and Mrs. Elin are both experienced social creatures, the impression given at dinner is almost one of heartfelt and unforced conversation. The meal is served in the small dining room, an eight-sided room with hand-painted wallpaper, crystal chandelier and wall lights, Gustavian furniture, softly shining silver candelabras, autumn flowers, and warm plates. Toasts are given to the

164

new pastor and his wife-to-be, to the reverend's encyclopedic efforts, and to the doctor's wife, who has just become a grandmother, despite the fact that she is seventy.

However, a ghost suddenly goes through the room and strikes holes in the brittle atmosphere of festivity and assurance. It is the Works manager, who, in answer to a question by the doctor, retorts that the blast furnaces, the rolling mill, the steam hammer, and the forge were out of action that afternoon. The workers had at first gathered in the harbor warehouse, since it was raining heavily, but had been driven out by the guards. Then they had broken into one of the buildings due for demolition down by the rapids. The manager and two office clerks had gone there and threatened the men with the police, but Nordenson said they could stay if they sent away the agitator and returned to work on the third shift.

"What is happening?" says Henrik. Nordenson turns a surprised face to the pastor: "Not much, really," he replies, smiling politely. "If you were more aware of the political situation, Pastor, you would know that we haven't had a week's peace since the general strike. For a hundred years or more, here at the Works we have had a core of good, respectable workers who understand our difficulties and want to help us and themselves out of a difficult situation. Now we have a new generation: loudmouths, agitators, criminal elements pushing their way in between us and the workers. They live off class hatred and lying propaganda. They spread terror and uncertainty.

Henrik: I don't understand how they can get people to listen if they don't speak the truth.

There is a moment's silence. Nordenson's smile deepens as he turns to the Reverend Gransjö.

Nordenson: One can only regret that young priests are not given any kind of political education before they are let loose on the market. I think that a discerning churchman could be of some importance as an opinion maker, anyhow among the women and indirectly through them . . .

Reverend Gransjö: My dear brother, it's actually part of our assignment to be troublesome. "I come to you not with peace but with strife" the Master once said, when he was dissatisfied with his bickering disciples.

Nordenson (*calmly*): Let's not mince words: *Riffraff and rabble!* One should call things by their proper names. That simplifies matters and clarifies them. Let's also be honest. They want to take my heritage away from me. They want to drive me out onto the highway. Make no mistake. They want to kill me and my family. I accept their hatred. I am even impressed to some degree by the force of their lies and their empathy. But make no mistake: Their hatred is returned in spades! I am perfectly capable of taking my rifle down from the wall and shooting them like mad dogs. You should know, Mr. Pastor, that the time of consensus is past, and strife is upon us. One might possibly wish for an enemy who fought with cleaner weapons, but that's surely too much to ask of a rabble smelling blood. I would have been grateful if this subject had not been brought up. It has undoubtedly disturbed our ladies. At bedtime, I shall be reprimanded by my dear wife for having demanded political awareness of a man of the cloth.

Henrik: I had no idea the situation was so inflamed.

Nordenson (*laughs*): "Inflamed" is an excellent word, gleaned from the noble art of healing! As if it were a question of a disease of the afflicted and the innocent! But that is not so! It's *revolution*, sir! And we who are sitting here are the losers. It will be our heads that roll!

Elin (*laughs*): My husband is being far too macabre! I suggest we conclude this pointless conversation and leave the table. Coffee will be served in the green drawing room.

Reverend Gransjö: Allow me first to turn to our hostess and, on behalf of myself and the other guests, thank you for what has been, as usual, an exquisite meal. We do indeed live in times of change and threat — what was it I wanted to say? — a good dinner is and remains a good dinner — I really wanted to say something else and better — I wanted to state that a good dinner, thoroughly enjoyed, is a cornerstone in the barricade that it is incumbent on us to raise against — yes, exactly — to raise against violence, chaos, and disorder — I had really meant to say something cleverer, but it escaped me just as I had it on the tip of my tongue. Ah, well, that will have to do. Here's to you, Elin, and thank you.

Nordenson (*suddenly*): Bravo, brother, bravo. As always, you find the right words. Here's to you, Pastor, and you, the enchanting young fiancée! Forgive a shaggy old wolf whose tail has been bitten once too often. Youth and beauty are things we thirst for out here in the wilderness. Then cleverness can take a back seat.

They all toast one another and the engaged couple. They all rise and repair to the green drawing room. Henrik leans quickly over Anna and kisses her ear as he takes the letter (with a heart drawn on the envelope) out of his top pocket and presses it into her hand. She smiles conspiratorily and slips it into her bag. "Read it before you go to sleep." "Are there tedious things in it?" whispers Anna. "Mostly love," says Henrik.

Elin: And tomorrow, Pastor, you and your fiancée are to inspect the chapel and the parsonage?

Anna: That's the program, yes.

Elin: I'm truly sorry I can't be with you. I'm going to Stockholm to see an old friend who has been taken ill.

Magda: I shall go with the young people and show them everything there is to show.

Elin: There are a great many repairs to be done and things to put in order. Please don't be appalled. The chapel has been out of use for two years and the parsonage even longer.

Anna: We've been both prepared and warned.

Elin: If Magda's to be with you, I feel better. (*To Magda*) You'll look after our children, won't you, Magda, and see that they don't run away out of sheer horror? I must say in all truth that the parsonage is in a very bad state of disrepair.

Magda: We have the go-ahead from the Church Council for total repairs. Then we can certainly do the remodeling as we see fit, isn't that right, Elin?

Elin: Of course, Magda! Ah, I think our daughters have come back from their dancing lessons. Can you imagine, Pastor, we have succeeded in arranging a course in modern ballroom dancing in Älvnäs, ten or so kilometers away from here. Young people of the same age can get together once a week and have some fun. These are my two daughters, Susanna and Helena.

The girls greet them with well-bred politeness. Susanna is fourteen, small, dark, and like her mother. Helena is thirteen, thin and gangling. Mrs. Elin takes Henrik's arm and guides him lightly into an adjoining room, which is dimly lit. "I have something I wish to say to you, Pastor. It is important."

Elin: Susanna and Helena don't go to school. They have private tuition. We have a teacher, a kind and competent person. She couldn't join us this evening. She has just had an attack of gastric catarrh and

167

preferred to have her meal in her room. Susanna is fourteen and Helena thirteen. Eventually they will go to school in Upsala or Gävle, but they are the darlings of their father and he wants them to stay here at the Manor as long as possible. Are you going to have pupils, Pastor? I mean, take confirmation classes?

Henrik: I presume so. I haven't actually . . .

Elin: Good. (*Exalted.*) I passionately want the children to be confirmed. It's my *only yearning*!

Henrik (*surprised*): That should be no problem.

Elin: But it is, Pastor. Their father does not under any circumstances want the girls to be confirmed. He gets so furious if I bring the subject up, it frightens me. An unreasonable anger, Pastor. I don't understand it.

Henrik: What do the girls want?

Elin: Oh, Pastor, there's nothing they want more.

Elin: I suppose I will have to speak to Mr. Nordenson. There can't be any great . . . ?

Elin: No, no. You really mustn't speak to my husband. I will speak to him myself. Sooner or later he will have to give in.

Henrik: Are things that difficult?

Elin: Yes, they are. Some time, some time . . . (*Stops.*) I can't talk to the Reverend Gransjö. He and my husband are old friends. He's bound to take my husband's side.

Henrik: How strange.

Elin: A lot of things have become strange over the years. Come now, we must go back to the others. Someone may begin to wonder.

A minor drama is being enacted in the salon. The Works manager has severe pains in his left side. He is sitting breathing heavily and sweating on a low chair, while the doctor undoes his collar and his wife hunts for the tube of tablets in the inside pocket of his tailcoat. Smiling with embarrassment and stammering apologies, anxious and panting, the man drags himself toward the door, supported by his wife and a servant. Nordenson follows him, patting his arm all the time: "You just forgot to take your pills, you careless old thing. You'll soon recover, you'll see. Have a stiff brandy when you get to bed. No, no, I'll go out to the carriage. I'll be back soon."

The cheeks of the doctor's wife have become redder and redder throughout the meal, and now she hurries up to Anna and Henrik, presses Magda's hand, assuring them in a whisper that it'll soon be *the end!* Her husband has made a thorough examination and says it could be the end *at any moment.* Drop dead, as they say. The Works have broken him. He'll be the first victim, but certainly not the last. Everything's on the brink of ruin, and what'll happen when Nordenson throws in the sponge?

A few hours later, after Anna has retired to the comfortable bishop's room, she takes out Henrik's letter and reads it carefully, at least twice. Then she sits down at the secretary and writes her answer on some pages she tears out of her diary. The moon is as white as ivory and almost circular, its cold light so strong it overpowers the walls and floor of the room. The paraffin lamp shines mildly down on Anna's hands and the words she is forming in her rounded, disciplined handwriting.

> Dearest, I can't reply directly to your letter. There's so much I don't understand. Yes, I understand the words, but for obvious reasons, I don't understand the *reality* behind the words. I have lived as a spoiled child and you have lived as an exposed child, and now those children are looking testingly at each other. I don't know why I like you so terribly much. How can one know that? Yes, you have a lovely mouth and kind eyes, and you like me because I am good to hold, that's obvious. But why have I grown together with you? Why do I think I understand you even when I don't understand? Why do I imagine I am thinking your thoughts and feeling your feelings? That's a mystery and perhaps when all is said and done, it is "the mystery of Love." So you see how philosophical I become as I sit here in the bishop's room writing to you in nothing but my nightgown and a cardigan and bedsocks. It's icy cold along the floor, but the reason I am so solemn may have something to do with all the episcopal thoughts that have got absorbed into the walls over the years. Good night, my darling husband! I also think we live in a dream, but I wake up again and again and realize with a shudder of joy that I've woken to another dream, which is even better than the one I have just dreamed.

She signs the letter without reading it through, turns out the lamp, and plunges into the chaste, magnificent bed. She hasn't pulled down the blinds, and the moonlight is sharp against the square windowpanes.

The day is cold and clear, and there's nothing wrong with the lighting. The sunlight radiates around the yellow house and the birches. The house sits beautifully on the slope leading down to the swiftly flowing river and the rapids. In the overgrown garden there are fruit trees, berry bushes, and weed-filled beds for flowers and herbs. Against the west wall of the house is a lilac arbor, broken chairs, and a ruined table, and near the kitchen entrance there is a green pump standing on guard, a rusty bucket overturned on the cover of the well. The fire ladder has lost several rungs, and some of the kitchen tiles are missing.

The company consists of the future occupants of the house, plus Magda Säll and the churchwarden, Jesper Jakobsson, a taciturn man with a long face, faded eyes, and careful gestures. He has a bunch of keys and, according to Magda, is responsible for the repairs and upkeep of church premises.

At the very gate, before the visitors have had time to get out of the carriage, he turns around and says that *personally* he does not approve of the cathedral chapter's decision to provide the parish with another priest. He also considers it a waste of money to restore the chapel. Attendance at the big church is constantly falling, in contrast to that of the Pentecostalists and the Mission Society, which is increasing. Also, young people are prey to false doctrines and politics. Forsboda has been abandoned to spiritual and material desolation. Nothing can be done about that. Every attempt to halt the destruction is doomed to failure. Money down the drain, as they say.

Jesper Jakobsson's pallid face glows with mournful triumph. "Now we mustn't spoil everything for these young people," says Magda. "Let's try to be happy." "Far be it from me to do that," says the churchwarden. "Far be it from me to do that." He attempts a smile, which in fact makes him look even gloomier than usual.

Anna walks along the grass-covered gravel path and looks around. She turns to Henrik, who is still by the gate. "It's lovely here," she says. "As long as you can stand the rapids," says the churchwarden. "And you have to watch that the children don't fall in. There was a fence once, but it collapsed under the snow last winter." "Then a new fence will have to be put up," says Magda, somewhat irritably. "Yes, yes, of course," says the churchwarden, offended. "I suppose so." Magda takes Anna's arm and says she mustn't take any notice of Jesper Jakobsson. "He's a bigwig in the community, but a builder from Gävle has already been here and made a preliminary plan for improvements and repairs. The contract has been sent in and approved. You needn't worry, Anna. We can get you the list of what's to be done. Any further improvements (within reasonable limits, of course) can *all* be made. The work is to start in the new year and will be finished by the middle of May."

Jesper Jakobsson yanks open the kitchen door, which has swollen and sticks. A small square pane of glass has been replaced with a bulging sheet of cardboard. The kitchen is roomy, faces north, and has only one window. Mortar and brickwork have fallen down the chimney, the ancient iron stove is at an angle, and the larder door is off its hinges and now leans against a rusty sink and draining board.

"All this will be fixed up," says Jesper Jakobsson, suddenly benevolent. "I've said water should be brought in. One could make room for a pump by the sink, but they said no to that. Otherwise it will all be fixed, the chimney rebuilt and the stove changed. We have an excellent, almost unused stove in the office. It's to be moved up here. And the floor's to be relaid. It has gone rotten. The bearing beam has decayed over there in the corner. No, the kitchen will be to your satisfaction, all right, Miss Åkerblom, I can guarantee that." The churchwarden nods importantly, twice, and looks at Anna with his faded eyes.

He opens the door to a cramped little maid's room, inside which is a red-painted pull-out sofa. "For the maidservants," he says laconically. "They can sleep head to foot; otherwise we could put a camp bed in the kitchen." Magda Säll softens. "If you'll leave it to me, Miss Åkerblom, I can probably find you two good girls. I've already asked around." "Are we to have *two*?" says Anna, appalled. "What do we want with two?" "That's usual," says Magda. "There's always unexpected work in a parsonage, Miss Åkerblom, you'll see." Anna sighs silently. Henrik has not said a word all this time. Anna seeks his eyes, but he has turned away.

"And this would be the dining room and parlor," says the churchwarden. "The builder wants to make two rooms for reasons of heating efficiency, and the wall would be here, but I've objected, because there are many occasions when the pastor needs a large room for parish meetings. The church hall is over by the church and difficult to get to, especially in winter. So I've suggested we keep this room as it is today and put a larger tiled stove in that corner, where the chimney goes up to the first floor. So it'll all be warm and cosy, Miss Åkerblom." The churchwarden slaps the wall and rips off a piece of flaking wallpaper. "You mustn't worry, it'll all be warm and decorated. I can guarantee that."

Jesper Jakobsson opens another door. This is the hall to the front door. The stairs up to the first floor are to be turned around. It's rather peculiar that the front door faces the forest and the kitchen door the gate. "That's a little inconvenient for guests, particularly if they come in a carriage." Henrik looks straight at Jesper Jakobsson. "The house is simply oriented the wrong way," he says with sudden arrogance. The churchwarden is at once surly. "I didn't build the place," he says. Silence after that.

"The guest room," he demonstrates laconically, then goes up the sagging, creaking stairs. "Don't tread on that stair," he warns, pointing. "You can't trust that stair, and you could injure yourself. Watch out, Miss Åkerblom. Take my hand. Well, this is the upper floor, and it's not in too bad a state, if I may say so myself. We'll just paint and decorate here. Please go ahead. The bedroom. Not that large, but there is in fact a small washroom and the view is lovely. We could have a few trees cut down. We can't see the water now, but we've talked about doing some clearing. This is due south. And then the nursery on the right and the pastor's study on the left. The nursery and the study can naturally be exchanged to suit your needs. All you have to do is to say so, and it can be arranged, evening sun or morning sun." "And where is *my* room?" says Anna suddenly.

The depressed atmosphere, which has been lying in wait for some time, now becomes quite tangible. Magda Säll stares in astonishment at this little person in her elegantly tailored coat. Dark, serious eyes. Determined chin, resolute voice. "I'd like to know where *I* am to be? I'll have just as large a burden of work as my husband. And unpaid, too, all right, but where am I to go when I want to write letters and read and do the family accounts?" Anna looks at the churchwarden, who looks at Henrik, pleadingly. "I'm used to having a room of my own," the calm voice goes on. "I realize it may seem slightly spoiled, but I must actually demand one."

Now the amazement is total. Demand? What does the creature mean? Won't she come unless she gets a room of her own? What's this all about? "It's probably not usual for the pastor's wife to have a room of her own," says Magda Säll conciliatorily. "Oh, really. Well, I couldn't know that," says Anna. "Would the guest room be an idea?" says the churchwarden, clearing his throat surprisingly submissively. "You could have the guest room as your room, Miss Åkerblom. What do you think?" "I suggest that Henrik take the guest room as his study," says Anna decisively. "I want to be near the nursery." "It might be a little disturbing with everyone going in and out," says Mrs. Säll cautiously. "The pastor has to be undisturbed when he is preparing his sermons." "Then he'll have to put cotton in his ears," says Anna, smiling at Henrik. Say something, Henrik dear! her eyes are saying. You're master in your own house. You decide. But Henrik is struck dumb. "Does this have to be decided here and now?" he mumbles.

"Mr. Jakobsson and I will go out and look at the outbuildings," says Magda with sudden insight.

So Anna and Henrik are left to themselves. *I was only joking,* says Anna, laughing. "It was only in *fun* because everything is so dreadful and we were getting depressed." She flings her arms around Henrik and holds on to him tightly. "Laugh now, Henrik! It's not a major catastrophe. We'll make a lovely home and I — can — wind — Jesper — Jakobsson — around — my — little — finger! You could see that, couldn't you? Now you're laughing, thank goodness. I thought for a moment you were angry."

Mrs. Säll and the churchwarden note that the young couple come out into the autumnal sunlight in a good mood. Together they view the woodshed, the carpentry workshop, the outhouse, the sawdust-covered stack of ice, the storage shed, and the little earth-cellar. "There'll be lots of wild strawberries on the top of it, I see," says Anna.

After that, the chapel is to be inspected. Henrik unlocks the tall, plain iron door. "I borrowed the key from Jakobsson. I said we wanted to be on our own when we went into our church for the first time."

Forsboda chapel had been built at the end of the eighteenth century and was intended to house the park's palms in winter. The room has high, slightly vaulted windows with stained glass in the chancel, thick walls, and a flagstone floor. All around the chapel is a churchyard now no longer in use, partly overgrown, the tombstones barely visible in the long yellow grass.

Henrik and Anna go into the church. Pigeons fly up and make their way out through a broken windowpane. The benches have been cleared away and stacked in a murky heap along the far wall, and the flagstone floor stretches bare and echoing toward the raised space for the altar. The altar cloth is gone, and the wooden stand gapes emptily; a hole has been dug in the corner. Numbers hang on the hymn board: two hundred and twenty-four, second verse:

Strive not for fortune, bread or honor in this world.
Let sorrow not consume you, for this thy short time on earth.

"That's almost like an exhortation," says Henrik, his arm around Anna's shoulders. The sunlight falls sharply on the plastered wall and forms squares and elongated shadows of trees. At the entrance door, a builder's scaffold goes right up to the roof, which soars in a gentle curve. Bird wings. Sun shadows. Somewhere the wind grumbling. Dead leaves have blown in through the broken and partly nailed-up window.

"The pulpit is sixteenth century," says Henrik knowledgeably. "Look at that lovely carving! Peter and John, and there's the Archangel with his sword and the sun and the eye. I wonder where they've taken the reredos. Perhaps in the sacristy."

But the sacristy is empty, nothing there but a stained cupboard with its doors wide open and paintpots and brushes standing on the floorboards, the window wall already painted, the cracks and sores in the wall already healed. "They're getting on with the repairs, you see," whispers Anna.

Then they examine the organ, which is under a cover to the right of the altar. It's a tall, finely carved structure with two manuals and a great many stops, two foot-bellows at the side. "Shall we see what it sounds like?" says Anna, sitting down at the organ.

Henrik pushes the tarpaulin to the floor and stamps on the bellows. Anna pulls out some stops and presses the keys in a C-major chord. The instrument emits a tremendous but frightening discord. "The organ will also have to be repaired," says Anna, taking away her hands. "I wonder if Jesper Jakobsson has thought of that little detail? It's a fine old chancel organ. Where do you think it was before it landed up in exile here? By the way, perhaps the reredos is over there in that corner, under that cloth?"

They lift the dusty cloth and open the closed doors of the reredos. In the middle part is the Lord's Supper, clumsily carved, but dramatic, the disciples rolling their eyes, the Master raising a disproportionate hand, the corners of his mouth drooping. The face of Judas is dark, weighed down by his approaching crime. On the right is Christ nailed to the cross, his head hanging. His wounds are terrible, and the Roman soldier is just thrusting his lance into his side, the blood gushing out. On the left is the Annunciation, Mary with her hands on her stomach, with a menacing figure with flapping wings stretching out a long forefinger and wagging it officiously. In the background the sun is shining above a peacefully grazing lamb.

All these images, all this goodwill and tenderness, are perishing. Dust from the wood flies about; pieces have fallen to the floor; patches of damp have faded the colors; mice and insects have partaken in Holy Communion.

Anna and Henrik stand there mournfully and appalled. Carefully, they replace the stained draperies.

Now I shall describe a quarrel that is soon to explode between Anna and Henrik. Right here, in this decaying palm house, which on a

174

whim became a House of God and on another whim has once again decayed. It is always hard to trace the real reason for any conflict. The origin and outburst are seldom identical (just like the actual scene of a murder and the place where the body is found). One can imagine quite a number of alternatives, both random and fundamental. Go ahead, you can browse and speculate; this is a party game. Two facts, however, are established. First of all, we are witnessing the first heartrending conflict between our two main characters. Second, Luther is right when he says that words flown out cannot be caught on the wing. Meaning that certain words can never be taken back, nor forgiven. Words of that kind will be exchanged in the argument described here. In reality, I know practically nothing about what transpired that Friday afternoon in the ruins of Forsboda church. I only remember a few words of my mother's. "We were in the chapel for the first time, and we quarreled. I seem to remember we even put an end to our love as well as our engagement. I think a long time went by before we forgave each other. I'm not sure whether we ever forgave each other, wholly and fully."

It should perhaps be pointed out that all her life, Anna was quick-tempered and equally quick to make up. She found it difficult to reconcile that hot temper with the Christian concept of turning the other cheek. Henrik was slow to any visible rage, but when the barriers were down, he could reveal a terrible brutality. And he was almost comically unable to forgive things easily. He never forgot an injustice, although with pronounced acting talent, he managed to show a smiling face to whoever had wounded him.

At any rate, this scene now starts, and I maintain it starts at this very moment: Anna is standing by the covered reredos, her head down, her arms hanging by her sides. Then she slowly starts putting on her gloves, which she had pulled off when she had made an attempt to play the organ. Henrik goes up to the altar rail and its stained and worn kneeler. He is standing with his back to Anna and looking at the stained-glass windows in the cruciform. Lighting? It's dramatic and full of contrasts! The sun has stopped going down at a snow-laden cloud, which has appeared above the edge of the forest. The cloud forms a blue-black wall and the light is white and merciless, but only over half his face. The compensatory light on the other half has turned to gray.

Henrik: Anna?

Anna: Yes, my dear.

Henrik: I want us to . . . . (*Falls silent.*)

175

Anna: *What* do you want?

Henrik: When we get married . . . can't we get old Samuel Gransjö to officiate?

Anna: Yes, of course. If you like.

Henrik: Here.

Anna: Here?

Henrik: Yes, here in the chancel of our unfinished church. Just you and me. And two witnesses, of course.

Anna (*mildly*): I don't know what you mean. Are you saying our wedding should take place here?

Henrik: Just you and me and old Gransjö, then two witnesses. Mrs. Säll, for instance, and the churchwarden. Then we'd be dedicating the church and dedicating ourselves to this church. Can't we do that, Anna?

Anna: No, we can't.

Henrik: Can't? What do you mean?

Anna: You and I are to be married in Upsala Cathedral, and the dean is to marry us. He's promised. And we're going to have a proper marriage with bridesmaids and pages and ushers and guests and the Academic Choir and lots of family and dinner at the Gillet. We've agreed on all that, Henrik dear. We can't change it.

Henrik: Can't change it! We're getting married in March, and it's only September!

Anna: What do you think Mama will say?

Henrik: I thought you no longer cared what your mother thought.

Anna: I've invited my whole nursing-school class to the wedding. Nearly all of them have accepted. Henrik, dear, we've already talked about this before.

Henrik: You've told me what it'll be like. I have had to keep my views to myself.

Anna: It was you who wanted the choir. You and Ernst have already decided on the program. You can't have forgotten that?

Henrik: What if I ask you now to abandon all that? Is that so impossible?

Anna: Yes, it's impossible.

Henrik: Why should it be . . . ?

Anna (*incensed*): *Because I want to have a proper wedding!* A really splendid, impressive festivity. I want to celebrate. I want to be joyful. I want a terrific wedding.

Henrik: And the wedding I'm suggesting?

Anna: Let's stop this stupid argument here and now. Otherwise we'll start quarreling. And that really would be unfortunate.

Henrik: *I'm* not quarreling.

Anna: No, not you, but I am.

Henrik: Think it over. (*Pleads.*) Anna!

Anna: I *have* thought it over, and of all the idiocies I have endured for a very long time, this latest whim of yours is the worst. If you don't see that, you're more idiotic than I thought you were, and that's not saying much.

Henrik: And if I don't want to?

Anna: Don't want to what?

Henrik: If I don't want to be part of this spectacle in the cathedral? What'll you do then?

Anna (*angry*): Well, I'll tell you, Henrik Bergman. Then I'll give you your ring back.

Henrik: But this is mad.

Anna: *What is it that's mad?*

Henrik: Are you sacrificing our life together, *our life*, for a shabby ritual?

Anna: It's *you* who's sacrificing our life together for a foolish, theatrical, melodramatic, sentimental . . . I don't know what. My *celebration* is anyhow a *celebration*. Everyone will be happy, and everyone will be aware that you and I are at last properly married.

Henrik: But we're going to live *here! This* is where we're going to live, don't you see? It's important that we start our new life here, just here, in this church.

Anna: Important to you but not to me.

Henrik: Don't you understand at all what I mean?

Anna: I don't *want* to understand.

Henrik: If you loved me, you'd understand.

Anna (*angry*): Don't give me that! I might just as well say that if you loved me, you'd let me have my wedding.

Henrik: There's no limit to how spoiled you are. Don't you understand that this is *serious?*

Anna: I shall tell you what I understand . . . you don't like my family. You want to humiliate my mother as much as you can. You want to demonstrate your new power. Anna, come with me. Anna, don't bother about what your family thinks any longer. You want to get even in a very hurtful and sophisticated way. That's what it is, Henrik! Admit it!

Henrik: It's amazing how you can misinterpret things. Horrible and amazing. But of course, it's good now that I really know . . .

Anna (*even more angry*): . . . don't stand there looking like that. What's that stupid grin all about?

Henrik: All I can see is that you're on your family's side, *against me.*

Anna: Are you *really and truly* crazy? I nearly killed my mother in order to come to you. And Papa, what do you think he thought when . . . ?

Henrik: . . . I'm only asking a silly little sacrifice of you.

Anna: You're still crazy. You know *what*, Henrik? Sometimes you seem to me to be painfully lower-class. You've a way of making yourself worse than . . .

Henrik: What did you say?

Anna: You make yourself out to be stupider than you are. You put on an act that doesn't suit you at all. Do you know what? You flirt with your poverty and your wretched miserable childhood and your poor wretched mother. It's disgusting.

Henrik: I remember when you asked me what Frida did, and I told you she was a waitress. I remember your tone of voice. I remember your expression.

Anna: It's not necessary to wear dirty shirts and have holes in your socks. It's not necessary to go around with dandruff on your collar and dirty nails.

Henrik: I *never* have dirty nails.

Anna: You aren't always clean, and sometimes you smell of sweat.

Henrik: Now you've gone too far.

Anna: Of course. The pastor can't stand the truth.

Henrik: I can't stand your being cruel.

Anna: Don't trample on me, Henrik.

Henrik: I'm glad this conversation occurred *before* the wedding.

Anna: So am I! Now we both know where we stand. We almost made a huge mistake.

Henrik: So you're prepared to throw away . . .

Anna: Am *I* throwing it away?

Henrik: No, the awful thing is we're both . . .

Anna: Well, it was remarkably easy.

Henrik: Terribly.

Anna: I want to cry, but I can't. I'm far too miserable.

Henrik: I want to cry, too, I'm so horribly miserable. I don't want to lose you.

Anna: It didn't sound like that just now.

Henrik: No, I know.

Distance, geographical as well as spiritual. The sunlight has gone into the blue-black wall of snow slowly looming up over the forest. The daylight is gray but sharp. Anna sits down on the altar rail's dirty kneeler. Henrik sits down on it, too, but at a distance — several steps away. Their grief is palpable, but so are the anger and the poisonous words just spoken, and what has not been said. This story of good intentions could end here, as the main characters now

179

consider themselves abandoned, alien, and alone. Anna is thinking with revulsion about that man's body and his smells. Henrik is thinking with distaste about this cruel, spoiled child. Both are thinking (perhaps) how terrible to have to live together for just one day, one hour. Humiliating. Unworthy. Frightening.

Anna: Henrik?
(*Henrik says nothing.*)

Anna: *Henrik.*

Henrik: No.

Anna (*holds out a hand*): Henrik!

Henrik: Don't be affected.

Anna: I'm miserable.

Henrik: Are you? Too bad.

Anna: I said terrible things.

Henrik: Yes.

Anna: Can you ever forgive me?

Henrik: I don't know.

Anna: So this is the end?

Henrik: I think so.

Anna (*sigh*): It feels like it.

Henrik: Words flown out can't be caught on the wing.

Anna: What do you mean?

Henrik: That's Luther. He means that one can say anything. But not *just* anything. Certain words are irretrievable.

Anna: And you mean that now I've . . .

Henrik: Yes.

Anna: But that's terrible.

Henrik: Yes, it's terrible.

Anna: But you're a priest.

Henrik: My profession has nothing to do with . . .

Anna: You *must* forgive me.

Henrik: I can't. I'm furious. I hate you. In fact, I think I could hit you.

Anna: Well, at least that's clear.

Henrik: You're welcome.

Anna: Here I am, sitting here humiliating myself and . . .

Henrik: No one asked you to.

Anna: . . . and going on about you — that *you* should forgive *me!*

Henrik: If I were capable of it, I'd get up, go out that door, slam it shut, and never come back.

Anna: Are you crying?

Henrik: Yes, I'm crying, but I'm crying because I'm in such a rage. No, don't come any closer. Don't *touch* me.

Anna touches him. He knocks her arm away, the blow striking harder than he had intended. She is frightened and falls back against the altar rail. Astonishment and horror.

Anna: You hit me!

Henrik (*pure rage*): I may hit you again! Go away! I never want to see you again. You're vile. You torment me. You torment me because you *want* to torment me. Go away. For *Christ's sake.*

Anna: What a coward! Now I'm beginning to understand why Mama was frightened of you. I'm beginning to understand . . .

Henrik (*interrupts*): . . . oh, yes, that's really good. Your mother and you will fall into each other's arms and thank God you've escaped with nothing but fright and loss of virginity.

Anna: God, how *crude* you are. It wasn't just Mama and Papa, I'll have you know. Ernst warned me too. Constantly. He said you were a dual personality no one could . . .

Henrik (*white*): *What* did he say? What did Ernst say?

Anna: That you were untrustworthy. That you were a liar. The worst kind of liar, because you never knew when you were lying. He said you were incapable of telling between the truth and a lie. That was the real reason you became a priest.

Henrik: Did Ernst say that?

Anna: No.

Henrik: What did Ernst say about me?

Anna: Nothing. He likes you. You know that.

Henrik: *Now* I know nothing.

Anna: I think you should go back to Frida. Carl thought she'd be a good wife for a priest. For Anna Åkerblom, this will have been an instructive interlude.

Henrik: Stop acting. You do it so badly. And leave Frida out of this squalid . . .

Anna: Miss Frida made no demands. She loved her dear Henrik. Her motherliness no doubt knew no bounds.

Henrik: Shut up.

Anna: Your crudeness is really . . .

Henrik: . . . on a level with yours.

Anna: Yes, maybe so.

Speechlessness and anger, they are almost audible, echoing in the darkening church, freeing themselves from the protagonists and striking against roof and walls, maybe even breaking windows and rushing like searing flames along the stone flags.

Henrik: I'm beginning to recognize my life now. It's at last coming back, and it looks as it has always looked. I was dreaming. Now I am awake.

Anna: Sometimes you sound like a novel. A cheap romance.

Henrik: I don't know any better.

Anna: And we were supposed to have children! Three children! Two boys and a girl. How filthy everything is. And stupid. This is all crazy. Here I am, sitting in a decaying palm house in the wilderness and it's getting dark, and I think it's starting to snow. *Me*. This is really crazy. A strange man shouting at me, hitting me! It's all quite mad.

Henrik: How can we go on living after this?

Anna: Oh, I'm sure that's possible.

Henrik: You don't see the worst of it?

Anna: And what would that be?

Henrik: Our love. We've thrown it all away on a . . .

Anna: . . . a trifle.

Henrik: I don't care about that wedding. It can be anywhere. At the North Pole.

Anna: I don't care either. You can decide.

Henrik: No, no. That ritual means more to you than to me. And also, it's stupid to make your mother more miserable than she already is.

Anna: She could come here.

Henrik: Your mother and my mother! Here? Then a gigantic binge, in which everyone drowns in a sea of theatrical idiots, would be better.

Anna: Let's not get married. I'll be your housekeeper.

Henrik: Thanks for the offer. I'll take it into consideration.

Anna: Henrik!

Henrik: Yes. Anna.

Anna: Now we've shouted and quarreled before God. What do you think He says about it?

Henrik: I don't know. The place is a little odd.

Anna: Do you think this is a sort of marriage?

Henrik: No, I don't. We were heading straight for the destruction of our love.

Anna: To think that we go around with so much hatred in us.

Henrik: Yes. I'm so tired, Anna.

Anna: So am I. How shall we get away from here?

Henrik: Come and sit down here beside me.

Anna: You're not going to hit me anymore!

Henrik: Anna!

Anna: Is that all right?

Henrik: Give me your hand. It's icy cold. Are you cold?

Anna: Not really. Only inside.

Henrik: There. Is that all right?

Anna: I have to cry.

Henrik: I'll hold you.

Anna (*cries*): Do you think we'll be any wiser after this?

Henrik: I don't know. More careful.

Anna: . . . more careful with what we've got?

Henrik: Something like that.

They are close together as dusk falls.

My parents were married on Friday, March fifteenth, 1913, in Upsala Cathedral in front of a large congregation of relatives, friends, and acquaintances. The Academic Choir sang, and Dean Tisell officiated. Bridesmaids and ushers assisted, and the little bridesmaids trod on the veil. After the wedding, a dinner was given at the Gillet in their large banquet room. However much I search through albums and the family photographs, I cannot find any photographs of the wedding. This is remarkable considering that the Åkerbloms were very much a photographing family and innumerable, less important gatherings are recorded. In our home, an abundance of happy brides and handsome bridegrooms sat on stove mantles and small tables, but I have never seen any photographs of my mother and father's wedding. There are explanations, the simplest being presumably that my mother (who loved saving things and sticking them in albums) did not think the bride sufficiently beautiful, or that the wedding dress was not becoming, or that the young couple simply looked fatuous. Another explanation is that the photo session was canceled. Something got in the way; someone felt ill, sad, or perhaps simply annoyed. A third (just as unlikely) explanation is that the photographer bungled the job, none of the photographs came out, and one cannot really dress up with the wedding crown and bouquets all over again. That is an extremely unlikely possibility. Wennerström and Son on Upper Slottsgatan was the town's most prominent photography studio, and it is inconceivable that it could make a mistake of that magnitude.

The fact is, however, that no wedding photographs exist in albums or archives. Also, I never asked my parents about their wedding. On the whole, I asked my parents far too little about everything. I regret that, especially now as I sit here with considerable gaps in my documentary material. I regret it in general. All that indifference and lack of curiosity. So foolish and so very like the Bergmans!

In any event, the wedding was splendid and the dinner festive. I possess a yellowed invitation card (very beautiful with the bridal couple's initials intertwined on the front and the actual invitation in elegant print on the inside). The speeches were doubtless excellent, moving, and amusing, the waltzes dazzling, and the food exquisite. If the producer has plenty of money, he is very welcome to portray all these festivities on film. Things of that kind are called "production values," after all.

Let's now look at a short scene on this sunny wedding day in March. The setting is the dining room in the Trädgårdsgatan apartment house. The big table with its lion feet has been pushed up against the bulging stomach of the sideboard. A full-length mirror has been moved from Mrs. Karin's bedroom and placed between the windows in the dining room. In front of the mirror, right in the middle of the flood of light, is the bride, ready, on her head the crown from the cathedral and the veil from the family bridal chest. Mrs. Söderström, employed by the most distinguished fashion house in Stockholm, is on her knees putting right a hem that has been trodden on (from nervousness). Anna is gazing at her image with matter-of-fact attention, rather like an actress just about to go on stage in an incomparable, brand-new part, thought up and written for her alone. Her breathing is under control, her heart thumping, her face pale, her gaze wide-eyed.

The dining room door opens, and in the mirror, Anna sees her brother Ernst in a well-cut morning coat and usher's emblem. The siblings look at each other in silence for a few moments, then Ernst takes a few steps forward and tenderly embraces his sister. Mrs. Söderström bites off the thread and sticks the needle into the left shoulder strap of her apron, then she quietly moves aside, an important actress in the drama of the day, but nevertheless a shadow. With a firm hand, together with three highly professional women, for weeks she has been shaping this masterpiece and on this very morning brought her creation to Trädgårdsgatan. She is standing with her forefinger against her lips, tall, broad shouldered, and dark complexioned, her black hair in a heavy knot on the top of her head. She has good reason to be pleased with her handiwork, since the young bride has to move with great dignity and much more slowly. Mrs. Söderström is sure to have pointed that out after the brother has left the room.

185

Ernst: Well?

Anna: Good.

Ernst: Really good, or are you just saying that?

Anna: You'll have to guess.

Ernst: You're beautiful.

Anna: So are you.

Ernst: But you're pale, sister dear.

Anna: I'm probably terrified.

Ernst: You've got what you wanted. In everything.

Anna: I'm sorry Papa . . .

Ernst: Yes, it's sad. Still, had he been here, he would have been sad. His darling leaving him. You can imagine. (*Falls silent.*)

Anna: When are you leaving?

Ernst: The day after tomorrow.

Anna: And coming back?

Ernst: In a year — maybe. It's a major expedition.

Anna: Then you're going to stay in Christiania?

Ernst: My work is in Christiania.

Anna: Mama'll be lonely now.

Ernst: Sometimes I think she *wants* to be lonely.

Anna: Has Henrik come?

Ernst: He's a wreck! I had to give him a large brandy.

Anna: Tell him I'm coming in a moment. Has anyone fetched his poor mother from the hotel?

Ernst: Be calm, now, sister dear. There's an organizer lying in wait around every corner. This festival of rejoicing is not to be allowed to fail.

Anna: Mama's coming.

A light tap on the door. Without waiting for an answer, Mrs. Karin enters in dusky red brocade and the family jewelry. She is calm and smiling. She has put on weight recently and in some strange way seems broader in the shoulders, though that's perhaps an illusion. Her gait is just as energetic, her movements as usual light and under control.

Karin: Ernst, would you be so kind as to make sure Carl doesn't get drunk? He's just come and doesn't seem to be all that well.

Ernst: All right, Mama.

Karin: My dear Mrs. Söderström, what a masterpiece!

Mrs. Söderström: Thank you, Mrs. Åkerblom.

Karin: I would like to be alone with my daughter for a little while.

Mrs. Söderström: Of course, Mrs. Åkerblom.

And so mother and daughter are alone together. Mrs. Karin sinks into one of the high-backed dining room chairs that are scattered around looking rather lost (now that the table has been shifted up against the sideboard).

Karin: I'm feeling rather moved, I think. But that's all part of it.

Anna: You know how grateful I am, Mama, for this splendid wedding.

Karin: You don't have to be grateful, my heart.

Anna: It's a pity that Papa . . .

Karin: Yes, yes.

Anna: I believe he's with us at this moment. I can feel it.

Karin: Do you think so?

Anna: Mama, there's one thing I must tell you.

Karin: Yes?

Anna: Henrik and I have postponed our honeymoon. Ernst was kind enough to cancel the train tickets and hotel rooms.

Karin: Oh, really. Was that why he disappeared all morning?

Anna: Yes.

Karin: And what are your plans now, if I may ask?

Anna: Were you sorry to hear that?

Karin: My dear child, honeymoons are supposed to be a pleasure.

187

Anna: Henrik and I can go to Italy another year. Can't we? We can save that trip?

Karin (*rather weary*): Naturally. What are you going to do instead?

Anna: We're going straight to Forsboda.

Karin: Tomorrow?

Anna: Tomorrow. First thing in the morning.

Karin: Oh, I see. Oh, really. This is rather sudden.

Anna: Mama, don't be sad!

Karin (*lightly*): I'm not.

Anna: We've spoken to Mrs. Säll. She's invited us to stay at the parsonage. In the bishop's room. It's quite grand, I have to tell you. Like any old bridal suite. She says everyone's pleased we're coming straightaway.

Karin: I see. In that way you can supervise the repairs of your house.

Anna: . . . and of the church.

Karin: That's a very good idea! Do you think you'll be coming to the summer place in July sometime?

Anna: Of course. For at least a week.

Karin: We said three weeks, if I remember correctly.

Anna: I think Henrik is very anxious to get going earlier than he agreed to. And I want to be with him from the start. That's important for us both.

Karin: I understand perfectly.

Anna: I have to give in a little, too. Henrik's had to give way on so many points.

Karin: Has he? (*Smiles.*)

Anna: Yes, but we won't talk about that.

Karin: No, let's not, Anna.

Karin goes up to her daughter and carefully holds her face. They look at each other.

Anna: You might just *try* to like Henrik. For my sake. Just a little.

Karin: The past is all forgotten.

Anna: I wish it were.

Mrs. Karin's eyes darken. She kisses Anna on the cheek and forehead. Then she leaves the room. Anna turns slowly around toward the mirror.

Anna (*silently to herself*): What a fuss! What arrangements! I'll do as I like. No honeymoon? Oh, really! No summer with them all? Oh, really! Do I really want all this? I don't know. Do I know what I want, or do I just want a whole lot of nonsense in general? Have I even *got* a will of my own at all? Do I ever think through whether *this* is what I want, and so I get my own way? Have I the same kind of willpower that Mama has? That's doubtful. *Do I want Henrik?* Yes, I think I really do. But do I want to get married? I don't know. Doubtful. One has to be on guard against wanting too much, particularly now, when Mama and all the others are starting to listen to what one wants.

The door opens a little, and Carl's aging clown face comes into view. "Come on in," says Anna, pleased to have her unprovoked monologue interrupted. Carl comes right in, his morning coat not entirely a perfect fit on his chubby figure, his forehead beaded with sweat and his pince-nez misted over. He has a glass of brandy in his hand and makes a gesture toward his eyes.

Carl: You dazzle me.

Anna: Ernst has just gone to look for you.

Carl: I escaped him. (*Drinks.*) Do you want a sip?

Anna: Yes, please. Phew!

Carl: Phew! You can say that again! What have you done, Schwester-chen?

Anna: Isn't it *terrible?*

Carl: I'm becoming intoxicated and have no views.

Anna: Can't you wait until dinner?

Carl: Yes, yes. Don't worry. I shall not bring shame on your party. By the way, do you want Mama to put me in the hands of a guardian?

Anna: What do you mean, guardian?

Carl: Guardian. Power of attorney. Mama and brother Oscar are going to take my money and hand it over to a guardian. What do you say to that?

Anna: Poor Carl.

Carl: I'll have to sign for a monthly allowance.

Anna: Is that such a bad idea?

Carl: You don't think so?

Anna: You know you're careless with money.

Carl: Do you want another sip? You're so pale.

Anna: Please. (*Drinks.*)

Carl: Stop, for God's sake. You must leave a few drops for me, too. Sit down here. On my lap.

Anna: I can't sit down. My skirt'll get creased.

Carl: Then I'll lie down.

Four chairs are standing in a row. Carl lies down, propping his head on his hand and regarding Anna with a sorrowful, cracked smile.

Anna: Why are you looking like that?

Carl: When I look at you and delight in your prodigious beauty, Schwesterchen, I have comical visions. I see Milky Ways and galaxies and the insane polka of the planets. And then you are standing there! (*He sighs.*)

Anna: Are you all right, Uncle Carl?

Carl: Oh, yes. I'm fine. (*He sighs.*) And then there you are, all earthly beauty radiating around you, and I am dazzled, tears coming to my eyes. Do you know why?

Anna: You must tell me quickly, because I must soon . . .

Carl: Well, you see, you contradict meaninglessness. Just now and at this very moment, little sister, you contradict the icy meaninglessness of winter streets and the merciless emptiness of the universe. If I stand beside you like this. No, look now, don't look at the clock. Look at us two! Look at our images in the mirror. I correspond to highly placed demands for galactic meaninglessness. And then we look at you, my flower, and you are overflowing with meaning and content. One could

190

almost become religious. One could say you characterize God-given thought, a concealed but nevertheless perceived meaning. That was amusingly and nicely put, wasn't it? Do you understand what I mean?

Anna: It sounded very moving. But I mustn't start crying. You and I are the best of friends, aren't we?

Carl: Do you think I'm *really* an idiot? Feebleminded?

Anna: Why do you say such stupid things?

Carl: Approaching eclipse? Dementia?

Anna: You're the kindest, wisest, best . . .

Carl: I'm probably sick, you know.

Anna: Are you sick?

Carl: Yes, but that's not a fit subject of conversation.

Anna: Isn't it as you say?

Carl: No, oh, no.

Anna (*cautiously and quietly*): We must go now.

Carl: If I close my eyes, I can immediately imagine eternal Death. If I open my eyes, I see you and see incomprehensible magnificent Life. That's just it.

Anna: Come on, dearest brother Carl. Take my arm, and we'll prop each other up. Then we'll march together out to our guests and what is to come.

So they march into the salon. The sun sparkles in the chandeliers and wall brackets. The family is already assembled and chatting cheerfully. The actors know their lines, and everyone is in the right key for the drama. As the bride enters, the players rise with enthusiastic cries and scattered applause. Anna glows from the smiles and bathes in the looks and comments. There is Henrik in his new well-fitting cassock. Tears suddenly come into his eyes. Whether of joy or pain or both is not easy to know.

The wedding night without a honeymoon is discreetly and swiftly transformed into an organizational matter of urgency. Mrs. Karin ordered an extra bed to be put in Anna's childhood room, ignoring all assurances that this would not be necessary. The bright room was decorated with a small fraction of the flowers from the festivities, two small bouquets of lilies-of-the-valley on the pillows, and a collection of telegrams and letters in a neat pile on Anna's white desk. However, Martha's suggestion of champagne and appropriate sandwiches was decisively rejected.

For a few hours, the disquiet in the house dies down, the streetlight shining through the light, painted blinds, the fire glowing gently. The cathedral strikes the quarters and the hours, followed by the large salon clock far away in the apartment. The beds are a short distance apart. Anna and Henrik hold hands across the chasm.

Anna: What did it strike?

Henrik: Four.

Anna: I can't sleep.

Henrik: Neither can I.

Anna: I'm too wound up.

Henrik: And I — am — probably — too wrought up.

Anna: It's like when you were little and it was the night before Christmas.

Henrik: I feel — well, what do I feel?

Anna: Just wait. Just think about us occupying the bishop's room. What kisses!

Henrik: Tonight was more like brother and sister.

Anna: Best that way.

Henrik: We'll be on the train in three hours.

Anna: Marvelous.

Henrik: Aren't you at all sad?

Anna: No. Not in the very smallest corner of my heart.

They lie with their eyes closed, holding hands, Anna smiling, Henrik rather solemn, the flowers giving off scents, the fire crackling and glowing. The superintendent of traffic may well be somewhere out there in the hovering darkness.

Henrik: I've been thinking about your father all evening.

Anna: Me, too. (*Sits up.*) Damn!

Henrik: What is it?

Anna: Damn! Do you know what we've forgotten!

Henrik: The photographer. The wedding photographs. Damn!

Henrik: Everyone forgot the photographs!

Anna: Carl's brandy!

Henrik: What?

Anna: Just as we were off to the church, he came creeping in with a glass and said: Take this; it'll calm you down and help. I drank nearly all of it.

Henrik: I thought I could smell brandy up at the altar. I thought it was the dean . . .

Anna: And so we forgot the photographs.

Henrik: Do you mind?

Anna: Not in the slightest. (*Lies down.*)

Henrik: We can get ourselves photographed in Gävle. (*Lies down.*)

Anna: We have an *inner* photograph.

Henrik: I do believe I'm falling asleep.

Anna: Me, too.

In front of me on my desk are two photographs dated spring 1914. One of them is of Mother and Father, Mother smiling with soft lips, as if often kissed, her hair in slight disorder, her head against Father's shoulder. Maybe she doesn't feel too well, for she must be in her fourth month. Father is grave and obviously proud, standing very upright in his neat cassock. His figure, which used to be rather thin, has become more solid. He is holding a protective arm around Mother's shoulders (you can't see that, only suspect it). The photograph expresses harmony, growing self-confidence, and modest happiness. The other photograph is of Mother sitting in an uncomfortable armchair, leaning slightly forward, as usual elegant in an ankle-length skirt with buttons down the side, handmade high-heeled boots, a finely patterned blouse, and a gold brooch at her neck. Her hair is neatly done, but nevertheless unmanageable. In front of her is Jack, a rather muscular, almost square Lapland dog.

The expression on his face is that of a samurai devoted unto death. Mother and Jack are looking smilingly at each other. On all previous photographs, Mother has never been laughing. On this one she is cheerful, relaxed, amiable. From these testimonies, one can draw the not too dangerous conclusion that Anna and Henrik got on relatively well together during those first years, something which in fact was confirmed by both my parents.

What possibly spoiled their pleasure was that Anna's mother never went to see them at the parsonage. In her letters, she pleads various obstacles. In July, the young couple pay a short visit to the summer residence. Dag-Erik was born in October at the Academic Hospital in Upsala. After a few weeks' convalescence, the family returns to Forsboda. Their firstborn is healthy and yells at night, a fact mentioned in letters with weary cheerfulness.

On New Year's Day, 1915, brother Ernst announces that he is coming to see them. He intends to go to Stockholm from Christiania, but takes the route over Falun, changes to a narrow-gauge track at Mackmyra, and arrives at Forsboda at about two in the afternoon.

Huge drifts of snow, clear and windless, the sun going down in burning mist, footsteps crunching, the engine billowing smoke, the heating pipes in the train cars hissing, the whole little train enveloped in damp steam. Because of that, Anna can't see her brother, and he embraces her from behind, a violent, wordless joy. They have both changed, but not that much: handsome, kind, decorative, warm, still untouched.

Yes, Ernst has married, a dark, plump beauty of upper-class extraction, accepted from the very first moment by Mrs. Karin and the rest of the family. They live in the neighboring country and are seldom seen; even their wedding was not allowed to be a family affair. They had a civil ceremony, a new idea at the time, and at once went to Egypt. The families received the news in the mail. Comments were surprisingly good-tempered. Well, Ernst has his own ideas. You can't decide things for him. Alternatively, Maria has gone her own way. One has to accept that. Ernst and Maria were established favorites. They all shook their heads, but smiled at the same time. Now Maria is pregnant and is staying behind in Christiania, so Ernst is alone. After his trunk has been checked out and loaded onto the back of the sleigh, brother and sister bed down in the fur rugs, a tall red-haired girl sits up on the driver's seat, and they are quickly and lightly carried off into the ice-blue dusk.

I presume their conversation is slightly exalted — it has been such

194

a long time. Expectations have been great. There's so much one doesn't write in letters and trivialities fly, but that doesn't matter, for now they have four days together and that's a long time!

Anna: Henrik sends his regards and says I must give you a special hug from him and say you are *his* brother, too, and he's very pleased to be seeing you again, old Laban. By the way, is it true your friends called you Laban? I never knew that. Just like you and all your women. I never even knew about half of them.

Ernst: Maria sends her love, too. She has terrible morning sickness, so doesn't want to travel. We want you to come and stay with us next summer. We've got a summer place in Sandefjord right by the sea. Well, it's Maria's place, of course. Her father gave it to her as a wedding present. You'll like Maria, I promise you. She's very much like you, but taller. Since I couldn't marry you, it had to be Maria. And so far I've had no reason to complain. You'll see. I have some very good photographs.

Anna: Are you cold? Yes, your ears are cold. You silly . . . take my shawl and wrap it around your head. It was twenty-three below this morning and is going to be colder this evening, at least thirty below. No, stop it. Take that silly hat off, and then I can wrap you up in the shawl. Now you look fine. You always look fine. I wonder whether you're not the best-looking creature in the world. I've missed you terribly, you can't imagine! Just because things are so good for me, you see. When you're as happy as this, you become insatiable!

The parsonage welcomes them with burning torches on the gate-posts and the steps, lighted candles in the windows, the smell of Christmas still hovering. "Welcome to my home," says Anna after they have stepped over the threshold and are peeling off their outdoor clothes and boots. "You're to have my workroom," she goes on and opens the door. Inside, a paraffin lamp sends a flickering light on the pale furniture and wallpaper, and anyone with eyes in his head can recognize various items from Anna's room as a girl in Trädgårdsgatan. The huge trunk is maneuvered in by red-haired Mejan and dark-haired Mia, big girls, sisters, neatly clad in blue, giggling cheerfully, industrious, and perspiring. "You must have some coffee now, and some of Mia's fresh buns," says Anna. "But first you must come and see Dag-Erik. Come on, come and have a look at your nephew."

"He's fine, isn't he?" says Ernst without interest. "I think he looks like brother Carl. Only the pince-nez is missing." "He cries all night and sleeps all day," says Anna. "Just wait, you can hear him all the way down here, too." "He must have got his night habits from Carl as well," says Ernst. "You may not look at him any more," whispers Anna, pushing him out the door. "Come on, now! You didn't appreciate him enough and I'm rather hurt, but you can have some coffee all the same. Henrik's the kindest and best papa one could wish for. If I didn't stop him, he'd be changing his son's diapers." "Why shouldn't he, if he enjoys doing it?" says Ernst. "Oh, no, that wouldn't be right," Anna rebukes him. "Come and sit here! We'll light the candles on the tree after dinner."

Outside the windows and their airy curtains, the northern lights are swirling and looming, the rapids can be heard like a distant organ note, and there's a rumbling resonance behind the doors of the iron stove, the warmth smelling of Christmas and birchwood.

Anna: And how's Mama?

Ernst: I went to see her last month. In the middle of December, actually. She seemed in good spirits, I thought.

Anna: Did she seem lonely?

Ernst: I don't know what you mean by lonely. Miss Lisen was there. They were very busy with all the Christmas presents that had to be sent off.

Anna: So she was going to be alone over Christmas?

Ernst: Not alone. She and Miss Lisen, of course.

Anna (*impatient*): Yes, of course. I mean, wasn't anyone going to visit her? Wasn't she invited to any of the brothers or sisters?

Ernst: I don't think so. Anyhow, she said nothing about it.

Anna: Couldn't you and Maria have considered having her over Christmas?

Ernst: That wasn't possible. We were to spend Christmas with Maria's parents.

Anna: Couldn't you have . . . ?

Ernst: Why didn't you invite her yourself?

Anna: You know the situation with Henrik. I didn't even dare suggest it.

Ernst: Does he still hold grudges?

Anna: He finds it hard to forget humiliations.

Ernst: Oh, well, we weren't all that nice to him at the time.

Anna: No, we weren't.

Ernst: Time heals all wounds. (*Pats her.*)

Anna: He was sorry our child was born at the Academic Hospital in Upsala and not here at home. The moment Mama came to see me, Henrik left. And vice versa. He wasn't just sorry. He was furious. And he refused to go to Trädgårdsgatan. He kept telling me I had let the women in the parish down. The midwife in Forsboda wasn't all that pleased, either. My milk ran out for a few days, I was so miserable. Though it's all right again now. But he keeps bringing up a whole lot of things from the past. I don't understand how someone like Henrik, who's so kind, can go around carrying so much hatred in him. I want to help him, but . . .

Anna falls silent and runs her hand down her face from forehead to chin and throat.

Ernst: Mama talked kindly about Henrik. She didn't mention any of what you've just told me. She just said you were happy, and she was pleased you seemed so content.

Anna: Yes. (*Silence.*) Henrik had a letter in October, in shaky, almost illegible handwriting. It was from his grandfather. (*Silence.*) His grandfather was asking for a reconciliation. (*Silence.*) The old man was ill, seriously ill. (*Silence.*) He wanted Henrik and me to go and see him. (*Silence.*) Henrik showed me the letter. I asked him what we should do. He answered quietly that he could see no reason to seek reconciliation with the man.

Ernst: And you?

Anna: Me? What could I do? Sometimes I can't make head or tail of anything. Sometimes a chasm opens up. I keep away so as not fall into it.

Ernst: *Can* one keep away?

Anna: *I* keep away. And *say nothing*. A few hours later everything's normal again, and Henrik is the kindest, happiest, sweetest — well, you'll see.

Ernst: Anna!

Anna: No, no. He's coming.

(I write what I see and hear. Sometimes it all goes well, and I forget to listen to tones of voice, which might be more important than the words. Could there possibly be a note of sheer suppressed anxiety in Anna's voice? Does Ernst take in her possible uneasiness? Did Anna have in mind Henrik's carefully concealed and seldom revealed wounds, the inflamed unhealed wounds of the mind? Or is she much too occupied with the present, with all that is new and unexpected? Anna has a talent for lighthearted recklessness. Henrik is tender-hearted, loving, and mostly happy. The day runs its course. Without thinking about the course, they become concepts of each other. "I can't tell," says Anna apologetically. "How could I understand?" says Henrik in astonishment. "Surely one can't *always!*" protests Anna. "I don't know why I should have a guilty conscience," mumbles Henrik.)

Henrik comes into the hall stamping his feet. "Is Ernst here? Has he come?" He is wearing a short military sheepskin coat, a knitted cap on his head, and a wool scarf around his neck. His trousers are stuffed into sheepskin-lined boots, and in his hand he has a square leather bag containing his cassock, vestments, and a little wooden box of the sacred requisites for communion. The Lapland dog, Jack, is circling his legs.

As Ernst appears in the doorway to the dining room, Jack goes rigid with resentment and growls. "Quiet, Jack!" cries Anna, pulling at his collar. "This is Ernst, you stupid dog. My brother. We have the same scent, if you could trouble yourself to take a sniff!"

"Dear old Laban, how welcome you are here," says Henrik, embracing his brother-in-law. "Dear old Luvern, let me look at you. God, you've filled out!" says Ernst, patting Henrik's cheeks. "You're beginning to look like a real pirate. Where's that elegiac poet got to now?" "Living in the forest's good for you," says Henrik, pulling off his gloves, cap, scarf, coat, and boots.

He flings his arms around Anna and Ernst and suddenly says: "This way I'm happy!" He is fiercely moved and lets his arms fall, orders Jack to say hello to Ernst, saying that Jack is his armor-bearer. "The way things are around here, you need something of Jack's caliber to defend you." "Jack's church-inclined, too," says Anna. "When Henrik's preaching, he lies at the door of the sacristy. He's quite familiar with altar service as well as communion. We really must have dinner now! The women are coming at seven." "What women?" says Ernst. "We have a sewing bee on Thursdays, when womenfolk, young and old, from all over the parish come. Sometimes forty souls. Henrik reads aloud, and we have coffee, and everyone brings something to eat. You wait and see, it's not bad at all. When we came here, they were all stuck out on their own in their homes. Now you could say there's some sort of *communication* going on! Wait and see!"

My mother told me quite a lot about her sewing bee. As soon as they took on the parish and had got the house in order, they had systematically gone around and introduced themselves. She had said that every Thursday at seven o'clock, there would be open house at the parsonage, a sewing bee, reading aloud, and evening prayers.

The suspicion they met with was unmistakable: Oh, yes, indeed, new brooms! Pentecostalists and Mission Society members all declined. This was seduction of the devil. The communists were unfriendly. Were their womenfolk to have coffee with the church, the moneybags, and the military? Inconceivable! The unemployed shook their heads. What? Bring something to eat? Who could do that when you didn't know how to get from one day to the next? So at first the number of people who came to the meeting was fairly minimal. A few church people from the bigger farms came, and three older women from the workers' quarters, possibly in defiance of views held in the kitchen at home. Gradually (but very slowly) curiosity got the upper hand. And it should not be forgotten that my mother was a trained nurse and it was twelve kilometers of bad roads to the provincial doctor, the midwife nearly always out on her rounds. Mother had a good hand with people's ailments, children, animals, and flowers. She consulted with the doctor and was able to acquire a set of instruments and administer some harmless medicines. There were plenty of ailments, and Mother felt needed and energetically active. Father, according to Mother's testimony, made modest but effective progress.

It all began with an accident in the forge. A worker had his arm torn off and died from loss of blood before the doctor and ambulance could get to the place. The men wanted to stop work and go home, as was traditional when a death occurred. The management refused to allow it, citing delivery dates and the pressure of time (it was wartime, and important goods were being manufactured). Suddenly the men's anger exploded. There was still much antagonism below the surface after the humiliations of 1909 and the local conflicts that followed. The main switches were turned off, the machines stopped, and an iron-gray dusk descended over both workshops and men.

When Nordenson finally made his way down to the office, the pastor was already there, sitting on a bench by the wall with some of the older men. People were standing, sitting, or lying on the floor — it was warm, at the end of August. Nordenson spoke calmly and politely, one knee shaking violently. No one replied. He appealed to the pastor, who remained as silent as the others: dusk, silence, heat. Nordenson left the foundry and telephoned to the minister himself. The minister then summoned the pastor and severely reprimanded him, referring to the Master's rather obscure words, render therefore unto God the things that are God's and unto Caesar the things that are Caesar's.

This episode was much discussed at the Works and on the farms, and possibly overvalued. The pastor was regarded as "one of us." He also got on well with people, had a good memory for faces and names, visited the old and the sick, talked to them in a way they understood, and sometimes sang a verse from a hymn or something equally appropriate. Without telling anyone, he reformed the confirmation classes and told his pupils both what would be asked and what the answers should be at confirmation. He abolished their homework and talked to them about things that interested both them and him. He held parish evenings once a month, often at the parsonage, for the chapel was difficult to heat. He ordered lantern slides and printed lectures from the diocesan publishers. He sought out the chairman of the Mission Society and suggested working together. That was an inappropriate step. The minister forbade such contacts, and the pastor of the Mission Society declined with harsh words.

Steadily, modest spiritual activity began to grow in the parish, a fact that was good for both the Mission Society and the Pentecostalist movement, for competition increased and the battle for souls intensified. Once the early curiosity had waned, the pastor had preached to a fairly empty chapel, and in the big church the desolation was even more evident. Slowly, extremely slowly, people began to come to morning service and evensong.

Mother and Father were also a handsome couple living in obvious harmony on the brightly lit stage of the parsonage, its doors all open. No one doubted their good intentions.

The sewing bee, particularly in the winter, is a lengthy but functional procedure. On this evening, at seven o'clock, twenty-nine women assemble at the parsonage. They are all well wrapped up and have brought with them handwork bags and food (everyone brings a basket, in the basket a thermos of coffee, cream, sugar, cup, spoon, plate, and buns and cakes of varying richness and quality). Mia, Mejan, and some confirmands see to the baskets. The dining room table quickly becomes a coffee table, the coffee all poured into the big household copper pot (because it is the third winter of the war, the coffee is mostly chicory). Then they unwrap themselves, and outdoor clothes pile up on the chairs in the hall and on the stairs. They blow their noses politely, smooth down their hair in front of the mirror, and there is a quiet mumbling and buzz of talk. Anna and Henrik stand in the doorway greeting them. There are paraffin lamps, candles, fires in the tiled stoves, tables moved in, and all the chairs in the house assembled or borrowed from neighbors. "Good evening, good evening, how nice, Mrs. Palm (Gustavsson, Almers, Flink, Danielsson, Berger, Ahlqvist, Nykvist, Johansson, Tallrot, Gertud, Karna, Alma, Ingrid, Tekla, Magna, Alva, Mrs. Dreber, Gullheden, Ander, Märta, Mrs. Flink, Werkelin, Kronström) that you could come. We're going to be quite a crowd tonight despite the cold. This is my brother, Ernst Åkerblom. He's just come from Norway, where it's even colder at the moment. A cup of coffee would be really good now, wouldn't it? I've got a packet of real Java coffee from my mother. We've put it in the pot. I'll come and see you tomorrow, if that suits you, Mrs. Werkelin, then I can take a look at your mother-in-law."

Anna finds that Mrs. Johansson is holding her left hand behind her back, two fingers bandaged with linen cloth and string. "I burned myself badly on the stove ring." "We'll see to that. I have some ointment the doctor gave me. We'll do that when the reading starts. I've also got some pills for the pain." "Yes, it hurts something awful," mumbles Mrs. Johansson.

They all bustle around together with ceremonial politeness. At last the big copper pot is on the table. The intensity of the talk rises by a few decibels; there's a rattle of spoons and porcelain. This is the prelude to long notes and controlled tempo.

Henrik takes his place by the window table, sharing a paraffin lamp with Miss Nykvist, Mrs. Flink, and the good-tempered Alva, who is simpleminded but good at all kinds of handwork. He opens the book and asks for silence. Then he recaps what happened in the last chapter. His choice of literature is unconventional, not to say bold. *Anna Karenina* by Tolstoy.

Henrik (*reading*): "The same day that they came, Vronskey went to his brother's, where he also met his mother, who had just arrived from Moscow on certain errands. His mother and sister-in-law received him as usual. They asked him where he had been abroad and talked to him about mutual old acquaintances, but they said not a word about his relationship with Anna. His brother, on the other hand, who came to see Vronskey on the following day, asked him about her, and Alexey told him that he regarded his connection with Anna as if it were a marriage, and that he hoped to effect a formal divorce so that he could then marry her, but that even before that, he regarded her as his wife."

While the reading was going on, Anna had retreated into the kitchen with Mrs. Johansson, fair-skinned, plump, blue-eyed, her usual red cheeks pale from the pain in her hand, her lips trembling when Anna exposed the burn, now already infected. The skin is already gone from the inside of her middle and third finger. They have to get her rings off. Anna and Mrs. Johansson are alone in the kitchen, except for Jack, who is asleep under the sink. "I'll fetch my brother and a sharp pair of pincers," says Anna decisively. "This can't wait until morning. Gangrene might set in." Ernst turns pale, but arranges the pincers and cuts the rings, which are then forced apart. Then Anna spreads ointment on the burns, bandages the hand, and makes a sling. Ernst fetches brandy and pours it out. Mrs. Johansson nods gravely, and Anna and Ernst nod back. They empty their glasses in one draft, almost to the bottom.

Anna: You'll have to keep your left hand still. How can you do that?

Mrs. Johansson: I suppose I'll manage.

Anna: Then I'll phone the doctor and ask him if he wants to see your hand. I wouldn't dare take the responsibility myself.

Mrs. Johansson: Yes, please.

Anna: Take some of these painkillers at night; then you'll get some sleep, Mrs. Johansson. But try to put up with it in the daytime.

Mrs. Johansson: Thank you, thank you, I expect it'll be all right.

Anna: Shall we go back to the reading?

Mrs. Johansson: I suppose we should.

Anna: What's the matter, Mrs. Johansson?

Mrs. Johansson: I don't know. I don't know whether it's worth mentioning.

Anna sits down. Ernst has withdrawn from the circle of light round the kitchen table and sat down by the sink, smoking a cigarette and cautiously making Jack's acquaintance, with some success.

Anna: We can stay awhile.

Mrs. Johansson (*after a silence*): Maybe it's nothing. The children have grown up now. The girl's a nursery-school teacher in Hudiksvall and the boy's in the Navy and called up forever. He wants to be an officer, so he'll probably be all right. Johannes — my husband, that is — and I have been on our own for two years, and that's fine. Just fine. Johannes has had a lighter job since his lungs went bad on him — he's got a job in the Works office, and that's all right. (*Silence.*)

Anna: But there's something that's not quite all right?

Mrs. Johansson: I don't know. I don't know how to put it.

Anna: Would you like my brother . . . ?

Mrs. Johansson: No, no, heavens no. I'm probably making things more complicated than they are. (*Takes a deep breath.*) It's like this. My niece who's married in Valbo has a little boy of seven. His father went off a few months ago. The marriage probably wasn't all that great. But you never know who's to blame when you're on the outside, so I'm not making judgments. Anyhow, Johannes and I thought the boy could live with us. His name's Petrus. My niece has gone to the father's parents in Gävle, where she's got work in the kitchen at the big hotel there. The father's vanished without a trace, but otherwise things are fairly good. Now Petrus is to start at the school here in Forsboda, of course. That'll be in the autumn, won't it?

Anna: He's seven, is he?

Mrs. Johansson: He'll be a little old for the class, but I've talked to the teacher and she says there shouldn't be any problems. There are children who're even older when they start . . . (*Silence.*)

Anna: *Is* there something about Petrus?

Mrs. Johansson: I don't know.

Anna: Does he have difficulties? Is he . . . ?

Mrs. Johansson: Oh, no. He can read and write and do sums. He's more . . . what shall I say? . . . forward, advanced. He's mostly good and helpful and obedient. And he seems to be fond of Johannes and me. My husband has a little workshop on the farm and likes . . . when Johannes is free, he and Petrus are always together in the workshop.

Anna: But something's wrong, all the same?

Mrs. Johansson: The teacher is nice, but she's retiring next year. So I can't talk to her. I tried, but I didn't get very far and hardly even got started.

Anna: Is Petrus sick?

Mrs. Johansson: No, no. (*Uncertainly, quietly.*) He's *tormented*. My husband doesn't notice, but I . . .

Anna: Tormented?

Mrs. Johansson: His eyes look confused. Not always, but if you look, so to speak. Runs and runs until he . . .

Anna: Perhaps you'd like to bring Petrus here, so we could talk to him.

Mrs. Johansson (*nonplussed*): Yes.

Anna: It may be his age.

Mrs. Johansson: Yes.

Anna: Or that he thinks his mother has . . .

Mrs. Johansson: Maybe.

Anna: Bring him here one day next week, Mrs. Johansson. We have the bazaar on Saturday, so at the moment there's . . .

Mrs. Johansson: Of course, of course. At the moment there's lots to . . .

Anna: Shall we go in to the others?

Mrs. Johansson: Don't say anything about this.

Anna: I must talk to Henrik.

Mrs. Johansson: Yes, of course.

Anna: Come now. The pastor will be wondering whether we don't like his reading.

An hour or so later, Henrik closes the book and gets up. The fires have gone out; the homemade candles, which burn down so quickly, are almost down to the candlesticks; the paraffin lamps have grown sleepy and are smoking slightly. It's nice and warm, and one or two people are dozing. Henrik claps his hands and reads the blessing. Then he suggests that they sing Jesper Svedberg's hymn, "Now the Day Is Over" . . . We know that one, don't we? Anna sits down at the piano. Henrik and Ernst sing first, and the assembled company follows in the heartfelt assurance that the streets of heavenly Jerusalem are paved with gold:

Now the day is over,
Night is drawing nigh.
Shadows of the evening
Steal across the sky.
Jesus, give the weary
Calm and sweet repose.
With thy tend'rest blessing,
May our eyelids close.

At half past ten the last guest has wrapped herself up and tumbled out into the night with her handwork bag and emptied basket. Mejan and Mia have cleared everything away, together with Ernst and Henrik. Anna wakes her slumbering son and changes him. As she sits down on the low chair in the bedroom to feed him, the dog lies panting at her feet. His field of responsibility has increased. Previously, two gods had to be defended and attended to, but now they have become three, and that's difficult. Yawning and slobbering, Jack is working on his jealousy.

When Anna and Jack come down from their duties, Ernst and Henrik are sitting at the cleared dining room table, drinking milk and eating crispbread and soft whey cheese. The gramophone, brought from Trädgårdsgatan, is wound up and ready with a Victor record of the latest tune on it. "There you are," says Ernst. "A present for Anna, a late Christmas present, really." "What is it?" says Anna inquisitively. "It's a one-step," says Ernst challengingly. "The very latest from New York, the very latest dance. It's called the one-step." Out of the gramophone's red horn leaps Coal Milton's syncopations. "This is what you do. It's great fun," says Ernst, demonstrating. After a few minutes, Anna imitates him. He pulls her to him, and they dance the one-step together. Henrik and Jack watch, noting the siblings' delight, their affinity, their enthusiasm and laughter. "Again, again," cries Anna, winding up the gramophone. "You and me, now," she says, overweeningly, tugging at Henrik's arm. "No, no, not me," protests Henrik, pulling back. "Come on, now, don't be silly, it's fun, I tell you." "No, no, it's more fun watching you and Ernst dancing." "Let's all dance," cries Anna, beginning to insist, her cheeks red. "We'll all dance. You and I and Ernst — and Jack!" "No, no, let me go, Anna. I just get embarrassed." "What do you mean, embarrassed?" laughs Anna, who has now kicked off her shoes, her hair loosened and down, with some help from Ernst, who has scooped up some hairpins and two combs. "This is how things should be," she cries, raising her arms.

"This is how things should be! Come on, Henrik, you who were such a one for dancing. Remember the Spring Ball." "That was waltzing," protests Henrik. "All right, then, we'll dance a waltz although it's a one-step," says Anna, embracing her husband. "It's the cassock that's in the way. Let's take it off the pastor!" She starts unbuttoning the cassock from the middle down. Ernst winds up the gramophone. Henrik flings his arms around his wife. "You're squeezing me to death," she cries, with a touch of anger. He lifts her and drops her, pushing her lightly in the chest so that she takes two steps back and stumbles over a chair. Then he shakes his head, goes out, and slams the door.

Ernst lifts the gramophone head off and smiles with embarrassment. "Henrik's not the only one who doesn't like the one-step," says Ernst rather lamely, taking the record off and putting it back in its green cover. At that moment the door is flung open and Henrik comes back in again! "I know I'm an idiot," he says quickly and apologetically. "We were only having a little game," Anna says gently. "I'm a great spoiler of games," says Henrik. "I can't help it."

"Let's get the fire going and sit around and talk," Ernst suggests as a diversion. "Jack and I were probably feeling out of it," says Henrik in a feeble attempt at a joke. "Jack and I both tend to be jealous. Isn't that so, Jack?"

The fire crackles with renewed vigor, the little doors of the tiled stove are open, the paraffin lamp glowing faintly on the round table by the window. They sit in a row on the sofa, Ernst, Anna, and Henrik. Ernst fills his pipe and slowly lights it. Jack has fallen asleep at a suitable distance, occasionally raising one eye or directing an ear, keeping his two gods and their untrustworthy friend under supervision.

"I've flown in an airplane," says Ernst suddenly. "Our institute hires a Farman Hydro from the Norwegian Defense Forces. It's a two-engine biplane that takes off and lands on water. Our people go up daily and make observations on weather fronts and measure temperatures and air pressure. They also photograph cloud formations from above. Sometimes they go up to a height of three thousand meters, but then we have to have oxygen — otherwise it's hard to breathe. One day we went up to four thousand meters and the sky was dark blue, almost black. There was no color left, and the sound of the engine got fainter and fainter." "Aren't you scared when you go up?" says Anna. "Scared? No, the opposite. It's an incredible feeling of . . . well, I don't know what to call it . . . a feeling of power. No, not power. Of being perfect. Of being almost crazed with joy! I want to throw myself out into that sea of air and sail on my own. And I think, this is what the Creator felt on the seventh day, when he found his work good."

It may be appropriate to relate here how the seven-year-old Petrus Farg came to stay at the parsonage. It was at the end of January, and the cold had turned to a gray icy thaw with sudden sharp showers of rain and beating snow. What strange weather! One night they had a thunderstorm, and the Works transformer was struck by lightning.

One morning, Anna comes down to breakfast at half past seven (Henrik has already gone off to the village to be on duty at the pastor's office, which opens at eight). When Anna comes into the kitchen for breakfast, Mrs. Johansson is sitting at the table with a cup of coffee and some bread and butter, and Petrus Farg is sitting on a stool by the woodbox. Mejan is going in and out of the larder. She has a big baking day ahead and is only moderately amused by the visit. Mia is cleaning somewhere, and they can hear her singing. She likes to sing when she's in a bad mood. Mrs. Johansson at once gets up and makes a little bob. Her hand is still bandaged. Petrus gets up and bows when told to. Anna has completely forgotten her promise and is a little confused and rather short, at which Mrs. Johansson immediately apologizes for intruding. Anna collects her big cup and saucer and some bread and butter and urges her guests to come with her into the adjoining dining room.

Petrus Farg is standing at the end of the table with his hands behind his back. He is slim and gangling, with thick lips and large expressionless eyes, a high forehead, straight protruding nose, cropped hair, and large red ears. He is properly dressed in a thick jersey with too-long sleeves, dark blue shorts with a large patch in the seat, and well-knitted long stockings. His boots are on the porch. He is sniffling with a cold, and out of one nostril runs snot, which he discreetly licks up whenever necessary.

Mrs. Johansson again apologizes. She hasn't announced her visit. She has come far too early in the morning. Anna drinks her tea and mumbles politely that it doesn't matter in the slightest, she had promised, and it's good that Mrs. Johansson has at last decided to come, and asks about her hand.

Yes, the hand is better; she can move her fingers, and the doctor was pleased with what the pastor's wife had done.

Anna puts down her teacup and calls to Petrus. He at once turns around to her and steps forward, but still with his hands behind his back. He looks at her without fear or shyness, but at the same time almost blindly, as if he really were blind. "May I look at your hand?" says Anna. He holds it out and puts it in hers, a long hand, long fingers, clear veins, dry rough skin and bitten nails, the middle finger-nail chewed right down to the flesh. Mrs. Johansson shakes her head. "It's terrible the way he bites his nails. I put mustard on them and I reprimand him and I promise him rewards, but nothing helps." Anna doesn't answer but turns the boy's hand over: the inside is crisscrossed with faintly red patterns and lines, an old man's hand.

Anna: So you're starting school in the autumn?

Petrus: Yes.

Anna: What do think about that?

Petrus: I don't know. I haven't been yet.

Anna: But you can already read and write?

Petrus: And do sums. I know my multiplication tables.

Anna: Who taught you?

Petrus: I taught myself.

Anna: Didn't anyone help you?

Petrus: No.

Anna: Not Uncle Johannes?

Petrus: When we're in the workshop together, Uncle Johannes asks me questions and I answer.

Anna: Have you any friends?

(*Petrus says nothing.*)

Anna: I mean have you any boys to be with?

Petrus: No.

Anna: So you're lonely?

(*Petrus says nothing.*)

Anna: Perhaps you like being on your own?

Petrus: I suppose I do.

Anna: And what do you read?

(*Petrus says nothing.*)

208

Anna: Have you got any books?

(*Petrus says nothing.*)

Mrs. Johansson: We've got some old Christmas magazines, and sometimes my husband buys the *Gefle Dagbladet*. So he mostly reads a reference book we've got, though only a part, "from J to K." It's a trial volume Johannes bought for seventy-five öre.

Anna: I think I've got some books you'd like, Petrus. Wait a moment, and I'll see.

She goes over to the white, glass-fronted bookcase and hunts along the bottom shelf for a while, then pulls out a fat, red, clothbound book with a gold-worked spine and gold lettering on the front. It is *Nordic Sagas*, "edited and published for children." There's an illustration on nearly every page, some of them in color. "Here you are," says Anna. "You read that, and when you've finished it, I've got some more books that are just as good. Take it, Petrus! We'll just make a cover for it, like they do in school, so it doesn't get dirty."

Mrs. Johansson: Say thank you properly, now.

Petrus: Thank you.

A few kilometers south of the parsonage, where the Gräsbäcken flows into the Gävle River, is the Sawmill, which, like the Works, belongs to the estate. The Sawmill employs twenty-two men who live with their families in ramshackle rows of cottages above the timber chute. The sawn timber is transported to the Works harbor along a narrow-gauge railway and all around the timber-roofed sawing sheds that lean toward one another are stacks and stacks of fragrant planks. The dust above the Sawmill is thick, and thin streams of water spurt through the closed hatches all summer and winter.

One day in the middle of February, this is what happens: The foreman announces abruptly that Arvid Fredin has been dismissed on the spot and told to get out of his house within a week. To start with, there are no protests or comments, and work goes on as usual inside the Sawmill and out on the stacks and the freight cars. At the eleven o'clock break, some of the men doing the sorting start talking about the dismissal, and it is considered unjust. True, Arvid Fredin is a loudmouth, and it is also true he's careless with his drink, but he's also a good worker who has never been guilty of absenteeism or drunkenness at work.

Arvid himself is standing in the yard, his arms at his sides, and he is unusually silent, his expression one of astonishment and distress. His wife opens the window at regular intervals and tells him to get going, go on down to the office and talk to the manager, complain to Nordenson. No one should submit to things like this!

During the break and on their way to the afternoon shift, a lot of the men stop by to see Fredin. "You've been sacked for what you said at the meeting on Monday," says Måns Lagergren, one of the oldest men, who has become increasingly involved in social-democratic politics. "I warned you not to let your tongue run away with you." "I was no worse than anyone else," protests Arvid. "Maybe not, but you read something you'd written. A sort of *manifesto*, or whatever the hell it's called," says Måns, lighting his cold pipe.

Another ten or so men have assembled in the muddy yard. "They're making an example of you," says Anders Ek, starting off toward the Sawmill. "Come on now, for Christ's sake; otherwise there'll be more trouble." No one moves. No one goes.

Henrik is paying a sick call. One of his confirmands is ill with the present rampant sickness and is in bed, coughing and having difficulty breathing. It is probably not just a chill, but something else, and worse. Henrik has just agreed with the mother that he must talk to the doctor and promises to phone that afternoon.

Henrik looks out the window and sees the crowd. "What is it now?" he asks Mrs. Karna. "I don't know," she says irritably. "There's always trouble these days. I think they've sacked Arvid. Arvid Fredin. I'm not saying anything. He's a real agitator and drinks and fights. He says we should all join world communism and shoot Nordenson or hang him from the bell tower. I don't know, and it's best not to know anything. Last week he sat here jawing away with Larsson, wanting him to sign something. We had to get the neighbor to help get him back up to his place. So I've nothing against him going."

Henrik says good-bye and goes out to the yard. The foreman has just come up the slope but has stopped some distance away. He's trying persuasion. "Come on, men. It's high time. We don't want no more trouble than we've already had." Everyone stands still, some of them to their own surprise. "Wait a few minutes, and we'll be along," someone says. "Well, then, I'll go on down and wait for the time being. I don't want to hear any more of that rubbish." "If you go down, you can send the others up."

The foreman doesn't answer, but turns his back and moves off. He could telephone the office, for there's a sort of local phone, but he doesn't.

"This isn't about Arvid Fredin," says Johannes Johansson. "It's a matter of principle. We must tell them we won't agree to . . ." "Yes, to what?" says someone. "We won't agree to Arvid getting fired, although he drinks and talks shit?" Disapproving mumbling. "They're making an example," says Anders Ek stubbornly, his voice hoarse. "Because he can write and express himself. He's dangerous, of course, so they're kicking him out. Not because he drinks and is a shit."

This is all said in a friendly way; even Arvid is smiling. "Anyhow, we can't accept this Arvid business," says Måns Lagergren firmly. "We must state that clearly, but by all means politely. There's no point in yelling and screaming. We've had enough of that. The agitators from Gävle have been no help. On the contrary."

They listen to Lagergren and agree with him. Actually, no one really likes Arvid Fredin. He may be good and thorough at work, but he's a loudmouth and reads extracts of books no one's ever heard of.

Nothing is said for a while. They ought to go to the afternoon shift, and it's already very late. The foreman is a decent man, and they all know him well. He is a local. He doesn't make a whole lot of unnecessary fuss, but things may get bad for him if the work doesn't get started. Despite this, they stand around, dispirited and indecisive. "Can't we have a meeting and talk about this properly?" says Johannes. "There are various sides to this question, and we solve nothing by standing around here with our mouths open." Mumbled approval. "Then the question is, where can we meet?" Johannes goes on. "We ought to get the men down from the Works to meet with us — it shouldn't be just us. If we use any of the Works premises, they'll throw us out, and there'll be trouble about that, too. We can't be out of doors in this god-awful weather, and it's colder in Robert's barn than it is outside."

"We could use the chapel," says Henrik, without thinking. "We can be warm in the chapel, at least on Sunday after morning service. The stoves are on all morning. The chapel holds a hundred and fifty people, and that's big enough, isn't it?" Henrik looks around, a question in his eyes. Closed, mistrustful, surprised faces. "In the chapel?" says Johannes. "What d'you think the minister'll say about that, Pastor?" "I have the right to arrange meetings and assemblies. That's actually my right." "Oh, yes," says Lagergren, with surprise in his voice. "Well, shall we accept the pastor's offer? Suppose we could, so long as you don't regret it, Pastor." "I won't regret it," says Henrik, as calmly as he can. "Shall we say Sunday at two o'clock?" says someone. "That's all right," says Henrik. "Will you be coming, Pastor?" "Yes, of course. I've got the key."

That same night, Anna and Henrik are awakened by a thunderstorm over Forsboda. It's like continuous gunfire over the Storsjön, the ridges and mountains, hailstorms coming in waves over the roof. "I've never seen such peculiar weather," whispers Anna. She lights a candle and fetches Dag, who has slept all through the racket. So all three of them are lying in Henrik's bed. "Thunder in February is like the final judgment," says Henrik.

The racket gradually subsides and is now just flashes of lightning and softly rustling rain. "What's that down on the veranda?" says Anna, suddenly wide awake. "It's nothing. Your imagination." "Yes, I can hear something, someone knocking on the pane of the outer door." "Who could that be? A ghost?" "No, listen, can't you hear?" "Yes, you're right. There's someone on the veranda."

Anna lights a paraffin lamp, and they put on dressing gowns and slippers, the stairs creaking. Now they can hear the knocking quite clearly, faint and irregular. Henrik unlocks the door and opens it. Anna holds the lamp up. On the steps, a dark figure is crouching, faintly outlined against the blurred snowy light of the yard. It is Petrus, in a much-too-long woman's coat, a large peaked cap, and boots. He is just standing there, motionless, his arms hanging loosely at his sides, the peak of his cap hiding his eyes, his mouth half-open. Anna stretches out her hand, pulls him into the hall, and takes off his cap. The blue eyes are expressionless, the face pale, lips trembling. "Are you cold?" says Anna. He shakes his head. "What have you come for?" says Henrik. Another shake of the head. "Come on, I'll heat up some milk," says Anna, temptingly. "Take your coat and boots off." Obediently, his head down, the boy slouches along behind her.

The next morning, Mia is sent with a message to the Johanssons, who have awakened to find the boy gone. There is a very early meeting in the parsonage kitchen. Johannes and his wife are standing in the middle of the floor apologizing. As one of them draws breath, the other starts up. Mia is seated at the table eating her breakfast porridge; Mejan is busy at the stove. In vain Henrik begs his two guests to have a cup of coffee or at least sit down. Anna has gone to the guest room to wake Petrus, which turns out to be unnecessary, for he is already awake, curled up at the head of the bed wrapped in a red blanket. Above the blanket is a bloodless face and two wide-open, watery eyes, a blind whirlpool right in the center of his gaze, the dry lips clamped together. Anna takes a chair and carefully sits down opposite her strange guest. "You must come now," she says kindly. "Your parents have come to fetch you."

Petrus: They're not my parents.

Anna: They're like your parents.

Petrus: No, they're not.

Anna: They're nice to you, Petrus.

Petrus: Yes.

Anna: Things couldn't be better for you, Petrus.

Petrus: No.

Anna: No one's angry with you, you know.

Petrus: Why should anyone be angry?

Anna: No, no, you're right.

Petrus: But I don't want to.

Anna: You can't decide that for yourself, Petrus.

Petrus: No.

He gets up meekly. Anna lets him keep the blanket. Obediently and sorrowfully, he trots along behind her through the hall and the dining room, then out into the kitchen. When he sees his foster parents and the others in the kitchen, he stops and draws the blanket tighter around him. Anna is behind him and tries to push him forward, but with no result. He stays put, immovable.

Mrs. Johansson has been saying something meek and sorrowful, but at once stops. "Come, now, Petrus," says his foster father, taking a step toward Petrus, who at once turns to Anna and clings to her, pressing his face into her stomach. She stands still, nonplussed, gently stroking the back of his neck. Johannes carefully tries to loosen his hold, but when the boy persists, the man takes a firmer grip and Anna falls forward welded to the boy. Then Johannes grabs hold of him, pries loose his arms, takes him around the waist, and lifts him up. Without a sound and with fierce strength, the boy tries to fight his way free, wriggling and jerking, kicking and scratching, trying to bite his foster father's hands.

"Let him go," says Henrik. "Let him go. That's not the way to do it." Johannes lets the boy go, and he at once clings to Anna again. Mrs.

Johansson is rigid, as if paralyzed, her hand to her mouth. Johannes is breathing heavily, his face red and tears in his eyes. "I don't understand" is all he can say. "I don't understand. We're such good friends, Petrus and me. Aren't we, Petrus?" But the boy doesn't answer or even move, simply clutches Anna. She has her hands around his head. Mia is sitting there openmouthed, her porridge growing cold, and Mejan forgets to rake the ashes out of the stove.

"Perhaps Petrus had better stay for a few days," says Henrik in the end. "He needs time to calm down and think." "He's welcome to stay a few days," says Anna. The foster parents look helplessly at each other, perhaps humiliated, anyhow deeply embarrassed. They accept the pastor's offer with no signs of gratitude.

The community consists of four small parishes around the much-too-large church built at the beginning of the nineteenth century. The parish office has been in the west wing of the minister's house for many years. The actual office is a long bare room with three desks in a row along the window wall, accommodating the assistant minister, the pastor's curate (Henrik), and the clerk, who sits nearest the entrance. Along the opposite wall are a long wooden sofa covered with worn leather, two chairs, and an oak table. On the table is a carafe of water and church magazines. On the far wall, an iron stove wages war on the drafts from the old windows, and the three gentlemen have permission to wear their overcoats, overshoes, and felt boots. There's another door by the sofa, leading into the minister's private room, and a short corridor that leads into the records office and a small library. Worn linoleum on the floors, a picture on the wall above the sofa in a black wooden frame of the Good Shepherd with a lamb and a lion. There is a smell of damp, mold, and thick outdoor clothes.

The office is open every weekday between eight and ten. Practical matters are dealt with: baptisms, burials, weddings, churching, certificates for moving away from, and moving into, the parish. The care of souls is confined to regular mediations between warring married couples. These are carried out by the minister in his room. Other so-called private conversations go on in the records office, in which there are two rickety wooden chairs.

This is a morning in March, 1915, icy rain pouring down the dirty windows, the light fleeting and reluctant.

The clerk, who is the organist and also works part-time in the school, is correcting writing books. Henrik is occupied with a moving certificate, a young couple standing in front of his desk, the woman heavily pregnant. The assistant minister is planning a funeral. The widow and her sister and brother-in-law are deep in murmured conversation. A chair has been put out for the weeping, black-clad widow, who is mumbling incoherently. The Reverend Gransjö has his door slightly ajar and is speaking in a loud voice on the phone, his white beard wagging, his glasses glinting.

The door to the porch opens violently, and Nordenson comes in. He is wearing a short fur coat with a belt, his trousers tucked into heavy boots, and he has snatched off his Persian lamb cap, so his iron-gray hair is now on end. His head is thrust forward, his nose red from the wind and a cold. His quick black eyes immediately find the person he is looking for. Right across the room, he says in irrefutable tones that he wishes to speak to Pastor Bergman — immediately. Henrik replies that perhaps he would be good enough to sit down and wait a few minutes; "I'll soon be finished with what I'm doing." Nordenson makes an impatient gesture and flings his gloves down on the table among the church magazines, at first remaining standing as if considering leaving the room in fury, but then sighing and sitting down on the creaking sofa. He fishes out his glasses and for a few moments studies the latest issue of *Our Watchword*, but at once flings the magazine down again and lights a cigarette. "I'm sorry," says the clerk. "But smoking is not allowed in the parish office." "Well now it is!" says Nordenson, drawing his lips up into a grin that does not get as far as his eyes, at which the clerk's courage fails him. He gestures lamely at a printed notice on the door and returns to his exercise books.

The minister has finished his telephone call and from experience realizes that something is happening in his office. He comes out, sees Nordenson, who gets up and greets him with a hearty handshake: "I haven't come to see you. I want to talk to your curate," says Nordenson, pointing with a long finger. "Go right ahead," says the minister politely. "No, he's pretending to be busy," says Nordenson. "Come over here, Bergman. The clerk can do that. Please come on over."

Henrik looks up from his writing and reluctantly but obediently gets to his feet. "Mr. Nordenson wishes to speak to you. You can use my room if you like. I'm just going for my breakfast." The minister looks at his watch: "It's ten o'clock, so . . . do come on in! You'll be undisturbed in here." Nordenson sits down in the visitor's chair and lights another cigarette. Henrik does not sit down at the desk but moves up a heavy chair with a high back. The window has stained glass in it, and a wall clock ticks.

Nordenson: I've spent the whole of my life up here by Storsjön and have never known such weather in February before. It's as if the devil had got loose.

Henrik: People say the influenza comes from the weather. I don't know what to believe.

Nordenson: It's not the weather. It's the war, Pastor. Millions of corpses rotting. Infections are carried on the winds. But it'll be over soon. The Americans will find a reason, and then it'll end. Believe you me.

Henrik: A year, two years, five years?

Nordenson: Fairly soon. I was in Cologne a few weeks ago. Nothing's the same. Food's running out. Trouble in the streets. No one believes in victory anymore. Which is bad for us.

Henrik: Bad?

Nordenson: Of course. As long as the war lasts, we've got a living. When the war ends, our living goes too.

Henrik: Is that so certain?

Nordenson: I presume you're not very familiar with the situation, Pastor?

Henrik: No, indeed.

Nordenson: I thought as much.

Henrik: You wished to speak to me, Mr. Nordenson?

Nordenson: It was more of an impulse. I was just passing the office and thought I'd look in and have a chat with young Bergman. How are things going for the girls?

Henrik: Well, thank you.

Nordenson: I hear you've abolished homework for your confirmation classes.

Henrik: More or less, yes.

Nordenson: Are you allowed to do that?

Henrik: There aren't any specific rules about how the teaching shall be done. It just says "confirmands shall be prepared in an appropriate manner for their first communion."

Nordenson: I see, and now you're preparing my daughters? I suppose

216

you know that this is happening against my express wishes? No, no, for God's sake. Don't misunderstand me! There's never been any trouble over this. Susanna and Helena and their mother decided. I just pointed out that I'm against all that hysterical nonsense about the blood of Jesus. But my little Susanna persisted, and then my meek little Helena was not to be outdone, so the girls persuaded their mother, who is a little — how shall I put it? — romantic, and that was that. What has a scruffy old heathen to say with three young women assailing him? Not a damn thing, Pastor!

Henrik: Susanna and Helena are making great progress.

Nordenson: How the hell one makes progress without doing any homework, I can't imagine!

Henrik: Some of the pupils make discoveries, which they can then make use of in their everyday life. We talk.

Nordenson: Talk?

Henrik: About how one lives. About what one does and doesn't do. About conscience. About death and spiritual life . . .

Nordenson: Spiritual life?

Henrik: The life that has nothing to do with the body.

Nordenson: Oh, so there is such a thing, is there?

Henrik: Yes, there is such a thing.

Nordenson: My wife has started saying evening prayers with her daughters. Is that an expression of what you call "spiritual life"?

Henrik: I think so.

Nordenson: When the girls have gone to bed, my wife goes into their room, closes the door, and they kneel down and say the prayers you have taught them.

Henrik: They don't use my words. They are St. Augustine's.

Nordenson: I don't care whose words they are. I'm only concerned that I'm left out.

Henrik: You can always join in on the prayers, Mr. Nordenson.

Nordenson: What the hell would that look like? Nordenson on his knees with his females?

Henrik: You could say, Maybe I don't believe this, but I want to be with you. I will do what you do, because I love you.

Nordenson: I promise you, Pastor, the ladies would be even more disturbed at their prayers.

Henrik: You could try.

Nordenson: No, I couldn't.

Henrik: Well, in that case . . .

Nordenson: . . . in that case it's hopeless?

Henrik: I think Susanna and Helena understand the difficulty. Just as their mother does.

Nordenson: Just as their mother does? Have you talked to my wife about me, Pastor?

Henrik: Your wife came to see me at the parsonage and asked for a private talk.

Nordenson: Did she now? Elin went to see you, Pastor? Couldn't she be satisfied with the minister, the old goat? Who lives in walking distance? Eh?

Henrik: Anyone seeking a spiritual adviser has a perfect right to choose whoever he or she wishes and is in no way bound by geographical considerations.

Nordenson: Isn't she in any way bound by consideration for her nearest and dearest, either?

Henrik: I don't really understand what you . . .

Nordenson: Forget it. So you talked about me. And what was the conversation about? If I may ask.

Henrik: You may certainly ask, but I cannot possibly answer. Priests and doctors are, as you know, bound by an oath of silence.

Nordenson: I'm sorry, Pastor. I forgot about that oath of silence. (*Laughs.*) Yes, it's comical.

Henrik: What is it that's comical?

Nordenson: I could also say a thing or two. But I'll keep quiet. I'm not going to sit here blackening my wife.

Henrik: I don't think I am breaking my oath if I say that your wife talked about her husband with the greatest tenderness.

Nordenson: She talked to *you* about *me* with "the greatest tenderness." Oh, really. With tenderness. Good God!

Henrik: I'm sorry I even mentioned that conversation.

Nordenson: Oh, that's all right. Don't worry, Pastor. Slip of the tongue. That's only human.

Henrik: I hope that Mrs. Nordenson will not suffer . . .

Nordenson (*smiles*): What? You can rest assured, Pastor. Of all the complications between my wife and me over the years, this is one of the minor ones.

Henrik: That's good to hear.

Nordenson: Then you know our secret, Pastor.

Henrik: I know nothing of any secret.

Nordenson: But you know, of course, that my wife left me? Twice, to be more precise.

Henrik: No, I didn't know.

Nordenson: Oh, really? (*Pause.*) How did the meeting go on Sunday, by the way?

Henrik: I presume you sent your own reporters, Mr. Nordenson. Anyhow, I noticed at least one of the men from the Works office there.

Nordenson: It was splendid of you to give the Sawmill workers a roof over their heads, Pastor.

Henrik: Not in the slightest splendid, just logical.

Nordenson: Has the minister said anything about it?

Henrik: Yes, indeed.

Nordenson: May I ask what?

Henrik: The Reverend Gransjö was very definite. He said that if I ever again allow church premises to be used for socialist or revolutionary meetings, he would have to report me to the cathedral chapter. He went on to say that he had no intention of agreeing to the House of God being a refuge for anarchists and murderers.

219

Nordenson (*amused*): Really, is that what the old goat said?

Henrik: Unfortunately the meeting was pointless. Arvid Fredin got fired after all.

Nordenson: I know.

Henrik: I should have spoken up, but I said nothing.

Nordenson: Never mind, Pastor. Next time you'll be at the barricades.

Henrik: I'll never be at any barricades.

Nordenson: Was it perhaps the case that your little wife didn't like your rash decision to lend the chapel?

Henrik: Roughly that, yes.

Nordenson (*amused*): You see, you see!

Henrik: What do you see?

Nordenson: I won't say. What would you say to some kind of cooperation, Pastor?

Henrik: Cooperation with whom?

Nordenson: With me. Next time there's any trouble, you get up in the pulpit or on a soapbox or a machine and speak to "the masses."

Henrik: And what should I say?

Nordenson: You could, for instance, say that what was most important now was not to try killing one another.

Henrik: The people at the Works are badly treated and humiliated. Are you saying *I* should advise them to let themselves be badly treated and humiliated?

Nordenson: It's not that simple.

Henrik: Really? How is it then?

Nordenson: I don't think you and I should continue this conversation, Pastor.

Henrik: I have plenty of time.

Nordenson: It hasn't been particularly profitable.

Henrik: I've mostly been frightened.

Nordenson: Really?

Henrik: Some people frighten me.

Nordenson: Has it ever occurred to you, Pastor, that I might be just as frightened. But in another way?

Henrik: No.

Nordenson: Maybe you'll learn, Pastor.

Mr. Nordenson gets up and shakes hands without saying anything. Henrik goes with him to the door and holds it open. Sleet is falling outside, the road gray and icy. Henrik remains standing by the door, watching the black figure going toward the gate. He suddenly realizes that he has met a person who intends to kill him.

IV

VI

Spring-cleaning at the parsonage, the inner double windows taken out, rugs beaten, wardrobes aired, floors scrubbed, books dusted, paraffin lamps polished, summer curtains put up. Sun and mild winds, blue shadows under the trees, the birches coming out day by day. The rapids thundering and the river below the slope running high, white clouds rushing hurriedly by. Jack at the bottom of the steps, lying stretched out in the sun, guarding and keeping watch, the carriage with Dag-Erik sleeping in it nearby. In a large apron and with her hair in disorder, Anna is beating sofa cushions, Mia and Mejan shaking out blankets, the dust flying. A neighbor's wife and her daughter are scrubbing floors and stairs. The pastor keeps out of the way.

The Reverend Gransjö appears in the middle of Anna's well-organized tumult. He has with him a bunch of spring flowers and keeps apologizing, but his errand is important, yes, it concerns Anna just as much. He wants to speak to Anna and Henrik immediately. He won't be long. No, nothing unpleasant; on the contrary, really. No, the buggy can wait by the gate. He has borrowed it from Nordenson. Anna says that Henrik is probably fishing down by the river. She tells Petrus to go and ask him to come at once. Then she asks the minister to come in, takes him up to the first floor, offers him coffee, which he declines, takes off her big blue striped apron, and sits down.

Gransjö: The Farg boy is still with you. Is he any trouble?

Anna: I don't know what to say. He refuses to go back home and seems to like it here with us. He's good and obedient and attentive. He's very patient with Dag-Erik and likes playing with him.

225

Gransjö: No difficulties of the kind that . . .

Anna: He's sometimes very preoccupied. His eyes wander, and he doesn't hear what you're saying. But not all that often. He's moving into the little room above the shed for the summer. He likes it there.

Gransjö: I suppose the problem will be solved eventually?

Anna: Yes, yes, if only one knew how.

Gransjö: You look well, Anna.

Anna: Yes, I am, thank you.

Gransjö: Liking it?

Anna: Why shouldn't I? We've everything we could wish for. And at last the summer's coming!

Gransjö: After an unusually rough winter.

Anna: We'll forget that. (*Laughs.*)

Gransjö: . . . we'll forget that. (*Smiles.*)

Anna: I can hear Henrik coming.

She goes to the door and calls down, "We're up here. In your room. But take your boots off because the floors have all just been scrubbed. Where on earth did you find that old jersey? I thought I'd hidden it away well enough." Henrik is wearing a long, shabby old jersey, baggy working trousers, and is in his stockinged feet. He is sunburned. The minister and his curate greet each other warmly, if somewhat formally. They all sit down.

Henrik: Haven't you offered the minister anything?

Gransjö: Thank you, but I won't have anything, thank you. I'm disturbing you quite enough as it is.

Henrik: And to what do we owe this honor?

Gransjö: I've had a letter.

He opens his rather worn black briefcase and searches among the papers, then pulls out a envelope with the Church Commission's emblem on it.

Gransjö: Yes, I've had a letter. (*Long-winded and quite cheerful.*) It's from my old friend Pastor Primarius Anders Alopéus of the Church Commission in Stockholm. Pastor Primarius is also senior court chaplain in

226

the parish of the court. It is in the latter capacity that my old friend and colleague has written to me.

The minister pauses deliberately and looks at Henrik and Anna though his thick spectacles.

Henrik: Oh, yes?

Gransjö: I considered the contents of the letter so important that it should at once and with no unnecessary delay be brought over. (*Holds up the letter.*)

Henrik: That was very good of you.

Gransjö: Exactly, Pastor Bergman.

Anna: And it concerns us?

Gransjö: Please let me read it aloud to you. (*Adjusts his glasses.*) Well, the beginning is all personal matters, that's to say, more personal. Here! We can start here. Listen carefully now. "As you probably know, the Sophiahemmet was founded by Queen Sophia. She took a lively interest in Swedish health care and wished to found a model hospital adhering to the highest European standards. Her Majesty succeeded in setting up an institution that, by dint of her own considerable efforts, is today famous and much renowned for its great contributions to medical science. During her lifetime, she was chairman of the board, a position which on her passing was taken over by Her Majesty Queen Victoria." Yes, well . . . and so on. But to the point now! "Her Majesty, in consultation with the board, has now decided to create a permanent part-time chaplaincy. The assignment will be to lead and organize the spiritual work within the hospital and — as time permits — to teach in the college of nursing and thus provide for the spiritual education of the pupils. It has been agreed with the Reverend Källander, the minister in Hedvig Eleonora parish in Stockholm, that the projected chaplaincy at the hospital shall be complemented and supplemented by a suitable post in the aforementioned parish, so that the stipend corresponds to conditions and circumstances of a minister. The board is also planning to build a parsonage with all modern conveniences on the grounds of Sophiahemmet." Yes, well. Yes. Now — here comes the very nub — the nub itself — if I may put it that way. (*Pause.*) "Owing to her delicate state of health, Her Majesty the Queen lives largely abroad, and a few weeks ago paid a visit to her country on urgent family business, in which the undersigned participated in a humble capacity. At a meeting, Her Majesty happened to mention Sophiahemmet, whose problems have always been close to her heart. Her Majesty was particularly concerned about the proposed chaplaincy and emphasized how important it was to find the right man. Our archbishop, who was present on this occasion, immediately exclaimed: 'I think I have the right man!' On closer questioning, the archbishop named a young priest by the name of Henrik Bergman."

The Reverend Gransjö, now playing his role of dramatic reader to the hilt, pauses triumphantly, then repeats the name with feigned surprise, nodding in confirmation. "Yes, it really does say Henrik Bergman, and that must be the same person sitting opposite me with the sun in his eyes." Anna has grasped Henrik's arm, her delight more evident than Henrik's.

Henrik: Good gracious!

Gransjö: To be brief, the archbishop happened to remember that Henrik Bergman was now a curate in Forsboda parish. Pastor Primarius remembered that he was an old friend and fellow student of the parish priest's and at once wrote this letter. I should perhaps point out that farther on in this eight-page missive, Pastor Primarius points out that if I consider Henrik Bergman unsuitable for this extremely distinguished assignment, then I ought to disregard this letter. After which he calls down God's blessing on me and my house.

Henrik: Good gracious!

Anna: It's not true. It's not true.

Gransjö: Yes, young Mrs. Anna, it certainly is true. Since I received, read, and digested this missive, I have taken the liberty, at my own expense, of making an expensive and adventurous telephone call to my friend Pastor Primarius. He confirmed what he had written and told me, to make doubly sure, that the archbishop had met Henrik Bergman early one morning many years ago in the minister's garden in Mittsunda. They had had a conversation that had made an impression. In addition to that, the archbishop had heard the young Bergman preaching and from that had been singularly convinced.

Henrik: I don't know what to say.

Gransjö: You don't have to say anything. You must now think it over and discuss it with Mrs. Anna.

Henrik: When do we have to decide by?

Gransjö: As soon as possible. If your decision is positive, Her Majesty has requested a meeting before she departs for her annual stay in Borgholm. In other words, you will fairly shortly have to put on your best clothes and go to Stockholm to take afternoon tea at the palace. The palace administration will pay your fares and sojourn. (*Points to the letter.*) There's a postscript here. (*Reads.*) "It is particularly emphasized that Her Majesty wishes to meet both the pastor *and* his young wife." Well, now look at this, he's written along the side. I didn't see that. "The young wife Anna, née Åkerblom, received her training and excellent testimonials at Sophiahemmet's school of nursing in the spring of 1909." It says that here. I hadn't noticed that.

Anna: But I fell ill.

Gransjö: It says nothing about illness here. It just says "excellent testimonials." Well, that's the lot, and quite a lot it is, too, so now I'll leave you two young people in what I hope is more joy than confusion. At the same time, I would like to be the first to congratulate you, despite the fact that I myself am by no means to be congratulated, for I shall lose a young colleague whom I have come to like and a young wife whom I also like and who makes a delightful addition to the work of our parish.

The Reverend Gransjö holds out his old hand and pats Anna on the cheek. Then he pats Henrik on the cheek, though harder.

Henrik: I suppose it not forbidden to refuse.

Gransjö: It is not forbidden, but almost impossible. Such distinguished offers are not made often and are of vital importance.

Henrik: Yes. No doubt it's of vital importance.

Gransjö: Now I must be off.

Anna: Then we must really thank you for coming. (*Curtsies.*)

Gransjö: Good-bye, Mrs. Anna. My regards to your son.

Henrik: Good-bye, sir.

Gransjö: Good-bye, Henrik Bergman, and God be with you both in your important decision.

The blossom on some of the fruit trees in the garden is out. Anna and Henrik are sitting on a white, somewhat scratched bench; Dag is slumbering on a rug. Petrus is lying on his stomach with his hands over his ears, reading a book. Jack the dog has placed himself strategically so that with a minimum of effort he can watch over his wards. It is Saturday (the decisive day), and the chapel bell is ringing in the Sabbath. Below the grassy slope, the river flows silently along, glittering in the sun, and the rumble of the waterfall can be heard in the distance. Mild scents, mild wind, the insects industrious. Henrik is smoking his pipe, Anna crocheting a jacket for her son. The silence is peaceful, but charged with spoken questions and unspoken answers.

(*Henrik laughs silently.*)

Anna: What are you laughing at?

Henrik: I was thinking about great-grandfather, who was a great preacher and regarded as almost a saint. Whenever he had to make a difficult decision, he opened the Bible and always seemed to find the right answer.

Anna: And that's what you've just done?

Henrik: For fun. (*Leafs through a pocket Bible.*)

Anna: Well?

Henrik: Listen now. I landed on the Revelation of St. John the Divine, chapter three, and it says: "Be watchful, and strengthen the things which remain, that are already to die: for I have not found thy works perfect before God. Remember therefore how thou hast received and heard, and hold fast, and repent!"

Anna: I'm sure you cheated!

Henrik: I promise I didn't.

Anna: And what is the message?

Henrik: I can only interpret it in one way.

Anna: That we shall stay in Forsboda?

Henrik: No doubt about it.

Stillness. Bees buzz, the chapel bell falls silent, a newly arrived song thrush tries out a few notes. Henrik closes the book and relights his pipe. Anna smooths out her crochet work and examines it carefully.

Anna: You don't ask what *I* want.

Henrik: I don't ask because I know.

230

Anna: Are you sure?

Henrik: Absolutely sure.

Stillness again. Anna puts her work aside and peers up at the sun and the swaying branch of blossom above her head. Henrik leans forward and calls to Jack, who at once comes over, sits down at his master's knee, and has his neck scratched under his collar.

Anna: In this, my wishes are subordinate. You must follow your conscience.

Henrik: Are you really sure?

Anna: Yes, I'm sure, Henrik.

Henrik: You won't regret it?

Anna: Of course I'll regret it a thousand times, but then it'll be too late. You needn't . . .

Henrik (*interrupts*): . . . at the moment, it's like paradise. In a few months, it'll be thirty degrees below zero and impassable and pitch dark almost all day and red noses and hacking coughs.

Anna: . . . and the church will be empty, and there'll be trouble at the Works, and Nordenson will be going on about anarchy and strife. And ice on the water in the jug.

Henrik: . . . and we'll forget we've got each other.

Anna: No, we'll never forget that.

Anna takes Henrik's hand between hers. He puts down his pipe, which has gone out, and closes his eyes tightly.

Anna: But I must admit it would have been fun to have tea at the Royal Palace with Her Majesty the Queen.

Henrik: Most of all it would have been one in the eye for our friends in Trädgårdsgatan.

Anna: And fun suddenly to say to each other, let's go to the Royal Theater tonight and see Anders de Wahl.

Henrik: . . . or to a concert and listen to Beethoven.

Anna: Or buy a silk blouse at Leja's.

Henrik: Well, we can fantasize like that.

Anna: Dangerous fantasies, Henrik! (*Smiles.*)

Henrik: Dangerous? Why dangerous? (*Smiles.*)

Anna: No, of course not. We've decided, haven't we, or rather that book has decided.

Henrik (*lightly*): Are you perhaps being slightly ironic?

Anna: No, not in the slightest! I'm as serious as any woman in Selma Lagerlöf's books. The decision has been made. And it's a mutual decision.

Petrus has stopped reading and started listening. He is crouching down by the bench, and his pale, strangely blind face is turned toward Anna.

Petrus: Are you leaving?

Anna: No, on the contrary, Petrus.

Petrus: I thought you said you were going to leave.

Anna: You weren't listening carefully. We've just decided to stay.

Petrus: Then you won't be leaving?

Anna: Don't be so silly, Petrus. We're staying.

Petrus's ancient seven-year-old face is distrustfully sorrowful: "I thought it sounded as if you were going to leave," he says almost inaudibly and pretends to go back to his book. Tears come, and he sniffs as quietly as possible.

Henrik: Apropos that! You had a letter from your mother, didn't you?

Anna: Yes, I forgot to tell you. She wrote to ask whether we were coming to the summer place for your holiday. Ernst and Maria are going to Lofoten with some friends. Oscar and Gustav have rented a place in the archipelago. There would be only us and brother Carl.

Henrik: What do you think?

Anna: What do you think? Mama will be rather lonely.

Henrik: I thought she liked being on her own.

Anna: Well, then.

Henrik: What do you mean, well, then?

Anna: That was answer enough.

Henrik: It's better here. (*Pause.*)

Anna: Only for a week?

Henrik: Do we have to?

Anna: No, no. Mama didn't think we'd come. She mostly asked for form's sake.

Henrik: Weren't we going to have another child, by the way?

Anna: Yes, we were.

Henrik: You don't sound like you want to any longer. It was your idea!

Anna (*laughs*): There's been so much to think about. My poor little head becomes so confused.

Henrik: Shall we go in? It's getting chilly.

Anna lifts up her son, who wakes up and starts whimpering. Henrik gathers up the rest of the things, rattle, rug, pipe, and Bible, calls Jack, and sets off toward the parsonage. Halfway there, he turns around.

Henrik: Come on, Petrus.

Petrus: I'm just finishing.

Henrik: It's getting chilly.

Petrus: I'm not cold.

Henrik: Don't forget to bring the book in.

Petrus: No.

Henrik: Come on, now. We'll have a game of chess.

Petrus: I'll just finish reading.

Henrik: All right, do as you like.

Anna has gone up the steps to the veranda. She stops and smiles at Henrik. Petrus is staring steadily at her. The veranda door closes. Petrus rolls over on his back and stretches his hands upward — spreading his fingers out wide.

One warm early summer's day in the middle of June, 1917, Anna and Henrik Bergman are waiting in the Green Salon in the queen's private apartment. It is in the left wing of the palace, with a view out over the waters of Strömmen, the National Museum, and Skeppsholmen. Pastor Primarius Anders Alopéus, a handsome, ruddy churchman of considerable proportions, is also present. They are standing at one of the big windows and talking in low voices about the striking view. "But it's drafty," says Alopéus. "You can feel the drafts. Even the curtains are swaying, but then the wind always blows in this direction. Lucky it's not winter."

In the background, two liveried court servants in white gloves are busy at the tea table, moving soundlessly and communicating with each other with subdued gestures.

The room is well proportioned, almost square. It is furnished elegantly but far too richly in the style of the eighties: bulging sofas and chairs covered in shimmering materials, hand-painted silk wallpaper, a wealth of stucco on the ceiling and the lintels above the tall doors, gilded mirrors facing each other and making the room seem endless. High crystal chandeliers, elaborately draped floor lamps, thick carpets muffling footsteps on the creaking parquet floor. Dark pictures with ornamental frames, palm trees and pallid sculptures, spindly tables crowded with ornaments, a piano covered with an oriental shawl and laden with photographs of various lesser or grander nobility.

Anna is wearing a new tailored gray-blue costume and a hat with a turned-up brim and a little white feather. Both gentlemen are in clerical suits. Henrik's shoes are far too new, far too shiny, and far too tight. He is staring in terror at Anna and fumbling for her hand. "My stomach keeps rumbling. It'll be disastrous." "You shouldn't have had that game soup," whispers Anna. "Try breathing deeply." Henrik breathes deeply, his face pale and gray. "I should never have agreed to this, I ought . . . "

A door opens and Chamberlain Segerswärd appears. He is in uniform, and his radiant smile reveals a row of teeth of marvelous whiteness. He smells of fine pomade and condescending amiability. His little hand is pale and flabby: "So this is the pastor's little wife. Welcome to you, and to you, Pastor Berglund, welcome. The court chaplain and I met earlier today. We serve on the same charity committee. There are just one or two small things I should like to point out. Her Majesty should be addressed as 'Your Majesty' if that should arise. One ought to avoid direct address if possible. Her Majesty will ask the questions and guide the conversation. It is inappropriate to make your own digressions. I would also like to say that Her Majesty is not well and is very tired. I suggested with all humility that this

234

meeting should be postponed until another and more suitable occasion, but Her Majesty is extremely dutiful and very much concerned about everything to do with Sophiahemmet. So Her Majesty rejected my suggestion. On the other hand, this means the meeting will be very brief. Matters of a practical nature should be discussed with our friend Pastor Primarius here, who is intimately *au fait* with the situation. Do you have any questions? No questions. Her Majesty will come through that door. I suggest — it is customary — that her guests place themselves here. Her Majesty will first greet the court chaplain, then the pastor's wife, which entails as deep and elegant a curtsy as can be achieved. Finally, Her Majesty will greet Pastor Berglund."

Alopéus: Bergman. Henrik Bergman.

Chamberlain: Have I really . . . ? It's not possible! It must have been a misprint in my list! I do apologize, my dear Pastor Bergman. Please excuse an old man!

A dazzling smile, wide-open gray eyes, the pudgy, flabby hand touching Henrik's arm, the pendulum clock on the mantelpiece above the marble fireplace striking three. The door opens, and Queen Victoria makes her entrance. She is tall, thin, and broad shouldered, her graying hair gathered into an elaborate knot on the top of her head. Her face is pale, and there are lines of pain around the dark blue eyes. Her thin lips are pressed together with self-restraint and infinite weariness. She is wearing a draped, soft gray silk dress with lace at the neckline and breast, the only jewelry a single strand of pearls around her neck, small pendant diamond earrings, and a diamond ring between her engagement and wedding rings. She is accompanied by a lady-in-waiting, who silently closes the door. Countess Bielke is small, plump, white-haired, and pink-cheeked, her eyes radiating childish and genuine cheerfulness. She is wearing a long, dark green skirt and a shantung blouse with a cameo brooch at her throat, and is carrying a light cashmere shawl over her arm.

The queen walks slowly, and slightly unsteadily, across to her waiting guests. She holds out her hand to Anna, her smile quick and shimmering. Anna curtsies nicely (she has practiced). After that, the queen greets Henrik and finally the court chaplain.

With a slight accent, she says that it was pleasant that they could meet and it was kind of them to come such a long way, and "shall we all sit down? I hope you would like a cup of tea. We actually still have some of the genuine article. I am very fond of tea made with apple blossom and chamomile."

The livery-clad servants serve while the queen inquires about their journey, their son Dag (she has been well briefed), and whether they were considering an evening at the theater. She herself had been to a performance of *Everyman* a few days before, a disturbing experience, like divine worship. "We simply could not applaud."

The pain-filled expression gives way to gentle amiability, and color comes into those pale cheeks. Her voice is low, occasionally hard to make out, but gentle. When she speaks, she looks steadily at Anna and Henrik, her face open and vulnerable.

The Queen: And now we are entertaining great expectations.

Henrik: My wife and I are still a trifle frightened. Everything has happened so quickly. Nor do we know what is required of us. I mean, what is *really* required of us? All we know is that we shall do our very best.

The Queen: At our last board meeting, our architect produced a report on the construction work to be done in the coming years. Professor Forsell will have the most modern X-ray institute in the world, and our chaplain and his wife will have a parsonage of their own. Where is the envelope, Countess? Ah, yes, there. Here you are. This is a pencil drawing of the proposed house. It will be situated on a small hill with extensive forest lands outside — Lill-Janskogen. It will be like living in the country, although in the middle of town. Ideal for the children.

Anna: I know exactly. It's opposite the home for retired nurses. Solhemmet.

The Queen: Yes, of course you know, Mrs. Bergman. You were at the nursing school, a few hundred meters away from your future home. Three big rooms on the ground floor and a well-equipped kitchen. Four rooms on the first floor. The nursery in the corner, I should think. Where there's sun all day. And naturally all conveniences. It will all be ready within a few years. Meanwhile, Hedvig Eleonora parish will provide you with living quarters.

Anna: It's all overwhelming.

The Queen: I realize it will be difficult to leave Forsboda.

Henrik: Yes, it will be difficult.

Anna: At first we were worried and unsure. It seemed to us we were perhaps escaping from our task.

Henrik: . . . our life's task.

Anna: I wasn't as afraid as Henrik was.

Henrik: I thought I was leaving people in need . . .

The Queen: The need in a hospital can be just as great, Pastor Bergman.

Henrik: Yes, I know. (*Smiles, shakes his head.*) I know.

The Queen: Tell me something, Pastor Bergman. Do you think our suffering is sent to us by God?

Chamberlain Segerswärd cautiously sucks on his false teeth. He finds Her Majesty's question obscene, and his face is stripped of every conceivable expression. The nice little Countess Bielke has tears in her eyes, but then she is easily moved. Pastor Primarius leans back and burdens the fragile back of his chair with his not inconsiderable bulk. He glances urgently at his younger colleague, his smile professional and adapted to the question in hand. Anna swiftly sees that this tall, tormented woman has asked a question beyond the boundaries of convention.

Henrik: I can only say what I believe myself.

The Queen: That was why I asked.

Henrik: No, I don't think our sufferings are sent to us by God. I think that God looks on his creation with grief and horror. No, suffering does not come from God.

The Queen: But suffering is said to purify us?

Henrik: I have never seen suffering to be of any help. On the other hand, I have seen instances of suffering destroying and deforming.

The Queen (*to her lady-in-waiting*): Countess, would you please be so kind as to hand me my shawl?

Countess Bielke at once gets up and puts the light shawl around the queen's shoulders. For a few minutes, she sits with her eyes closed, her right hand to her breast.

The Queen (*looks at Henrik*): If it is as you say, Pastor, how can it be possible to console one single person?

Henrik: All consolation is momentary.

The Queen: . . . momentary?

Henrik: Yes. The only possibility is to persuade people, those seeking help, to make peace with themselves. To forgive themselves.

The Queen: Shouldn't we ask God for forgiveness?

Henrik: That's the same thing. If you forgive yourself, then God has forgiven you.

The Queen: Is God so close!

Henrik: God and Man are indivisible and one and the same. It's a terrible cruelty to separate God from human beings! God as authority, as a punishing authority at that, as a dogmatist. That's the exact opposite of everything Christ taught us. And he knew!

The queen has once again closed her eyes. She is leaning slightly back, her lips apart and pale. "I'm terribly tired today. You will have to excuse me, my friends." She rises laboriously, staggering slightly, her lady-in-waiting discreetly supporting her. "Thank you for your honesty," she says, smiling faintly.

Then she turns to Anna: "Make sure that your husband goes to the new parsonage. I think you'll find it a rich field of activity, both of you."

She nods at Pastor Primarius and the chamberlain. The two servants step forward, move the armchair, and open the door. "I beg you to excuse me," says Baron Segerswärd, holding out his fat, flabby hand, unable even to smile with his brand-new denture. "Jansson, would you be so kind as to see our guests out?"

He wiggles away beyond the mirrors. Their departure is rapid and wordless. The guests are handed their outdoor clothes and guided by Jansson to the West Arch, quickly and with no further comment. Brief bow and closed door. Pastor Primarius steps out into Borggården and peers up at the sun. The wind is warm and strong.

Primarius: Well, yes, then, yes, it'll soon be five o'clock. I've got a service. I hope you young people will manage without an old man. Good-bye, Mrs. Bergman, good-bye, Pastor Bergman. I congratulate you on your exceedingly unorthodox trial sermon. It obviously made a great impression on Her Highness. New tunes, new tunes indeed, very harsh and fresh: God grieves for his Creation. Why not? Times change, and bold personal interpretations are the fashion of the day. I was thinking about whether in my youth . . . (*Laughs.*) No, I mustn't stand here talking nonsense. Congratulations and good luck to you! If you wish to discuss practical details, Pastor, Minister Källander is quite *au fait* with everything.

He shakes hands with them, raises his hat, and wafts away across the sunlit desolation of Borggården. For a moment, Henrik stands watching the prelate waddling off, then he starts walking toward Lejonbacken, quickly, with violent movements, breathing heavily. Anna is angry and asks him to slow down as she can hardly keep up with him.

Anna: What's the matter with you? What is it? Why are you so angry? It went well, didn't it? You mustn't be angry over that Primarius. He's nothing but an old fogey. He was envious, you could see that. Don't run, Henrik. I can't keep up!

Henrik: No! No!

Anna: What do you mean, no? What are you saying no to?

Henrik: It's no, no, no! I'm not moving to Stockholm. I won't take the Sophiahemmet chaplaincy. I'm not going to talk to court chaplains and chamberlains and queens. I'm going to stay in Forsboda. I've been an idiot. An idiot twice over. An idiot in all directions. I can see that quite clearly now. Thank God for that Primarius. Thank God for that Distinguished Lady. Does suffering come from God? The grandiose-ness of grandeur and the triumph of silliness. Did you hear me bab-bling all that nonsense, flattered, mendacious, conceited! I must get back to the hotel and clean my teeth. What was I thinking about? I must be crazy. Dazzled and seduced, Anna! Dazzled and seduced by that poor lady with her nasal amiability. No, no. That's the end of Bergman's stupidity. Now we're going back home to Forsboda to tackle our stony fields and sullen, poverty-stricken, sulky fellow human beings. I say no, and no again. I say no. It's no.

Anna (*furious*): *Stop*, I say!

She pulls his sleeve, grabs his arm, and makes him stop. She stands in front of him below the obelisk on Lejonbacken, diminutive, raging, and out of breath.

Anna: If only you could hear yourself! But naturally you should be pleased to escape such an experience. I and I and *I!* I say no. What the hell is that kind of damned rubbishy talk—that's it, rubbish, *sheer tripe!* We're actually *two*, or perhaps you've forgotten that down there wher-ever you keep your grandiose visions. My name's Anna, and I am your wife. *I am one of us.* And I actually have a right to say what I think. And I think you're behaving like a hysterical prima donna. What is it you keep going on and on about? What decision is it you have taken? How dare you decide about — vital decisions — about what is vital — vital decisions, Henrik! — without consulting me. I am your wife, and I must have the right to say what I think. And now I'm crying, and if you think I'm crying because I'm miserable, you're mistaken, as usual. My tears are because it hurts when you *trample* on me. You trample on your most faithful friend, and I'm crying because I'm so angry! I am furious and raging and would like to slap your face right here in front of your church, you . . . you camel!

Henrik: Don't shout. People can hear. You've lost your mind! We can reason calmly, can't we? (*Starts laughing.*) You really are so sweet when you're angry like that.

Anna: Stop that stupid superiority! Stop grinning! If you say one more word, I'll leave you and go back to Trädgårdsgatan and won't speak to you again even if you crawl on your hands and knees all the way to Upsala.

Henrik (*suddenly kind*): Anna, forgive me.

Anna (*more graciously*): Frightened, were you?

Henrik: God in heaven, how angry you were!

Anna: I have a furious temper, I'll have you know. And in the future, if there is any future, I'm going to make a habit of being angrier than ever.

Henrik: In all humility, I have a suggestion.

Anna: So you have a suggestion.

Henrik: I suggest we go and buy a strawberry ice-cream cone and then take the ferry over to Djurgården.

Anna: You mean, not discuss this?

Henrik: Anna, my dearest dearest. This is so serious for you, and so serious for me, and we are so close to each other. We must, for God's sake, find a solution.

Anna: Of course, an ice cream might be calming as well as cooling.

The Djurgård ferry is fussily steaming along, rumbling faintly and trembling gently, the water glossy and oily with reflections of the sun in the swell. Anna and Henrik have a whole bench to themselves right up at the front, a kindly wind fanning their cheeks. Anna has taken off her hat and put it down beside her on the bench. They are eating their ice-cream cones.

Anna: Take your hat off.

(*Henrik takes his hat off.*)

Anna: May I have a taste of your ice cream?

Henrik: Let's exchange. (*They switch cones.*)

Anna: You start.

Henrik: I have nothing to say.

Anna: Ten minutes ago, you had quite a lot to say.

Henrik: I can repeat what I said.

Anna: But in a more friendly tone.

Henrik: In a more friendly tone.

Anna: I'm listening.

Henrik: As usual with me, it's a *feeling*. This time I saw it in capital letters, gigantic letters, N O. Nothing else. And I was miserable and angry with myself and that fat slob of a Primarius. (*Falls silent.*)

Anna: And then?

Henrik: I don't know. Nothing.

Anna (*quietly*): What shall we do?

Henrik: What do *you* want?

Anna: I don't know any longer. It's such a responsibility. Why can't one take life a little lightheartedly?

Henrik: We aren't that sort.

Anna: *You* aren't that sort.

Henrik: I can't force you to live in Forsboda all your life. If you sacrificed your ideas of a good life, you'd just be miserable and angry. And vengeful.

Anna: So would you, Henrik.

Henrik: Yes, yes, I probably would.

Anna: Yes.

Henrik: I can't tell you how much this conversation pains me.

Anna: Someone has to give in. Oh, I know it'll be me. I don't even understand why we're arguing. You follow your vocation, and your vocation is to live and die in the wilderness among heathens and cannibals. That's the vocation you have to follow — and I follow you.

241

Perhaps that's *my* vocation. But I'm not as certain as you are. I thought life was to be colorful and brilliant. *Great* sacrifices and *great* feelings. Not being buried alive. Do you remember how we fantasized about the priest and the nurse and suffering humanity?

Henrik: It has turned out as we had dreamed.

Anna: No, Henrik. *We did not dream about Forsboda.*

Henrik: Is it so terrible?

Anna: Not until a few weeks ago. Then there was no alternative. (*Sighs a little.*) Oh, Henrik, I thought it was going to be so marvelous. (*Smiles.*)

Henrik: Poor Anna. Your stupid priest turned out not to be a particularly enchanting dream prince. You should have taken Torsten.

Anna: But it is strange, isn't it? I didn't want Torsten in the slightest. I just wanted you.

Henrik: You didn't want Torsten because your family was crazy about him.

Anna: Do you think so? You may be right.

Henrik: So you took me because your mother detested me.

Anna (*smiles*): That sounds possible.

What follows is an extract of a letter from Pastor Primarius Alopéus to his dear friend and colleague, Samuel Gransjö, parish priest of Forsboda.

> When I received your worthy missive of the thirteenth of this month and had thoroughly taken in its message, I hurried to request an audience with Her Majesty the Queen. I must confess that Her Majesty professed *profound disappointment* over young Bergman's *refusal*, which was as surprising as it was unwise. I nevertheless ventured at this painful moment of perplexity to suggest a slight *retardation* of our plans. In all humility, I put it that it might be possible that we had acted all too precipitately and *possibly* ought to give our young friend and his fair wife a period of time to think it over, let us say, *a year*. Her Majesty was pleased to find my idea worth considering, and so I am suggesting to My Highly Honored Brother that on some *appropriate occasion* he return to Her Majesty's offer. I am convinced that My Honored Brother, with all conceivable wisdom, will turn our young friend's thoughts in the *desired direction*, thus not forgetting the

delightful Mrs. Anna's quite certainly *decisive* influence on her husband's feelings and thoughts. It is indeed possible that I am mistaken, but the young wife seemed to me quite *enthusiastic* about the possibility of a brilliant and honorable Advancement. Her Majesty the Queen *particularly* requested me to send her regards to My Honored Brother and say that with confidence she entrusted this delicate task into the *experienced hands* of My Respected Brother. Finally, I call down on you, My Beloved Brother in Jesus Christ, and the whole of Your House, the Grace and Blessings of God. Tuus Anders Alopéus.

The Reverend Gransjö read the letter through twice, then went to rest on his couch, pondering in his heart on what he had read and deciding to bide his time until the right moment. After which, he fell asleep and slept until dinnertime, when, with gentle taps on the door, Mrs. Säll woke him to new potatoes and salmon. Although it was wartime, neither the potato fields nor the river were showing the slightest signs of crisis.

On the Saturday before Midsummer, the pastor assembles his confirmands to decorate the chapel with flowers and budding birch twigs. Anna and Henrik have already set off from home early in the afternoon, followed by Mia and Mejan, Petrus, their son Dag, and the dog Jack. All except Jack have great armfuls of blue and white lilacs they have gathered from the arbor, which is giving out bountiful scents and colors. The master of the house and his whole family are on their way toward the chapel. Suddenly Anna puts her left arm around her husband's waist, presses her forehead against his shoulder, and says she's happy. "I'm happy now, Henrik. I feel I'm really happy again now. You were probably right, the way you felt about that offer. I was dazzled by the brilliance, you see. Now I feel I've got over all that, those childish things. You were the wise one — which doesn't mean you're *always* wise. But on that particular occasion, you were wise and I was stupid."

Anna says all this in a whisper as she clasps her husband around the waist and adjusts her steps to his. Now they're walking with quick, even strides, she in a white summer dress with a high waist and wide skirt. She has unlaced her boots and taken off her stockings, and so is barefoot and bareheaded, her thick brown hair in a braid down her back. Henrik says without thinking that he has often wondered what paradise might look like, and there's presumably no such thing as paradise, but *if* there is a paradise then it exists here on earth in June on Saturday afternoon in the parish of Valbo. "Here I am, Henrik

243

Bergman, wandering in the Garden of Eden in utter bliss. I would never have believed it. I never believed it could happen to me. Never. And angels! And the paradise dog! It's not possible! It's unfathomable!"

They number fifteen, the confirmands, seven boys and eight girls, some from the workers' quarters around the Sawmill, some from the Works, the doctor's youngest son, and Nordenson's two daughters, Susanna and Helena. The last two are the oldest of the bunch, Susanna seventeen and Helena sixteen. All of them are busy decorating and cleaning under the supervision of Magda, who is wearing a dark blue apron over her light summer dress, and a wide-brimmed straw hat.

Then the pastor and his household arrive, so now there are twenty-one people in the little chapel, plus one dog. Work stops for greetings and chat. Anna sits down at the organ, Petrus tramps on the bellows, and von Duben's summer hymn is sung:

In this pleasing summer time,
Go out my soul,
Rejoice in all the Almighty's gifts!
See the earth in all its glory!
See for us its beauteous bounties.

No one notices Nordenson coming into the chapel and stopping by the door. He is wearing an elegant summer coat, a light suit, and a neatly tied necktie. He has his hat in his left hand. His face is pale, and he is thinner. The right-hand corner of his mouth is twitching, his eyes veiled, and the thin gray hair is neatly brushed, smooth, and pomaded.

Henrik is the first to notice the visitor, but he is saying the blessing after the hymn. Then he takes a few steps toward Nordenson, and everyone sees him, looks at him, the chapel now quiet.

Henrik: You are welcome, Mr. Nordenson. Would you care to sit down? Or perhaps you would like to help? There's still a great deal to be done.

Nordenson: I'm sorry to disturb you, but I've come to fetch my daughters.

Henrik: That was very thoughtful of you, Mr. Nordenson, but Susanna and Helena will be busy for another hour at least. We are to go through the questions and answers before tomorrow.

Nordenson: I realize it'll complicate matters, but I'm afraid my daughters must decline.

Henrik: I'm sure Mrs. Säll will be willing to take the girls home as soon as we've finished. You needn't wait for them, Mr. Nordenson.

Nordenson: I've come to fetch my daughters. My daughters. Susanna and Helena.

Henrik: I realize you've come to fetch your daughters. But unfortunately, that can't be done for another hour. The girls are occupied with other things.

Nordenson: Really. They are occupied. With other things. Helena and Susanna are occupied.

Henrik: So they'll not be ready to be fetched for another hour, you see, Mr. Nordenson.

Nordenson: Susanna! Come over here!

(*Susanna does not move.*)

Nordenson: Helena! Come over here!

(*Helena does not move.*)

Nordenson (*calmly*): Come now, my girls. I can't wait forever.

Henrik: I suggest we two go out into the churchyard and sort this problem out. There must be some kind of misunderstanding.

Nordenson: I can reassure the pastor on that point. There isn't the slightest misunderstanding. Regardless of the time of day and the locality, it is Susanna's and Helena's imperative duty to obey their father.

Henrik: There must be some solution.

Nordenson (*calmly*): Absolutely, Pastor Bergman. The solution is that my daughters come with me. *This moment!*

Henrik: And if they don't obey?

Nordenson: I know they'll obey.

Henrik: What will happen if I ask you to leave the church?

Nordenson (*quietly*): Then I'll use force.

Henrik: Force against whom?

Nordenson: Against anyone.

Henrik: It's not possible.

Nordenson (*conciliatory*): Stop playing this game now, Pastor Bergman. I am asking you politely to tell my daughters to come with their father.

Henrik: You're intoxicated.

Nordenson: So are you, Pastor Bergman. But in a much more dangerous way. You are intoxicated with your power over my daughters. You have consciously humiliated me in front of the children. In that way you are thwarting Susanna's and Helena's chance of participating in confirmation and communion.

Henrik (*short pause*): Susanna and Helena, go to your father.

The girls stop what they are doing. Without looking around, they go to their father, come to a halt in front of him with their arms at their sides, faces turned away.

Nordenson: Your order came exactly half a minute too late, Pastor Bergman. Fifteen seconds ago I decided to stop their participation in your blood rituals. One day they will thank me for that.

Henrik: You may not do this.

Nordenson: What may I not do? May I not stop my children from being exposed to emotional rape, a vile idiotic game, a stinking orgy of tears and blood? What is it I may not do, Pastor Bergman?

Henrik breaks the choreographic pattern and takes the few steps up to Nordenson. He is very pale; blue shadows have appeared under his eyes; his mouth is trembling.

Henrik: You are a base creature. You are vengeful, jealous, and repulsive.

Nordenson (*immobile*): How interesting to hear a priest denigrating a father in front of his children in the presence of witnesses. How almost fascinating to hear a man of the cloth using such words in God's own house. God is love and love is God, isn't that so, Pastor? The House of God and Love. A love house, so to speak.

Henrik: I'll kill you.

Nordenson: What? You speak so quietly, Pastor. I thought I heard the word "kill." Is it possible! Knock me down. That's easily done. I have no intention of defending myself. You're young and strong! Hit me. I'm old and tired, and as you say — drunk.

Anna: Henrik! Stop it, now!

Her voice comes from a long way away and scarcely reaches him. Weighed down by hatred, Nordenson turns and leaves. His daughters follow him.

Winter comes early. At the beginning of October, the first blizzard hits Forsboda and cuts off the electricity, telephone network, and rail communications. After the storm, an arctic cold descends, thirty degrees below zero at the Sawmill and in the forests around the Iron Works. The lake and the waterways freeze over; only the rapids and the racing current below the parsonage stay open, the furrow made by the current black between the edges of ice and the rapids roaring in the distance.

Added to this unusual and extraordinary cold are the trials of wartime life, perhaps not so evident in the countryside as in the towns. Bread and coffee are rationed. (People have been drinking dandelion coffee for a year now). Carbide has disappeared, and there is a shortage of candles. Paraffin is in short supply. But there is timber in the forest, and they can keep their kitchen stoves and tiled stoves going fairly well. Forsboda more or less manages. The Works and the Sawmill are going full tilt; people have enough to eat; they can keep their houses and cottages warm, and ration cards can be disregarded. But it grows dark and still in the arctic night.

Henrik's mother at last pays them a visit. She seems pleased and fairly well. The severe cold is not good for her asthma, but the tiled stove in the guest room burns day and night. Mrs. Alma prefers to sit in a rocking chair with her book or handwork, and Dag plays quietly on the rug on the floor, or stands at his grandmother's knee to listen to her telling a story. Mrs. Alma likes telling stories.

One sunny afternoon at the end of her visit, Alma has a pain in her side and takes her tablets, but they do not help. She gets out of the rocking chair to call for help but falls to the floor. In order not to frighten the child, she laughs a little and says poor fat old grandma is a really clumsy old thing and perhaps Dag should go and fetch Mama or Papa.

But Dag stays where he is, staring solemnly at his prostrate grandmother. "Are you going to die?" Then he sits down on the floor quite close to her and puts his hand on her forehead. She closes her eyes and thinks that perhaps this is rather good, this too. But the pain in her left side returns, and she is finding it hard to breathe. She opens her eyes and says quite sternly to Dag, "You *must* fetch Papa or Mama now, or some other grown-up who can help your grandmother into bed."

Reluctantly Dag gets up and goes off to find Mama in the kitchen. Anna has just put Jack into the tub and is washing him with soft soap. Mejan is making cabbage soup, Petrus sitting at the kitchen table with a book about Indians, and Mia has gone off on the sled to the post office.

Alma is picked up off the floor. Her lips are blue and pains increasing, creeping out toward her shoulder blade, and again she is finding it difficult to breathe. Together Henrik and Anna undress the heavy woman and get her into bed. Petrus and Dag stand out of the way, solemnly watching this strange drama but with no particular terror. Jack has crept out of the tub and shaken the water off his coat, and the kitchen is rather wet. Then he goes and hides under Mejan's bed in the maid's room.

Henrik tries to telephone the doctor, but the exchange tells him the lines to Valbo are down because of the snow, but says they'll no doubt be repaired by the end of the following week. Because Henrik is a good skier, it is decided he will set off immediately. He expects to be back with the doctor within less than two hours. Mejan looks after the boys (and Jack, who has to be rinsed and dried). There is still a little cocoa left at the bottom of the tin. Mejan makes hot chocolate and cuts two big slices of bread. Calm once again descends on the parsonage. The wind has dropped over all that whiteness, and the sun is resting on the edge of the forest. The guest room (which is actually the nursery) is still light. (Dag is sleeping in his parents' bedroom during his grandmother's visit, which he likes.)

Anna is sitting by the bed holding the old woman's hand. As the pain subsides, she dozes off for a few minutes. Total silence reigns in the sky and on earth. The sun shines. The dining room clock strikes two. Mejan and the boys laugh. Jack barks. Then it's quiet again.

Alma: Anna.

Anna: Yes.

Anna leans forward, quite close, and sees the soft hand criss-crossed with fine lines and scratches, the closed eyelids trembling slightly, her breathing scarcely audible, her pulse slow and getting slower, a little saliva in the corners of her mouth, the thin hair in a gray strand across the low, broad forehead. The hand.

Alma: Do you think the boy was frightened?

Anna: I don't think so.

Alma: I mean when I fell over?

Anna: He's in the kitchen having hot chocolate with Petrus and Mejan. And Jack.

Alma: I'm so clumsy. I lost my hold. It was an awful crash.

Anna: It was silly that no one heard anything.

Alma: Do you think Henrik'll be back in time?

Anna: It's not that far. The doctor has a horse and sleigh, and the road's been plowed.

Alma: Are you going to leave Henrik?

Anna: No.

Alma: I have such a strange feeling.

Anna: We've had our difficulties. But everything's fine now.

Alma: I don't understand why I worry.

Anna: Things are fine now, Grandma.

Alma: Henrik is . . . no.

Anna: Lonely?

Alma: Shut in . . . no. I don't know. I don't know.

Anna: I'll never leave him. I promise you.

Alma: You see, it was like this . . . when Henrik was really small and his father had died, and I had no idea how we were going to survive . . . (*Falls silent.*)

Anna: Yes.

Alma: I did a terribly stupid thing.

Anna: We don't need to . . .

Alma: Yes. It's so terrible. For a whole year we lived with Henrik's grandfather on the farm. Henrik's grandfather and his brother lived up there, you know. Hindrich was a minister and the other one, the tall one, was a member of Parliament. Not then, but he became one later on. We had nowhere to go, and so we were allowed to live on the farm. I stood in the doorway and watched Hindrich thrashing my boy. He was about the same age as Dag is now, three or so. It was supposed to be the way to bring him up. Hindrich said it was for the boy's own good. Henrik's grandfather was watching but said nothing. I was beside myself. I just stood there.

Alma is talking calmly and clearly, with no emotion, as if the memory of those punishments had been emptied of all feelings, a strange image that for some reason it was important to bring back.

Anna: Did it often happen?

Alma: Hindrich was obsessed with "upbringing," as he called it. His children were grown. A daughter, the stay-at-home daughter, didn't protest. She just said, "You can be sure he means well. It won't do any harm. We were thrashed, too, and it didn't do us any harm. You're so soft," she said. "The boy's become as soft as you. He has to be hardened." That's how she talked. Henrik's grandmother was kind, but she was afraid and she never dared . . . yes, occasionally.

Anna: But you didn't stay?

Alma: No. One day I took the boy with me and went to Elfvik, you know, the sisters at Elfvik. It wasn't as grand in those days. But grand enough. Blenda lent me a little money. She was the sensible one. She didn't want me to live there, because she didn't like me. But she lent me some money. So we moved to Söderhamn.

Anna: That was brave of you.

Alma: Brave?

Anna: Would you like something to drink? A little tea?

Alma: Yes, please. My mouth gets so dry from those tablets.

Anna puts Alma's hand back on the quilt. She is lying quite still. The sun is shining but has sunk between the trees, and the shadows in the room deepen. The cold is green above long, narrow, motionless clouds.

In the kitchen, all is calm and cheerful. Petrus is reading aloud to Dag as they sit close together at the kitchen table. Mejan has sat down with her handwork. The cabbage soup is steaming fragrantly. Jack is lying flat, newly scrubbed and exhausted, on the floor. The day sinks.

Mejan: How is the old lady?

Anna: I think she's asleep.

Mejan: She was in quite a lot of pain.

Anna: Yes, I'm sure she was. We must make her some tea.

Mejan: It won't be long.

Anna: It's time for Dag's rest now. I'll take him up and put him to bed. Henrik and the doctor should be here any moment now.

Recovered, regained ordinariness. Calm voices, practiced actions, work, and duties. Anna persuades her son, who reluctantly leaves Petrus and the story. Jack moves his tail to show that at least he's awake, though very tired. Mejan brews lime blossom tea, which she pours into a large flowery breakfast cup, and then puts a few long hard-baked scones on a plate. Anna lifts Dag into her arms and carries him up the stairs. "I want to walk by myself," he says sorrowfully but doesn't bother to resist. Now he is standing on his bed, jersey and trousers hauled off. "Do you want to wee?" "No, I've weed." "You've a big hole in your stocking. We must change them." "No, thank you, new stockings prickle." Down into bed. "There we are; give Mother a kiss; that's it. Where do you want *your* kiss? Oh, on your nose. All right. There!"

Anna puts the green screen round Dag's bed. "Is Grandma going to die?" the boy says quietly. "No, she's not. The doctor's coming any minute now."

"If death comes and fetches Grandma and loads her up on a cart, might he perhaps fetch someone else at the same time?" says Dag. "What are you talking about?" says Anna, still standing by the screen. The light glimmers strongly in the white room, the light from the snow shadowless and floating in and out through the windows. "Maybe he'll get the wrong person and take me instead. Or you, Mother." "Death doesn't come with a cart," says Anna. "Where did you get that from?" "Father read it aloud from a book to the ladies!" "Oh, and you heard that, did you? But that's just a story! Death doesn't come in a cart, and death doesn't get the wrong person. If Grandma dies, it'll be because she's so tired and in such pain." Dag listens with attention to his mother's explanation. Then he says: "Do children die, too?" Anna says nothing for a moment, thinking she hears Henrik outside the house, taking off his skis and stamping the snow off his boots on the porch.

"Father's back now," says Anna. "Go to sleep, little boy; then we'll talk about all that one day when we have more time." She strokes him hastily over his forehead and cheek, and he dutifully closes his eyes.

251

Henrik: The doctor wasn't at home, but Sister Blenda promised to tell him the moment he got back. Some accident at the Forge.

Mejan: The old lady is asleep. I took the tea tray up, and she said she felt sleepy and wanted to go to sleep, but she took a little tea. I helped her.

Henrik is on the porch unlacing his boots, his face red with cold. He has dragged in some snow, and his short sheepskin coat and cap are lying on the woodbox. He's snuffling.

Anna: I sat with her for a long time, and she was quite clearheaded. Maybe the attack is over for now.

Henrik: I'll go up and look in on her.

Anna: Better if I do! You're terribly sweaty. I've put dry clothes out for you in front of the stove in your room.

Henrik: Can we have dinner a little earlier today? I have a meeting at six o'clock with the churchwarden and the others down at the chapel.

Mejan: We can eat in ten minutes.

Anna: I was going to go with you. It was about the Christmas bazaar. You'll have to tell them why I couldn't come.

Henrik pads up the stairs to change his clothes, and Anna cautiously opens the door to where Alma is sleeping. She sees at once that the old lady is dead, but to make sure, she goes up to the bed to check, quickly and professionally. She closes the dead woman's eyes, crosses her hands over her chest, and brushes the hair back off her forehead, which is still warm and slightly moist. Then she lights a half-burned candle on the bedside table and another on the tall, green chest of drawers. She goes over to the bed and looks at the dead woman, trying to work out what she is feeling. Yes, solemnity. Pity. The majesty of death. Out of your womb, Henrik was born.

She hears Henrik's steps on the stairs and goes out to him, closing the door behind her. He sees at once what has happened and for a moment stands without moving on the last stair, then takes Anna's right hand and starts crying, loudly but with no tears. It's a strange and penetrating sound. At first Anna is puzzled, then she pulls him with her to the dead woman's room. He stops in the doorway, his weeping suddenly over, as if forbidden, to be controlled as soon as possible.

Anna: She fell asleep. You can see that.

Henrik: Yes, but alone. Alone. She was always alone.

At the beginning of November, the countryside around Storsjön is hit by blizzards that, with a few interruptions, continue for almost a week. The cold is like a searing flame over the people and their dwellings, etching its way into the very marrow of their bones, thirty degrees below zero and snowstorms. A kind of hell, like the end of the world.

One morning at dawn, Anna vomits into the pail. At first she thinks it is that herring, oily and horrible. Then she vomits again and turns sweaty with fright. It's not the herring. Henrik is now holding her forehead, standing there in his long underpants and vest. He has just started shaving and has shaving soap on his face. "It's that sausage you had on your bread last night." "I didn't have any sausage." "Well, I don't know then. Maybe you got a chill on your stomach out in the privy." "No, I don't think so," mumbles Anna, pulling down her nightgown and exposing her left breast. "Look!" she says. "What? What am I supposed to see?"

Anna: Can't you see it's become . . . ?

Henrik: Prettier?

Anna: Idiot! Can't you see it's different?

Henrik: Overnight?

Anna: Supposing I'm with child!

Henrik: But we've been . . .

Anna: . . . so careful. Though I don't know what you *really* mean by careful.

Henrik: You said you *wanted* children.

Anna: That's the sort of thing one says.

Henrik: When Mama . . .

Anna: Oh!

Henrik: Some veins have appeared there.

Anna: . . . it's become huge overnight. I'm going to be sick again.

Henrik: Kneel down. I'll hold your forehead.

Anna: Nothing comes.

Henrik (*sits on the floor*): Come on, I'll hold you.

Anna: I'm cold. Why is it so cold all the time?

Henrik (*wrapping a blanket around her*): Now you'll be warm.

Anna: You're getting shaving soap all over me.

Henrik: Darling heart. Go on whining and complaining!

Anna: I'm so unhappy, Henrik.

Henrik: Are you *so* unhappy?

Anna: Why does it have to be so hideously cold and so hideously dark? Can you answer that?

Henrik: We chose this life.

Anna: And so quiet. And so lonely. Can't we *go away* somewhere? Just for a few weeks. Just for a week.

Henrik: How can we afford that?

Anna: *I* can afford it. I'll pay.

Henrik: I can't go away when old Gransjö is in bed with the flu. You know that.

Anna: Oh, God, I do feel sick.

Henrik: Do you want to crawl back into bed?

Anna: No, it's better like this with you. (*They embrace.*)

Henrik: Complain some more!

Anna: I miss Mama! I know it's crazy, but I miss Mama.

Henrik: Then I'll write a polite letter and ask your mother to come and see us: "It would be a great delight to us, dear Karin, if you would at last take the trouble to come and see us up here in the wilderness."

Anna: That'd be dreadful.

Henrik: Then I don't know what to suggest.

Anna: I miss Trädgårdsgatan. Mama and Lisen and Trädgårdsgatan. And *Ernst!* (*Cries a little.*) I miss my brother terribly!

Henrik: My poor little darling.

Anna: Do you *want* another child? Answer me honestly now. Do you want another child?

Henrik: I want to have ten. You know that.

Anna: Preferably girls.

Henrik: Since you're asking, I'd like to have a girl this time. You'd also prefer a girl, wouldn't you?

Anna: I have absolutely no desire to be with child.

Henrik: I'll be extra nice.

Anna: You are what you are.

Henrik: What kind of tone was that?

Anna: You're so childish, Henrik. I want to have a fully grown, mature man at last.

Henrik: So that you can be little and childish.

Anna (*kindly*): That was both silly and banal.

Henrik: If you want to go back home to your mother for a few weeks . . .

Anna: And give her that triumph? Never!

Henrik: Well, then I don't know what.

They sit on the floor and hold each other, wrapped in the big quilt from their bed. It grows lighter; the snow rages and swirls, soundlessly and mercilessly.

Thursday evening at the beginning of December. The sewing bee at the parsonage. Everything is as usual, but the guests are fewer than usual — only five — which cannot be blamed entirely on the cold, the state of the road, or the shortage of paraffin, candles, coffee, and other necessities.

To introduce those present: Gertrud Tallrot is seventy and has been a widow for many years. Her husband had worked at the Forge. Nowadays, she assists at the Post Office when extra help is needed. She is tall, thin, and bent, her eyes clear behind the pince-nez, her hair thin, chin large and slightly whiskery. She is good-humored and has a deep voice. Big cardigan and boots. She scratches in her ear with her knitting needle, an alarming sight.

Alva Nykvist is in her fifties and has been employed for many years in the Works office. She is plump, pasty-faced, and good company, her eyes black and inquisitive. She likes passing on news of local disasters and interesting rumors. She is unmarried and looks after a simpleminded cousin without tenderness. She is well-read, Christian, and takes journeys abroad. She belongs to the upper class of the Works, so to speak, for she lives off an inheritance from her father, who had been a successful wholesaler in Gävle.

Over the years, Mrs. Magna Flink has become a friend of the parsonage family. Her husband spends most of the year traveling as a representative for a machine tool firm with its head office in Enköping. Magna is a dark, handsome beauty, determined, and well aware of her importance. She organizes the community's lotteries. Her children are grown and studying in Upsala. If there is anything unfavorable to say about her, it is that she is both jealous and possessive, a fact she hides with some skill.

Märta Werkelin is thirty and the new teacher at the village school. She is convincingly kind, quiet, and has blue, rather protruding eyes. She looks permanently surprised, has thick ash-blonde hair, and is feminine without knowing it. Because she is a newcomer to the district, she is not particularly well informed.

Tekla Kronström is married to a worker at the Sawmill and is mother to five children. Sharp gray eyes, broad forehead, high cheekbones, large mouth (still has all her own teeth), large breasts, and big backside. She has a turned-up nose, her hair is short, and she is small.

These five women are participating in the evening's sewing bee, drinking dandelion coffee, and listening to the pastor reading aloud.

Henrik (*reads aloud*): "Far from discouraging him, Lucien's rage over this defeat of his ambitions gave him new strength. Like all people who are borne by instinct into a higher sphere and arrive there before they are able to manage it, Lucien continued to sacrifice everything to remain in high society. During his journey, he pulled out, one by one, the poisoned arrows he had received. He talked aloud to himself. He snubbed the blockheads he came across. He found witty answers to the stupid questions asked of him, and grew vexed over his wit becoming as it were *post festum* like that . . ."

Henrik falls silent, turns the page, new chapter, closes the book with a little bang, and puts it down on the round table by the paraffin lamp. Anna gets up and gives him some coffee. They all seem to be absorbed in whatever their hands are doing. Henrik takes a sip of the bitter drink and puts down the cup.

Henrik: I think, in contrast with Balzac's hero, I will come straight to the point.

None of his guests appear to react. Anna goes around and fills up cups. Jack yawns.

Henrik: I'd like to find out why we have become so few recently.

Silence.

Henrik: At the beginning of the autumn, we were between twenty-one and thirty-five. Now we're (*counts*) five. Plus Anna and myself, and Jack, of course.

Silence.

Henrik: Let's blame the cold and the state of the roads, but I don't think that's the whole explanation.

Silence.

Henrik: I would very much like to know if there is any other explanation. If any one of you could find another explanation.

Silence. Everyone is busily occupied.

Henrik: Then I'll ask you directly. What do you think, Mrs. Tallrot? (*Pause.*) You work at the Post Office and meet lots of people.

Addressed directly, Gertrud Tallrot scratches her big chin and peers over her pince-nez.

Gertrud: I don't really know what to say. (*Pause.*) To me, it seems people are slightly afraid, or how can I put it? I don't know, but that's what I think.

Henrik (*astonished*): Afraid?

Tekla: I'm not one of those real churchgoers, I'm really not. But you can't escape noticing certain things.

Henrik: No, people aren't coming so often.

Tekla: The one doesn't necessarily have anything to do with the other.

Magna: I don't think so, either.

Some of the other women agree: no, there are probably different reasons. Silence.

Henrik: No.

Märta: It could be that preacher at the Pentecostalists.

Henrik: Let's leave out the church and talk about our Thursday evenings. You say people are afraid, Mrs. Tallrot. Why should anyone be afraid?

Alva (*brightly*): Everyone knows that.

Henrik: I don't.

Alva: There's a *list* down at the office of everyone who comes to the sewing bee.

Henrik: Is that true?

Alva: I've never seen it, but Torstensson at the office said there was a list and that it was locked in Nordenson's safe.

Henrik: What would Nordenson want with such a list?

Tekla: That's not difficult to figure out. If it's true.

Alva: Why shouldn't it be true?

Tekla (*angry*): Because that Torstensson is a shit. He invents things to frighten people. Just like his lord and master.

Henrik: I still don't understand. Does Nordenson . . . ?

Alva: I've heard talk about a list, too. But has *anyone* been harassed or treated badly?

Gertrud: Yes, indeed. Johansson and Bergkvist and Frydén have all been fired with no explanation, and Granström has been transferred and been given a worse job at lower pay.

Tekla: The foreman, I mean Santesson, came and asked my Adolf if I still went to the pastor's Thursday evenings. "Does your old woman still go to that old woman-pastor's old women's Thursdays?" Adolf was angry and said that Santesson was the worst old woman of the lot and he should . . . well . . . what his Tekla did on Thursday evenings was no damned business of his.

Henrik (*pale*): But this isn't possible!

Märta: Everyone thinks about when Nordenson was at the chapel last Midsummer.

Gertrud: Yes, of course. That's probably true.

Märta: I know Helena, his elder daughter, a little. Helena said several times that her father can't forgive that. Nordenson can't forgive that humiliation in front of the confirmation pupils.

Henrik (*frightened*): But why hasn't anyone . . .

Tekla: Why hasn't anyone said anything? That's asking a lot, isn't it, Pastor?

Alva: Quite a lot has probably been said, but not to you, Pastor. Nor to your wife.

Anna: Magna, have you known about this? And never said anything to us? That's . . .

Magna: I've heard a lot of gossip, but I've never paid any attention, because I think . . .

Anna: But you've seen that our Thursdays . . .

Magna: Yes, I've noticed all right. But I think there's a better explanation.

Anna: A better explanation? What do you mean?

Magna: We can talk about that another time.

Anna: Why not now?

Magna: Because that would upset Mrs. Tallrot and Mrs. Kronström, and I don't want to do that.

Henrik: I'd like . . . I insist. (*Agitated.*) I *insist* that you tell us what you know. Or think you know.

Tekla: She needn't worry about me. I'm already as angry as I can be.

Gertrud: If it's that business we *all* know about, then it's just as well we ask the pastor directly.

Alva (*suddenly*): Though on my part, I think there's a third explanation.

Henrik (*really frightened*): Magna, you maintain you're a friend of ours. Tell us what you know.

Magna: The Reverend Gransjö told his housekeeper, Mrs. Säll, that Henrik and Anna went to see Queen Victoria at the palace, in June I think it was. Mrs. Säll passed that on to some members of the Women's Corps. I suppose they were all singing Henrik's praises, and then she probably said that we won't be keeping him for long, because he's been offered the *court chaplaincy*. Well, then summer and autumn went by, and everyone was talking about it, and some people were probably upset, I presume. Some probably thought Henrik was false for not saying anything about leaving us.

Anna: Why didn't you say anything yourself?

Magna (*hurt*): If you're both thinking of leaving without saying anything, then I'm not the kind to run after you with a whole bunch of questions about the reasons why.

Anna: But, Magna!

Magna: Maybe I heard a word here and there. But that's nothing to go on and on about, is it?

Anna: But Magna! We've *turned it down!* Henrik was asked in the spring. It wasn't to be court chaplain at all. He was to be the priest for a big hospital of which the queen is chairman of the board. We were tempted, which isn't all that surprising. But Henrik *turned it down*. I was much more uncertain. But Henrik *turned it down!*

Magna: Oh, did he? (*Still offended.*)

Anna: Well, now you know everything. Surely there wasn't much to tell you.

Magna: There could be different opinions about that.

Anna: Nothing has changed. We're going to stay here. We've decided.

Magna: As a kind of sacrifice?

Anna: We want to *be here*.

Magna: That's nice of you.

Henrik: I can't figure out why you're so angry.

Magna: I'm not angry. I'm miserable.

Henrik: I don't understand why you're miserable.

Magna: No, of course not.

Tekla: When you two came here to Forsboda, we were pleased. I don't mean just the regular churchgoers, but most people were glad.

The door opens and Mia comes in with a basket of wood. She blows on the embers in the stove, puts in more logs, and the fire flares up.

Gertrud: We suddenly thought there was some kind of fellowship.

Märta: Pastor, sometimes you came down to us at the school and held morning prayers, or took over the scripture lessons. That was a great joy, I assure you. Both for the children and for me. We always looked forward to you coming. We said to each other: The Pastor hasn't been for a long time, so he'll be coming soon.

Henrik: Why didn't anyone say anything?

Märta (*confused*): What should we have said?

Henrik: You could have said, Please come back soon.

Märta: Should we have said that?

Henrik: For instance.

Märta: Excuse me, Pastor, but it wouldn't have been appropriate. It would have been obtrusive.

Henrik: We thought we belonged.

Silence. Gertrud Tallrot smooths out her knitting on the table, shaking her head. Alva Nykvist is hemming, her needle moving quickly. She bites off the thread with her short white teeth, her eyes quick and inquisitive. Magna Flink is doing nothing, her large hands in her lap, her embroidery bag beside her on the table. She is upset; her cheeks are red, and she keeps swallowing. Märta Werkelin has reached out for the book they are reading and leafs through it without looking. She sighs cautiously. Tekla Kronström turns her heavy body and looks at Anna, who is standing behind her with the coffeepot. Henrik is clutching the arms of his chair, an involuntary display of an emotion: What is it that is happening at this very moment, here in our familiar dining room, in the light of our kindly ceiling lamp, which is smoking a little, the paraffin so bad nowadays? I must go over to the table and adjust the wick so the ceiling doesn't get blackened. Henrik gets up carefully and goes over to the table, raises his arms, and turns down the reddish smoking flame.

Henrik: It's smoking.

Gertrud: It's the paraffin that's so bad.

Alva: You can't get any paraffin at all in Gävle. I heard that down at the office.

Tekla: I suppose we'll soon all be sitting in the dark, like primeval savages. Chewing on old bones.

Märta: My father wrote to say that we're bound to get involved in the war. To help Finland. And then the Russians will come with their fleet and attack Söderhamn and Gävle and Lulea and ravage and pillage just like the last time.

Anna: The war must come to an end soon.

Tekla: It won't stop until the people take over and kill all the generals.

Silence falls again. Henrik sits down on his chair by the dining room table and runs his hand over his face, the sense of vertigo persisting.

Henrik: So Anna and I have just been imagining things.

Tekla: What do you mean, Pastor?

Henrik: We thought that we . . . (*Falls silent.*)

Gertrud: No one is reproaching you or your wife, Pastor. One does one's best. There's nothing wrong with your good intentions. In the end, the skein gets tangled anyhow.

Tekla: If I'd been in your shoes, Pastor, I would have accepted that offer and gone from here as quickly as possible. There's nothing to be had from Forsboda.

Anna (*quietly*): We thought we might be useful.

Tekla: Sorry, what kind of useful?

Anna: Be useful. (*Helpless.*)

Tekla: How touching. Really touching.

Gertrud: Now, Tekla, don't be nasty.

Tekla: What would a nice little pastor and his lovely wife be able to do this far out in this wretched place?

Gertrud: Now you're being a Bolshie, Tekla.

Tekla: Oh, what nonsense! Listen. Gertrud, you don't have to defend anyone at this moment. Least of all, you don't have to defend the pastor. He's in no need. He's got his regular income from the state.

Alva: I've heard another explanation.

Tekla: No one's interested in your explanations. And now I must go home before I start talking any more nonsense.

Tekla Kronström sighs, then starts ceremoniously gathering up her belongings. Finally she takes off her glasses and puts them into a worn case. She looks steadily at Anna for a long time.

Anna: May I ask you something, Mrs. Kronström?

Tekla: Please do.

Anna: Why have you come here every Thursday? I mean, if . . . ?

Tekla: There's no connection between us and you. You don't understand how we think, and you don't understand us. That's what it's like all the way.

Anna: You didn't answer my question.

Tekla: Oh. No. The answer is simple. I suppose I liked the pastor and his wife. I liked listening to him reading aloud out of those novels. I suppose I wanted to sit here for a few hours with the other women. I suppose I thought it was lovely.

She shakes hands without saying any more, then nods to the other women. Departure, taciturn and embarrassed, the words hanging in the room like wet dishcloths. Alva Nykvist makes herself useful, clears the table, brushes off the crumbs with a little silver brush, and helps to fold up the tablecloth. Suddenly, she says: "Oh, the others have all gone, and I'm the only one left." Anna and Henrik are stunned and not looking at each other.

Alva: Quite a bit's been talked about tonight. And then there's that *list*, of course. But I think there's another reason. A much worse one. It's all talk, of course, just like everything else.

Anna, Henrik, and Alva Nykvist remain standing. Henrik is trying to light his pipe. Anna has picked up the poker to stir the embers in the stove. Alva stands with her arms folded and head slightly back, peering through her half-closed eyes. Neither Anna nor Henrik have asked her to stay or to say anything.

Alva: If I didn't know that what I'm going to say is just shameful, yes, shameful slander, then I wouldn't say a word, that's for sure. You must understand that.

She is expecting some reaction, but there is none. She clears her throat and lowers her head, now looking at her shoes sticking out from beneath the hem of her skirt.

Alva: What's *most poisonous* is probably what no one wants to say. I feel very sorry for both of you now. Especially sorry for the pastor's wife, of course.

She waits for a few moments, but no one says anything. The dog Jack gets up and goes and stands by Anna's knee.

Alva: It's probably that many people think this *secret* mixing with Nordenson is the worst of all. They mean most of all mixing with Mrs. Nordenson. A lot of people are upset. A lot say they understand why Nordenson is so hateful toward the pastor. I mean all that business with the daughters. It probably had nothing to do with the daughters. A lot of people say it's hard on Nordenson. A pity and a shame. I'm not spreading gossip. It's generally known that Mrs. Nordenson, that Elin, is quite flighty. She's so lovely and smooth, is Mrs. Nordenson. And she smiles in such a friendly way, but there's a stench, yes, a stench of lechery about her. And then that list, if it exists at all, is probably not the real reason why people don't go to church or come to the Thursdays.

All this is said in courteous, matter-of-fact tones. Mrs. Alva Nykvist is not agitated, nor is she in any hurry. Her dark eyes go from Anna to Henrik and back again; sometimes she smiles quickly and apologetically. When she has finally come to the end of her information, she makes a helpless gesture with her hand: "Now I've said everything. It was painful but necessary, forgive me, we don't believe all this terrible . . ."
Henrik nods in confirmation and holds out his hand.

Henrik: Thank you for that information. It has been very valuable. Anna and I are extremely grateful. What an *evening*, Mrs. Nykvist! I'm overwhelmed. *We* are overwhelmed. And grateful. (*Smiles.*)

Alva Nykvist finally leaves. The hall door closes. Henrik locks up and turns to Anna. His face is pale, but he laughs.

Henrik: Now, Anna! Now I know for certain. Now I know how important it is that we do not let these people down, Anna!

He embraces her with much emotion, so does not see her face. Suddenly someone scratches on the glass pane of the porch door, then there's a discreet knock. Anna extracts herself from the embrace and opens the door.

Märta Werkelin is standing on the steps. She is upset and has tears in her eyes. "Excuse me for troubling you, excuse me, but I must say something important." Anna lets her in. She stops inside the door beneath the ceiling lamp, leans against the wall, and bursts into tears as she takes off her thick gloves and large fur cap, the ash-blonde hair tumbling out and falling over her shoulders. Anna and Henrik stand there, astounded and reluctant. "Shall we go in and sit down?" says Anna lamely.

Märta Werkelin energetically shakes her head and blows her nose. "No, no, I must go at once. There's just something I must say first." They all remain standing, Märta propped against the wall, Henrik with his hand on the banister rail, Anna by the door into the dining room. Märta tugs at her long shawl.

Märta: It's all so terrible, and I'm so miserable. Why do things have to be like this evening? It's . . . it's grotesque. It's . . . it's sick. And I'm ashamed. I'm ashamed because I didn't dare come out with what I was thinking all the time. I was thinking that what is going on now, at this moment, is *exactly* like the story of my blouse.

She blows her nose again and is surprisingly beautiful in her agitation, tears in her slightly protruding eyes, her lips swollen with crying, and the shiny hair over her shoulders.

Märta: It's like my blouse. One day I put on a lovely blouse. It was in the spring, and the weather was beautiful. I wanted the schoolchildren to see that their teacher could be well dressed. They were to be allowed to see something beautiful. The blouse is of genuine lace with a high collar and Russian buttoning, if you know what I mean, and widens over the sleeves, and the cuffs are of another material. The lace is openwork, and there's red silk under the lace. Then I put on the gold brooch I've inherited. I pinned it at the neck and then braided my hair into one thick plait that hung down my back. Then I went down to the children, and we went out onto the bank below the school, and we sat there and had our lessons, which was nothing special. Then came the talk. About the blouse. Never directly. And I was so terribly ashamed. It was almost as if I'd done something indecent. But no one ever came to me and said anything directly (*pause*), and tonight, it was *exactly* like that blouse. I don't know how I can explain what I mean, but it's the

265

same thing. What kind of hatred is it? What kind of animosity? Things are difficult enough anyhow out here in the darkness. And now the pastor'll leave, I can see that. You don't have to tolerate this vileness, either of you, or this darkness. But I have to stay. I don't have any offers to be a teacher at the palace. (*Laughs.*) That sounded like envy, but I'm not envious, forgive me! I don't begrudge you leaving. I must go now. You poor things, you must be dreadfully sad after all that nastiness this evening, and then I come here bawling on top of everything else. Good night and forgive me. No, please don't say anything. I'm grateful to you both for listening to me so patiently. Good night.

Märta Werkelin holds out a delicate hand and says good night once again. Then she vanishes into the arctic night, half-running down the slope to the gate, and is gone.

Anna turns out the lamps in the dining room and closes the stove doors. A heavy, wordless fury is slowly moving inside her. Henrik turns out the lamp in the hall. The nightlight is burning flutteringly on the upstairs landing outside the bedrooms and the workroom, moonlight coming through the window to the right of the stairs. There are toys and building bricks on the rug on the floor. Petrus and Dag have been using the landing as a playroom, which has actually been forbidden since the day Dag fell down the steep stairs. Henrik goes into their bedroom and lights the candles by the beds. He quickly pulls off his clothes and washes in the basin, then cleans his teeth. The stove is still warm after the evening fire, the curtains carefully drawn across.

Anna picks up the toys and bricks. She goes back and forth across the rag rug on the landing. She is not systematic or quick. She flings something into the big wooden box, and he can hear it. Then she leaves it all and opens the door of the room where Dag and Petrus are asleep. (This is really Anna's room, which had been turned into a nursery while Alma had been staying with them. After her death, no one had got around to converting it back again.) The boys are sound asleep and undisturbable. Dag is in Petrus's bed. Anna lifts her son up and tucks him in his own bed, letting her hand rest on his head, on his hair, his cheek. An anger without words. Petrus is breathing soundlessly, his face smooth, his mouth half-open, his eyelids twitching, a pulse beating in the stretched neck. Could he possibly be awake? Is he pretending to be asleep? No, he is almost certainly asleep.

Anger with Henrik, wordless and blind. It fumbles and stumbles. The child moves inside her, uneasily, without softness.

She closes the door and returns to clearing the landing rug. Wooden trains, fir cones, and a sheet of paper, building bricks, a large tin soldier, a teddy bear with one ear missing. Henrik is cleaning his teeth and spitting into the basin. She's asked him ten times to spit into the pail. Anna shifts her feet, barely muffled by the rag rug. Henrik stops cleaning his teeth and pours the water into the pail. It turns quiet, as Anna has stopped. She is holding a rag doll in her hands. Moonlight.

Henrik (*invisible*): Are you coming?

Anna: Soon.

Henrik (*invisible*): *Is* there something?

Anna: No. What do you mean?

Anna takes a few steps, stops indecisively, goes back, stops again, and throws the rag doll into the box.

Henrik: You're making a terrible noise stamping about out there.

Anna: Am I now?

Henrik: But your shoes are nice. (*Looks out.*) High-heeled.

Anna: Less appropriate, perhaps?

Henrik: What do you mean?

Anna: With reference to tonight's meeting.

Henrik: What? What do you mean? (*Stands, short pause.*) Are you coming?

Anna: Soon.

Henrik (*puzzled*): I'll go to bed then?

Anna: I'm coming in a minute.

Henrik: All right. (*Disappears from the doorway.*) Well, yes . . . (*Pause.*)

Anna: Henrik.

Henrik: Yes. (*Fiddles with the pillows on his bed.*)

Anna: We must send Petrus away. The sooner the better.

Henrik: Anna, dear. Let's deal with that tomorrow, shall we?

Anna: No. *Now!*

She is standing in the bedroom doorway, starting to take out hairpins, her face half turned away, her voice slightly out of control. She has to breathe.

267

Henrik: Why all this hurry with Petrus, poor child? He doesn't bother anyone, does he?

Anna: I never promised that he could live here forever. I never promised to be his surrogate mother. You'll have to speak to Mrs. Johansson.

Henrik: Yes, of course. (*Amenable.*) I'll speak to Mrs. Johansson.

Anna (*shaking inwardly*): It is hard enough anyhow. I can't take the responsibility for another child, you must see that.

Henrik: Don't be so angry, Anna.

Anna: I'm not angry. Why should I be angry?

Henrik (*sits up in bed*): Come over here and sit down.

Anna: I'm quite happy standing.

Henrik: I'll speak to Mrs. Johansson.

Anna: At once. First thing tomorrow.

Henrik: As soon as possible.

Anna: I've tried to like that poor little thing, but I can't. He's like a *dog*.

Henrik: But you like dogs.

Anna (*smiles slightly*): Idiot.

Henrik: Yes, he's strange.

Anna: He's definitely a strange sort. We'd better clear the matter up as quickly as possible.

Henrik: It'll be a wretched business, of course. Poor boy.

Anna: We're actually going to have a child of our own.

Henrik (*humbly*): Yes, of course.

Anna: He kicks and makes himself felt all the time.

Henrik: She. It's a girl.

Anna: Petrus is . . . he looks at me with his puppy dog eyes and I get angry, and then I'm angry with myself, because you shouldn't be antagonistic to a child.

Henrik (*wearily*): This has been a heavy evening, and I have to get up at six. Can't we go to sleep now?

Anna: Do you understand what I mean?

Henrik (*ready to drop*): Of course I do.

Anna (*lies down*): Then we'd better go to sleep. Good night.

Henrik (*kisses her*): Good night, angriest.

Anna (*kisses him*): Good night, Pastor.

She blows out the bedside candle. Moonlight. Petrus Farg is standing quite still out on the landing. He is wearing a long nightshirt with a red border, and bedsocks.

The morning is icily still and misty, and it is snowing slightly. At the parsonage, the indefatigable Mejan is in bed with a high temperature and a rasping cough. She has a stocking around her neck, and her face is red, her eyes feverish. Mia, who shares the bed and sleeps head to toe with Mejan, also has a cold, but she's at the kitchen table preparing the midday meal. (At the parsonage they have breakfast at half past seven, porridge, eggs, and bread and something on it. At one o'clock, they have a hot drink, bread with something, a cooked dish, and that's rightly called the midday meal. The evening meal is taken at five o'clock and is two cooked dishes. Before going to bed, they have tea or milk and crispbread with cheese on it.) So Mia is preparing the midday meal at the kitchen table, spreading bread with drippings and slices of sausage, setting the table and putting things straight. The yardman has brought in wood and is stacking it in the woodbox. Anna and Petrus are both carrying a basket of kindling for the insatiably greedy tiled stoves. Dag is already sitting in his chair sucking on a rusk, whining and sniffling.

Anna (*comes in*): . . . from today on, we'll stop lighting the stove in the living room, the dining room, and the nursery. We'll have to be content with keeping the kitchen, the girls' room, and the upstairs rooms warm. I wonder if Dag's got a temperature.

Mia: His nose is certainly running.

Anna: How are you, Mia?

Mia: Mejan is worse. She coughs so hard that the bed shakes. I don't get much sleep.

Anna: You'll have to move in with Petrus and Dag. We'll get out the camp bed.

Mia: As long as Mejan gets better.

Anna: She must have hot drinks and keep warm.

Anna pours Ems salt and hot water into a cup and goes in to Mejan, who blinks red-eyed, her lips dry and her cough rasping.

Mejan: I feel better, so I think I'll be able to get up for dinner.

Anna: Drink this and stay where you are in bed.

Mejan: But maybe I have to go out to the privy.

Anna: You'll have to use the bucket. That can't be helped.

Mejan: Oh, this is terrible.

Anna: It could be worse. We can keep warm, and we have food, and the paraffin hasn't run out yet. Now, let's look at your temperature. Exactly thirty-nine, so it's gone down a bit. You'll see, we'll have you up again in a few days.

Mejan (*coughs*): I've probably got consumption.

Anna: You have not got consumption, Mejan. I promise you that.

Mejan: You've been a nurse, so you ought to know.

Anna: Exactly. Now lie down again. I'll bring the cough mixture.

Anna goes out into the kitchen and closes the door of the girls' room. Mejan coughs. Mia has put on her outdoor clothes and boots.

Anna: Where are you off to?

Mia: To the Post Office. The pastor is waiting for the newspaper.

Anna: Are you going to go out in this weather with that cold of yours?

Mia: I'll take the sled. The road's been plowed.

Anna: I'll go and make the beds. We'll be eating in an hour. Will you be back by then?

Mia: I'm sure I will.

Mia trudges out and disappears toward the gate, scooting along on the sled. Anna picks out a storybook with illustrations and gives it to Petrus: "Sit down here and read to Dag while I go up and make the beds. You and Jack look after Dag and each other." Jack, who had been dozing by the warm stove, at once gets up and attends to his responsibilities.

Anna pulls her big winter cardigan around her and hurries through the living room and dining room, both now really cold. She runs up the stairs to the upper landing, where the wooden box of toys is still on the rag rug. She lifts it up and carries it into the boys' room. She at once starts making the beds with swift and irritable movements. Henrik is standing in the doorway.

Anna: Come in and shut the door so that you don't let the warmth out.

Henrik (*obeys*): I've been thinking about our conversation.

Anna: Which conversation?

Henrik: Which conversation? We were talking about Petrus.

Anna: Oh, Petrus. There's no hurry, is there?

Henrik: Last night he was to be sent away immediately.

Anna: Really.

Henrik: I can't sit in there writing my Sunday sermon, knowing I am to send Petrus away. I can't.

Anna (*friendly*): Do as you please.

Henrik: Can't we decide together?

Anna: Yes, of course. We decide together, and then you do as you please. Your Sunday sermon is actually important. (*Without irony.*) We have to think about that.

Henrik: Petrus is a fellow human being.

(*Anna stops making the bed, looks at him.*)

Henrik: What is it?

Anna: Nothing.

Henrik (*takes hold of her*): Anna, don't be so difficult.

Anna: I am also a fellow human being, although I happen to be your wife.

Henrik: Can't we help each other?

Anna: Help each other?

Henrik: Anna!

Anna (*friendly*): Yes, of course! We must help each other. You go on in there and write your sermon, then we'll let the subject rest for the time being. Is that all right?

Henrik stays where he is, sucking on his cold pipe, which squeaks faintly. He is wearing a spacious jersey and a shawl over his shoulders, crumpled trousers baggy at the knees, slippers, thick socks, his trouser legs tucked into his socks. He presumably wants to say something more, but Anna is making beds and has turned her back on him. So he slopes off to his sermon and evangelical text, which he has paid for in order to stand in the pulpit and interpret: "The signs should appear in the sun and the moon and the stars, and on the earth anguish will descend on the people. They will find themselves helpless in the thunder of the sea and the waves, now that the people give up the ghost in terror and anguish when faced with what transcends the world." I shall stand turned toward a handful of people, see into their faces, and speak of the Unfathomable, thinks Henrik. He bites a ragged nail; he has started biting his nails again, as he had in childhood. And then Anna being so awkward and pregnant!

Anna has gone into the bedroom to finish straightening, the rough movements doing her good: Poor Henrik, how nasty I am, behaving like a real harridan. She laughs to herself, straightens up, and looks out the window.

At first she doesn't understand what she sees, but then she understands and screams. It's like in a dream. She sees Petrus running in his stocking feet, bareheaded and with no coat on. In his arms he has Dag, whose arms are clasped around Petrus's neck. Jack is running after them in great circular movements. Petrus is slithering and running and sliding down the cleared path toward the jetty where they do the washing. Petrus fleeing with Dag in his arms. Toward the river.

Anna rushes downstairs and tries to cut off Petrus by crossing the slope, but sinks to her knees in the snow and sees Petrus getting farther and farther away, the last bit of the road dropping quite steeply toward the water. She plunges and struggles up and down through the snow, apparently never getting any farther, as if in a dream. She screams at Petrus to stop. He turns his head, but goes on. Then he slips and falls on the slippery slope. She sees Henrik coming racing down, choosing the plowed stretch of road, then falling headlong, getting up, slipping and falling again. Petrus has disappeared down the hill, holding Dag in front of him very carefully, and Dag is screaming. Jack is leaping around in circles, uncertain of the content of the situation.

At last Anna extricates herself from the deep snow, tumbles

through the drift of plowed snow, and slides down the slippery slope. Henrik is standing on the riverbank with his son in his arms. Petrus is sitting on the ground. His nose is bleeding and his lip split, blood dripping onto the snow. He is sitting with his head down, leaning forward without complaining, the palms of his hands pressed to the snow. Anna takes Dag, who is still screaming, and tries to calm him, tears and snot pouring out of him, snow in his hair. Beyond the jetty, the current keeps the water open, rushing along and frighteningly black against the white edge of ice. Henrik pulls Petrus up by the collar, and they stand there, panting. Anna is on her way back to the house, followed by Jack. She turns her head and looks around. Henrik is hitting the boy in the face, hitting hard, and Petrus falls. Henrik pulls him up again and strikes again and again; the boy falls to one side and lies there.

Henrik jerks the boy up by the collar so that he is on his feet and drags him along the road. He'll kill him, thinks Anna indifferently. Petrus is not crying. His face is swollen and bloody, his hands too.

The next morning, Mrs. Johansson is sitting at the kitchen table at the parsonage. Henrik is standing in the kitchen doorway. He has pulled on his boots and the short coat, the knitted cap in his hand. Horse and sled are waiting out in the yard. Anna comes into the kitchen, pushing Petrus ahead of her. They stop in the middle of the floor. Jack is uneasily wagging his tail and padding around.

Anna: Good morning, Mrs. Johansson.

Mrs. Johansson: Good morning, Mrs. Bergman.

Anna: I'm sorry everything is in such a mess here. Both the girls are ill.

Mrs. Johansson: It's the same everywhere. Only half the men are at work at the Sawmill and the teacher at the school is ill, so the old teacher has come in her place.

Anna: I think Petrus has all his belongings with him. I have packed a few books too. Petrus likes reading.

Petrus is standing in the middle of the floor, not looking at anyone. His blind gaze is expressionless. There is a swelling by one eye, and his lip is split.

Mrs. Johansson: The pastor has told me everything. There's nothing much to add.

Anna: I hope you understand, Mrs. Johansson, that under the present circumstances we dare not . . .

Mrs. Johansson: No, no, of course. There's no question of it.

Anna: Good-bye, then, Petrus.

Anna pats his cheek. He turns his head away.

Mrs. Johansson: I think we'd better go.

She gets up heavily and takes Anna's proffered hand. "Thank you very much for all your patience and care." Anna looks away. "It was a pity it had to end like this." Mrs. Johansson is embarrassed. "Anyhow, you and the pastor couldn't have looked after the boy forever."

They all stand around. Finally, Mrs. Johansson puts her hand on the back of Petrus's neck and pushes him toward the door. Henrik reaches for the suitcase, and they leave in silence. Jack follows. He likes riding on the sleigh. Henrik helps Mrs. Johansson and Petrus up, tucks the fur rugs around them, and gets up on the driver's seat, urges the horse on, the bells jingling. The sleigh disappears up the slope toward the gate.

Anna watches them go. Her darkness is great. Gradually, she forces herself out of her immobility and knocks on the door of the maid's room, where things are very cramped. Mia's cot is blocking the doorway, and she is lying curled up, her forehead beaded with sweat. Mejan is sitting up on the pull-out sofa, knitting and coughing dully. The stove pings; the iron doors rattle; the room is steamily hot and smells of sweat and body odors.

"I'm getting up tomorrow," says Mejan determinedly. "Only if you haven't got a temperature," says Anna. "How's Mia?" "I think she's delirious. She says such peculiar things, I have to laugh," says Mejan. "Maybe you ought to air the room," says Anna. "It's rather stuffy in here." "I'm not letting out all this nice warmth," says Mejan, coughing. "Have you drunk your Ems water?" "Oh, yes. And Petrus had to go, did he?" "Yes, Petrus has gone." "I never liked that boy," says Mejan decisively, rattling her knitting needles. "Are you sure you don't want me to do the dishes?" "You stay there!" says Anna, and goes out into the kitchen and closes the door.

There is a copper cistern of hot water by the stove. Anna turns on the tap, and the hot water steams and splashes into the washing-up bowl. She adds cold water and mixes in a slick of green soft soap (shortage), then lifts the bowl onto the bench. She can feel that in her back, but she is deep down in her darkness and tears are pouring down her cheeks. She starts washing the dishes from yesterday's evening meal. Then she stops abruptly, wipes her hands, and sits down at the kitchen table. The stove rustles and crackles, but otherwise it is quiet. A gigantic quiet lies on Anna's shoulders, rising like a column toward icy space.

She has sat there quite a long time, perhaps even dozing off for a few minutes, when she hears the sleigh bells up by the gate and the neighbor who has lent them the sleigh coming. Henrik speaks to him and hands over the reins. They exchange a few words, and then Henrik is stamping the snow off his boots on the steps. Anna gets up and stretches, bending back. Sometimes her back aches, or else she has been sick, but that's not surprising. The door opens and closes. Anna washes dishes. Henrik is standing over by the door, taking off his coat. Anna washes dishes. Henrik sits down on a chair and pulls off his boots. Anna washes dishes in a clatter of glass, china, forks, spoons, and knives. Henrik sits down by the window, his coat across his knees, his boots on the floor beside him. He is looking steadily at Anna, who is washing dishes. Jack lies down under the kitchen table.

Henrik: It was best that way.

(*Anna washes dishes.*)

Henrik: We couldn't possibly keep him here.

(*Anna washes dishes.*)

Henrik: I think he understood.

(*Anna clatters.*)

Henrik: He didn't even cry.

(*Anna puts the plates into the bowl.*)

Henrik: Why don't you answer?

(*Anna doesn't answer.*)

Henrik: We can't go on like this, Anna!

(*Anna washes dishes.*)

Henrik: You've no reason to behave like this.

(*Anna stops washing dishes, stands still.*)

Henrik: It's as if it were all my fault.

(*Anna shakes her head, washes dishes.*)

275

Henrik: *Stop washing dishes* and turn around!

(Anna stops washing dishes and doesn't turn around.)
(Henrik says nothing.)
(Anna says nothing.)

Henrik suddenly gets up and walks across the floor to Anna, snatches the plate out of her hand, and bangs it down on the draining board so that pieces fly in all directions. Then he grabs her by the shoulders and turns her to him, breathing heavily, his face trembling.

Henrik: *Speak to me!*

Anna: You've cut yourself on the plate. Your finger's bleeding.

Henrik: I don't give a damn.

Anna (*calmly*): Come on, let's get out of here. There's no point in the girls hearing us.

She wipes her hands on her apron and goes ahead of Henrik into the living room. It is bitterly cold, and their breath turns white.

Henrik: Can't we go up to my room? It is so damned cold in here.

Anna: No. I have moved Dag into our bedroom. We're only going to heat the bedroom and your workroom. What did you want to say?

Henrik: You must speak to me.

Anna: There's no point.

Henrik: Anything, Anna. Anything's better than saying nothing.

Anna: And *you* say that?

Henrik breathes, and his breath billows out. Anna is standing with her back to the window, her hands under her woolen cardigan and her arms folded across her bosom. Mejan's blue apron is too large. Her hair is untidy, her face gray.

Henrik: Anything.

Anna: I have a responsibility. I am responsible for Dag and the child that is coming. My *responsibility* tells me that I must leave here. My responsibility to the children is more important than my loyalty to you.

Henrik: I don't understand.

Anna: I must take Dag with me and go away. You want to stay, as that is your conviction. I respect your conviction but do not share it.

Henrik: And where are you going?

Anna: Where shall I go? Home, of course.

Henrik: Your home is here.

(*Anna says nothing.*)

Henrik: You can't do this to me.

Anna: I have already written to Mama.

Henrik: What a triumph. For her.

Anna: So that's your first thought.

Henrik: I forbid you to go.

Anna: You forbid nothing, Henrik.

Henrik: And how long will you be away?

Anna: When you have come to your senses, then perhaps we can talk about the future.

Henrik: What future?

Anna: I have spoken to Gransjö. Or rather he has spoken to me. He pointed out that the offer still stands.

Henrik: So you've gone behind my back, have you?

Anna: You could say that, yes.

Their breath comes steaming out of their mouths, the cold pressing against their faces and their bodies. They remain inexorable, Anna with her back to the window, Henrik inside the door.

Henrik (*calmly*): I shall never forgive you for this.

Anna: So now we know that. Now I'm going to the kitchen to finish the dishes.

She walks past him. He turns around and grabs her by the arm to stop her, but she frees herself and laughs. He hits her in the face, and she stops, staring at him.

Henrik (*panic*): Just go away! (*Shouts.*) Go away, *for Christ's sake!* I never want to see you again! Go away! You've lied and gone behind my back. (*Shouts.*) *Go away!* Just go away!

He hits her again. She staggers back and slowly brings her hand up to her face, staring steadily at him, more astonished than really shaken.

Anna: You're insane.

Henrik: I knew it would be like this! I knew you'd leave me! *I knew it!*

She isn't listening to him, but goes out into the kitchen and closes the door behind her. Henrik starts walking across the floor, the cold penetrating through the floorboards, through his legs, stomach, and chest, up into his throat, mouth, eyes.

Three days later, everything is organized for an undramatic departure. Anna says she is taking her son with her to visit her mother in Upsala, something everyone finds quite natural. Husband and wife speak politely to each other in friendly tones. The dog Jack weeps quietly over the suitcases. Anna catches herself singing as she packs. Mia and Mejan have recovered, and the everyday domestic order is more or less restored.

The pastor accompanies his wife to the station. It's windy, the loose snow swirling about in silent clouds, the sun as red as a sore, the time half past nine in the morning. They have taken shelter in the waiting room, a large room with brown walls, fixed wooden benches, and a huge iron stove glowing more than producing heat. Mia is busy checking in the many suitcases; then she puts them on the platform where the guard's van stops. Henrik and Anna are alone in the waiting room, sitting beside each other on the wooden bench. Dag sits on Henrik's knee but wants to get down on the floor. Nothing is said. Then the train hoots and clatters across the points, thick white clouds of steam billowing in the cold.

The prayer house is a bare hall with four high windows facing the snowstorm and the arctic night. The wooden walls are unadorned and painted green. On the platform there is a lectern and a pedal-organ. (*Instant savior.*) Behind the lectern is a cross painted black. Two tall iron stoves take care of the heating. Eight carbide lamps hang on iron hooks from the ceiling and spread a strong bluish white light. The hall contains fifteen long benches with no backs. Despite the bad weather, everyone has come. It is a full house, more than full, and people are standing in the aisles and sitting on the floor. It is suf-

278

focatingly hot, and they are all sweating profusely.

Now they are singing:

> When the sinner blindly rash,
> Hastens to destruction,
> He is preceded by Thy Grace.
> Thou hastens to his meeting, calls:
> Stop sinful bondsman!
> See salvation for wretched soul!
> Waken and see your peril!

Henrik looks around. He is squashed up against the wall. They are all singing, the storm crashing against the windows, the carbide lamps shining sharply down on the pale faces, old people, young girls, families with children, boys in uniform.

They all sit down, shifting and making room, a gentle coughing buzz. Pastor Levander gets up on the platform and says a silent prayer. Then he raises his eyes and looks at the assembled crowd without ingratiation and speaks in a light but penetrating voice.

Levander: And they brought to him one who was deaf and almost dumb and bade Jesus lay his hand upon him.

Congregation: Yes, yes, praise the Lord!

Levander: Then Jesus took him aside from the people and put his fingers in his ear and spat and touched his tongue.

Congregation: Hallelujah! The Lord be praised!

Levander: . . . and looked up at the heavens, sighed and said to him "Effata" — "open up."

Congregation: Effata, Jesus, thou my savior!

Levander: Then his ears were opened and the bands on his tongue loosened, and he spoke plainly and clearly.

Congregation: He spoke, he spoke, Oh, Jesus! Jesus!

Levander: And Jesus forbade them to tell of this to anyone, but the more he forbade them, the more they told of what had happened!

Congregation: Come to me, Jesus! Open my heart!

Levander: And the people were amazed beyond all things and said: "He has brought about everything. He lets the deaf hear and the dumb speak." Hallelujah, sisters and brothers, let us together praise the Lord

Jesus Christ for the miracles he creates with us daily and always. May we with rejoicing raise our voices in praise and prayer.

The organ squeals and squeaks and is at once drowned.

All (*sing*): Crushed by the threat of law, by your hand I'm guided, to the throne of grace, to the foot of the cross, where salvation is prepared! Here am I purified in the blood of Jesus. Here I find another courage. Here life in faith is given!

Levander: The Grace of God and Peace be with you all, but especially with those of you who come from the extremes of darkness, especially those of you who are slaves of your deeds, especially those of you who think yourselves rejected and weep tears of blood, those of you who are choked by your evil words and your evil thoughts, those of you who carry earth in your mouth and the poison of serpents in your mind. Grace be with you! The Grace of Jesus Christ be with you. And may He have mercy on you this night and grant you peace.

Congregation: Hallelujah! The Grace of God! The Love of Jesus!

Levander: You who have gone astray, may you be taken by the hand of the Father. You who are lonely and think yourself spurned, may you already this night see the great light in the name of the Father, the Son, and the Holy Ghost. Amen.

Congregation: Amen, amen, amen.

Henrik tries to make his way out, almost suffocated by the heat and the crush. The congregation is now rising, and a trumpeter is on the platform. It is Tor Axelin from the village store. He is a member of the band of the Volunteer Defense Corps.

Congregation (*roaring*): The blood of Jesus my guilt doth take away. Jesus hast all reconciled. Jesus all good for me doth exhort. That I was mercifully spared. I a certain refuge find, in the deep wounds of Jesus. Jesus helps us out of need. Out into life and into death.

Henrik has reached the door and squeezes his way out. He sees surprised faces, a smile, someone whispers. Then at last he is away from that huge mysterious crush of human bodies. Icy nails in his face, the pain a release.

Mrs. Karin Åkerblom is waiting for the train, which is late because of the snowstorms in North Uppland. The two women meet on the platform, but there is no time for emotions. The grandchild is whimpering, and overseeing things now assumes vital importance, so a porter, arranged for in advance, takes the luggage tags, and a hired cab sits waiting.

Lisen is standing at the front door. She has never seen the son. Light everywhere, warmth. Supper is on the table, which is laid with the hand-painted English cups and saucers. Anna and Mrs. Karin make a hurried tour of the apartment, which is unrecognizable. The dining room has been halved and turned into a study with desk and bookcases, and, at the moment, with a sofa bed made up for the night. "I'm sleeping in here," says Mrs. Karin. "Then you and the boy can have my room. Have you ever seen such a nice room! I took away a third of the drawing room and got a pleasant bedroom. We've managed to get a cot for the boy. I hope he'll like it here."

After they have eaten, Dag is to go to bed. He falls asleep before he has time to say his prayers. Lisen is puttering around in her room (the only room that remains unchanged). Mrs. Karin and Anna have closed the door. "Now at last, I really must take a look at you," says the mother, her arm around Anna's waist. "Now I really must have a good look at you."

The two women are standing on the green carpet in the drawing room, the light in the chandelier out and the mirrors behind the wall brackets reflecting the gentle candlelight. "I've so longed to be back," says Anna. Her mother shakes her head and strokes her daughter's forehead and cheek. "Now you are."

Anna: I got so exhausted, you see.

Karin: That's natural, you're in the third month.

Anna: They were all ill. I was frightened.

Karin: When is it due?

Anna: The doctor thought July.

Karin: You must go to Fürstenberg. I've spoken to him. He'll see you on Monday.

Anna: Mama?

Karin: Yes.

Anna: I'd better . . .

Karin (*after a pause, carefully*): What is it?

Anna: I'm confused and just want to cry.

Karin: You've been traveling all day.

Anna: I'm not going to break up my marriage. I'm not going to leave Henrik. Perhaps you got the wrong impression from my letters.

Karin (*quietly*): Come, Anna, let's sit down here on the sofa. Just like in the old days. Would you like a little glass of sherry or a brandy? I'm going to have a stiff brandy — you too, won't you? After all these emotional upheavals.

Her mother pours out their drinks and puts the glasses on small, round silver platters, after which they sit down on the indulgently bulging green sofa. Mrs. Karin puts her feet up on a stool, Anna kicks off her slippers. She tucks her feet under her. A small lamp with a painted shade is on the low table, the small doors of the tiled stove open, the embers winking and flickering, crystal flowers of ice just visible behind the embroidered screens on the double windows. Anna closes her eyes. Mrs. Karin waits. A sleigh jingles down on the street below. The cathedral clock strikes the three quarters of the hour, distantly.

On the twentieth of December 1917, the Iron Works goes bankrupt and all payments are suspended. That same morning, Nordenson is found dead in his study. He has shot himself through the mouth with his hunting rifle. Half the back of his head is spattered all over the bookcase.

In the unsettled icy morning light, more than a hundred men gather outside the Works office, the doors of which are locked, a neatly written notice on the board outside — No Payments. Two policemen from the Valbo force are posted outside the manor gates. The local policeman and his colleague are in the drawing room trying to speak to Mrs. Elin. Her face is expressionless except for a small polite smile, and her head is turned away as she answers yes and no and I don't know. He didn't tell me anything about his difficulties. He didn't talk at all recently. My husband did not want to worry me. I know nothing.

At the pastor's office, it is bitterly cold, and in order to share fraternally the insignificant warmth warring with the freezing drafts from the badly fitting windows, the Reverend Gransjö has left the door of his private room ajar. At the moment his assistant is busy on some errand in the course of duty, and the organist is on his way to the church to repair, if possible, one of the keys. As soon as air reaches the organ, it lets out a high-pitched sound, which must be silenced.

The Reverend Gransjö calls to his curate and asks Henrik to please come in and close the door. "Do sit down. Where is the new organist? He can't just go out like that without saying where he is going. But he's new, of course, and sings well. He's got a good voice, that boy."

Henrik: He went to the church to repair the organ. Some key in the top manual has fallen down. He thought he could silence it.

Gransjö: Henrik, please go up to the Works and see if you can be of some help, outside or inside. I'll stay here and hold the fort. When it's this cold, my hip aches and I can hardly move. I'd only be a nuisance over there.

Henrik: I'll go at once. (*Gets up.*)

Gransjö: Do you know whether the Nordenson girls are at home, or whether they've gone to their grandmother's?

Henrik: They've gone.

Gransjö: Sit down for a moment.

Henrik: Yes.

Gransjö: How are things with you?

Henrik: Excellent.

Gransjö: I hear that Anna has gone to Upsala.

Henrik: Yes, that's right.

Gransjö: With the boy?

Henrik: Anna's mother will at last see her grandson.

Gransjö: Is she coming home for Christmas?

Henrik: I don't know.

Gransjö: Henrik, do you know *in general* when she's coming back?

Henrik: No.

Gransjö: What has happened?

Henrik: I'm sorry, but I'm not prepared to make any kind of confession. May I go now?

Gransjö: Of course.

Henrik: I have no wish to be unfriendly, and I am grateful for your interest, but I consider the occasion ill chosen to discuss my private griefs when the whole Works is faced with disaster.

Gransjö: The disaster at the Works is a fact. Your disaster might possibly be avoided.

Henrik: Was there anything else?

Gransjö: I just want to point out that the offer still stands.

Henrik: The offer? As far as I am concerned, it doesn't exist.

Gransjö: So may I write to those concerned and tell them that whatever the circumstances you are not interested? Is that what you want?

Henrik: I would be singularly grateful.

Gransjö: Singularly grateful. I have noted that.

Henrik: I know where I belong.

Gransjö: And your wife?

Henrik: She has also decided.

Gransjö: Go now, Henrik Bergman. And make yourself useful.

Henrik bows politely to the old gentleman and goes through the pastor's office. He buttons up his short coat and pulls on his gloves, picking up his fur cap in the porch. His eyes are dry and smarting from lack of sleep. As he turns off toward the Works, he meets Magda Säll, who greets him kindly.

Magda: Are you on your way to the Works?

Henrik: Your uncle sent me.

Magda: There's a lot of talk about sending for the army.

Henrik: Is it that bad?

Magda: I don't know. It was just something I heard. When's Anna coming back?

Henrik: I don't know exactly.

Magda: We have to discuss the bazaar. I suppose it'll have to be postponed now.

Henrik: Your uncle is still at the office.

Magda: I was just going to fetch him. He finds walking so difficult when it's cold. And he's in pain all the time, poor thing.

Henrik: I'll let you know.

Magda says something, but Henrik has already started off along the hilly road toward the Works. An engine and some empty goods wagons are standing at the railway station. No one in sight. The daylight has gone, and the light is leaden.

Outside the office and outside the yard walls, it is black with people. The policeman has climbed onto a ladder leaning against the warehouse wall and is speaking in a loud voice, saying it is pointless to stay there. Everyone should go home and wait for information that might come the next day or at the earliest the day after tomorrow. A special delegation from the Unemployment Commission is on its way, and starting up the Works again in the new year is being discussed. The Works has outstanding orders, and the creditors are meeting in Gävle at this moment planning to continue production. "So please go home. I am asking you to go home. Go home, please. There's no real reason to worry. Most of all, we don't want any trouble."

A hard snowball hits the wall. The policeman looks with astonishment at where it landed, then back at the silent crowd. Perhaps he is wondering whether to say something, but he doesn't, and gets down from the ladder. People make way for him. Henrik is dispirited and stays where he is. He recognizes his parishioners but doesn't dare go any nearer. He walks through the silent groups, occasionally greeting someone, and they greet him back.

Nordenson is lying on his leather sofa in his study. His head is bandaged, his face protruding from the bandages, that great nose standing out more than ever, the thin lips half-open, exposing his top teeth, his skin discolored, the stubble dark and eyelids red. He is still wearing his stained dressing gown, a shirt with no collar, baggy trousers, and slippers. The overhead electric light is on, but otherwise the corners of the room are in darkness.

Elin: This is his farewell letter. Perhaps you would like to hear what he says, Pastor Bergman (*doesn't wait for an answer and starts reading in a calm voice*).

In recent years, anyhow for the last two years, almost every evening I have gone into my study, locked the door, and put the barrel of my gun into my mouth. I can't say that I have been particularly desperate. I have just had a desire to train my will for the inevitable. It will be a great relief to go into final, and as I see it total, loneliness. I have made provision for my nearest, for Elin and the girls. They will not be affected by the financial situation. I have no reason to apologize for my death, even if it will cause some practical and hygienic problems. Neither have I any reason to apologize for my life. As is well known, I was attracted by all kinds of gambling. I won occasionally and that was fun, but on the whole I was indifferent to it. Life itself was one of the more banal gambles, a gamble I mostly had to take on someone else's conditions. It wasn't a question of chance. Perhaps I was occasionally my own opponent. In that case, that would be the only really comical point. Now I am drunk, sufficiently drunk, and so put a full stop.

Mrs. Elin lowers the letter and breathes jerkily, a kind of dry sob. She smiles in embarrassment.

Elin: Do you wish to say a prayer, Pastor?

Henrik: No, I don't think so.

Elin: You don't think . . . ?

Henrik: I don't think Mr. Nordenson would like it if I stood here and read a prayer. (*Pause.*) Have you spoken to the girls, Mrs. Nordenson?

Elin: They're staying with my mother over Christmas.

Henrik: Is there anything I can do? (*Helpless.*)

Elin: No. No, thank you. Please give my regards to the Reverend Gransjö and say I will come to the office early tomorrow morning, so we can discuss the funeral.

Henrik: I'll tell him that.

Elin: I must thank you, Pastor Bergman, for taking all this trouble.

Henrik does not reply, but simply shakes hands and bows. On his way home, he goes past the Works office. It is still closed, but lights are on in the windows and strangers in hats and overcoats are moving about inside, talking to one another, looking in files, sitting at tables, and leafing through papers. The wind has got up, and snow comes drifting in thick chunks from the dark icy wastes of Storsjön. A greenish uncertain strip of light is hovering above the edge of the forest. The harbor area and the road are deserted. People have gone home. There had been no trouble. Someone had just thrown a snowball, which hit nothing.

Anna has put on a high-waisted, ankle-length, dove-gray silk dress with a broad belt under her breast, wide sleeves, oval neckline, high-heeled shoes with straps, lacy stockings, necklace, and earrings. She has done her thick hair into one braid that comes down to her waist. She has put on perfume and blackened her eyelashes. For the first time, her son is wearing a sailor suit, white knee-stockings, and shiny new low shoes. Mrs. Karin has put on a gray dress of thin wool with a lace collar and high cuffs. She has gathered her white hair into a graceful knot on her head. In honor of the day, Miss Lisen has put on her black dress and a brooch, small gold rings in her ears, a genuine tortoiseshell comb in her hair, and her best boots, which creak.

Thus clad, the three women and the boy are to celebrate the most deplorable Christmas in the history of the family. The Christmas tree between the windows in the drawing room is decorated with customary finery and numerous candles, despite wartime shortages and rationing. Presents in colorful wrappings lie under the tree. The chandelier sparkles, and the mirrors behind the wall brackets reflect innumerable flames. A Christmas crèche of the biblical scene and small figures are set out on a table, a concealed electric bulb covered in red tissue paper letting the light come from the Virgin and Child. A fire crackles, shooting glowing sparks at the protective brass guard.

On the stroke of five, there is thunderous knocking on the door, and Uncle Carl comes tumbling in dressed as Santa Claus. "Isn't it terrible?" he cries. "Isn't it terrible! I'll go mad. What! Well, for God's sake. Are there any good children in this house? Or only bored old women and runaway wives? No, no, Mammchen, I'll be serious, but I nearly die laughing when I see all your efforts. It's quite mad. So, *Eyes front!* Is there a Good Little Boy here?" Uncle Carl turns his terrifying mask toward the four-year-old, who immediately begins to cry. Carl snatches off the mask, takes Dag up on his knee, and plays a tune on his lips as he trumpets with his nose. The boy stops crying and stares with fascination at the swollen benign face grimacing and playing tunes. "I've earned a drink now," sighs Uncle Carl, putting on his pince-nez. "My God, the way you ladies have got dressed up! I can hardly believe my own eyes."

"Then let's go and eat," says Mrs. Karin, taking the boy by the hand. "You're to sit by Grandmother."

Everything is as it always has been in the kitchen. "No sign of wartime and food shortages here," says Carl, clapping his fat hands. "We decided not to celebrate Christmas at all this year," says Mrs. Karin. "But then we had second thoughts. The boy is to feel Christmas is just as usual."

A few hours later, they have used up all their strength and the masks have cracked, the candles flicker and die in their holders and candlesticks, the fire dies down and glows, half-light. Dag has fallen asleep in his still-far-too-large bed, surrounded by his Christmas presents. Uncle Carl has collapsed on the green sofa, his speech slurred, and he keeps dozing off. Lisen is sitting on a straight-backed chair, her hands lying on the silk of her dress as she stares at a candle on the tree, which flares and goes out, flares up again, and suddenly the flame is a bluish colour.

Mrs. Karin and Anna are in armchairs around the tiled stove, gazing into the embers, allowing themselves to be enveloped in the warmth, which already smells of ashes.

Karin: I've taken to having a glass of brandy before I go to bed. It helps, and is also warming.

Anna: Helps?

Karin: I find it hard to sleep.

Anna: But you've always slept well.

Karin: Not any longer. In the stormy days I slept well. It's more difficult nowadays. (*Drinks.*)

Anna: Thank you for a lovely Christmas, Mama dear.

Karin: I thought it was quite deplorable.

Anna: Dag was pleased.

Carl (*grunts*): I'm also hugely pleased, Mammchen.

Karin: Thank you, Carl dear, it's kind of you to say so. (*Stretches.*) I'm not really particularly sentimental, but I felt like crying. Several times. So I said to myself, Don't be silly, Karin Åkerblom, what are you whining about?

Carl: One has to be brave. (*Grins silently.*)

Anna: I had a letter from Henrik this morning.

Karin: I didn't want to ask.

Anna: He sent his regards.

Karin: Thank you. Please return them when you next write.

Carl (*sniffing*): I warned him. You bloody well watch out for the Åkerblom family, I said to him.

Anna (*ignoring him*): He's preaching in the big church for the early

288

service. They've closed the chapel for the time being. The stove's broken down.

Karin: So things are all right with him.

Anna: It seems so. He has sent Mejan and Mia home over Christmas. He and Jack go on long skiing trips.

Karin: How does he manage for food?

Anna: He's often invited to dinner with the Reverend Gransjö.

Karin (*drinks*): I'm glad things are all right.

> (*Anna cries.*)
> (*Lisen turns her head and looks at Anna.*)

Carl: The time has now come for Santa Claus to take himself off to his hotel. Thank you for this evening, Mammchen dear. Thank you for this evening, Miss Lisen. Thank you for this evening, Anna, little crybaby (*tenderly*). You really are a muddle. There you are, a big wet kiss. Cry away, my heart! Women cry so that their eyes are more beautiful. Yes, yes, Mammchen, I'm going. We won't see each other tomorrow because I'm taking the early train to Stockholm. No, no, I can manage. Stay where you are, for God's sake. I'm not very drunk. I'll leave the fancy dress at the hotel. Regards to the brothers, by the way, and wish them a Happy New Year from me. No, *don't* give them my regards. There is a limit to my capacity to lie. This evening has reached it, gone beyond it. I have no more allowance until the new year.

The front door slams, and Carl goes whistling down the stairs. Lisen gets up on a chair and blows out the last candles on the Christmas tree. Then she wishes them good night and disappears into the kitchen, where she cleans up and puts things away. Karin holds out her hand and takes her daughter's.

Karin: Are you cold?

Anna: No, no. I'm warm.

Karin: Your hand.

Anna: Yes, I know. Whenever I'm miserable, my hands and feet get icy cold. You remember, don't you? (*No pause.*) I'm so upset about Henrik. I have such a terribly guilty conscience.

So Henrik has sent Mejan and Mia home for an indefinite period of time. At the same time, he shows some practical and organizational talents, among other things by contracting his living space and moving into the abandoned maid's room off the kitchen, thus enabling him to combat the cosmic cold. The fire in the stove is on all day and night, and the stove wall and the tiled stove stay warm. His household routine is otherwise meticulous. The dishes are done every day, the sofa bed made, the paraffin rationed and topped up, his cassock brushed, trousers pressed, and he eats a properly cooked meal in the middle of the day. Necessities of life are brought by his neighbor, who goes to the store daily. Every morning, Henrik makes his way to the pastor's office on skis, a half-hour journey if the going is fairly good; then he sets off for home at dusk. The dog Jack goes with him and stands guard, though he does indeed grieve over Someone's incomprehensible absence. But he fulfills his duties.

Henrik writes his sermons at the kitchen table, in his usual everyday clothes, a large cardigan with long sleeves and collar that is as warm as a fur coat, his trouser legs tucked into gray socks and wooden shoes on his feet. He has let his beard grow, but trims it with Anna's nail-scissors, which she has left behind. He has brought a bookcase into the room and filled it with important books. Tolstoy, Rydberg, Fröding, Lagerlöf, Walter Scott, Jules Verne, Albert Engström, and Nathan Söderblom.

His alarm clock measures the time, an ancient monster of tin and brass, its bell capable of waking the dead, but at the moment ticking peacefully, the fire roaring in the stove, the pastor sitting at the kitchen table preparing his New Year's Day sermon. It's about the reluctant fig tree and the conscientious vineyard worker. "Lord, let the tree stay this year as well, and meanwhile I can dig around it and manure it, so maybe in that way it will bear fruit next year."

He lights his well-broken-in pipe: he has real tobacco, a Christmas present from Gransjö, who has just given up smoking, and he breathes in the mild, sweetish smell. Jack is asleep on his piece of matting under the table, his legs twitching, and he is growling faintly. Suddenly he leaps up and goes over to stand by the door. Someone is approaching by the gate, someone on a sled. Henrik opens the kitchen door to the porch and closes it behind him to keep the warmth in. Magda Säll jerks open the outer door, for the kitchen steps have become a snowdrift during the night's bad weather.

Magda: Hello, Henrik, and may the rest of this holy week be as good. I've brought you and Jack some goodies. Uncle Samuel sends his regards and says you are welcome to celebrate New Year's Day with us. We won't be all that many, seven or eight perhaps.

Magda holds out the basket she has with her. This tall, broad-shouldered creature fills the kitchen porch, her graying hair sticking out from under her shawl and curling down over her forehead, her cheeks and the handsome nose red with cold. Her very dark eyes are looking at Henrik with no dissembling, her mouth smiling: "Surely we don't have to stand out here," she says, laughing in a friendly way. "Have you got something warm to offer, Henrik?" She pulls off her felt boots. "My toes are frozen stiff. Despite my boots. Can I put them in front of the stove? It's nice and warm in here. Oh, so Henrik's moved into the maid's room and made the kitchen into his study. Oh, and I can see you were preparing your sermon, and I'm sure I'm disturbing you, but I won't stay long. I must just sit down for a moment or two and get my breath back. Is the coffeepot warm? Do you think it'd be all right if I take a cup? I see you're keeping the place neat and tidy, Henrik. And you do the dishes, too."

She has wriggled out of her thick winter coat and the shawl crossed over her chest. "I stole this jersey from Uncle Samuel, and my skirt's twenty years old but is just right for this weather. Why is Jack growling? Is he angry because I'm disturbing you?"

Magda: How are things?

Henrik: Fine. Excellent.

Magda (*smiles*): That's good.

Henrik: I see from your smile that you don't believe me.

Magda: But, Henrik dear . . .

Henrik: How *could* a lone man manage on his own, abandoned by his wife? Out of the question, isn't it?

Magda: It was only a polite inquiry.

Henrik: And so you'll be given a polite answer. Fine. I'm well. Things are all right. I have adapted.

Magda: You sound angry.

Henrik: I can't help my tone of voice. You come storming along on your sled, up to your eyebrows with compassion. That embarrasses me. I cannot fulfill your expectations.

Magda: Henrik, my dear . . . (*Laughs.*)

Henrik: I'll tell you something, Magda. I am the loner type. In fact, I've always been alone. The time with Anna and my son confused me. For instance, I imagined that there was special happiness intended just for me and always waiting round the corner. Anna made me believe in something of that sort. Anna and Dag. I was almost comically grateful. And as I said, confused.

Magda: You sound convincing — but nevertheless I think . . .

Henrik: There is no "but," Magda! As you see, I am quite calm and am speaking calmly. If I seemed irritable, that's just temporary. I don't like anyone pawing at me. If you keep your paws off me, I'll be nice and conversant.

Magda (*smiles*): I must admit I'd expected a sad, disconsolate fellow human being, whom I could console with friendly words and the remains of the Christmas ham.

Henrik (*smiles*): It was kind of you to go to all that trouble. I'm glad you came.

Magda puts her coffee cup down on the stove, gets a chair, and sits down opposite Henrik, then looks at him thoughtfully.

Magda: I've had a talk with Uncle Samuel. You know that I like you. He's beginning to be rather poorly. Well, we talked about you, and we've begun to realize that you are determined to stay here in the parish, despite all the difficulties. (*Henrik wants to say something.*) Wait a moment, Henrik. Let me finish. Uncle Samuel and I came up with a suggestion. Now you're supposed to ask what kind of suggestion, and also appear slightly interested.

Henrik (*graciously*): What kind of suggestion?

Magda: Quite simply, that you should move in with us down at the parsonage. Without too many complications and very little expense, we could turn the right wing into a place for you to live in. (*With controlled eagerness.*) You'd have a living room and kitchen down below, a bedroom upstairs, and a study with a view over the lake across the landing. We could arrange for some help with the cleaning and cooking. She could live in the big house. We've several rooms in the attic. (*Controls her eagerness.*) I think the Church Council and the old boys on the Parish Council would be terribly pleased. Then they could close the chapel without a guilty conscience and also shut up this parsonage.

Henrik: Is the chapel to be closed?

Magda: At least for the winter.

Henrik: I hadn't heard that.

Magda: Jakobsson came to see Uncle Samuel yesterday. They talked about the possibility of closing it. For the winter. The heating costs so much.

Henrik: That's astounding news.

Magda: Don't be offended. It's not news, just discussions. Nothing will be decided without consulting you. You must know that?

Henrik: And if Anna comes back?

Magda: Do you *believe* she's coming back?

Henrik: Nothing's definite. She's gone to Upsala for a few months. The child is due in July.

Magda: And then she's to come back?

Henrik: Don't sound so distrustful, Magda dear. Why shouldn't she come back? Why shouldn't two young people have the right to be on their own for a few months and try separately to test out their feelings?

Magda: A moment ago, you sounded quite convinced.

Henrik: Convinced?

Magda: Convinced of your solitude. "I've always been alone. I always will be. My life with Anna confused me." And so on.

Henrik: That is what I feel like *at this moment*. In a few months or perhaps tomorrow, I may have changed my mind.

Magda: You like contradicting, don't you?

Henrik (*laughs*): At the risk of contradicting you, I say, no, no, not at all. Ordinarily, I am just vague, nice, and rather cowardly. I mostly think everyone else is right, and I am wrong.

Magda: Your beard suits you.

Henrik: An expression of my true personality? Or perhaps just idleness. I don't have to heat water every morning. I don't have to shave.

Magda: Don't you think it'd be nice if you moved into the wing of the parsonage?

Henrik: Do *you?*

Magda (*smiling*): Playing chess, playing cards, making music, reading aloud, eating well. Being together? Henrik?

Henrik: Yes, of course. Of course.

Magda: What are you thinking about?

Henrik: I was thinking about what I was going to say when you confused me by talking about my beard.

Magda: I'm sorry. (*Smiles.*) What were you going to say?

Henrik: I think that I'm best at living on the Extreme Edge of the World. Both metaphorically and literally. Then I attain that hardness, that sharpness . . . I can only find banal words for something important. Magda, try to understand me. I have to live in privation. Then, and *only then*, can I possibly be a good priest. As I *want* to be, but have never been *able* to be. I am not created for larger contexts. I'm not terribly bright, no, I say that with no false modesty. But I know that I'd be a good worker in the vineyards if I could live without sidelong glances.

Magda: Now you're being very convincing. I shall retreat.

Henrik: You sound ironic?

Magda (*gently*): I'm not being ironic. I feel like crying.

Henrik: Yes, so many tears will have to be shed.

Magda (*stroking his face*): I must go now before it's too late. I mean, it's already getting dark. Good luck with your sermon.

Henrik: The sermon is about the fig tree that refused to bear fruit. And its owner said, cut down that tree. It stands there year after year and sucks good out of my soil.

Magda: Yes, I know, I know. And the worker in the vineyard said, let me look after the fig tree especially well, then we can see if it doesn't bear fruit . . .

Henrik embraces her, and they stand there swaying together for a few moments, speechless. Then she frees herself and pushes her hair back from her forehead with her big hand.

Henrik: Things *are* all right here, Magda. It's not particularly nice, but good. I have to face myself every day. That's fairly dismal, but an invaluable experience.

Magda: But you can come to dinner on New Year's Day nevertheless, can't you?

Henrik (*smiles*): I don't think so.

Magda: Good-bye, then.

Henrik: Thanks for coming to see me.

Magda has started putting on her outdoor clothes. Boots. Shawl around her head. The heavy coat, gloves. Jack has got up, pleased their guest is leaving.

Magda: Nordenson's funeral is going to be in Sundsvall, where there's a crematorium. Uncle Samuel insists. We have to go. They were friends in some peculiar way. I saw them leaning over the chess board, a rare sight, I assure you. Uncle Samuel so gentle and angelic. And then Nordenson, a lost soul from hell, a demon. Your beard really is delightful. I hope Anna will enjoy it.

Henrik: Anna doesn't like me having a beard.

Magda: Oh, dear me, how unfortunate!

Henrik: You're sure to be home before it gets dark.

The kitchen door closes. The outer door resists, the snowdrift has grown. The door shuts again with a dull thump. Magda walks briskly toward the gate, shoves the sled in front of her, and scoots off. She has left the basket behind on the draining board.

So Henrik is alone.

Does he scream? No.

Does he begin to cry, leaning over the bench? Unlikely.

Does he walk up and down in the cruelly cold dining room?

He might have, but he doesn't.

What does he do?

He sits down at the kitchen table and bends over his half-finished sermon.

He lights his pipe. He lights the paraffin lamp.

He looks out the window for a moment.

The roving light of dusk, the snow.

The cold.

The game could come to an end here. Every ending and every beginning has to be arbitrary, for I am relating a piece of life, not an invention. Nevertheless, I have decided to add an *epilogue*, which is entirely invented. There is no documentation from the first six months of 1918.

So now it's spring, early summer, the month of June. The students have taken their exams, celebrated, feasted, sung, and vanished, the professors and lecturers have pulled down their blinds and gone out to the country. The streets are silent and the parks full of blossoms and their scents. The shadows of the trees deepen. The Fyris River trickles gently along. The trams reduce their timetables by half, and the little black-clad old ladies who have stayed indoors all winter now suddenly appear. They tend their graves, peer into their hidden window-mirrors behind the curtains, sit on the benches in the botanical gardens or the city park, and let the warmth of the sun flow into their joints and bones.

At seven in the morning, one sunny Thursday at the beginning of June, a freight train from Norrland stops at Upsala Central Station's freight platform. At the end of the train are (that's what it was like in those days) two ancient passenger cars with wooden seats, spittoons, and iron stoves, but no trace of comfort. One lone passenger gets out. The station restaurant has just opened, and he orders a simple breakfast (there isn't much available because times are bad). Then he goes to the cloakroom and washes, shaves, and changes his shirt. He is wearing a neat dark suit with a waistcoat, stiff collar, and black tie. He is carrying the barest necessities in a shabby black briefcase, which he deposits in the luggage room together with his hat and raincoat.

Then he sets off at a slow pace up Drottninggatan and turns off onto Trädgårdsgatan. There he takes up a post directly opposite building 12, well concealed behind the gates of the school yard. There is no one in sight. The little tram screeches and disappears down the hill. The ducks quack in Svandammen. The sun shines, the shadows shortening. The cathedral clock strikes ten.

The entrance door opens, and Karin Åkerblom steps out into the strong white light. She is pushing a baby stroller, Dag walking beside her with one hand holding firmly onto its arm. Then the person who has been holding the entrance door open appears. It is Anna. She is heavily pregnant and is wearing a light-colored dress and white boots. She is bareheaded. Her summer coat is on the stroller. The little company turns to the right and at a slow pace sets off toward Svandammen. They don't see Henrik, who slowly follows them along the opposite pavement, hidden in the deep shadows of the trees and buildings. The two women stop, and Mrs. Karin lifts the boy onto the stroller. He kneels facing forward and surveys his surroundings with a satisfied expression. They set off once again. Mrs. Karin says something to her daughter, and Anna slants her head to the left and smiles. She answers. Both of them smile. They have presumably said something to the boy.

They walk around Svandammen and stop in front of the Flustret, which has just opened its outdoor service. The wind is blowing through the big trees, and Henrik is standing on the other side of the pond. Dag is feeding the ducks, Anna giving him small pieces of bread out of a paper bag. Mrs. Karin says something, and Anna laughs. He can hear her laughter, although he is quite a long way away. It is windy, and the laughter is carried on the wind.

Anna takes her summer coat off the stroller, and a book, then leans down and ties up a bootlace, turns to her son and says something, and kisses him. Then she gets up, nods to Mrs. Karin, and slowly strolls over toward the leafy quiet of the town park. Henrik follows her.

She sits down on a bench in the shade of the lime trees. On the other side of the gravel path is a fountain surrounded by resplendent flower beds. She sits down heavily, then bends backward, pushing her hair off her forehead and opening the book.

Henrik hides nearby. Perhaps he is invisible, perhaps he is here only in his mind, perhaps this is a dream. He looks at her: the bowed neck, the dark eyelashes, the soft mouth, the braid down her back, the hands holding the book, the huge stomach — what a huge stomach — the boot below her hem. She turns the pages, stops reading, raises her eyes, the fountain splashes, the wind blows in the limes, there's a buzzing in the flowers in the flower beds, a song thrush obstinately repeats the same set of notes, and far away a steam whistle blows. *I'm here, quite close, can't you see me?* She lowers the book, lets it lie on the bench, rests her hands flat on the bench. *Can't you see me?* No. Yes. She turns her gaze in his direction. She sees him, hides her face in her hand, sitting quite still.

Anna: What do you want?

Henrik: Just an impulse. I heard there was a night train running.

Anna: What do you want?

Henrik: I don't know. That is, I . . . . (*Falls silent.*)

(*Anna says nothing.*)

Henrik: I think about you and the boy all the time. I yearn too much.

Anna: I'm never coming back.

Henrik: I know.

Anna: Never. Whatever you say.

Henrik: I know.

Anna: I have been filled with terrible anguish. I have felt like a traitor. Things are better now. Don't come and tear it all up again. I couldn't face it.

Henrik: You'll never have to go back again, Anna. I promise you. I have written to Pastor Primarius and accepted his offer. We're moving to Stockholm in the autumn.

He falls silent and looks over at the fountain. Anna waits. They are agitated and trembling, but speak calmly, their voices calm. She is sitting here, and he is sitting there. Each on a separate bench.

Anna: What did you want to say?

Henrik (*smiles*): I'm not a talented martyr. Good intentions are not enough.

Anna: Perhaps we'll never be able to forgive each other.

Henrik: So you want us to go on?

Anna: You know perfectly well I do. I don't want anything else. That's all I want.

Then they don't know what ought to be said or can be said. So they sit in silence for a long while, each on a separate bench, sunk in their own thoughts.

Anna is surely occupied with practical considerations about the coming move. Henrik is doubtless wondering about how he will ever be able to look his parishioners in the eye during his remaining time in Forsboda.

Fårö, Sweden